Bloody London

Bloody London

Reggie Nadelson

Thomas Dunne Books
St. Martin's Minotaur
New York

THOMAS DUNNE BOOKS.
An imprint of St. Martin's Press.

BLOODY LONDON. Copyright © 1999 by Reggie Nadelson. All rights
reserved. Printed in the United States of America. No part of this
book may be used or reproduced in any manner whatsoever
without written permission except in the case of brief quotations
embodied in critical articles or reviews. For information, address
St. Martin's Press, 175 Fifth Avenue, New York, N.Y. 10010.

ISBN 0-312-24372-3

First published in Great Britain by Faber and Faber Limited

First U.S. Edition: December 1999

10 9 8 7 6 5 4 3 2 1

To Verity Lambert

Thanks to Chief Inspector Tom Pine of the River Police at Wapping (Thames Division of the Metropolitan Police) for a view of the River, insight into the threat of floods, and some terrific stories.

Bloody London

London: November 5

London! The exhilaration, the anticipation washes over me and a light layer of gooseflesh ripples up my arms. I can't shake it, in spite of everything, this thrill of travelling, that I'm allowed to go wherever the hell I want. Just going makes me happy. All it takes is the dough. If, like I did, you grow up in a lousy land-locked city with walls the height of the world – it's how Moscow felt when I was a kid – you never lose it, the sheer physical pleasure of going.

Suddenly, the plane coming in now, there's a hole in the clouds. I cram my face against the window. England looks like it's on fire. I'm looking down and I see it, the landscape dotted with remote fires, like war breaking out in the suburbs. It seems prehistoric and post-nuclear at the same time. But then the clouds come up again in fast black-gray rolls, the fires disappear, the PA system crackles with pilot babble, Enjoy your Stay. No one mentions the fires. Then the cabin lights go out.

We're down.

Welcome to London.

I've never been to London, or Europe either, not really, not unless you count East Berlin when I was a kid or a couple of days' vacation in Poland once. (Some vacation!) I'm here to finish something that started at home in New York when Thomas Pascoe was murdered in a swimming pool on Sutton Place. The answers are here in this foreign place.

Around me, everyone is busy with the stuff of arriving, rubbing their eyes, yawning, scavenging for things they dropped under the seat, stuffing duty-free into their carry-ons. No one on the plane knows me or why I'm here. I'm just a guy in a crumpled tweed jacket and a denim shirt. My legs, too long for these seats, are cramped up and I'm trying to unfold myself and stretch, and thinking at the same time I'm glad I bought some decent Scotch at the duty-free and that too many people are dead.

Too many people died in New York, Frankie Pascoe most of all. And I owe her. I think about her, waiting for the fatso ahead of me while he shuffles off the plane. I owe Frankie, and the obligation gnaws at me. In my pocket I can feel the sharp edge of my passport against my fingers, and the envelope with British cash in it and keys for a borrowed apartment. I wish to God I had a gun.

I don't have a weapon. Can't, not here. Anyway, I'm unofficial, an ex-New York City cop with a license to work private cases in America and that's about it. No gun. I don't know my status here, but I miss the gun like hell, like you miss a body part.

My fingers fidget with the Swiss Army knife in my pocket. The woman next to me with the spiky racoon hair says 'What's so funny?' and I shake my head and say 'Nothing' because I'm laughing at myself. What would I do with a little red Swiss Army knife? Threaten the bad guys? Mostly I use it for the corkscrew attachment, to open wine. A cop with a corkscrew. I could have been a waiter.

'Welcome to Britain. Enjoy your stay.'

The guy at immigration stamps my passport, I ride the escalator down, grab my suitcase off a luggage carousel, head out into the raw London night and climb into a square black taxi. I leave the window open. I want to see what England feels like without glass between it and me. The air is dank as hell. In front of me all I can see of the cabbie is his beefy shoulders and a pony tail. He's a talker.

'American?' The cabbie says without turning his head. 'Where from?'

'Yeah.'

Again he says, 'From?'

'New York. What's with the fires?'

He chuckles like he knows I missed the joke. 'Guy Fawkes,' he says. 'Back, you know, 1600s or something. Bloke name of Guy tries to blow up Parliament. They trussed him up, burned him. Something like that. Bonfire Night every year, a bit like your Halloween, only now we have that too.'

We cruise along a highway and into town and it's late, there's not much traffic.

Now I'm hanging out the cab window and laughing. Everything, every car, cab, lamppost, mailbox, street sign, billboard, every store and café is foreign, even McDonald's and the GAP seem different, especially at night in the harsh air. I even hum 'A foggy day' just for the hell of it.

London's big. Planet London. I watch the blur of unfamiliar places, small houses, big boulevards, department stores. The driver points out Buckingham Palace, then a long avenue leading away from it, green spaces on either side.

Big Ben, the clock face lit up, slides into view between trees, like a postcard. Then Parliament. I tune out the cab driver and lose myself in the passing city. The cab turns left, drives fast along an embankment, the river's on my right, a few boats are winking on it in the distance. In a square on my left, behind a low iron railing, a bonfire is burning, dying out. Then I see the figure.

The driver points it out, a scarecrow or ragdoll, perched on the spikes of the iron railing. The light turns red. He slams on the brakes.

'Penny for the guy?'

It startles me, this soft, ugly, ragdoll face coming through the half-open window. It brushes against my face. I pull back. A couple of drunks are pushing the thing in my window, in my face, yelling 'Penny for the guy?' They laugh, a drunken slurry giggle, then stagger away to some cronies, three other guys drinking beer on the sidewalk. One of them sticks the dummy back on the spikes.

The light changes, but my excitement's gone, punctured by the creeps with the doll. A faint feel of gauzy dread takes its place. My feet and lips buzz with it and I grab a cigarette out of my bag, light up, take a couple of fast drags.

The river, when we cross it, has a silver-black surface, hard, flat and dark. Behind me, when I twist my neck, I can see the Tower of London. I slept through history when I was a kid, but I remember the Tower of London. Murderous place.

The narrow lane where the cab turns in, in spite of the renovations and fancy shops, feels claustrophobic, closed-in, old, melancholy. The shops near by are mostly dark, except for a restaurant where yellow light dribbles into the street.

'This is it, mate,' the driver says. 'Butler's Wharf. Very nice.' He pulls up in front of a renovated warehouse.

I stick some cash in his hand, haul my suitcase out of the cab, into the building, which is slick enough, the lobby, the elevator. The apartment is on the top floor.

The hallway's silent. Somewhere a dog whimpers. Fumbling the unfamiliar keys, I get the door unlocked. Inside, the place is dark, a quiet, empty place no one lives in. I scratch around the wall for the light.

There are light wood floors, white walls, an open kitchen, a table, a few canvas chairs, not much else. There's a bedroom and bathroom, bed, dresser, closets. A digital clock next to the bed. I can hear the numbers flip over.

Suddenly I feel dog-weary, sit down hard on the bed. Next time I look at the clock, it's three in the morning. My head's thick with jetlag and fatigue, eyes cruddy with sleep.

The duty-free Scotch is in my bag and in the kitchen I find a glass and pour some out. Somewhere, from another apartment, I can hear music, very faint, very far away, a dreamy ballad, maybe a show tune, and I take my drink and head for the sliding glass doors. On the balcony outside are a pair of wicker chairs, the kind with high curved backs.

The door isn't locked. I slide it open. The wind's blowing hard now. Below the balcony, the promenade that runs along the river is deserted. Lightbulbs strung between the lampposts along the riverfront tinkle against each other, glass on glass, an eerie noise, like the metal bits on a flagpole, clinking, warning me. Balancing the drink in one hand, I reach out to push the door wider. I need some air.

It's ten, twelve days since Pascoe was murdered; it seems longer. He was on his way to London the day he died. The Pascoe murder's infiltrated my life; whatever killed him, I want it over. I want to stop it all before it crashes over everything. I feel like a surfer in a huge wave. I don't know why this image keeps coming to me, I've never done any surfing in my life, but it's suffocating, the wave breaking over me, breaking my arms and legs, people I know around me on their own boards, yelling for help. Somehow I have to find the right coins to put in a slot that will make the water recede. If I don't find them, if I don't stop it, it will drown everyone I care about.

The Scotch is mellow in my mouth. Then the lights in the apartment flicker and go out and I reach for the switch on the wall. A fuse has blown, but I don't care, I'm going to bed after a smoke, and I feel in my pocket for cigarettes and a lighter, go further out on the balcony and grab a chair. Under my hand, the smooth wicker is oily from the damp.

You know when something lousy's coming, you think you sense it before, but maybe afterwards you can't remember if you really knew, if it was the anticipation that made your gut turn over and your skin crawl, or if it came to you later. Later. After you saw it.

It's coiled up inside the wicker chair. One of the stuffed figures like a scarecrow, a dummy, and it's the size of a baby. There's a photograph stuck to its head with pins. The picture is cropped. Only the features show: mouth, nose, eyes. There are holes punched in the eyes. I've seen this before: a picture, the eyes cut out. It's a warning. They throw acid at you or cut out your eyes, it's an old curse. They make you blind, then they kill you.

The damp night is making the skin on my arms crawl like there's ants on it and I grab the crumpled picture and hold my lighter up so I can see it better, but the light goes out in the breeze. Again, somewhere in the building, a dog whines.

I get inside, shut the balcony door, flick on my lighter again. The flame makes shadows jump on the piece of paper I'm holding. There's a peculiar smell, now I get a whiff, something musty in the apartment, maybe just a mouse that passed through and died here, maybe that's all. I gulp the rest of the Scotch in my glass and ignore the stink. The paper I'm holding has been swiped out of a file and printed off the Internet, and when I hold the lighter closer I can see the face.

The wind is coming through a crack, and I open the glass door again then slam it so hard it rattles. Then I lock it.

Where's the fuse box? I bang around looking for it. I want the lights on now. The photograph I ripped off the dummy is in my hand.

I've never been in London before in my life, no one knows I'm coming, this is a borrowed apartment. But the dummy in the wicker chair on the balcony was intended for me. To spook me, and I know it. Where's the goddamn fuse box, I think again, holding my lighter up high, squinting at the picture that I know was left for me because the face in it, the eyes cut out leaving only brutal holes, is mine.

PART ONE

New York, October

Chapter 1

Blood floats. It was the first thing I noticed that morning. It spread slowly outward over the water in the swimming pool uptown.

The stink of chlorine was intense. The lights the cops had rigged made their faces flat and white as they worked the edge of the swimming pool, maybe twenty guys, like the sorcerer's apprentices, some slow, some brisk, homicide, forensics, photographic. The pool was a large rectangle, the tiles, at the bottom and around the rim, dark blue with gold flecks in them. On their hands and knees, the crews took water samples, dusted, sifted invisible shreds of cloth, hair, skin, determined, hopeful, doubtful, like men panning for gold in permafrost. Whenever I'm at a scene I usually think about it in metaphors, men digging in permafrost, that kind of thing; it passes the time and keeps you sane.

The morning Pascoe died, it was a Monday, I was drinking hot black coffee at the fish market before it was light, watching Italian guys in big rubber boots unload a crate of red snapper onto a bed of cracked ice. I was working a possible case at the market, a theft. Just a job. But I like the fish market early in the morning. The sun comes up. The East River turns pink, the breeze that day was soft as powder and when the mist burned off, the sky was bright blue. Then my beeper went. I looked at it, and twenty minutes after I got the message I was at the swimming pool on Sutton Place.

The body, already bagged, lay on the slippery tiles. Catch of the day, I thought. I heard one of the guys crouched by the pool hum a Beach Boys tune to himself. 'Little Surfer Girl', he hummed. In New York City, the terrible and comic always lie, as my first boss used to say, side by each. But all Sonny Lippert said to me when he looked up and saw I'd arrived was 'I got a Russian for you.'

'Dead? The dead guy's Russian? On Sutton Place?' I looked at the body bag.

'No, man. The Russian's a witness. The dead guy's a teabag. And rich. Very very rich, very important, very connected, very dead also. You heard the name Pascoe?'

'Yeah, I maybe read something.'

'Thomas Pascoe. British. Pushing eighty. Big time. Investment banker. Lawyer. Charities up the wazoo.' Sonny paused to let it sink in.

I let it sink. 'And?'

'Head of the co-op here. Thomas Pascoe was head of the fanciest co-op in New York City. I bet there's plenty of people mad as hell at him.'

'How'd they do him?'

Sonny chuckled. 'That's the kicker. They tried to whack his head off. I swear to God. Head of the co-op. In the pool. Where the old lady found him, the Russian. Come on.' He looked at his watch. 'She's in shock. They said give it an hour, I'm still fucking waiting.'

I could already write the headline in the *Post*: WHACK! HEAD OF CO-OP LOSES HEAD. It was gonna play big.

Sonny Lippert's a federal prosecutor with a lot of connections and a special interest in Russians; there was a Russian involved, I could speak the language, Sonny feels I owe him in perpetuity, so here we were again.

'Homicide victims, if they got dough, Art, they're like cannibals, they eat your life.' Sonny pulled me away from the technicians. Impatience drove Sonny as he looked at the scene and tapped his foot.

He was a small, compact man, like a bantam, a fighter, with a tight hood of black curls, arms and legs pumping like a wind-up toy. I don't know if Sonny dyes his hair, but he's probably close to sixty and he looks forty-five. That morning, he wore tobacco suede Guccis, no socks, faded jeans and a white T-shirt. A black cashmere crewneck was knotted around his neck. He was small but lean; Sonny works out religiously, usually at night. He doesn't sleep good.

I took hold of his arm. 'I'm glad as hell to see you, Sonny, but I was on a job.'

'What kind of job? Sniffing the swordfish? Trying to figure if some wiseguy's pushing tuna past its natural prime?'

I laughed. 'Snapper.'

'An old Russian, calls herself a princess, you know? She finds the body. In the swimming pool. Bangs right into him, head bobbing around, man, I mean, she starts yelling. She's been here fifty years, pretends she doesn't speak English, no one understands what the hell she's saying, but they can see. Severed almost. Like a piece of fruit. Pineapple on a stalk. The head, I mean. Pascoe's head.'

'And?'

'One of the janitors says she's down here most days early, doesn't like swimming with other people. What do I know, maybe she figures the rest of the residents are proles, maybe she hates herself in a swimsuit.' Sonny changed his tone. 'You're looking very good, Art, man. Lost some flab there, been working out?'

I could read the flattery: Sonny needed something. It used to grate, the style, the tone – he addresses everyone as 'man' – but it mostly makes me laugh now. A lot of water went under the bridge with us and I'm used to Sonny Lippert.

'You saw her already?'

He looked at his watch. 'No, I been here since, Christ, six-thirty this a.m., but I didn't see her yet. Medics were working on her, she must be eighty. I want to hear how come she's in the pool and what she knows about this piece of real estate, you dig? Art, OK?'

'The swimming pool was part of the original 1920s building design. Influenced by Rosario Candela, but maybe better,' said Lippert, who's a pedagogical asshole. 'You know about Candela? He did a lot of great buildings up around here, this was a tribute. One of his students.' Sonny looked at his watch again.

I was staring at the pool, trying to imagine the scene: Pascoe down for a swim; someone goes for the neck with a saw, a sword, a knife. The old woman who finds him going nuts. I said, 'What else we got on Pascoe?'

'Like I said, he was head of the frigging co-op here,' said Sonny, as we made our way through other basement rooms, some now used for storage, all with old cold stone floors. 'So maybe it was symbolic, you know? Maybe they whacked his head 'cause he was head of the co-op. Maybe they didn't like his rules.' Lippert was already working up one of his arcane theories.

I followed Sonny and the small procession of special squads, looking for access routes and broken locks. There was nothing out of place. A photographer snapped every possible angle.

The ceiling seemed to vibrate. I said, 'What's up there?' and a short guy answered in halting English. 'Generators,' he said. 'Air con.' Like the other back-of-the-house guys, janitors, supers, handymen, he was Spanish speaking. He leaned against the wall, waiting until we finished. He worked on a scratch card.

I grinned and said, 'So, you win, you're gonna buy a place here?'

He was a small man with straight black hair and a Yankees cap on. The face was smooth, high boned; Peruvian, maybe, I figured; there was Indian in it, anyhow. He swivelled the cap so the peak faced forward. 'You must be kidding, man, you think I wanna live in here?'

'How come? They treat you bad?'

He covered his eyes, then his ears and mouth and laughed. 'They treat me like a monkey, I make like a monkey.' He added, 'Is OK, you know, most of the tenants. Front-of-the-house, Irish guys onna door, management, treats us like garbage sometimes, you know what I mean? They's under-educated, the Irish. You a cop?'

I shrugged. 'What's your name?'

'Pindar Aguirre,' he said, and I slipped him twenty bucks and said, 'What time's the pool open usually?'

He said, 'Seven o'clock.'

'Anyone ever come down before?'

'I don't know, I go off usually by six, I'm a night guy. Sometimes I seen Mr Pascoe coming in. Only Mr Pascoe. Only him allowed before opening. He OK, Mr Pascoe.'

'What about the elevator?'

'Regular elevator from the lobby got an operator and goes up. Elevator to the pool for residents only.'

'Automatic?'

'Yeah.'

'What were you before? Back home, I mean?'

He said something to himself in Spanish, then glanced up at me and said, 'A poet.'

It reminded me of the big Moscow buildings when I was a kid: those Stalinist palaces, it was always the poets, brooms made of twigs, who cleaned the floors. The Nomenklatura, the bigwigs with a name, partied; the poets wiped up the shit.

We got to the elevator. Sonny grabbed my arm.

'Art?'

'You were saying?'

'I don't think anyone broke into this place. I think someone had access. You saw the security. I looked at the key system. Brand new. Electronic.'

'Yeah, Sonny. It's some kind of fortress. Whoever did what's his name – Pascoe – probably knew his way around. Or hers. Anyway, New York City, we ain't got no crime, doesn't exist now, right, Sonny?'

He got in the elevator and gave a tight little smile. 'Yeah, right. Coulda been a female?'

'Sure. You don't need that much heft if you get the right kind of knife and your victim's not expecting you. Coulda been a female. Coulda been a kid, for that matter, you got the right kind of weapon.'

'Shoulda coulda woulda, yeah, but what kind?'

I said, 'Remember Brighton Beach, they got those knives could take your head off in three seconds flat. Chinatown too.'

'But it ain't gonna be your first choice of weapon unless you want to make a statement.'

'Unless you're nuts. I assume no one found the weapon.'

Lippert shook his head.

I said, 'I talked to a guy says the pool opens at seven. What time did the old Russian find Pascoe?'

Lippert looked at me. 'Before seven. I was here by six-thirty. Jesus.'

'So if she went to the pool before it opened, maybe someone invited her.'

'Like Pascoe himself.'

'Or whoever sliced his head.'

'Yeah, that too.'

'One other thing.'

'What's that, Art?'

'So they left Pascoe's eyes intact? Or they cut them out?'

Chapter 2

'No one except New Yorkers would take the shit these co-ops hand out, you with me here, man?' Sonny Lippert looked irritably around the lobby. 'Goddam Russian princess lives in a couple of maids' rooms at the top of the building, she has to use the service elevator, Christ, man. Jesus.'

In the lobby the mayor, baseball jacket zipped to his throat, worked the room like election day. The morning crackled with cellphones and walkies. A tenant pulled a wellbred pup with attitude to the elevator; the animal yapped so loud I wanted to stick it with a fork. Through the window I saw a camera crew get out of a van.

A doorman, six feet four of middle-aged Irish condescension, held court. The name tag on his uniform said he was Ryan Sweeney. He had a silver pompadour like Boris Yeltsin and he was big.

The young cops listened to Sweeney hold forth; they were intent, earnest, hopeful of a collar. My official ID still shows me like that, face solemn, dark blue shirt, hair ruthlessly slicked down under a blue cap. It expired when I finally quit the NYPD last year; I keep it in my pocket anyhow for luck, like a charm.

Sonny Lippert ignored the doorman's supercilious gaze, then cracked his own knuckles; it sounded like he was crushing the bones of little animals. He began pacing the dark lobby, appraising the bronze lampstands, the worn oriental rugs and I followed him, cooling my hand on a marble plinth that supported the bronze figure of a languid girl with a whippet on a leash.

Lippert was restless. This wasn't his kind of job. It was homicide, but there was no politics except of privilege, and the victim was British, which didn't count in his book. He likes their novels, the Brits, but that's it. Once, Sonny Lippert would have killed to get in on something like this, the mayor calling him in special, the brass asking his opinion. All that changed a coupla years back when the sweatshop downtown burned. A hundred women died in it. It changed him.

'Look at that.' Lippert put his hand on a small brass plaque on the wall.

I looked at it. 'Middlemarch. So?'

'You never read George Eliot? It's a great book, man. A-list, top of the line. It's not an Eastside kind of thing, a building with a name. Central Park West, they got the San Remo, the Majestic, the El Dorado, Beresford, whatever. Here they got tasteful stuff, River House, like that. I read once the guy who built this place was a big-time bootlegger with a daughter who liked books. He indulged her, that's how the place got its name.'

'Look, Sonny, I got a job to do.'

'Stick with me, OK?' Sonny was nervous. He bunched his shoulders up and unknotted the sweater, then tied it around his neck again.

I made conversation. 'So why'd they leave the name plaque up?'

'I don't know, man. How do I know why they left the fucking name plaque up? Who knows, maybe they think it's a piece of goddam history. Christ, what's taking so long? I'm going up, I don't want her dying on me before you see her. Come on, man.' He was walking and talking, headed for the elevator when it opened and a woman emerged.

She said, 'I'm Frances Pascoe, and you're right, it is a piece of history, the name of the building, that is.'

Mrs Pascoe was tall, slender, big shoulders like an athlete, five ten, maybe more. Great silky skin. She wore a tailored white shirt, cuffs folded stylishly back over the freckled wrists, gray slacks, cream-colored sweater unbuttoned but tossed over her shoulders, wide gold wedding band.

Gliding forward from the elevator, hand outstretched, she greeted me and Sonny like she owned the building. She had her part all ready: gracious lady was the role, and there was a script in her head. You need a script these days; even for grief we get our manners off the TV, even death. Christ.

Lippert's jaw line twitched, the veins in his neck stood out, and he said to her abruptly, 'I was looking for you earlier.'

It was hard to read Mrs Pascoe's age. The cheekbones were world class, the good skin was like a girl's, the dark hair was short, but her long thin hands were freckled. The eyes were lighter than hazel, like seawater, and wide set, one slightly larger than the other; she fixed me with those green-brown lamps for a few seconds, then took some shades out of her sweater pocket and slid them on.

Thomas Pascoe, the dead guy, was a Brit. His wife Frances was too, but the accent had faded, bleached by years in New York. Brit-Lite, I thought; I'd met a few like her. She gestured for us to sit; instinctively she arranged the seating so we sat in the sun, the light in our eyes, and she was in the shadow, watching us.

'I've already talked to three different detectives this morning,' she said. 'How can I help you?'

'We're going up to talk to Mrs Ulanova,' Lippert said.

'You can't do that.'

'Why not?' Sonny was pretty blunt. He didn't offer condolences; Mrs Pascoe didn't look like a woman who wanted them either, not from strangers, not from anyone.

'When she found poor Tommy earlier, something happened, an embolism probably.'

Sonny said, 'I knew that.'

'They took her to the hospital an hour ago.'

'How the hell did they get her out? Why didn't anybody tell me?' Sonny was furious.

'Service lift. And there's a side door,' said Mrs Pascoe. Her laugh was harsh. 'You could say she blew her top. Who can blame her? I'm sorry.'

Sonny said, 'Yeah, so am I.'

'I meant for myself. Sorry for myself. Madame Ulanova might have noticed something. Told us something. About Tommy. I don't think she'll do much talking now.'

Sonny stood up. 'We'll get to her in the hospital. Art, you ready?' He turned back to Mrs Pascoe. 'Your husband was head of the co-op here, is that right? He virtually ran the building?'

'Yes. My husband was head of the co-op board here for almost forty years, but you knew that.'

– 19 –

Sonny said, 'Yeah, OK, while I get on to Ulanova, you could help me out, make me a list of everyone who tried to get an apartment here the last couple of years.'

She said, 'We don't keep lists. I don't suppose you'd have a cigarette?'

I tossed her a pack; she lit up, sucked in a lung full of it and grunted, 'Thanks.'

I got the impression Mrs Pascoe was ripped on something; the queer calm, the pupils of her eyes – the peculiar sci-fi headlights – that turned into pinpricks. Then she said, 'We were going to London tonight, you see. It was planned.'

'But you'll stick around now. Won't you?'

'I thought I might bury my husband. If that's all right.'

Sonny Lippert saw the mayor signal to him, got up and said to me, 'You talk to her.'

Mrs Pascoe stood up too, then stumbled. I put out my hand. She ignored me. I lit a cigarette for myself and said, 'What about financials?'

'Everything's paid in cash.'

I said, 'A list, some names, it would help us out.'

'I told you, there isn't any list. Everyone who was interviewed for an apartment was known to us.' She looked at the lobby. 'This was our home. Ours.'

'OK,' I said. 'So I'll put the word out we're looking, see who shows up. All right?'

Frances Pascoe got the message. 'I'll see what I can do.' She stubbed her cigarette out in an ashtray on a table, turned to go, then added very softly. 'We were already packed.'

Outside, Sonny Lippert looked up at the fourteen-story limestone building. I followed his gaze, both of us shading our eyes, looking at the bronze Art Deco sculptures of stylized women – the Muses maybe – carved in the façade, gilded by the sun off the river. Sonny put on sunglasses and said, 'They built it back when there wasn't any air conditioning. They built so when it got hot the building was always in the shade. So the rich people could stay cool.'

We stood on the river side of the building on the little piazza that faced the water. The place was festooned with yellow police tape like Christo was getting ready to wrap it, and now Sonny lifted some tape for me to pass. I walked to the railing and looked at the water.

From the piazza, the drop to the East River was terraced, like a vincyard. A flight of stairs led down to a pocket park and then again to the river front. There was a jetty on the water, once used by residents for their private craft: men who went to work on Wall Street by boat, bootleg guys who unloaded supplies for the rich, spies, crooks. Once upon a time. Now a helicopter buzzed the scene, and if I listened hard there was the mild chop that splashed the seawall and made a smacking sound like babies chuckling.

I said, 'You were pretty rough on the wife. How come you're so obsessed with who wanted an apartment? There's a million possibilities on this one.'

'There's rumors all over town. Real estate. Market's too volatile. Up. Down. People wanting in. Management companies embezzling funds. Bribes. Maybe other stuff. The rules are off,' he said. 'So go get me a witness, Artie, man, OK? I don't care if you have to dress up and play doctor to get into the Russian's room, but please? OK?'

'I'm freelance now. I'm expensive.'

Sonny said, 'You're worth it,' which surprised me.

'Where's the money coming from?'

'We got a law and order mayor in residence at Gracie Mansion, which is just up the street – you think he wants this kind of shit in his neighborhood when he has his eye on national office? Gimme a break! Thomas Pascoe was a player. For an uptown job like this there's always money. Anyhow, you speaking Russian, I can make a case I need you on the witness.'

He hurried across the piazza and around the building to the street, where a crowd had gathered. Sonny got to his black Lexus, then opened the car door. 'I just gotta ask myself, Who wanted in? Who did Pascoe reject? Who got shafted by the co-op board? Who had to sit with the sun in their eyes for an interview?'

Across the street a homeless guy sat on the curb, face to the sun, squinting at the spectacle. A supermarket cart was beside him, piled with empties. Men and women in suits emerged from the buildings that lined Sutton Place, the insular, elegant riverside avenue. They looked up at the blue sky, smiled, and went to work. A trio of private-school kids loitered near by. They were maybe fifteen and they gaped at the crime scene, caught some morning rays, drank coffee out of Starbucks containers, smoked.

The two boys, shirts untucked, ties at half-mast, were still kids, and I felt for them. The girl in a yellow blazer and a pleated skirt flipped her shiny hair, hiked her skirt higher on her fleshy thighs, pushed out her hip at the boys, taunting them.

But the sun shone, the streets up here were clean as a fucking whistle. No garbage bags sat out on Sutton Place, and the air off the river was fresh, clear, almost succulent. Paradise in Manhattan, except for the dead man in his tower.

I turned to look at the building again. All those rich people stacked up in their limestone castle overlooking the East River. A tribe in its own right. And the headman was dead. The taboos would be tough to break.

I unlocked my bike where I'd left it hitched to the railing that divided the street from the townhouses and the private gardens. I said to Sonny, 'You're telling me someone tried to chop Pascoe's head because of an apartment in a dumb-ass co-op?'

'You checked out of reality since you left the department? You think because the media assholes say the city's safe from fear, and Disney gobbles up Times Square, nothing's happening? Evil don't go nowhere, or greed, or ambition neither, babe, nowhere at all.' Sonny waved an arm at Sutton Place. 'These people express themselves by which building they got a piece of or who they rejected. Human nature,' he said. 'Nowadays, all ideology been replaced by money.' He ducked into his car and sat and looked out at me.

Sonny Lippert held the car door open. 'Read your Gorky, or Darwin, man. We are talking Darwin here, we are talking Hobbes.'

I said, 'Jesus Christ, Sonny.'

A tiny smile twitched at Sonny's mouth. 'I don't think so, man. Mrs Pascoe does a nice line in gracious living, but it doesn't stop her living in a building that never takes Jews.'

'You really want to nail her, don't you? I mean, is this personal, or what?'

Sonny Lippert got in his car. 'Yeah, man, well I like to see rich people squirm.'

Chapter 3

It was quiet as a sunlit tomb up on the rich-people floor later that day at New York Hospital, light from the river streaming in, carrying motes of silvery dust. I went home first to dump the bike, pick up my car; I wasn't going out on this kind of job like some copcycle from the Parks Department. Shucked the jeans and sweatshirt, put on a good Hugo Boss jacket I got for peanuts on the designer rack at Century 21, listened to some messages, three of them: a possible job on a missing persons deal; a message from Lily; Tolya Sverdloff, only his mobile number, nothing that couldn't wait.

I called Lily's answering machine – I call sometimes even when she's out because I like hearing her husky voice on the machine – and ignored the others. By the time I got uptown, the hospital was in gridlock from a smash-up on the FDR and also a lot of leftover bagel cuts from Sunday. The thing they see most on Sundays at the Upper Eastside ERs is bagel cuts. People slice their bagels too fast, they lose a piece of finger.

It took me a while to negotiate my way, but I slipped inside, ducked into a supply closet, found a white coat, tossed it on, felt like a fool in it. There'd be security for Ulanova, I figured, so I put on the coat.

Where was she? The Russian who blew her lid when she found Pascoe dead in the pool, she could be anywhere – the operating table, the morgue. Anywhere. Sonny would explode if I screwed this up.

I walked through the corridors, looking for the old Russian, but thinking about Frances Pascoe and the building itself. From a nurse's station, a pumpkin grinned at me. I snatched a handful of candy corn from a tray. A pretty nurse saw me do it, grinned at me. Halloween at the end of the week. A million people coming into the city. Celebrate the dead.

I peered at the name cards slotted into doors. No one stopped me. Some of the doors I passed were ajar; I got a glimpse of beds, patients, some asleep, others half sitting, peering up at the TVs that hung from overhead arms. The cathode glow of the screens caught my attention and I stopped and looked at a set. The Pascoe story was already running. I turned a corner.

From one of the rooms came a soft moan now: someone crying in pain, muffled by medication. And the alien antiseptic smell, insidious, the ammonia, the sick flesh, the weird sour smell of stainless steel – bedpans, sinks, bedrails.

Too many times in the last year I'd smelled it. Friends died. I had waited in the hallway and smelled the sour smell.

Behind me there was the quiet squish of rubber soles on linoleum. Hospitals spook me. Something goes wrong. An alarm shrieks. A hunk of human flesh in intensive care malfunctions. There's the sudden noise, the officious thud of a phalanx of medics when they appear.

Where was she? Ulanova. There'd be a cop on duty. Then I saw it. The name was on the door. No cop. I pushed the door open softly, but the bed was made up tight and empty, the lights doused. She must be dead.

I dug some chewing gum out of my pocket. I wanted a smoke, but I was committed to three a day and I'd already had four. I glanced in the bathroom and the closet. Someone had supplied her with a toothbrush and there was a cheap watch on the bedside table, a hairnet and a little wooden icon. I wondered how the hell she got hold of the icon before they brought her in, and I sat on the edge of the bed looking at it, the sad, crappy souvenir, and felt pissed off that I was too late.

What the hell. With the story running this big, other witnesses on this one would come out of the woodwork like cuckoos out of a clock.

In the mirror, I caught my reflection. Like Sonny said, I had dropped some weight, I was tan from a day of fishing off Sag Harbor the week before. I'd cleaned up my act and my eyes were clear. I'm six one. Hair still dark.

'You look like an American,' my mother always laughed, way back when I was still a kid in Moscow. When I got to New York, it made it easier to dump the past.

The last few years cost me. There was no ease in me for so long I didn't even notice. I thought I was a good-time guy when I was really dying. Too much pain, too much booze. I couldn't stop. People said, veg out, Art, chill. But I couldn't. I was locked into what I'd seen and done, with all the obligation, fury, guilt. I'd watched other guys my age drop dead from heart attacks. Strokes. You turn forty, you're in trouble.

But I was OK now, better than I'd been in a real long time. I'm solvent, more or less. Lily Hanes and me, we're good together, and there's Beth who's three already. Nothing was going to drag me back into the shit, and now, sitting in the silent, sunny room staring in the mirror, I hummed the Beach Boys tune that I heard the guy by the pool whistle.

'See anything you like?'

I saw Frances Pascoe in the mirror. I got off the bed, the cheesy watch still in my hand. There was a film of talcum powder on it.

I said, 'She's dead.'

Mrs Pascoe shut the door to the room. 'No, she isn't. She's gone home. I came in, like you, and found her gone. I spoke to the head nurse. Someone checked her out. When they brought her in this morning, it seems, she made a frightful stink and eventually got herself released against doctor's orders.'

'Who took her home?'

'I heard it was a nephew.'

'Doctors that accommodating around here?'

'Here? If someone's paying, yes.'

'He was Russian?'

'Who?'

'The nephew. Say I'm curious.'

'Apparently, yes.' She glanced at the icon in my hand. 'I'd better take her things.'

Like me, she'd come to pump the old woman. Mrs Pascoe gestured at the empty bed with a small yellow basket she carried. 'I'll get her things, then I'll take you to see her if you like.' She was polite and very cool.

I gave her the icon and she took it, then set her bag on the bed, put the hairnet and toothbrush inside. She pulled her sweater around her shoulders and pushed the short hair away from her eyes. A wry smile animated her cold, ageless face and I couldn't stop looking. Frances Pascoe was very sexy. I don't want anyone except Lily, but this was an interesting woman. Adhesive You wanted to touch her. She glanced at me, then at the bed and smiled.

I followed her into the corridor, where she said, 'You might want to get rid of your sleuth costume.'

I dumped the white coat in a laundry bin. 'My car's outside.'

When we got to the street, she put her hand on the door of my red Cadillac and said, 'Marvelous car.'

This was a woman who watched men: she saw where the soft tissue was; she clocked right away how I feel about the car. I reached over and opened the door for her, felt her sweater brush my arm, then her hand on my wrist, her letting me feel the cool light fingers, as she slid into the seat. She closed the door, shifted her thighs on the natural leather seat appreciatively, then waited until I got behind the wheel and said, 'You're wondering why I don't seem more upset about Tommy's death, is that it?'

I didn't answer her.

She said, 'I don't do grief, you see. It's not who I am.'

Ulanova's place was made up of a couple of maids' rooms; the bedroom was small and crowded with boxes, trunks, a narrow bed. The end of the line for the old woman who lay on the bed. Grimy white walls. On the mahogany bureau stood a gilded icon, the gold leaf mottled and flaky, the figures rubbed out.

Inert, emaciated, the old Russian lay on the narrow bed, head wrapped in bandages and a red silk scarf. A black woman in a white nylon uniform, face weary, sat thighs apart on a kitchen chair. I crouched next to the old lady's bed. The breathing was shallow, the face barely haunted by life. A noise came out of her mouth and I leaned closer; she spoke in short bursts.

I leaned my elbows on my knees and bent my head closer to the mouth. I whispered to her in Russian. I want to help, I said. Talk to me, please, I said. Suddenly her hand moved towards mine, the fingers crawling over the sheet like spiders. I put my hand in her claw and she dragged it up to her cheek. It felt like onion skin, thin, brittle, greasy. Her eyes stayed shut, but she forced out the words into a stream of venom.

The breath was putrid, her Russian was exquisite. Like some hideous metaphor for the whole goddam country.

I leaned closer. She whispered how much she hated Thomas Pascoe. He had stolen her apartment and left her the maids' rooms and she hated him for it.

The attendant said, 'That's enough.'

'This is important.'

'I'm sorry. You can come back tomorrow.'

I said softly, so the old woman wouldn't hear me, 'What if she's worse?'

'That's a chance you'll have to take, hon, all right? Let her be.'

But Ulanova pulled on my hair. My face was against hers.

'I came home,' she hissed in Russian. 'I had to come home from the hospital.'

I said, 'Why?'

She said, 'They planned to steal my home from me.'

Mrs Pascoe was waiting in the living room. It was small. It had one window, leaded panes, a rusted handle that didn't work right. It faced a brick wall. Under it was an upright piano with yellow keys, some of them missing. The room was jammed with black walnut furniture and carved statues, wooden crates, old books, battered icons, oil paintings, some of them stacked three deep, in piles, shoved against the walls, covered with drop-cloths and padded moving blankets. Seedy oriental rugs were piled on top of each other. Enough stuff for a mansion was crammed into the room; her life had shrivelled, was boxed in now, all that was left this lousy cluttered room.

I looked around and said, 'Miss Havisham's parlor.'

Mrs Pascoe, who sat on the edge of a straight chair, her legs tucked neatly together, raised her eyebrow very slightly.

I added, 'Yeah, I read books too.'

'I'm sure you do. Did you get what you wanted?'

I shrugged and said, 'You got anything for me? Some names? Some kind of list?'

'Names?'

'People who wanted apartments in this building.'

She got up and looked around. 'I hope the bloody nephew's coming to get her stuff. I hope to Christ he's got some sense and we can do business with him. At least we'll be able to clean this place out,' she said. 'Don't look so shocked, Mr Cohen. It's been hell dealing with her rubbish. Literally. We've been trying to get her out for years. Tommy would have been delighted.'

I said, 'She's not dead yet,' but Mrs Pascoe only said, 'As good as.'

She opened the front door. The hallway up here was bleak, no wallpaper, green paint peeling, the sour smell of age, disease, garbage. A mouse skittered by on the stained carpet. I said, 'All of them maids' rooms up here?'

Frances Pascoe said, 'Yes. The building's board has managed to buy them all, except for hers. To convert them to storage. She's stayed on like grim death.' She pushed the elevator button. It was a service elevator at the back of the building; we got in, rode silently to the second floor, where we got out and took some back stairs to the lobby.

I said to Frances Pascoe, 'This the way the help travels?'

She only smiled.

In the lobby, she gestured to a sofa in the corner. She didn't invite me home.

'Tell me how it really works, getting an apartment here. You advertise?'

'Never.'

'So?'

'We can't take everyone. We rarely have anything available.'

'You have complete control?'

'It's a co-operative. The residents own the shares. It's private. We have control.'

'So you look them over, the wannabes, according to the kind of dough they make. Right? So there will be records. You get an applicant for a co-op, you check out their financials first, and the references. Then you haul them in for an interview with the board that runs the building, right?'

'The apartments are paid for in full as I told you. I did tell you. There's no reason to involve banks for the most part.'

I said, 'OK, so references,' but she said, 'Most buildings, yes. Co-ops, as you know, are owned by the owners of the apartments, each has a share, each has a vote, which is how the boards are elected.'

I was getting impatient. 'Spare me the basics.'

'Fine,' Mrs Pascoe said.

'But there's references.'

'We don't ask for references.'

'What?'

She rubbed her hand across her forehead. 'We don't need them. Either people are known to us or not.'

'Known to you?'

'Yes. Can we go outside? I'd like to smoke.'

I followed her to the piazza, where a fountain decorated with stone mermaids spouted water and there were carved marble urns full of white geraniums. She walked down the stairs to the pocket park, where there was a little gazebo with a bench inside, then leaned on the railing and craned her neck towards the river. At the water's edge was a larger park; sun glinted off a bronze animal.

She looked down at it. 'It's a warthog, I think. The kids call it Warthog Park.'

'Kids?'

'Never mind. Let me have a cigarette.'

I gave her my pack and the lighter. She said thanks, lit up and glanced around.

'Expecting someone?'

'I don't know what you mean,' she said, but she was jumpy. Noise distracted her – the hoot of a boat on the river, the steady drone of cars on the Drive below us, the cars that swished over the 59th Street Bridge a few blocks north. The sun was warm, but Mrs Pascoe buttoned her sweater.

'You want to go in?'

'No, thank you.' She took my wrist lightly, then let go. 'I swear to you, we did try.'

I kept my mouth shut.

'Except for two apartments that were willed on when the occupants died, we've only had one come up in the last half-dozen years.'

'When? What year?'

'Last year.'

'Anyone make the cut?'

'We interviewed a few, I barely remember them. You know,

it's curious, most people are awfully good about it, they realize this building isn't for them, they rarely fuss. A few go a bit mad. They beg. A veiled threat. Offers to charity. The new rich always want to appear charitable, don't they, Mr Cohen? My God, one couple even offered us cash under the table.' She honked with laugher. 'In notes.'

I shrugged and kept quiet.

'It was a disaster really, all our efforts. I remember one couple, the fellow said, "We've got cash," and Tommy said, "But you work for your father-in-law. What happens if you and your wife should split up? You understand," Tom said – it was marvelous how he kept a straight face – "there's no financing ever," and the poor sod ran for the bathroom. He was sick as a parrot. We all heard him. It was humiliating for him, of course, but he shouldn't have lied to us.'

'Sure.'

She said, 'It did make us laugh, though. Tommy had such a sense of humor. One has to try, darling, he'd say before. Such frightfully unattractive behavior, he always said afterwards, after the interviews, when he had to have a second whiskey. He was right.'

'So what do these apartments run?'

'The market's been absolutely ridiculous, of course. I'm not being evasive, it just depends. Nothing under two million, of course. Am I a suspect?'

I watched the river. 'That's not my department.'

'I can't believe anyone killed Tommy on purpose.'

'Why not?'

'He was one of the good guys. He gave away money. He helped people. It's how he was raised. He sat on the boards of several schools. He rolled up his sleeves.'

'He was a good Christian.'

'Exactly.' Her tone was bland. She added, 'I wonder if this wasn't random, you see, an opportunity, someone he helped even, with an ax to grind, if you'll forgive the pun, or looking for cash.'

'In the swimming pool? I don't think you believe that.'

'Don't I? I don't know.' She stretched, and the bare skin of her midriff showed. It was tan and tight and she saw me looking. She smiled and said, 'I'm going inside.'

'You were on the co-op board along with your husband?'

'Not formally. I sometimes served drinks at the board meetings.' She started up the stairs towards the building. 'Will you tell me what Madame Ulanova said to you in Russian?'

'It's your husband, lady. He's the dead guy and you want to trade with me?'

Her eyes dilated, and when she raised her hand to brush the hair from her eyes, her mohair sweater slid up to her elbow. No needle marks. Maybe she was popping pills, but I was betting it was booze. The inside of her arm was soft and a little fleshy. I wondered how it tasted.

I walked her to the door. 'You have kids?'

'No.'

'So you get everything? The money, the apartment, all the goodies?'

'It was all mine to begin with.'

'You inherited it?'

'I earned it. Tell me what Ulanova said.'

Frances Pascoe assumed I was some schmuck detective who would do what she wanted, and she tipped her head inquisitively, locked the glistening eyes on me, said, 'Will you?'

I looked in the expectant face and said, 'No.'

She pulled her sweater tight.

I said, 'You mentioned only one apartment came up for sale. Who got it?'

'We did,' Mrs Pascoe said. 'It was next door to ours. Tommy and I. We bought it.'

'I'll tell you what. When you want to talk to me, give me a call, OK? I don't have anything personal invested in this, it's just a job.'

'Yes you do.'

'Do what?'

'Have something invested.'

'What's that?'

'Me.'

I was surprised and I said 'What?' but she ignored me, so I took it as a come-on and tried to forget it. She was used to getting her way, she'd say what she figured would work. How the hell could I have anything invested in this case? I'd never met

Frances Pascoe before in my life.

Before she finally went inside, she looked nervously around the piazza again and said, 'Do you see the world as a frightening place?'

'Not frightening,' I said, walking away. 'Unpredictable. I usually sit with my back to the wall.'

From the piazza, through the lobby window, I saw the doorman escort Mrs Pascoe across the lobby like she might break. Before she got to the elevator, she looked back out at me. She was irritated. Then the doorman leaned down and said something and she smiled. He pulled out some cigarettes from an inside pocket, gave her one, lit it for her.

It was warm out, almost hot. I walked from Sutton Place over to First when I left Mrs Pascoe. In the streets, nannies shared a smoke; their babies snoozed in their strollers. At sidewalk tables old guys sat and shot the breeze. In the sultry weather the neighborhood had a lazy, old-fashioned feel, a snapshot from another time: the elderly men wore Sinatra-style snapbrims made of straw; some of the women wore thin flowery dresses.

I walked as far as 67th Street and the One Nine, a precinct where most of what they see is property crime. Jewellery theft. Lost dogs. Down a couple of blocks, where I passed the gothic façade of St Peter's School, then back to Sutton Place.

I dated a girl once who lived around here and was nuts for its history. Sutton Place was a tiny enclave, almost hidden from the city, seven blocks long, tucked between the eastern edge of the city and the river. Not so long ago – in the 1700s – there were rocky bluffs where the East 50s are now. Rich Dutchmen who worked in downtown Manhattan came to escape the crowds and disease in the summer, and built their country mansions overlooking the river. Sloops sailed the East River on their way to Long Island Sound.

Later on there were inns and sightseers and then industry came: factories for making gun shot and cigars, breweries.

In 1900 the Queensboro Bridge, 59th Street Bridge, whatever you call it, opened, a dazzling, elaborate structure with stone piers, polished tiles, iron spires. The new rich drove their new cars across it en route to their palaces on Long Island. In the 1920s the rich built townhouses and apartment buildings here. Sutton Place always had a racy reputation. Scattered among the gentry were artists and actors and at least one famous porn star. It was a peculiar, insular place, even after they shoved the FDR Drive through and destroyed the riverfront. All that was left were the terraced walls, covered in ivy, that divided buildings like the Middlemarch from the highway below and the river beside it.

I looked up and down the street. There was something unreal about it in the hot, still evening.

Two TV vans were parked outside the Middlemarch and I went over to see what was up, when a young woman, Hispanic, Dominican maybe, emerged from the building and walked a few yards before she got out her smokes. I followed. We got to chatting. She was a maid at the Middlemarch. I asked if she knew a janitor named Pindar Aguirre. She said sure, but he was off that day. She knew that. She retailed some gossip: which maids stole; which nannies let their boyfriends in the service entrance; who tipped good.

After she finished her cigarette, she stubbed it out on the pavement and went back to the building, and I strolled across the piazza on the river side, leaned against the wrought-iron railing, watched the building. The lobby was empty now. Frances Pascoe was gone.

Sonny Lippert knows me; he knew what he was doing, putting me on this case. It wasn't just because I speak Russian. He wanted something.

I leaned against the piazza railing. My fingers touched the ornamental iron leaves entwined on the railing behind me. From where I stood, the fourteen-story building glowed. The light was fading and the evening sky made an almost visible frame for it. It was a pretty seductive picture. Rich people interest me.

I have this snapshot in my head, it's fading now, but I can still see the details, and in it I'm twelve years old. My Aunt Birdie takes me to a rich man's apartment in Moscow. He is a privileged foreigner and therefore fabulous. Exotic. An actual capitalist, a *bizinessman*, and we go up and a servant lets us in. There is beautiful light, rich wood panelling and furniture, some modern, some antique, but each piece is different, and there are soft Persian carpets and airy white curtains. Paintings unlike anything I can imagine, that Birdie says are by Marc Chagall, and lamps made of stained glass she tells me are from a place named Tiffany. There are American drinks, Jack Daniels for Birdie and Coca Cola for me, and chocolate chip cookies. I've never tasted such things. We were taught at school that Coca Cola tasted like shoe polish; it didn't. It tasted fine.

Most of all, I'm aware of the soft fabric of his sleeve when he shakes my hand, the great man, and of the smell. Moscow stinks of cabbage and the carbolic they use to clean up the drunks' vomit in buildings and on the street; you can always smell the vomit anyhow. Here the smells are good wood, wood polish, freshly washed linen and cookies baking. It smells clean and expensive.

In those days in Moscow, seeing the apartment was a kind of pornography: it turned me on. At twelve, I thought the light, the space, the smells were sexy.

Now, I stared at the lobby of the Middlemarch again. I wanted a look inside, but Frances Pascoe was gone. I stayed where I was, arms stretched out along the railing.

If someone from the outside murdered Thomas Pascoe, then the killer went in the side entrance and took the stairs up a flight and another set down to the pool. There were three elevators, one from the lobby with an operator, one for residents that went from the various floors straight to the pool and skipped the lobby, and a service elevator that went to the top floor where Ulanova lived but stopped on two. From two, you took the back stairs to the ground floor or the basement and the pool. God knows who dreamed up the arrangements, but I wanted a picture of the building in my mind, a cross section, like one of those kids' picture books that shows you how stuff works. I was betting whoever did Pascoe knew his way around.

I saw Sweeney go off duty at eight. A younger guy came on the door. I went around to the street side of the building and strolled inside in the wake of a guy walking a pack of fancy hounds. Then I slipped into the service door, the vestibule, through a second door and into the Middlemarch stairwell. I was in. Through the rabbit hole.

It was dark inside. I started down, missed a step, skidded a couple more. I put my shoulder against a door and leaned on it. Nothing happened. I climbed up a flight, but the doors opened into the stairs. I was trapped. I was like a rabbit in a vertical cage. I hate closed spaces. I was stuck in an elevator once with a couple of nasty thugs and it changed me.

I was sweating bullets as I reached the roof. 'Come on, fuck you.' I was screaming at the door. It was bolted. Then I remembered: there was access on Two. It was how the help travelled. I kept on moving, running back downstairs, when I heard it: a faint tap tap on the concrete steps, remote at first, then louder, coming closer, following me, up, down. The sound travelled in ways I couldn't follow. I had left the door propped open; someone had followed me in. The sound was closer now, behind me, on top of me. I turned and squinted.

The arm came from behind me and my head banged against the edge of the stairs. My adrenalin surged and I wanted to hit someone. I got my hand on my gun, wrapped it around the butt, got some momentum and hit out. Hard. Connected with hair and skull. A man whimpered in the dark and swore out loud in Russian. He couldn't stop himself; he cursed from the pain and cursed at me: keep your nose out of things, he said. I knew the curse: they cut off your nose. The accent was crude. Brighton Beach, I thought, and let him go.

He ran downstairs. Jerk that I was, I had made it easy for him. I heard him run out of the door and into the street. I ran too, but he was gone. I wasn't bruised bad, but I was pissed off. If Sonny Lippert heard I got banged up, he'd pull me off the case. I didn't want off. Already there was something that tugged at me on this one. I pretended it was just a job, but I wanted in. I went home and ignored Sonny's messages.

Chapter 4

I sat out on my roof that night, me looking through a telescope Lily got me for my birthday, Lily and Beth a few yards away. The end of October, but warm out. I didn't mention the Pascoe case, didn't tell her I was on it. It would upset Lily, me running into a creep.

On the barbecue, a butterflied leg of lamb sent up its delicious smoke. Through the telescope I could see a startling amount of stars. Space garbage drifted overhead too, in the spangled sky. From here, what was left of Mir looked glamorous, the last bright thing the Soviets ever made.

Around us, on low-lying roofs of warehouses, on fire escapes and balconies, in Chinatown and Soho, Tribeca and Nolita, people sat out late. There were colored lights, red, yellow, blue, green, strung up on makeshift clothesline. I saw some Chinese guys in their underwear playing cards. A half-naked couple rocked in a hammock. Somewhere a Stephane Grapelli album played.

I heard something splash.

A few feet away, in the blue plastic pool I fixed up on the roof, Beth paddled in the warm water and laughed. It had been warm all month and we ate out on the roof of the cast-iron building off Broadway where I have the loft. I got it early, when no one wanted rough spaces on the wrong side of Canal Street. Before I bought it, I lived in shitty rentals in Brooklyn and Alphabet City. It's the only place I've ever owned. I got real lucky. I can only tell Lily how I feel about my place, how I got it, fixed it up, scraped the floors myself, how it makes me physically happy to be in it. What I don't tell her is I'd kill anyone who messed with it.

I looked across the street. The windows were open in the building opposite mine. Girls on the nightshift in the sweatshop sewed and smoked and I could look in and see them work. Other windows had pumpkins in them, carved up into grinning faces. People in the street below were hanging out, making out, drinking beer.

No one could remember anything like it, weather so clear and warm for so long. A steady breeze blew pollution out to sea. Crime was down, the city was high. 'Can't last,' cynics said. 'The last good time.' People smiled. There was a blue moon that month.

I looked at Lily. She had on a pair of cut-offs and one of my shirts knotted up around her waist; she was barefoot and her long legs were still tan from the summer. She pushed her heavy red hair off her neck, fastened it on top of her head with a rubber band, then reached down, lifted Beth out of the pool and dried her with a yellow towel. Lily spread the towel on the roof and Beth sat on it for a while. She looked at Lily, then me, big black eyes wide, wondering what we wanted from her. She got up, toddled around the roof looking for someone to charm, returned to the towel, yawned a lot and dozed off.

Beth spent her first six months in a Chinese orphanage; the ability to divine what people liked was a survival tactic; for a baby girl in that hellhole, charm kept you alive. I went over and picked her up.

I had carried Beth home from China for Lily, and I couldn't hold her without remembering the heavy, warm sensation when I first picked her up out of a crib in the orphanage and put her arms around my neck. Then she pissed all over me. I laughed at the memory. I went from being a guy who worried if I had the right brand virgin olive oil in my kitchen to a guy who shopped for the right baby formula at K-Mart on Astor Place.

Beth was almost three now, big, beautiful, smart, spoiled, funny, a regular New York kid. They spend weekends with me here a lot of times, but it was Monday night. I'd take them home later. Lily, who's a freelance writer, works from home now. She keeps regular hours during the week. I didn't mind. I like the ritual.

Lily gathered up the papers that lay scattered at her feet, and I saw the headline in the *Post*. It was the headline I would have written myself, so I looked at it and grinned: HEAD OF CO-OP LOSES HEAD.

This being New York and a story about rich people uptown, it was big. Lily glanced at the papers and for a split second she looked worried, or maybe I imagined it. She took her glasses off. Then she crumpled up the *Post* into a ball, threw it across the roof, picked up a beer, drank, wiped the liquid off her upper lip and smiled at me. She makes me laugh. She's smart. She knows where I come from. Also, there's her legs. And the rest of her.

Lily Hanes opened a door I was looking for since I got to New York, an immigrant asshole, green, scared, desirous. I was looking for it for twenty years.

I knew I should tell her about the Pascoe thing. Tomorrow, I'd tell her. It might be over tomorrow and nothing to tell. There were a million guys on the Pascoe case already. I'd go back to the fish market. Back to a missing persons case I had for a bank in Austin, Texas. Nice safe stuff that pays fine.

For Lily I had finally quit the police department for good; it was our deal. Private stuff pays better, most of it's industrial so you don't get banged up. She didn't want the fear. I didn't blame her. Somewhere the music changed. Sinatra sang 'Moonlight in Vermont' from a roof near by.

I could see 360 degrees over the city, the rivers and bridges, the buildings, the midtown towers, their tops gilded with light. I could see the shape of Manhattan, the small island in the center of the New York archipelago, people obsessively territorial, fighting for a piece of turf, Eastside, Westside, downtown. 'My house,' New Yorkers always say, even when they live in a studio apartment the size of a dog kennel. I thought about the Middlemarch, people fighting to get a place in it, the board hanging on to the power.

We have a board down here too, but until a few years back we were just a bunch of people in an old warehouse building who couldn't afford anything else. Sometimes we'd get together. Mostly at the meetings we drank a lot of beer and ignored the plumbing problems. We let in anyone who wanted a place if they had the dough. Then the yuppies arrived on the fourth floor. Soho overflowed into Chinatown. Tribeca squeezed us from the west. Prices soared. We upped the maintenance. We started making house rules.

Lily ambled over, put her long arms around my neck. She said, 'Are you happy?'

I was happy. I was on the inside for the first time in my life, instead of looking in. It was the kind of domestic bliss I never figured for myself. The ambitious young cop trying to unload his past was gone. I could feel Lily's breasts against my back. I said, like I do around once a month, 'Let's get married.'

She leaned against me, and I could smell some perfume I gave her. 'Why tempt fate?' She laced her arms around my neck. 'Let's go somewhere nice next weekend.'

'Let's go somewhere very nice. What time is it?'

She said, 'It doesn't matter. Does it? Why does it matter?'

'No. It doesn't. Nothing else matters.' I kissed her for a long time.

After I dropped them on 10th Street, where Lily's lived all her life, I finally returned Sonny's call. He said, 'Where are you?' like he always does. He needs physical back-up for the elusive digital contact. Lippert can't do business by phone; he's a guy that needs to press your flesh, so to speak, and I said, 'In the car. On my way.'

Most of the cops who work out at Sonny's gym, the guys with a gut slung over their belt, were outside on the front steps, gabbing, enjoying the warm night, drinking a can of beer.

'How's business?' I called to a guy I used to know, who waved back and grinned and said, 'Lousy.'

Inside, the place smelled of sweat. It had breeze-block walls and basic equipment and a slick linoleum floor. A couple guys lifted weights on the other side of the room. Lippert was on the treadmill, reading Dickens. Sometimes he walks through the night.

Every year around this time Sonny does his annual criminology lecture. He tells the kids, you want to know law, crime, human nature? Read Dickens. Read Dostoevsky. Graham Greene. Updike. He draws a crowd. Now he broke out a smile and held up his paperback. '*Bleak House*. You read it?'

'I read it.'

'You saw her.'

'I saw her.'

'And?'

I got on the treadmill next to his and kept pace. 'Ulanova hated Pascoe is all I got. Thought he was going to sell her place out from under her. She's stroking out, Sonny, I don't know how much time she has. One thing's sure.'

'One?'

'She hated Tom Pascoc like it was religion. She was devout. Zealous.'

'Enough to set up a murder?'

I thought about the old woman, waxy claws, dead eyes. 'Where'd she get the dough? How'd she fix it? Why was she on the scene?' I pulled a crumpled fax out of my pocket and handed it to him.

It was a full-page ad from the *Times* for a real estate broker and I'd circled one of the offerings in red. 'Best address on Sutton Place, unique building, river views, Deco pool, top floor studio flat.' The Deco pool was a giveaway.

Sonny looked up. 'Where'd you get this?'

'I've got a few contacts. The point is, Mrs Pascoe told me they never advertise. She lied.'

'You're sure it's the Middlemarch?'

'Yeah. In which case, I'm thinking, top floor, studio apartment, it's the old Russian advertised her own place.'

'But why, man?'

'Money. Spite. Say they're giving her grief, she's scared, she wants to sell, but the board makes it impossible for anyone who wants to buy her place.'

'Unless she sells to, lemme guess, Thomas Pascoe. Who maybe invites her for a swim to do some business.'

I said, 'So she advertises to stick it to them, stir things up. I told you I talked to a janitor, right? Said the pool doesn't open before seven. So when you showed at six, six-thirty, Pascoe was already dead. But what's Ulanova doing there so early? Pascoe was the only one who swam off hours.'

Sonny stopped walking. 'You're thinking if she didn't set him up, it was the other way around. He sees the ad, invites her for a chat. It's her they intend to kill. They get him by mistake?'

'I don't know.' I thought about the creep in the stairwell. 'You think her being Russian's an issue?'

He laughed. 'You and me, we always think being Russian's an issue, man, but she wasn't that kind.'

For a few minutes, facing forward, walking his treadmill again, Sonny Lippert ranted freeform. 'I resent this, Art, I want it finished. Some teabag asshole named Thomas Pascoe had connections at Gracie Mansion. The Mayor's office says, Get Sonny Lippert. I tell them I'm busy, I got the Russian mob in Brighton Beach lubricating property deals in the boroughs, I got Russian hoods moving into Manhattan too, investing with Paine Webber, buying art galleries and real estate, the money disappears into the system, it's legit, we're fucked. They got white shoe lawyers now, Art, the Russians. And I have to worry about some goddamn Brit gets offed. Any luck with that list of wannabes?'

'I'm working on it.'

I watched him dry his face, then Sonny drew breath and said, 'We got Halloween coming up also. There's a million people coming into the city in costumes. We're looking at chaos. I want this stitched up before, otherwise it's dead. Stay with the program, Artie, OK?'

'You have enough on your plate, man, you don't have to take on Halloween,' I said.

'We're all taking on Halloween, Art. Every single law enforcement officer in or out of uniform in this town is working it. Me included.' Sonny climbed off his treadmill and threw me a towel. I got off mine and wiped my face.

'This ain't just the Russian. Is it? Sonny? What else you looking for from me?'

Sometimes Sonny Lippert catches me off guard and the old antagonisms get me like heartburn. The obligation, the requirements, the dues – he makes me feel I still owe him. When Sonny was a federal investigator in the Eastern District, he was in charge of nailing the Russian mob; he's still obsessed.

After I got to New York – we left Moscow when I was sixteen, spent a few years in Israel – I tried to make a buck as an interpreter, I ended up in Sonny's office. He helped me get my Green Card, then my citizenship, and a place in the academy. I was a kid, twenty-one, twenty-two. Sonny helped me, so I did stuff for him. He needed a cop who could speak languages; I can do Russian, Hebrew, some French. Everyone in my family's real nimble at languages, but it's just a knack, a gimmick.

So I was Sonny's cop and we went a lot of rounds over the years, even after he left Brooklyn. For years I figured his ambition ate him from the inside like cancer and left a corrupted shell. But I had been wrong, and after the Chinatown job, we became friends. Still, I see Sonny Lippert wants something, I get a tight feeling in my chest.

I hung over Sonny; I'm a lot taller. 'There's something else.'

He said, 'You saw the widow.'

'So?'

'Show her your baby blues, man, OK? Show them rich folk your dimples is what I want. It was always your thing, looking good, talking nice. You don't hold your utensils like they're weapons, you got nice suits, you read books. Help me out here, and I'll see you get paid good.'

It was a job. I'd do the work, cash the check and walk away. Maybe find the asshole that tried to beat me up for a bonus.

'I don't do back-room stuff, Sonny. You know that. I don't con bank clerks into telling me about their clients, I don't break open people's mail. I don't listen in or wear a wire, or use computers, I don't do your regular PI ruse, you know that, and I'm not going to start.' I felt in my pocket for gum and flashed him a smile. 'Not even for you.'

He headed to the locker room. 'I hear you. Uptown case like this, Art, there's a wall of lawyers, a lot of people don't feel compelled to talk to us. I can't ask some cop makes fifty, sixty grand a year and puts himself in the way of a bullet to interest himself objectively in people that make a hundred times as much for doing nothing. I can't trust Mrs Pascoe to some idiot out of a precinct. These people ain't scared of some two-bit detective. You I can trust, Billy I can trust, but he's in China on other business. You saw her. If it was me, I'd take Mrs Pascoe in right now. But I can't do that. I want you on this.'

'How old you figure her for, Sonny?'

'I don't know. Hard to read. Fifty? Forty-five? Why, you got a hard-on for her?'

'I want a look inside that building.'

Sonny leaned over a sink, put his head under a tap, gulped

some water. 'Art, man, listen to me. They got a division on the building, OK? Probably the FBI. For all I know, being as how Thomas Pascoe was a foreign national, they got the CIA, MI6, Scotland Yard and the British Prime Minister. Just find me who wanted a place up there at the Middlemarch, the wannabes, the hopeless, the desirous, OK, please.' He gave his version of a dirty chuckle. 'Stay on the women.'

On his way to the showers, Sonny peered at me. 'What's that bruise on your forehead?'

'Nothing.'

'All right, man, but take it easy, OK. These co-op boards got huge power. There's no oversight. One building I heard of, man, they threatened a guy with eviction if he did not stop his dog barking.'

'Yeah? So?'

'So he had the dog's voice box surgically removed.'

Chapter 5

The babe in black carried a dog the size and color of a corn muffin, and the doorman who held the door for her, hat and coat loaded with gold braid, resembled a footman in a Disney flick. I was surprised when he asked her in Russian if she wanted a cab. She shook her head, gave him a faint imperious smile, took the pup and left.

The building was on the west side of Sutton Place, up near the bridge. What I could see of it from the street, it was twenty-five stories of marble, brass and glass. A chandelier in the middle of the lobby dripped crystal.

Salvatore Castle leaned against the hood of his black Range Rover, watched the woman and dog cross the street and said, 'I've something fabulous for you here.'

'You got a lot of Russians up here, Sal?'

'This building, this side of Sutton, yes, some.' He was uneasy. 'Very nice people, of course, very high class, real aristocrats some of them. Is it a problem?' He was anxious to please. 'Several princesses and at least one count!'

Castle was an uptown realtor, a chubby man, black hair, face shaved so close his skin was soft and naked, like fruit. He was all smooth accommodation in the gray Zegna suit, orange Sulka tie, tasselled loafers. I showed him the newspaper ad again; it featured a full-length photograph of Castle himself standing in front of the Manhattan skyline, as if he were its agent.

I said I was only interested in the Middlemarch. He looked uncomfortable. 'There's never anything there.'

'You advertised. You put your picture on the page, Sal.'

'It was a mistake. Let me show you this one.'

'No thanks.'

'How about next door?' He gestured at a half-finished building, scaffolding still in place.

Castle had an aspirant face. He looked up at the building like a man who always looks up. 'Fabulous, this one, when it's finished, like the old days on Sutton Place. Look at the detail on the limestone. Libraries, billiard rooms, wine cellars. Servants' quarters too, for an extra four hundred grand. I've got a penthouse six thousand square feet, twelve million, including a swimming pool and wrap terraces. Or something smaller?'

'The Middlemarch. Level with me,' I said and showed him my old badge; he impressed easy.

'All right, look, like we figured, the apartment in the *Times* ad was withdrawn after a few days. I don't know who listed it.'

'How could that happen?'

'Someone at my office. It happens. We never even viewed it. Brokers get set up in this market. Extortion. Collusion. False advertising, and most of the time we play hardball.'

'But not with the Middlemarch.'

'Exactly.'

'It was a blind alley?'

'Yes.'

'Let's walk and talk, Sal,' I said and we strolled down Sutton Place. On the left was the row of townhouses, private gardens leading on to the river. In front of me were a pair of blue and whites, cop cars parked outside the Middlemarch.

I stopped and looked at the building. 'What's so great about it anyhow?'

Castle took off his little glasses, tapped his nose with them. He craned his short neck. 'Look at this street, the way it's set apart from the city, the river, the light, the history. It has the most desirable buildings in the best zip code in the country. Like the great buildings on Fifth and Park. The rooms are big, ceilings are high, the walls are thick, the service is gracious and this one has the pool. The rules are very very tough. Sweet Jesus, my grandmother in Cuba, and she was the old school, old Spanish blood, old Spanish manners, but when it comes to rules, she could have been a hippie compared with these people. I can't afford to offend this kind of people and they all know each other.' He saw the doorman watching us. It was Sweeney, the big Irish guy. Castle looked nervous. 'Let's go.'

'What did you mean, you can't afford to offend them? How's that?'

'I can put an apartment on the market, I can find a buyer, he has the money. Then he waits for an interview. Weeks. Months. The co-op board strings him along, then it rejects him. The deal's off. Rejection's the name of the game.' He laughed to himself. Not much humor in the noise he made.

I pulled a pack of cigarettes out of my pocket and held it out, but Castle shook his head.

'Manhattan is a very small island,' he said. 'It's the world's most expensive piece of turf now that Hong Kong's finished, and Hong Kong only counted for the money. This is the club. Limited membership. People will kill to get a decent place.'

'Literally?'

'There's nothing left. I can get a couple mill for a classic six "fixer upper", as they call it, for which read an apartment that needs a ton of work on not the best street. In, you know, an area that's adjacent.'

'What about financial criteria?'

'Insane. Some buildings require the full purchase price in cash and two to three times that much in liquid assets, plus five years' maintenance, say half a mill, in escrow. The country house doesn't count as assets.' He shook his head. 'That help you?'

A few Bloody Marys, and an early lunch at Billy's on First Avenue, loosened Sal's tongue even more. He ordered chopped steak. I watched him eat. I wasn't hungry.

'Do me a favor, Sal. Find out exactly which apartment it was.'

'I already did. It was a couple of lousy maids' rooms, a piece of crap on the top floor. I checked around. Madame Ulanova was there a long long time. She came over during the war, there was a tremendous housing squeeze and they cut up the old apartments. Rent control came in to ease the squeeze. After World War Two Thomas Pascoe began assembling shares. He put together the big ten- and twelve-room apartments, but Madame Ulanova, who inherited her shares from her husband, wouldn't play his game.' Castle started on his third Bloody, sipped it, patted the tomato juice off his mouth with a napkin.

'And Pascoe was in charge?'

'Pascoe ruled by intimidation, but it was subtle. He put people on the board who had secrets, people he could control, Jews, queers, excuse me. Society was pretty anti-Semitic back then. The only legitimate basis for rejecting applicants to a co-op, and it's in the city codes, are insufficient financial ability and bad moral character.'

'Moral character's a pretty subjective area.'

'Right. Thomas Pascoe *was* the board.'

'So when was the ad withdrawn?'

'There was a fax waiting for me this morning.'

I said, 'After Pascoe died. So it was probably spite. Now she's free to keep it or put it back on the market. It's hers to sell. With Pascoe dead, it frees her up. But who the hell sent you the message if she's stroking out?'

Castle clutched his drink and looked at me like I lost my marbles. 'I guess you haven't heard.'

'Heard what?'

'I thought that's why you showed up. Madame Ulanova died this morning.'

I left Sal Castle, went over to First, walked a while, past the florist, dry cleaners, a Korean deli, a muffin store and nail parlor. The nail parlor had a sign in Russian in the window. I shut my eyes and put my mind back on the case.

Ulanova was dead. The Russian was Lippert's excuse to keep me on the case: he could get the dough to run me if there was a Russian speaker. Now he'd pull me off it. I didn't want off. I wanted to see Frances Pascoe again. I went back to the Middlemarch and leaned over the railing at the edge of the piazza. Out on the river, a green and yellow water taxi cruised under the bridge.

The sun was in my eyes, but when I put on some sunglasses, I saw the boys in the little park a level down from me. Two of them. In the little gazebo they sat side by side, backs to me, curls of smoke going up.

And then one of them stood up and turned around very slowly. His back was to the river now. He put his hand over his eyes to shade them, looked up at the building, saw me and lifted his hand. Very slowly, he raised it, like a young prince, in a little wave.

The light caught the blue-black hair, the tanned skin, the yellow jacket – he was a rich, handsome boy – and made him glitter. He waved again, then laughed, and tossed his cigarette into the water. I recognized the jacket. St Peter's School. My neighbor's kid goes to St Pete's.

Someone was watching me watch the kids. My mouth went dry. I could feel someone on my back. On instinct my hand went to my gun. Very slowly, I turned around.

Frances Pascoe was standing behind me, looking. She held out a piece of paper with some names scrawled on it, handed it to me and said, 'The names you wanted. I hope it helps. I'll call you when I can,' she added, then disappeared back into the building. I wondered why she gave me the list and who she was protecting.

I went home, checked out the names on the list as best I could, then drove over to Sullivan Street. At Pino's I picked up a pound of prosciutto and some Newport steaks. I got smoked mozzarella at Joe's Dairy along with a loaf of semolina, and I went by Lily's for a late lunch and maybe dinner later on, and to tell her Sonny Lippert threw me a piece of the Pascoe case. I had to tell her.

'A little piece,' I said. 'Nothing much.' I poured us both a glass of wine.

She looked up from her computer in the corner of the living room. It was a big, square room, yellow walls covered with books, records, CDs, photographs and artefacts from jobs she'd done as a reporter – kitsch stuff mostly: a set of wooden Russian dolls featuring Stalin and Gorbachev; a Haile Selassie cigarette case; the mirror with Mao in it that lights up and plays 'The East Is Red'. Old despots make Lily laugh.

Beth was asleep in the other room and Lily was working, glasses on, distracted. She wore old white tennis shorts and a sweatshirt with the sleeves cut off. She was barefoot. The floor was piled with newspapers, the TV tuned to a local station, the sound muted. I turned up the volume and glanced at the news running on the TV. The Pascoe story was in its second day.

Lily grilled me about it lightly, joking, but her tone was brittle and her mood shifted as soon as I told her I was on the case. I flopped on her big white sofa, kicked off my shoes, stretched my legs.

'You heard the one about the guy who lost his head over an apartment?' I said and cracked up.

Lily didn't smile. I told her a couple more stupid jokes I'd heard on the phone. She kept working, then stopped, picked up her wine glass, drank off most of it. Finally she said, 'You think it's a joke, don't you? Some kind of uptown *grand guignol*, Pascoe getting murdered in the pool, the withered old woman in the attic.'

'It's pretty rich,' I said and went into the kitchen, put the steak in the fridge, sliced up the mozzarella and unwrapped the ham. I was starving. She followed me and stood in the door. She picked up a piece of mozzarella and ate it; the milk from it dripped down her chin. I reached over to wipe it away, grinning.

Lily backed off and said, 'How involved are you?'

'It's nothing. A couple interviews is all, and I'm out of it. There was a witness, a Russian speaker. Sonny called me in.'

'Was?'

'She's dead.'

'So what's that leave for you, on the case I mean?'

'A few loose ends. And a nice piece of change for the work.'

She ate some prosciutto slowly. Then she said, 'I thought you gave up being Sonny Lippert's errand boy.'

I drank the wine and kept my mouth shut.

'Murder at the Middlemarch,' she said. 'You think because it's rich people no one suffers? You think other people aren't involved?' Lily smiled, but her tone was forced.

I said, 'Hey, there's nothing gonna happen on this one. It's a piece of cake. Nothing even near dangerous. I promised you, I meant it.'

Lily looked up at me. 'That's not what I meant.' She stretched and kissed me, but she had turned in on herself. 'I have some work to do.'

'I'll make lunch.'

I figured she was pissed off I was on the Pascoe case, scared maybe. I was still in the kitchen when the phone rang. Through the swing door, I heard her talking. Someone in London. Lily had worked in London; it still has a lot of allure for her, and she was animated now, gossiping about people I don't know, laughing at jokes I didn't hear. Even her inflection changed.

Half listening, I fixed salad and sandwiches.

'Hi.' Lily appeared in the door, a bottle of her best wine in her hand like an offering.

We ate a late lunch with the TV on. Frances Pascoe appeared on the news in old pictures in an evening dress. Eventually I said, 'Who was it? On the phone.'

Lily said, 'There's some kind of job going in London.' She was a little shifty, fussing with her glass, smiling too hard. 'A sort of charity thing, you know, Lily-does-good kind of thing.' She laughed.

'You want to do it?'

Suddenly the glass slipped from her hand and shattered on the hardwood floor. Lily crouched down, picked up the pieces of glass, cut herself. A bubble of blood appeared, and I pulled her on to the couch, took her hand, put her thumb in my mouth. I tasted the blood.

I said, 'It's OK. Go to London if you want to.'

She slumped against me, head on my shoulder, as if she was suddenly heavy with fatigue. She closed her eyes.

'What is it, sweetheart? Tell me.' I held her. People think I'm a fool for putting up with her moods. I don't listen to them. It's not rational, this stuff, how I feel.

She said, 'I don't want to go, I don't, I'd rather stay here with you, it's just maybe something I owe, something I ought to do. I don't know.'

I held on to her. She pushed her red hair away, looked at me, light gray-blue eyes transparent, troubled. 'Bloody London,' she said. 'It sucks you in.'

I said, 'Owe who?', but Lily had closed her eyes. All she said was, 'Turn off the TV.'

Chapter 6

A picture of Thomas Pascoe came up on the TV screen. He had the right face for the job: long patrician forehead, aquiline nose, white hair, thin lips.

The TV was over the bar and I stood drinking a beer, watching it, waiting for Lulu Fine in the pub off York Avenue. Fine was top of Mrs Pascoe's list. Pictures of soccer stars lined the wall. I pulled some obits out of a file folder and put them on the bar.

Thomas Pascoe was born in New York, 1920, he had English parents who took him home before he could talk. He looked good for going on eighty. He looked great. He came back to New York during the war, some kind of hot shot in the OSS. By the time he was twenty-five he was a hero. He stayed on, joined an investment bank. There was a brief first marriage, no kids. Then, later, Frances. They met on one of his trips to London, he brought her back to New York.

She was a lot younger, but there were no birth dates. She'd covered her tracks that way. She'd been an athlete as a kid, played around as a journalist, decorator, hippie. The background bio was brief, but it read like she came from money. The money was hers, she said, when I asked her about it. 'It was mine,' she said. 'I earned it.' I didn't know if marrying Pascoe was that job that earned her the dough or it was really hers. But even as a kid she looked rich.

Later there were radical causes. In the file was a picture of her at a party for the Black Panthers in the late Sixties. In a fringed suede jacket, she looked very young.

I'd checked with Sonny Lippert. Forty-four apartments in the Middlemarch, not counting the Pascoes' and Ulanova's. A dozen guys had been on it around the clock. Owners had been interviewed; no one knew anything. I called the board members. All of them talked up Thomas Pascoe like he was a dead saint. The house employees I got to were also quiet. I got an address for Pindar Aguirre; he lived in Astoria; it could wait. Two wannabes on Mrs Pascoe's list were out of town, one permanently; a third was dead.

The story was like the geoplastic phase of those volcanoes you see on *National Geographic* on TV, like molten earth, the lava that keeps on coming at you, getting bigger, moving faster, eating everything in its path. The Pascoe affair, it was mayhem with parameters, so people lapped it up. It was fun. Papers loved it, *Post, News, Observer*, the magazines, the TV. The *Times* packaged the gossip as financial news and retailed it big in the business section because Pascoe was director of a bunch of companies. A very rich guy was dead in a midnight-blue Art Deco swimming pool with a gold frieze around the tiles; it was the fanciest building in the most exclusive neighborhood in town. A building that didn't take Jews, blacks, nobody from Jersey. They didn't say so; everyone knew.

Sally, Montel, Jerry, all of them lined up experts for daytime trash talk, put on 'Guys who try to behead their girlfriends', and asked, would it float? Sink? What would it take to sever the head from a body? A carving knife? I ordered another beer and my cellphone rang.

'Halloween, man,' Lippert said. He was on my phone relentlessly. 'Got to do this Pascoe deal before the weekend, or it goes cold. Please, man,' he said, pushing me, driven by his own bosses. He didn't mention Ulanova's death; he didn't cut the cord; I didn't ask. I wanted on this case.

'I heard you, Sonny,' I said into the phone for the fourth time, and looked back up at the TV set.

'Artie Cohen?'

I turned around. Lulu Fine held out her hand and said, 'Nice to meet you. You're the guy on the Middlemarch thing?'

I thought of telling her I was a reporter on the story, but I hate a ruse and it didn't matter. She was dying to unload. Lulu, who told me her real name was Larraine but she detested it, led me to a booth, ordered Campari and orange juice, put a bunch of quarters into the juke box on the wall, played some Beatles tunes. She was fortyish and small. She had a pelt of short, honey-blonde hair and wore creamy leather pants. Happy to talk.

'New York sucks,' she said. 'Who'd put up with this kind of housing crap anywhere else?' Her accent was part Brit, part New York. None of the pretensions of Mrs Pascoe's Brit-Lite. Lulu Fine was a cute woman.

'Do you want anything?' I said. The menu, which included fish and chips and shepherd's pie, was scratched on a blackboard.

She shook her head. 'A drink's perfect. I hope you don't mind, I come here a lot. It's where us down-market Brits like to hang out, you know? Feel at home, at least after I gave up wanting to be someone else. I was down at the Mercer already at lunch, I had enough of the horseshit high life for one day.'

I said, 'You're from England.'

She nodded. 'Yeah, just outside London. Essex, that mean anything to you?'

I shook my head. 'Been here long?'

'Christ, Artie – it's Artie, right? – almost ten years. My dad moved his firm over here. Gary was already running it, we came on over. I married Gary, must be twenty-five years now. I was nineteen, can you believe it? I still get homesick.'

Lulu Fine ordered another drink. 'I was vain. And stupid. You want to know about the Middlemarch, right? I tried to get an apartment in the Middlemarch last year. I was married then. I thought it would please Gary, him so anxious about moving up. He said it. He actually said it. Moving up, babe. Christ, I can see how pathetic we were then. I stepped into it like a blind man strolls into dogshit, and I took poor Gary with me. Poor bastard.'

She leaned across the table. 'Should I tell you my story?' Lulu asked, and I said 'Yeah, go on, tell me.'

Eight-thirty, a quiet winter night, snow melting, Lulu Fine remembered it very precise, she said. Every detail: the air heavy, wet, dark, dog-end of winter.

They left their rental apartment on Third Avenue, and getting into Gary's new Mercedes, racing green, tan leather interior, Lulu looked back at the building – the little beige bricks, the rows of sooty balconies, the predictable middle-class dullness. Finally they were leaving it behind.

Gary wanted somewhere better more than anything in the world and Lulu was helping him get it. They had the money now. She'd found it, the dream apartment.

She put her arm around the back of Gary's seat and gave him a little squeeze because he looked good; she made him get a haircut, he wore his plain dark-blue Armani suit and the black Gucci loafers.

'What?'

'You look really nice, Gar,' she said, and he said, 'Thanks, love.' He was really anxious. 'You think it will be OK?'

Lulu said, 'Sure it will. We have the money. We're fine.'

He'd done great too, even if it's her father's business; it was a bonanza couple years for the fur business and Gary on the cutting edge, excuse the pun. He saw fur would make a comeback and he was in there, meeting the fashion babes, talking up the product, organizing junkets to Norway so the young design kids could see how you worked fur.

The whole ride over to the building by river, they pumped themselves up. He said, 'I heard they're trying more of an open door policy, you know, take in some new blood,' and she said to him, 'That's right, and I mean, how many other people can get references from a top fashion editor and a designer like Isaac?' She straightened her demure, dark brown, well-cut mink that she put over a plain black Jil Sander suit. Plain dark tights from Fogal, the alligator Manolo pumps from Barneys.

'We look great,' he said. 'Why shouldn't they want us?'

Anyhow, the minute they got there, Lulu knew. Knew it was all wrong, the accents, the clothes, them. Too dressed up. She thought: I should have worn those stupid Belgian flats.

There were four of them on the board: Pascoe, a woman with red eye-glasses who repeated everything Pascoe said, a balding lawyer and an old queen. Also Pascoe's wife. She sat away from the others, poured tea and whiskey like it was a social occasion.

They shook hands all around, hello, how do you do? It was, of course, all cash the lawyer whispered, and Pascoe gave him a dirty look like you didn't talk about the money. But the lawyer ignored him, said to Gary – he talked to the man as if Lulu was a log – said they didn't permit financing ever, never, not in five, ten years. Gary went dead white. Him and Lulu's dad had worked it out; the old man had stuffed their accounts so they could ante up the cash, then finance later. Pascoe gave the lawyer another stern look and Lulu understood the lawyer was Pascoe's stalking dog. Did the dirty work.

Gary saw it all go up in smoke in front of his eyes. He ran to the can, didn't get the door closed all the way. They all heard him puke.

Lulu paused and I thought of Mrs Pascoe's words. 'Poor sod,' she'd said, 'but he shouldn't have lied to us.'

'You want me to go on?' Lulu said and I nodded.

'It was pretty awful. Before we got to the elevator, I heard Pascoe say, "Well, we were never serious about them, cash or not, were we?" And the wife said, "Of course not, darling," and they all tittered.' Lulu took a breath.

'I didn't get to the good part yet. While Gary's in the bathroom, Pascoe gets me to one side, offers me a drink, takes my hand, you know, that creepy way where it's like your hand's your tit and they're touching you up? Then he tells me I'm too good for Gary, and why didn't we meet up for a few drinkies. He said that, I swear to God.' She laughed, then raked her hand through her hair. 'That's how it is in New York fucking City, OK? It tore us apart, me and Gar. We split up a few months after.'

'I'm sorry.'

'Don't be. I got a much better place. You want to see?'

We stopped in a shop off East End Avenue that smelled of glue and cloth. The two old men who ran it worked late, coughing, listening to a radio while one of them wrote up bills and the other cut upholstery fabric by hand with a razor blade. Lulu gave the cutter some fabric samples and he looked up, his mouth full of pins, and nodded.

She led me out to the street, then glanced back at the tenement where the shop occupied the basement. 'Poor bastards. They're pulling these buildings down next year. That's them for the rubbish bin.'

The streets were jammed, people strolling towards the river. Every corner, the Koreans sold pumpkins alongside the other produce, shiny orange mountains of them. In the store windows, skeletons, witches, ghosts, politicians bared their fangs in rubbery masks. Our new national holiday, Halloween. Trick or Treat.

We went east on 57th Street, crossed Second Avenue and Lulu waved to the guy who stood in the door of the liquor store, eyes shut, enjoying a smoke. We crossed First Avenue, and on Sutton, she turned right and stopped in front of the huge building where I'd met Sal Castle. Now I got a better look.

The doorman, this time in evening gear that included a wing collar and even more gold braid, greeted Lulu effusively. The lobby itself included six kinds of marble: green marble, chocolate marble, white marble, pink, gray, black. The walls, floors, tables, and urns were marble and there were bouquets of pastel-colored silk flowers everywhere. A sweeping staircase had marble steps that were lighted from underneath by tiny bulbs and lit from above by the chandeliers that dripped crystal like a waterfall.

'Don't you love it?' Lulu said. 'The staircase ends in a closet. I love the fucker, it's so bloody vulgar. It drives the assholes at the Middlemarch bonkers. We call it the Staircase to Nowhere Building.'

The elevator opened. A burly, handsome man in a dark-blue suit, hand made, double vents, got out; his son followed. You could see the man's rough good looks, the dark hair, blue eyes, the surprisingly sweet smile, transformed into real beauty on the boy, who was about sixteen. Black hair like his father. No smile. I couldn't see the eyes: the kid wore a pair of designer shades. He had a yellow blazer over his shoulder.

The man whispered to him in Russian and the boy said, irritably, 'Talk English, will you?'

The doorman saluted them and went to hail a cab. Lulu got her mail from a concierge and we went upstairs. I had seen the boy earlier, hanging out in the pocket park, glittering in the sun. He had waved to me.

On the twentieth floor, Lulu unlocked her door and I followed her into a vast living room about forty feet square. At one end were some leather sofas and chairs, a glass coffee table stacked with magazines and books and a stray coffee cup. At the other were crates stacked neatly, shopping bags, objects covered with padded moving blankets, plastic sheets. Lulu picked one up and showed me German furniture in red leather and white suede, showed me French chandeliers with a million crystal drops tucked inside bubble wrap. There were bags of linens and blankets ('Frette,' Lulu whispered), china and silver, flowers made out of glass beads, oil paintings in gold-leaf frames so heavy they could crash the precious metals markets. Some bronze sculpture. Modern art.

Lulu looked at her watch, replaced the plastic, said, 'I'll let you in on my secret,' she said.

I said, 'What's your secret?'

'Russians.'

'Yeah?'

Lulu jumped up on to one of the packing crates and perched there, legs crossed, grinning. 'Well, you see, hon, it's rather brilliant. The market doesn't worry those girls, they got cash stashed place you would not believe. They got lotsa money, I mean up at the top of the heap, it's mega, and just starting out. There's quite a few in this building. Sometimes it's the babes, you know, they call 'em Natashas, though that's not always fair since it's the bloody Turks who gave them that name, the Russian hookers who work Turkey. Anyhow, mine are called "Ultra Natashas", gorgeous girls, but they come over from nowhere, from some provincial dump, they find a guy, and the guy isn't into shopping. Now someone has to purchase the Cristal, the Prada, the Hermès, the furniture, so I'm there to help. Sometimes I help them find the guy, nice banker, maybe. I get a nice deal on suites at the Four Seasons when they fly in. I get them a table at the bar. You're shocked?'

I shook my head.

'I can do decorating, auction houses. You ever pass Sotheby's? It's all Russians with mobile phones hanging outside on the steps. They like oil paintings. Big ones. You want to drink something?' she said, I nodded, and she disappeared then returned with a bottle of white wine. 'OK?'

She grabbed my arm. Gestured to the window. 'Superb, don't you think? Look.'

I looked. We were facing east toward the river. The Pepsi-Cola sign winked in the distance. Below us was the Middlemarch.

Lulu smiled. 'I can look down on them any time I like. Living well, as they say. And they bloody detest us, which makes it that much sweeter. You know the problem with the English here in New York, Artie sweetheart? At home we all know the game. You wanna break the rules, you know your cues. Here it's more like free floating. It took me a long time to figure that out. Here, some of them reckon they got a piece of the action, and they do, for half an hour in certain neighborhoods, but mostly, in the real world, nobody gives a shit. They don't get that.'

'And easier to get into.'

'What is?'

'A building like this.'

'Much much easier. We're a condominium so no one here has life and death power over the occupants. You pays your money, you gets your apartment. But even here they got to show, fuck me, everything, financials, credit ratings, even on a sublet. I'm on the board. I know.'

'You have preferences?'

'Friends, naturally. This is a very high-class condo, but we've got three hundred apartments. I have to say we're partial to artists, gallery owners, musicians, top models.' She reeled off some familiar names.

'Russians?'

She giggled. 'Like I said, we got a few.'

'They straight? Crooked?'

'Hon, this is New York – who can tell the difference? For all I know, we have indeed got a few high-tone gangsters. They make excellent tenants. They like spending. They want a piece of American pie. Don't we all?' Lulu added quietly, 'I give preference to people rejected by the Middlemarch. You know how the developers here got the land to build?'

'Go on.'

She snickered. 'One of Thomas Pascoe's relatives, I swear to God. He had a hunk of land he sold to the developer who built this place. I bet Pascoe was frothing like a dog.' She looked out the window again. 'They don't own the street. They don't own the views. They don't even own their own airspace anymore, not really, because at certain times of day we block out their sunlight.' She stretched like a little cat and glanced out at the river.

'They tried to strongarm the board here; it didn't work. Me, I'm queen of my condo now. Nothing happens I don't hear. Bloody marvelous, don't you think?'

Lulu delivered her zesty appraisal with gusto. It didn't completely hide the bitterness or the humiliation of the night her husband vomited in the Pascoes' bathroom. She looked at her watch.

I said, 'Thanks. You've been great.'

'Any time. Feel free. Come by. And Artie?'

'Hmmm?'

'So you're like some kind of private eye?'

'Some kind.'

'They all dress as good as you?'

'I hope not.'

'I better go change. We're having a reunion tonight, me and Gary. Pre Halloween. We're going to try to pick up the pieces, drink some good wine, go dancing maybe, celebrate. You want me to nose around for you?'

'Sure,' I said. I liked her. If I wasn't settled with Lily, if Lulu and Gary were not getting it together, I would have asked her to dinner.

At the door, I said again, 'What's the celebration?'

Lulu Fine's face lit up. 'Celebrate bloody Thomas Pascoe dying.'

Chapter 7

'This is Frances Pascoe,' the voice said into the phone. 'Please come.'

Frances Pascoe called and I ran. When I got to her building, she wasn't home and I was mad as hell. Most of the day – it was the day after I met Lulu Fine – I followed a paper trail, played cat and mouse with Mrs Pascoe and felt like an old piece of cheese. I ended up in Janey Cabot's office. Like Lulu Fine, Cabot was on Frances Pascoe's list. I looked at my watch. It was after six. When I finished with Cabot, I was going back to the Middlemarch. Mrs Pascoe was going to talk to me. I'm generally pretty easy about witnesses who are assholes, but I was major-league pissed off.

Cabot was late. She kept me hanging around and I sat in the waiting room of her office on 57th Street and thumbed through copies of the magazine she edited. House stuff. Shelter books, they call them, according to my pal and neighbor Ricky Tae, who knows this stuff back to front and keeps a finger in the style trade.

Eventually, a tall thin girl in a long black skirt appeared, looked me over, then turned, her boots going tap tap, stiletto heels hitting the floor, as she drawled, 'Janey says will you come please?' The accent was English, the voice nasal. I followed her into a corridor. She was so thin you could snort coke off her hip.

'What's your name?' I said.

Without blinking, she said, 'Neige.'

I kept a straight face and followed her.

More girls – you couldn't call them women – pale faces, concave chests, five-inch stilettos, strode hard along the corridors like they wanted to stick holes in the floor. Their eyes darted toward the offices that gave off the corridor. Rich kids. Twenty-somethings whose parents bought them a life in New York while they worked as assistants at magazines and publishing houses. They were erotic in a creepy way, something aggressive and vulnerable about the skinny bodies – the 'soulless size twos', Rick calls them. They made me think about mindless sex, kinky hardcore stuff – it wasn't just the starved bodies or bruised, smudgy eyes, but the braindead speech and furtive ambition.

The magazine shared offices with a fashion book, and Neige pushed past racks of clothing that included puffballs of fur in purple and orange, and big ballerina dresses in plastic bags that resembled fragile animals trapped in nets.

When I finally got inside Cabot's office, she looked like she was clutching razor blades. She glanced at me.

'It wasn't any bloody accident that they rejected me, you know. Bastards. Bastards!' Janey Cabot said.

Cabot's office had padded walls that looked like green silk, window sills lined with orchids in glazed blue pots, stacks of art books. Antique furniture. She said, 'Close the door,' and by the time I shoved it shut with my foot, she was looking hungry for attention.

'You haven't got a cigarette, have you?' Janey Cabot said, in one of those English voices that's rich as honey and cold as ice at the same time. Smoking was forbidden in the building, but this style queen was not a woman who shared her smokes out on the pavement with the secretaries and limo guys. She reached over to take one out of my pack. She was a good-looking woman if she would have smiled, tall, thin, legs up to her armpits, tight white suit. She said, 'Sit, for heavens' sake.'

For a moment she smoked and watched me, and I smoked and looked at the long shelf behind her desk. On it was a collection of old gold-colored glass. Then she gestured to some photographs on a low metal table. 'Tell me what you think of these images.'

I looked down at pictures of rooms stripped almost bare. Minimalist, you'd call it. Not a lot of comfort in those houses. I said, 'Expensive.'

'Very. That's the point. You can look but you can't quite touch. House and home, it's our pornography.'

Neige came back with a bottle of vodka and some glasses.

'Go home, Neige,' Cabot said and poured herself a drink.

She offered me one. I shook my head.

What was she? Forty? The great New York women, you can't tell. It isn't the face lifts or liposuction; it's the assurance, the assumption of life in the center of the universe, the money.

Cabot knocked back her drink and said, 'I'll tell you about the bloody Middlemarch if you're so interested.' She poured more vodka.

'Tell me,' I said. 'After all, it's your best shot at revenge,' I said, and I saw I'd made contact.

'They rejected me. Me.' She hissed when she said it and bared her teeth, plush red lips curled back over the gums. 'Rejected me as if I were what? A Jew? So I was friends with actors, writers, fags. But they don't tell you. The co-op board makes its own rules. I know about the board meetings where they blackball people.' She gasped for breath. 'I thought I was in.'

'You had the dough?'

'Of course I had the money. It's not that kind of building. No one asks to see your financials, you're simply known to them or you're not and I was, of course, I was, and then this.'

It was what Frances Pascoe said.

'It was in writing, that you were in?'

'You don't get it, do you?'

I played dumb. 'But you still want to live there?'

'Don't be ridiculous. You're invited to an interview, you leave, they talk about you. Tommy Pascoe liked it if you were involved, that's what he said.'

'Involved in what?'

'Charity. I had the magazine sponsor design competitions for his ridiculous homeless shelters, I sat on committees, ate the wretched dinners, then they rejected me. It's the most humiliating thing in my whole utterly miserable suck-up of a life.' Suddenly she looked up and stared at me. 'And they never tell you why.'

'What?'

'That's the point. They don't tell you why you're rejected.'

'Why's it matter so much? There's other places to live.'

'Everyone knows everyone. They live in the same buildings, the kids go to the same schools, they read the same columns. They all know, even the maître d's, even the fucking sales people selling overpriced crap on Madison Avenue who get write-ups in the *New Yorker*. They sit around, they dish! The PR queens, the Hollywood press agents, who are suck-ass idiots, scum you wouldn't wipe off your shoe. But it's early in New York, you start with London. Later, there's the Coast. That's how your news gets made. Even the bloody realtors hear. You have to compete to get the right real estate broker these days, you understand me? These people are celebrities now. You have to make the cut.'

'Like Salvatore Castle?'

'How the hell do you know Castle?' She opened her bag and pulled a neatly rolled joint out of it. 'Give me a light.'

Cabot shed her jacket, and her arms inside the sleeveless T-shirt were surprisingly muscular. It could have been a woman who killed Pascoe. Cabot had the muscle to use a heavy weapon, the kind someone used on Pascoe. She had the fury.

She leaned back in her chair, put her legs on the table, crossed her feet, which were encased in the skins of expensive reptiles. She inhaled. 'I was in. Then the bitch starts on my being single.'

'What?'

'It was the final straw. They said, "Oh and there's another thing, Cabot's a single woman."'

'Single.' I didn't get it.

'Don't be a dolt. It was an excuse. They said there would be men visiting late at night. Bitch.'

'So you want to let me know where you were early Monday morning?'

'I was home. Asleep.'

'Alone?'

'No. I've told them. I've told the wretched police. You can talk to my lawyer if you want, I wasn't alone, all right? Now bugger off.'

I got up. 'What bitch? I thought it was Thomas Pascoe who ran the building.'

She looked up. 'It wasn't him. It was her. It was Frankie Pascoe, all right?'

I got up to go; she called me back. 'Hey.'

'What?'

'You were with Lily Hanes, weren't you?'

'I still am. Why, it's something to you? You know Lily?'

'I know pretty much everyone. Lily's not exactly a wallflower. Anyhow, she was at the network in the Eighties in London, I was still there. I don't run into that many people who date cops, after all, do I? Word gets out.'

The air was thick with her rancor. 'You remember any of the board members other than Pascoe?'

'Yes. The most decent of them was Victor something or other. A fag and a Jew, but decent. Not a Yid or anything.'

'What?'

'Oh come on, you know what I mean, Mr Cohen. There are Jews and there are Yids, you know exactly what I'm talking about.'

I was half-way through the door. I thought about Pascoe and how he came on to Lulu Fine. On a hunch, I turned around and pulled the *Times* obit out of my pocket. It had a picture of Thomas Pascoe. I tossed it on her desk. She looked away.

'One other thing,' I said.

She snarled now. 'What?'

'You were screwing Thomas Pascoe, weren't you.' It wasn't a question.

Chapter 8

Frances Pascoe was waiting for me, and before I could open my mouth she said, 'You'll be wanting to know if my husband banged Janey Cabot or the others before or after he rejected them for apartments. Won't you?' In the background, very faint, I heard music.

I left Janey Cabot and went to the Middlemarch. Cabot's description of the Pascoes and their games left a sour taste in my mouth. I figured I was going in to see her, whatever she wanted.

Sweeney was at the door, but this time I dropped a couple names in his ear – my ex-boss was a famous Irish cop – and he let me in and I went up and found Mrs Pascoe's door already open.

It was Stan Getz playing in that apartment somewhere, very round, very sweet tones. It surprised me. I followed Frances Pascoe into a library. The music got louder and I saw an old-fashioned turntable where a vinyl played, a Getz version of 'How about you', Lou Levy on the piano, that I like a lot.

Two walls were covered with books, one had windows that looked out over the river and sky, the other was jammed with paintings. She pointed at a chair, then sat on the rug herself, feet under her, wearing gray flannel pants and a white cotton shirt.

'How come you gave me the names after all?'

'You're a nice guy.'

'How come you let me in?'

'I needed the company. And you apparently charmed Mr Sweeney.'

The paintings were lit right and they were something: a collage by Matisse; a picture by David Hockney of a woman by a window. An Edward Hopper. Things I would put on my walls if I had dough. I stared at them.

'Sit down. Please. Just sit down. I want to talk.'

I sat.

I said, 'You like that music?'

'Yes. But I knew him.'

'You knew Stan Getz?'

She said, 'Yes, I did, I knew Stan. I slept with Stan, if you want to know.' She laughed. 'Why? Does it make you like me better?'

I said, 'Yeah, it does,' and she said, 'Do you want a drink? I'm having martinis. Lots of them. I'm a prisoner, so I indulge. Half and half. My sort of half and half.' She held up a bottle of Gordons gin in one hand and a liter of Stoli in the other, and I shook my head. She smiled. 'I thought you might be my Prince Charming. Rescue me from the tower here. No martini? Something else?'

'A Coke would be OK. Thanks. Or a beer. What do you mean, a prisoner?'

'I go out, the TV people jump me, media comes at me like a shitstorm. There's a pantry down the hall, if you wouldn't mind. I think there's beer. I've given the maid the night off. Case the joint if you want,' she said, and I went and found some cans of Bud Lite in a small refrigerator, then took a tour, the music fading as I got further away.

The apartment occupied the whole floor. It was huge, twelve rooms, maybe more. I lost count. Two apartments had been joined, including, I figured, the place Cabot and Fine wanted. The apartment to die for or kill for. Christ. The place the Pascoes bought for themselves in the end.

Bedrooms, a formal living room, dining room, kitchen, library, a music room for chrissake with a beautiful Steinway grand. Ebony. Surface like silk. I opened it and hit a few keys lightly, wished I could play.

But it was Mrs Pascoe's bathroom that seduced me. It was big, it had a fireplace and a free-standing tub, and a dressing room with a half-dozen cherrywood closets. The surface was so rich and sleek you wanted to stroke the wood and I went down the row and touched the doors.

The closets swung open. Each was filled with immaculate rows of suits and dresses, racks of shoes, piles of linen shirts and silk blouses, all colors of white or cream or the color of bone. The scale surprised me; Frances Pascoe had worn the same things three days running, the gray pants, the plain shirts, but maybe it was her mourning gear.

All the main rooms had views of the river, the sky, the red neon Pepsi-Cola sign winking on the horizon, over the border in Queens.

In Thomas Pascoe's study I foraged in the papers, but Homicide had been all over the place already. There was a small sculpture on the desk, a pair of bronze hands. Begging hands, size of a child's. And lifelike. I picked them up and turned on the desk lamp. But the hands, in the light, were wrinkled, joints swollen. An old man's hands, and so alive I felt I'd touched real flesh.

Beer in one hand, the bronze in the other, I went back to the library.

She looked up. 'You enjoyed the tour of my apartment?'

'Very nice, but what can I really do for you? What do you want?'

I sipped some beer, watched her curl up on the sofa; in the low light she could have been thirty. I sat on a chair. Put some distance between us.

'You tell me,' she said, but her attention was taken up with the picture of herself that suddenly appeared on the small TV she had placed on the coffee table. In it she wore a black velvet evening dress, low cut, big skirt, and looked stunning.

'The Met. I think. The Whitney. The opera.' She peered at the screen. 'Some shit.' Frances Pascoe was pretty drunk. 'I want to know what you know. What Ulanova said. What the others tell you.'

I could play her game. 'It's privileged.'

'Bullshit. I gave you the names. It's your turn.'

I finished my drink. 'You want my help, then you help me.'

'Can I call you Artie? Where are you from? Where were you born?'

'Does it matter?'

'Make some conversation with me, all right? Humor me. I'm a widow. I need a friend.'

'I was born in Moscow.'

'I liked Moscow.'

'Why?'

'I was happy there. Tommy was posted there once very briefly by his bank and I was happy. Are you homesick?'

'You must be kidding.'

She sipped her drink. 'What do you hate now, then?'

'Nothing.'

She was drunk, we were going around in circles. I said, 'It's your husband. Talk to me, don't talk to me, but it's me or else some detective from a local precinct who's angry because you've got so much dough, or a hot-dog homicide guy who will retail it all to the *Post*.'

'I told you. Tommy cared too much for this building. In a way, towards the end, it was his life.'

'That bored you?'

She shrugged. 'I was much younger.'

'You said I had something invested in this case. You said it was you.'

She said, 'Did I? I don't remember.'

All the time I sat in her library, Mrs Pascoe seemed to circle me, like a animal with potential prey, charming, then withdrawn, then coming on heavy. She could eat you alive, I figured, and I reached for the gin and poured a shot for myself, then got up and went to the window, cooled my face against the glass. There wasn't much air in her hothouse of a co-op.

'Artie?'

'Yeah?'

'Help me, will you?'

'I'm trying. Your husband told you everything he did?'

'Obviously not. You've met Janey Cabot.'

'You knew.'

'Everyone knew, darling. Small town. He banged her a few times, so what? I suppose he met her at some charity thing. You were hoping perhaps that she applied for the apartment first and Tom took advantage. I mean, Tommy's philandering wasn't a real problem, if you'll forgive the old-fashioned word. Rather a good word, philandering, don't you think? He couldn't do much but he liked looking. It was nothing to do with me. It was a twitch, a neural itch. In fact, he had Janey after we rejected her. I suppose she kept on hoping.'

'I'm not getting this. You tell me your husband was a Christian guy, it turns out he's coming on to half the women who want apartments. He manipulates the board. He laughs at people who want to live here. He rejects them because he doesn't like the father-in-law.'

'You have all the answers. Can you do something for me?'

'What?'

'The police have sealed Ulanova's apartment. I'm not allowed in until the will goes to probate, I've got to get in there and see it's cleaned out before the rest of the building's infested.'

'I can't help you with probate. You'll have to talk to your precinct. Talk to your lawyers.'

Frances Pascoe lay on the sofa now, legs crossed, smoking. I went to the door, then I turned around and said, 'I think you're protecting someone.'

I'd put the bronze hands in my pocket. Now I put them on a table.

She looked at them. 'Take that away.'

'Why?'

'I hate the bloody thing, I think it's repellent.'

'Who did it? The hands.'

'A British sculptor.'

'Named?'

'Warren Pascoe.'

'Some kind of relative?'

'A distant cousin of Tommy's, I think. Gives me the creeps.'

'I think it's haunting.'

'Then for chrissake take the bloody thing if you like it so much. Take it out of here.'

She came down to the lobby with me. The bronze hands were in my pocket. 'Let me show you something,' she said and we walked out into the street. It was late. The TV crews had given up for the night. Frances Pascoe pulled her sweater tight.

She gestured at Sutton Place. 'It was our village,' she said. 'Ours. When Tommy first came here during the war, before they put the Drive through, it was a riverfront village. It's all over now,' she added.

The street was deserted except for the cop in his sentry box at the far end of Sutton Place, where the Secretary General lives in a townhouse.

We walked north. Mrs Pascoe looked up at the big buildings on the west side of the street. The lobby at Lulu Fine's building blazed with a million watts. Next to it, the unfinished building Castle had showed me loomed in the darkness, a massive hulk shrouded by the scaffold and metal nets.

She said, 'I just wanted you to see. Ugly buildings that blot out the sunlight and destroy the city's environment. We feel them on our neck. Literally. The market got hotter, people built these monstrosities. Condos they pay for with funny money. They steal our air.'

'Yours? Your air?'

'Yes. Tommy tried to stop them.'

'The old woman hated your husband, you know. She said she was his ghost. She stayed upstairs so she could haunt him. She also believed in saints and gangsters. She was afraid to stay in the hospital because she figured he might steal her apartment.'

A breeze came up and I could feel Mrs Pascoe shaking. We had walked back to the Middlemarch and she said, 'I'm in trouble here,' then wrapped herself with her arms. 'I've never been frightened of anyone or anything in my whole bloody life. But we both know it wasn't Madame Ulanova who killed Tom. It wasn't Janey Cabot or Lulu Fine, either. Was it?' She held my arm. 'Was it?'

'Probably not.'

She took the cigarette out of her mouth and tossed it on the street. The red ash flickered for a second and went out. She reached up and touched my face lightly. Tiny hairs stood up on the back of my neck. She said, 'What's the bruise?'

'Someone didn't like my face the way it was.'

'What do you want from me, Artie?'

'A look at the building. A look at the pool.'

Frances Pascoe led me to the service door and pushed a key in my hand.

She said, 'Promise me you'll finish this.'

'Finish what?'

'It won't end here.'

'Where will it end?'

'In London,' she whispered. 'Tommy said we had to go to London. There was a phone call, he started packing. We were packed.' She held my arm, urgent now. 'We were packed!'

'You said you were scared. Scared someone might come for you? What are you scared of?'

'Being alone.'

Chapter 9

The key slipped in easily. The lock on the service door, like everything else at the Middlemarch, was perfectly oiled. I reached for the light switch, but she pushed my hand away from it. 'No one's supposed to be here at night except for security, you understand? Please.'

For a few seconds she held the door and we stood inside the vestibule, a faint light coming in from the street. I listened for footsteps. I could hear my own pulse in my ears.

It was late. From the river I could hear the hoot of a tug somewhere, from the street the grind and rattle of a garbage truck. Then she pulled the door shut, and we were alone in the dark.

I ignored her warning and reached for a switch; the overhead light cast a hard, dull glare on the gray paint walls. I got my bearings. Frances Pascoe looked old under the hard fluorescent beam.

There was a telephone control panel on the wall and I opened it easily and saw even the phone wires were neatly coiled. In my own building downtown, you go in at night, you trip over stuff, ladders, stacks of newspaper, bags of empties, dead mice. This place had innards streamlined as an Olympic athlete.

The vestibule had an elevator on one side and a gray metal door on the other. I switched the light off and we stood in the dark one more time, then I pulled open the door to the stairs and we started down to the basement. I went first.

The building had a self-satisfied hum – the boiler, the generator, the central air, the pumps for the pool, the electricity meters, all running smooth.

'The doors open out into the stairwell,' she said. 'It's a fire precaution.'

I didn't mention I already knew and she led the way down another flight, then unlocked a door. We were on the pool level. I could smell the chlorine.

I said, 'I need some light.'

She said, 'No light. There's a super who lives here, a night watchman. The doorman comes down here to eat his supper.'

'And the janitor named Pindar Aguirre?'

She looked startled. 'He quit.'

'You've replaced him?'

'Not yet. Please leave the light off.'

'You're in charge now, aren't you? Now that your husband's dead, it's yours to run.'

'I imagine my presence in the swimming pool in the middle of the night would raise a few questions with your lot. Your Mr Lippert doesn't like me, does he? He'd be glad to hear I've been places I shouldn't be. I'm as good a suspect as any.'

'He won't hear. How much time have we got?'

She squinted at her watch. 'About half an hour before the doorman eats his supper and the night watchman makes his rounds next. I don't know about the police.'

We whispered.

The basement was a warren of rooms and closets. I'd had a glimpse the morning of the murder, now I got a better look. Empty kitchens, once used for residents who ordered meals sent up through the dumbwaiters. A staff cafeteria, empty now too. A clubroom, a few chairs draped in musty sheets, and lockers where crates of illegal booze were once stored.

There were wine cellars, servants' rooms, even shops. There had been a pharmacy, a grocery, a hairdresser. All empty now, or stacked with boxes and trunks and bikes.

I leaned towards her. 'No one wants all this space?'

She said, 'Only the wrong people want it.'

A radiation symbol was painted on a gray steel door further along the hall. The fall-out shelter. I walked in. It was empty, too, except for some shaky wooden shelves with six cans of creamed corn. I picked one up and read a handwritten label stuck on it. It was dated 1953.

The smell of chlorine got stronger now, and we went through the locker rooms and past a row of wide fluted columns.

We were in the pool. The gold frieze on the blue tiles glittered dully.

She said, 'They drained it.'

I walked carefully around the perimeter of the pool. Lippert had warned me off the building. Dozens of specialists had crawled every inch of this place.

I took Frances Pascoe's arm and we made our way to the deep end. Our footsteps echoed with a hollow ping. There was a bench and we sat on it. I said, 'He swam every day?'

She said, 'Every day, same time.'

'And the Russian?'

'Most days. She went to the pool, sometimes she swam, sometimes not. Sometimes she just stood up to her waist in the shallow end.'

'How do you know that?'

'I saw her. I occasionally swam with Tommy.'

'Anyone else?'

'No, of course not. Can you do me a favor, please?'

'Sure.'

'Call me Frankie. It makes me feel less old.'

'So he swam every day and people knew it?'

'Of course.' She reached into the pocket of her sweater and took out four vodka miniatures and passed me a pair. We sat on the bench in the empty pool, breathing chlorine and drinking vodka.

'I need to know.'

She opened the second miniature. 'What?'

'You knew the old woman advertised her apartment.'

The light-greenish eyes fluttered briefly, then she said, 'Yes.'

'Do you want to tell me when she did it?'

'I don't know.'

'But your husband knew.'

'Yes.'

'It upset him.'

'Very much.'

'She had a right?'

'Only legally,' she said.

I said, 'If you ask me, the old woman advertised her apartment, your husband got pissed off, he invited her to the pool for a chat and someone surprised them. You must be relieved she's dead.'

'Yes, I am. He was my husband, whatever else he was, and

Ulanova was an evil old woman. She inherited shares in the building from her husband, who was a contact of Tommy's during the war.'

I thought of Sal Castle and said, 'I know.'

She looked up. 'How do you know?'

'What else?'

Mrs Pascoe reached for her drink. 'Then she sold them. She made her bargain. She mistreated the help here, fancied herself some kind of aristocrat – it was all horseshit, actually. That lair she kept upstairs was filthy, roaches, mice, rubbish everywhere. All we wanted was to restore the building to its original integrity. We offered to get it cleaned for her, she turned her yapping disdain on all of us.'

'But you didn't evict her.'

'It was complicated.'

'She knew your secrets? You didn't want bad press.'

'We didn't want any press, good or bad.'

'Tell me about him.'

'Tommy? He had been a dashing chap, you know. An Englishman who was raised on Kipling and could recite *If* and fought in the Second World War and came to New York on some mission for the OSS. He believed all that imperial bullshit,' she smiled. 'Long time ago. And then Tommy was old. It goes so fast. People were polite, but the dazzle was gone. Give me a cigarette.'

I gave her the pack.

'It's why he went to London so often, I guess. Make believe people wanted to know him. People writing books, rewriting history, making television programs. He retailed his glorious exploits. The old days.'

'He kept his British passport?'

'Oh yes. Absolutely.'

'What about you?'

'I traded mine in as soon as I could. I hate England. I wanted to be an American for as long as I can remember. When I was still a little girl I wanted that.'

I said, 'Me too.'

She finished the rest of her vodka and smiled.

'You didn't want to go to London with him?'

'No.'

'But you didn't want him dead.'

She got up. 'I'm a rich woman. Why would I want him dead?'

'There's other stuff than money. Can we go over the alibi one more time, Frankie?'

Frankie Pascoe turned and smiled so sweetly I reached over and took her hand. She kissed me on the cheek and said, 'Thank you. I wasn't home is the thing, Sunday night. I was out. I didn't come home all night is what I'm saying.'

'You weren't far away.'

'I wasn't far, and Mr Sweeney, the doorman, called me on my mobile phone to let me know it had happened, then slipped me upstairs. Tommy was already dead. Ryan Sweeney's my lifeline.'

'You were out all night?'

'You're jealous. I like that. Out being a euphemism. Yes, I was.'

'Do you want to tell me who you were with?'

'Not unless I have to.'

'You're protecting someone?'

'Yes.'

I put my hand on her arm. The skin was cold as ice. 'You're not like rich people. Are you, Frankie?'

'What are rich people like, Artie? Is there some genetic coding? That we've haven't got problems, we're not allowed?'

'Someone else said that to me.'

She was suddenly alert, the eyes opened wide. 'Who else?'

'It doesn't matter.'

'No,' she said. 'I'm not like rich people. But I'm not like anyone. Do you want to come home with me?' She leaned heavily against me. 'What were you looking for here? Why did you want to see the pool? Artie?'

'I figured whoever killed your husband knew his way around here,' I said.

Without any warning, Frankie stood up.

'What is it?'

She stood silently for a minute, as if listening for something. someone. She fiddled with her sweater. Glanced around the pool, then locked her eyes on mine.

'What?'

'I thought I heard something.'

'There's nothing,' I said. To distract her, and because I wanted to know, I added, 'Tell me some more about Stan Getz.'

'You're wrong. There is someone. I can hear them. There are police everywhere, swarming on us, they think I'll tamper with the evidence. I've seen them.' Her voice turned shrill. She grabbed hold of my arm. I could feel the panic.

Somewhere in the basement was the faint drip of water and Frankie said, 'I want to go home.'

She walked rapidly now toward the door where we'd entered, past the columns, lockers, toilets. The sound of steps got louder. Louder. Someone running.

We got to the elevator. The doors opened. Behind us, the footsteps got closer, and I turned and squinted, peering into the dark basement.

When I turned back, Frances Pascoe was already in the elevator.

She raised her head. In the elevator's light, her eyes were wild lazy in their sockets, the lids half shut.

I put my hand out to hold the doors, but it was too late. She stared at me, threw up her hands in exasperation, fear, maybe both, and she said, 'I'll call you.'

Then the doors shut.

It was Thursday, one in the morning, when I got to my car. I'd checked out the basement after Frankie got in the elevator. She was right. There were a couple of cops making the rounds, guys doing security, keeping the scene clean. Why did it scare her so much, them being at the pool? It was her building after all.

I had been tempted pretty bad when she said, 'Come home with me.' Then her mood changed. She was protecting someone, I thought again, as I got on the FDR and headed home.

The highway was empty. I needed sleep, but when I pulled up to my building, I saw the lights on in the restaurant on the ground floor. Ricky Tae, who lives upstairs from me, sat at a table in the window of his parents' restaurant on the ground floor. I figured he wanted to talk, and yawning, I climbed out of my car and waved and pointed at the front door, but Rick darted out into the street.

'Don't go upstairs, Artie. Don't go.'

'What's going on, Rick?' I reached for the front door.

I ran up the stairs. Rick was behind me. 'Wait for me, please,' he yelled. 'Don't go in there by yourself.'

The locks on the door were bust. Broken glass was scattered on the floor. I turned on the lights. The couch and chairs lay on their sides, stuffing pulled out. The barstools I had stripped down and painted myself were smashed and scattered like pick-up sticks. Files, faxes, letters had been torn up and scattered.

They destroyed the paperwork, broke the glasses, smashed my laptop, took some cash I left on the kitchen counter. They never touched the CD player or the TV set, the usual stuff creeps want if they're ripping you off. It was some kind of message.

Feathers drifted from the bedroom. I went in. The pillows had been ripped. Books I'd had since childhood, the only things left from Moscow, were torn up in thick, rough chunks.

In the living room I saw Rick staring at the floor. Something heavy, a gun, brass knuckles, had been used to rip scars in the polished wood floors. The floors had taken me and Rick weeks to make beautiful.

'Christ, Artie, I'm so sorry. Stay at my place until we figure this out,' Rick said.

'Go home,' I said to him. 'Please.'

After Rick went, after I called an old friend who's a sergeant now at the First and got him focused on the situation, I swept up the glass, very careful, very methodical. If I'd caught them, I would have killed them. If I found out who did it, I would hurt them.

Someone wanted me off the Pascoe case enough to wreck my place. It had the opposite effect on me: I was in. I was in it for good.

Suddenly, I understood Thomas Pascoe and Mrs Ulanova and Frankie and Lulu Fine, their territorial sense of entitlement to their apartments. Their homes. Their piece of turf.

I wanted to call Lily bad, but it was the middle of the night. Maybe I would have called her anyhow if I didn't find the picture. It was stuck on the wall over my desk. It was a piece of newsprint. A picture of me from a case I worked in Brighton Beach a while back. The eyes were cut out.

I yanked it down. Then I got Sonny Lippert on the phone. He was still awake.

'What?'

'I already asked you, Sonny. Pascoe's eyes? Were they intact?'

'What's the matter with you, man, you sound crazy.'

'Just fucking tell me.'

'Yeah, sure, they left the eyes in. You there, man?' he yelled, but I hung up. I found a bottle of Scotch and drank enough to fall asleep with my clothes on.

Chapter 10

The phone was ringing.

A couple hours, maybe three, after I went to sleep, I stumbled out of bed. The sun streamed in through the big windows, and when I saw the damage in the hard morning light I wanted to hit something. I grabbed the phone. It was Lily. I looked at the mess in my apartment. I didn't tell her.

She said she was leaving for London. The job, she said, furtive, nervy. The morning flight. I looked at my watch. It was six in the morning.

'When do you go?'

'Soon. In an hour.'

I grabbed a shower and coffee, got dressed, then went to Lily's and took her to the airport. We didn't talk much on the way.

After a while, Lily said, 'You look like you didn't get much sleep. What's going on?'

'Nothing,' I lied and pulled up at the terminal.

She handed me a piece of paper. 'Phone numbers,' she said. 'I'll be back soon. Artie? You hear me?' She kissed me and said, 'I'm not angry about your case, I swear to God, OK? It's just I had the offer of some work and I owe someone and I want to do it. I told you.'

I was distracted by what happened the night before and I let her go. She had gone away like that before. She was restless. I watched her as she took Beth and they went through to the departure lounge.

Lily turned and grinned the rueful way she does that melts my heart, then, one hand in Beth's, she shrugged again, maybe by way of an apology for going without me or to say, What am I doing, me with a kid and a pink nylon backpack with Barbie on it? But she pushed her red hair on top of her head, fixed it with a rubber band, picked Beth up and held her high so I could see her and blow her a kiss. Then the two of them disappeared.

'You can't be who Lily Hanes wants, man, you know? A cop is who you are, the air you breathe.'

'Yeah I can. I'm crazy about her.'

'I'm sorry about that.' Rick poured out some coffee and slid the mug across the green marble counter that separates his kitchen from his living room. He lives in the penthouse. The terrace doors were open. It was warm again.

I shifted my weight on the high leather stool and drank the bitter liquid. I'd come back from the airport, we'd fixed my place as best we could. I didn't tell Lippert the thugs wrecked my place.

What's the point, I thought. Some Brighton Beach crumb wants me off the case, enough so he comes after me in the stairs at the Middlemarch, enough to fuck with my house. But there's a lot of low-level creeps out there that I offended one time or another. I couldn't see the connection to Pascoe's murder. Except for me.

'Artie, you hear me?' Rick leaned forward. 'You can't be somebody else.'

'She'll be back. She just has this thing for London, OK? You think I'm an asshole, don't you?'

'We all got our sorrows,' he said, but he smiled. 'You don't think Lily's reacting to the case?'

'Sure she's reacting. She's mad as hell I'm on it.'

'I didn't meant that. I meant the case itself.'

'Don't be an idiot.'

I took him through it: how Lulu Fine's alibi stuck to her like her leather pants; about Janey Cabot's fury. Rick, who looks smooth and slim as a young Noël Coward – Coward's his idol – dabbles in Cabot's world.

He listened carefully, then he said, 'What about your loft, man? I want to fix those floors for you.'

'I don't want to think about it now,' I said. 'Talk to me about Janey Cabot, about real estate, about what's going on in this city.'

He helped himself to coffee. 'There's still so much money swilling around this town. How do you get to show your status?'

Rick said. 'Clothes don't matter, no one's making clothes for people over twenty – I mean, you ever try a pair of those flat-front Gucci pants? I can't get my arm in the pants leg. Also, the old rich don't do clothes, never did, the new rich wanna look old. Ask yourself: what's selling?' He got up, went to the coffee table, came back with a stack of magazines, held them up one at a time. He laughed. 'Magazines, on the box, Martha Stewart, *This Old House, House and Home, Wallpaper, Kitchen Sink, Nest,* fantasy houses, real houses, houses for Barbie, gardens, cooking shows, the lifestyles of anyone you'd like to be.'

He stopped and picked up his coffee. 'It's where the dough is, sweetheart, it's where we put our money. Also, you don't want only a place in the city. You need something in the Hamptons for the summer, and Bedford for weekends, maybe the ski house in Montana or Jackson. You got family values now you're past thirty, right? You're not out in clubs. You gave up booze and smokes and coke and dope. Where you gonna put your dough if you can't buy a great co-op?'

I told him about the building, about Frankie Pascoe mainly. Rick's a guy that never judges; he has his own dark places. He stretched his legs now, and drank the coffee. 'You're telling me you wanted to fuck her because she once slept with Stan Getz?'

I didn't answer.

'I met Frankie Pascoe once, you know. Him too.'

I put down my glass. 'You met them?'

'Yeah. No big deal. I mean, half New York met these people, you know? Some charity affair. The sick, the homeless, the aimless, I can't remember. I was helping out on the food. All I remember is the outfits on those X-ray babes uptown who run these gigs, the high-heel ankle straps, the stick legs like they've been in the death camps. Frankie Pascoe stood out.'

'In what way?'

'Most of them you wouldn't touch with a ten-foot pole. She was very sexy.'

'Sexy.'

'Yeah. Hot. Dangerous. Like she wanted to take you into the toilet and put you up against the wall and fuck you, even while she was wearing her ballgown and the jewels. I remember the dress. Black velvet. Vintage Givenchy.'

'The one on TV. Jesus.'

'Eat you alive, babe, I thought. Gave even me a hard-on right there in the Metropolitan Museum, and I don't do it with girls if there's a choice. I thought, here's a woman that does everyone, men, women.'

'You ought to know.'

He smiled. 'Fuck you. Look, the thing is, I got the feeling she couldn't stand the husband. The appearance of upper-crust perfection was pretty spectacular, though. You want to get some dumplings or something? I'm starving.'

'I have to go uptown.'

'So we'll go eat with my cousin up on 86th Street, OK? Cheer you up. You OK? We'll fix your place like new. I got a couple good guys coming in to help with the floor. I swear to you, we'll do it like before.'

'Thanks, Rick. Thank you, man. I'm OK.'

'Pay your rent, asshole!' On the sidewalk near Gracie Mansion, a woman with a heavy cross around her neck hectored some demonstrators. The sun glinted off the cross.

We ate a late breakfast at Rick's cousin's, then walked a few blocks up. The demonstrators were a ragged bunch. A few had cheap Halloween masks on; a black guy wore a rubber parody of the mayor, the rictus grin, the flat head, the hair that looked like it fell off a tree.

The week before, the mayor had announced he intended killing all rent control for good. It would squeeze the poor who squeezed the unemployed. The homeless got hit worst. The homeless were like pus that oozed into the streets, someone said. 'We're the pus in the pimple on the ass of the good times,' one street-corner wise-ass cracked. He got a gig as a writer on a sit-com that featured three homeless guys.

'Pay your rent,' the woman with the cross shouted again, and this time the man in the rubber Giuliani mask looked at her and said, 'We ain't got no apartments to pay rent on, lady.'

'Look to God,' she screamed. 'God will provide.'

'He'll have to,' Rick said to me. He looked over at Gracie Mansion. 'I'm not betting on the mayor's having them all in for breakfast.'

'Jesus, in the eighties the homeless was a scandal, now it's like they're street furniture.' I turned my head and saw a cop I knew slightly. I looked at his badge. Santini. He was in uniform and he took off his cap and mopped his head and watched the demonstration.

The fallout from the Pascoe case, the fury over rent control, the stock market, landlords dying to evict, tenants terrified, prices on apartments heading north, not just fancy buildings, but everyplace, even the boroughs, made people scared. Five, six, ten grand to rent out a loft on the Bowery, or even down under the Brooklyn Bridge Overpass, what they're calling DUMBO.

'Like food in a famine, Art,' Rick said. 'Everyone's fighting each other for turf. Remember Pop used to tell us about the gang wars in the old Chinatown days? People would stick a knife in your heart to get the best stall in the market. Literally. Only now it's a piece of real estate.'

Santini, who'd been listening a while, laughed bitterly. 'Yeah, triumph of unfettered capitalism, right? Greedy pricks, all of them. I had the pleasure recently of helping out when one management company uptown was hauled in for extortion on contracts for some of the fanciest buildings in Manhattan. We even got a couple of big deal realtors implicated.' He grinned. 'I know all about housing scams. I grew up on Carmine Street. My great-granddad was the founder of the Italian Working-man's Coalition. I learned the rhetoric in the neighborhood. Carmine Street. Can't afford it now. So, Art, you still live in that great loft?'

I said. 'Yeah, I got in early. I was lucky. Hey look, man, when you made those arrests, the management companies, the realtors? You didn't come across a guy name of Salvatore Castle?'

'Yeah, sure. I wished I could have hung something on him, but nothing stuck.'

Rick went back to his cousin's, Santini went off duty and I followed the ragtag demonstration. It broke up, people drifted off, aimless. The black guy with the mayor's mask, he must have been past sixty, stopped in a bank lobby on First Avenue. It was empty except for one woman getting cash at the machine. She saw him, finished her business, scurried out of the door.

Through the glass, I saw the homeless guy sit wearily on the window ledge. He pushed the rubber mask off his face and on to his head, then he took off his shoes. He rubbed his feet like any bastard whose feet hurt him, minding his business. Someone had dealt him a lousy hand somewhere in his lousy life and I was sorry for him. When it comes to a guy with no place to live whose feet are killing him, I feel bad. Maybe some of the old Sov prop I learned at school – equality, property – kicks in.

I watched. I watched while a couple of goons, spotting him, went over and began pushing him, one hitting his arm, the other socking him on the shoulder. The black guy cringed. A goon slapped his face. They took turns now, then they shoved him across the lobby and out of the door.

I went over and gave him five bucks, and he looked back at the bank and said, 'It's what the city calls social outreach.' Then he put his mask back on and added, 'Trick or Treat.'

Sal Castle, the realtor with the Zegna suits, had been calling me every four hours like bad medicine. Wanted to help, he said. Updates, he said. But he never told me anything and he was nervous.

All along I had the feeling Castle knew who Ulanova's 'nephew' was. A Russian nephew who was going to inherit a share of the Middlemarch. I couldn't figure out how to get at Castle until the cop on the street – Santini – near Gracie Mansion gave me an idea. I found Castle in his office, writing letters in old-fashioned copperplate with a fountain pen. On the wall were framed ads; celebrity realtors.

I said to Castle, 'You've had a few problems – not you but your management company. A few people cut deals they shouldn't have. Put their hands in the maintenance money, cut funny deals with certain plumbers. Is that right, Sal?'

He looked up. He was a man who got a message. 'How can I help you?'

'Mrs Ulanova's nephew.'

'Who?'

'Come on, Sal. There was a nephew. I heard there was a nephew who would inherit. Russian, maybe.'

He looked at the window. Castle, jittery now, got up. 'Yes, all right. I met him. But that kind of thing's privileged. If it gets around, I'm dead.'

'What's his name?'

'I don't know.'

'Come on.'

'He was a big guy. Very very big. Six six.'

'Russian?'

'I think so. Yes.'

'What else?'

'Dimples.'

'What?'

'He had dimples. I'm sorry, but it was unusual. And an emerald stud in one ear.' Castle seemed to cower. He gripped the edge of his desk with his manicured nails. 'It's all I know, I swear to God.'

Before he was finished I was half-way out the door.

'I'm sorry. That's all I know, honestly,' he was saying, but I was in the street.

I should have returned the message, but I was drowning in stuff – the murder itself, Lily's leaving, Frankie's needs, the cretins who fucked up my loft. I took out my phone, dialled.

Come on! I said half out loud. Answer the phone!

'Comrade, darling!' The voice boomed in my ear in the kind of purring, cultivated Russian that twitched my soul and scared me with its seductions. I always figured I had climbed permanently out from my past; I was never really sure.

'Sweetheart, Artyom, you didn't return my message, where the fuck are you?'

I told him and added, 'Where the fuck are you?'

'I'm looking at you, sweetheart,' said Tolya Sverdloff. He gave me an address on Sutton Place. 'Come up.'

'Come down,' I said.

'I'll meet you,' he said.

Chapter 11

Around us in Mr Chow's were fat-ass Russian men with heavy gold rings, American bankers and the Natashas. The Slavic babes were exquisite, all six feet tall, all cheekbones and lips, some with fur on in spite of the weather, and Harry Winston diamonds the size of cherries. Like Lulu Fine said, these girls were Ultra-Natashas. I'd seen them around town, at Au Bar and Pravda, or shopping the Upper East Side where they were quick with the platinum cards their boyfriends gave them. Most were in their early twenties, and I watched them, covered in Chanel or Voyage, chattering and smelling of sex, Hermès bags on the table next to the Cristal Rosé. The crocodile bags cost thirty grand and there were waiting lists.

I helped out on a case once when a Natasha named Marina turned up cold as her own heart in a very fancy hotel. Also, I read Lily's fashion magazines in the can. Like great houses, fashion's my kind of porn. I thought about Lily on her way to London, shoved it out of my mind. She had a right. Fuck London, I thought. But I missed her.

By way of greeting, Tolya kissed me on the cheeks three times, then straightened his black mohair jacket as a maître d' seated us at a table. I ordered a Coke. Tolya ordered brandy to drink, then fried seaweed, Peking duck, lemon chicken and red wine.

'For lunch?'

He said in Russian, 'I'm hungry.'

He lit a cigarette and in the flame from his half-pound gold Dunhill, Anatoly Sverdloff's face was as big as an Easter Island statue but with dimples you could put a baby's fist in. He was six six, maybe three hundred pounds, hands that always looked big and juicy as veal chops. I'd met Tolya, what, three, four years ago, when he saved my ass on Brighton Beach, then again in Hong Kong. He drops in when he's in town, usually loaded with gifts for Beth, who adores him. Last I'd heard he had sold most of Macau and was purchasing beachfront property in Cuba for cash.

Now he held a piece of fabric between thumb and forefinger, showing me the material of his jacket. 'Versace,' he said. 'Custom. Thank God I got a couple dozen outfits made before – you know? Terrible tragedy.' He was talking about Versace's death.

I spoke English. 'You're the nephew, so called, aren't you? The heir to the apartment. I should have known when I got your message on my machine Monday.'

'You should have answered.'

'I was busy.'

He folded some duck and cucumber into a pancake, dipped it delicately in plum sauce and ate it. 'Me, too.'

'But you don't have a dead Russian auntie, Tolya, do you? Somehow you got hold of Ulanova and you talked her into leaving you the place. What's the game?'

He said, 'Very good, Artyom. I saw the ad, when? A few days ago, a week? Two? I'm a real-estate guy, I liked the sound. I discovered poor Princess Ulanova needed help. The asshole who runs the board threatened her. Told her no one she sold to would ever get board approval. We did a deal.'

'You gave her the money, told her she could stay as long as she lived, she made you her heir, you don't need board approval.'

Tolya nodded. 'I said to her, you live here the rest of your life, is OK. We made papers. Next day, before she removes ad, Pascoe's dead. She's sick.'

I'd thought about it before, that maybe the ad killed Pascoe. Maybe he saw the ad, got enraged, invited Ulanova to swim, set her up to get whacked and got it himself in the neck instead. It wasn't a scenario that played right with me, though.

I said to Tolya. 'So you took it off the market.'

'Sure, it was mine.'

'You didn't kill Pascoe, by the way, did you?'

'Artyom!'

'Why'd you want that dump of hers?'

He ate a piece of chicken. 'It's a special building.' Tolya

wiped his mouth, tossed a bundle of money on the tablecloth and said, 'Come, I have a surprise.'

It was the building next to Lulu Fine's, the half-finished limestone tower Sal Castle pitched me. A pair of hardhats, their legs slung over the scaffold, ate out of a bucket of chicken.

'What happened to your place on the park?'

'Too small.' Tolya savored the moment. 'And I like to buy. I go to see the Donald, you know who I mean, a few others. He is one weird guy. He hates shaking your hand. He likes you to bow instead. I bow, he sells.'

The building was unoccupied except for Tolya and a couple of others, he said. But uniformed flunkies manned the doors and operated the elevators. The place smelled of wet cement and plaster dust. Everywhere the painters' dropcloths fluttered on your feet, in your face, like ghosts.

On the top floor, the elevator opened into the penthouse. 'Real Estate, Artyom. It's the only thing that's any good, you know? Here, Moscow, London, Havana.'

'I thought the Hong Kong market collapsed.'

Tolya found a bottle of brandy he'd left out on top of a packing crate, poured some and handed me a glass. 'I bought Hong Kong, I sold Hong Kong. A few overpriced apartments in Hong Kong, the stock market cracks up, remember October 97? You have to play with it. Remember my father? He bored us to death talking about the land. I thought all you needed was love and a bass guitar, but he was right. This,' he said, sweeping his huge arms out to embrace the apartment, and maybe the entire city, 'this is my piece of land.'

He pushed a button and the room lit up. It was a large room with curved floor-to-ceiling windows on every side. The river, the city, the skyline, the buildings all seemed present inside the room. It was a virtual city, a hyper-real New York floating on bright blue sky.

We went out on the wraparound terrace, where there was a high-power telescope. I peered in it: you could see the whole city. To one side was the building with the staircase to nowhere; in front was the Middlemarch, the townhouses, riverfront, the river, burned silver by the sun.

Tolya followed my glance. He looked down at the Middle-march and said, 'Ah, yes, the old asleep in the shadow of the future.'

'You're a poet, man.'

He grinned. 'Thank you.'

We went back inside and Tolya showed me his newest toy. 'Custom-made Monopoly set,' he said. 'Look.'

I looked. The set sat on a couple of packing crates in the middle of the empty room. The board was polished slivers of dark and pale wood. The pieces were gold and silver, the houses and hotels tiny but exact models. Tolya scooped up some Monopoly money in his hand and I saw it consisted of gold Krugerrands.

'My property.' Tolya picked up a house and popped open the roof. 'Everything to scale. Look, furniture, people, everything. Eighteen karat. I buy something, I have a building made for Monopoly set.'

I thought about the lousy thugs who worked my place over. I wasn't in the mood for Tolya's games, but I humored him. I never knew exactly what Sverdloff's business was. He bought real estate, but I knew he'd done errands for Sonny Lippert in the past. He was a Russian intellectual, arrogant, funny, nuts. People like the Sverdloffs were the actors and musicians and writers who gave the fucking Soviet Union some shine, wrote its poetry, made it sing, and occupied its jails.

Tolya had been a rock-and-roll star in the former Soviet Union for ten minutes once. He tried to hump his Fender Stratocaster on stage, then went to jail for it. He also spoke great English and fluent Chinese; he made his name on radio broadcasting Russian rock music to the Chinese and got away with it because no one knew what the hell he was talking about. It was the early Eighties. I was already long gone. I never met him until later, but I had heard.

After the Commies went, Tolya's father gave him a piece of land outside Moscow; he discovered he was a natural-born capitalist.

'Parents OK?' I said.

He nodded. 'Yes, fine. You remember?'

I remembered: it was fall then too, in Nikolina Gora outside

Moscow. And beautiful – the white birch trees, the skidding yellow moon. We sat on the porch of the Sverdloff dacha, me and his cousin Svetlana.

I looked away from Tolya now and lit a cigarette. I almost married Svetlana, until she was blown up in a car bomb meant for me. She had on a white T-shirt and white jeans and a red shawl that night. Gold hoops in her ears. I remembered.

'Little Tolya?' Tolya Sverdloff's father was a famous actor; his son, Tolya III, was already a Moscow teen idol.

'He's got lead role in a big soap,' he said. 'I don't want to talk about it.' Tolya's mood changed. Mostly he talks about his kids all night long if you ask. Now he was curt, evasive, uneasy.

I said, 'Then let's talk about Ulanova, your Russian auntie. You have anything besides this brandy to drink?'

There was a half-finished bar in one corner. Tolya found a bottle of Absolut and a couple of glasses. He filled one and handed it to me. We sat on the packing crates.

'What's going on, Tol?'

'I tried to call you as soon as the Pascoe thing broke.'

'Yeah, I got a message, I was busy. So how come you were calling me about some old woman whose apartment you wanted? How's that?'

'I figured when Pascoe died and there's a Russian speaker involved, Sonny Lippert gets called, Sonny calls you. I have an interest. You want to talk?'

I talked. Thomas Pascoe in the Middlemarch pool. The building itself. The Pascoe co-op board, the rejects like Jane Cabot, who wanted an apartment bad enough to kill, and Lulu Fine, who didn't. Then I said, 'So maybe it was a handyman.'

'Artyom, please!'

'OK. Then who?'

'Your Mrs Pascoe?'

'I don't think so. She's not mine.'

He smiled. 'But you like this lady, Artyom? More than you should like her? How's Lily?'

'Mind your own fucking business. What do you know about Pascoe?'

'His bank bought big, London, Russia. Twenty years ago he was in and out of Moscow. Errands for the British. The Americans. Old-time spook stuff, but who gives a shit? Recently he was in on the oil in Baku. Mostly his people buy real estate. London mostly. My bank also buys. Small world.'

'Your bank? I thought most of the banks went bust when the rouble got devalued.'

'I'm smarter than most.'

'Do me a favor. Take possession of Ulanova's apartment.'

'You want me to plant a little bomb, flush out the opposition, meet with the co-op board?'

'Yes.'

'Anything else?'

'Someone tried to beat me up. Inside the Middlemarch. Someone with a Russian accent and a crude style.'

'What happened?'

'I hit him over the head instead.'

'So now some hood's even more pissed off at you.'

'Enough to fuck with my apartment and leave a picture of me with the eyes cut out.'

We talked, he drank, I drank. He left the room and came back with a satin bathrobe over his shoulders. He tugged the lapel. 'Belongs to George Foreman once. From Rumble in the Jungle. I bought at Christie's auction,' he said, then he took a Montecristo a foot long out of a box on the floor, slipped off his diamond-studded platinum Rolex, tossed it down. Tolya showed me his toys, he bragged and laughed like he always did, but it was an imitation. There was no gusto. The act was thin. There was something wrong.

The phone rang, he picked up his cellphone and went out on to the terrace to take the call. I got up and looked for a bathroom.

It was black marble. There was a dressing room next to it, and idly I looked inside Tolya's closets. His wardrobe was big: cashmere jackets, dozens of suits, the stacks of silk shirts and sweaters, the racks of identical Gucci loafers in twenty colors and a dozen skin types – red, green, purple, black, ostrich, alligator, elephant, all with solid gold buckles. Through a hidden speaker system, Sinatra sang.

A few minutes later Tolya Sverdloff appeared. He whistled along with Frank, 'South of the border, down Mexico way,' and gestured at the dressing room. 'You like it?'

'Sure I like it.'

'Let me show you something,' he said, opened a door, showed me a small steel plaque with a green key pad, then punched the buttons.

There was the sound of a motor. Bolts snapped into place. The door between the dressing room and the bedroom slammed shut. A small screen slid out of the ceiling. I looked up. It was closed-circuit TV; I saw the kitchen, then the living room. Tolya followed my gaze. He had his glass in one hand.

'What the fuck is this?' I said.

'This is my Just-In-Case Room. My Perhaps Room. You remember before, old times, bad times, everyone in Moscow had the Perhaps Bag?'

I remembered the old women with string bags wound around their hands. Soldiers with cardboard suitcases. Canvas sacks on wheels the old men dragged across the dirty snow. Everyone had a Perhaps Bag. Perhaps you might see toilet paper on sale, perhaps oranges. You would need a bag to take it home.

My mother made me carry a string bag and it embarrassed the hell out of me, but I managed to stuff it in the pants pocket of my school uniform. I never carry a bag home now. Lily thinks I'm nuts, but I'll give a kid five bucks to carry my stuff two blocks.

'So?'

'This is my Perhaps Room.'

'Perhaps what, for chrissake?' I was laughing, but I felt the hair rise on the back of my neck. We were trapped in a room with steel walls. 'OK, nice joke,' I said. I'm not good in shut-up spaces and he knows it. Tolya knows. 'Very funny, Tolya. So open the doors.'

Instead, Tolya punched a code in the wall plaque. A siren wailed. He turned it off. He showed me how the bullet-resistant walls were embedded in the wood. There was a short-wave radio. In the bathroom was a refrigerator filled with mineral water, canned goods and space food; there was an oxygen tank and a prescription safe stocked with antibiotics, sleeping pills, valium. There was a locked box behind the shirts that contained a dozen weapons. Another contained cash. He removed a semi from the weapons box.

'Perhaps what?' I said again.

'Perhaps terrorists show up, perhaps radiological spills, perhaps biological or a bomb or the bad guys.' Tolya polished off his drink. 'I am a businessman. People get crazy.' He went on with his list: 'Disgruntled employees, angry women. Riots, earthquakes, blackouts, floods.'

I snorted, 'Earthquakes? In New York City? How about plagues of frogs?'

'Also frogs. Look, Artyom, my favorite,' he said, and demonstrated the high-voltage cattle-prod technology underneath the carpet outside the dressing room. Under siege in his dressing room, he could activate the cattle-prod welcome mat; this would produce a violent kick, a nasty surprise for anyone who got past the front door. And the door was four inches of reinforced steel.

Tolya was laughing. I was sweating. What I felt the night in the stairwell at the Middlemarch, I felt again: the claustrophobia enveloped me.

He laughed some more. '"Forting up," they are calling this. Everyone has one. Not on blueprints. Installed the last minute of design.'

I kept it light. 'You're nuts, man. Certifiable.'

'It is dangerous out there.'

'I'd rather have a dog. Can we get out of here now?'

'Sure,' he said, but he didn't move.

'What is it?'

Tolya said, 'I'll do this thing you want, take over the old woman's apartment, OK, but be careful.'

'What of?'

'I called you Monday to warn you off this whole Pascoe thing, you understand? The thugs who went for you. It was a warning.'

'I got that. Of course I did. Jesus.'

'Maybe not a warning for you.'

'What?'

'For me.'

Press the button, I thought. Press the goddamn button!

I watched Tolya carefully. I'm big enough, but he towered over me. He was the color of uncooked meat. He didn't smile.

We were locked in a room with steel walls. My stomach churned. I had seen a room like this somewhere else.

I said, 'Open the fucking doors.'

Tolya looked at me. 'Don't be naïve, Artyom. You make a mistake here. You think because I am your friend, that I am like you, a law-abiding good little comrade,' he said. 'I am a free agent, faithful only to my bank account.'

'And your friends.'

He grimaced. 'Sometimes also my friends.'

A reporter in a bad linen jacket had stopped Frankie Pascoe a few yards from her front door. He was gesturing to a guy with a camera. I pushed him away. Signalled to a uniform on the beat nearby.

'Thank you,' Frankie said. 'I'm going home now.'

I kept pace with her up to the door, then she stopped. 'I said thanks.'

'Tell me something, Frankie.'

'I must go inside.'

I put my hand on her arm. 'No. Not until you tell me how come I think you've got a steel-clad fort in the middle of your apartment in New York City. With a button in your dressing room and closed-circuit TV. Your building has security. It has a doorman. You've got a whole precinct ready to jump through hoops if you need them.'

'It didn't actually do us any good, did it?' She looked towards the Middlemarch as if she were expecting someone, then back at me. 'You're absolutely right. I have got one. It was Tommy's idea. It made him feel important. He said he was always in some kind of danger, because of the work he'd done.'

'That's it? He was some kind of spy?'

She let out a raucous laugh. 'He liked to think so. He was only a banker, but he knew the Kennedys and Harriman and Kissinger, he knew the Soviets, the British. They let him run errands. He was very charming. The wives liked him. The husbands used to lock up their women, so to speak, when they heard Tommy was in town. He had them all.' The wind off the river ruffled her hair. 'I used to adore it when my politics irritated him. Fancied myself a radical. Kill the pigs, remember?

Long time ago.' She hummed 'Where have all the flowers gone?' and walked towards the front door. 'You must be the only cop in New York City who knows what in the fuck I am talking about. I said Cold War to someone recently, he didn't know what it was. Cold War Scrap, Tommy called himself.'

'I'm not a cop anymore.'

She looked up, saw the camera crew on its way back in her direction, hastily stubbed out her smoke and said, 'Christ, I really am sorry, Artie, but I must go.'

'Just fucking tell me.'

'The safe room made Tommy feel a big man.'

Chapter 12

It was another glamorous evening, sun falling into the river like a neon orange, as I drove out to Brighton Beach. I took the Belt out through Brooklyn towards the ocean. Sky and water slid by the car window and in the late afternoon light the harbor seemed as pristine as it must have looked when Giovanni da Verazzano had arrived for the first time; the Indians who met him, they say, were pretty dazzling: a fast-talking race with all colors of feather.

I went to Brooklyn to see a guy in security, maybe get a handle on Sverdloff. There was some way that Tolya Sverdloff was jammed up. And there were Russians on Sutton Place. Lulu Fine was running a virtual department store for Russians – oil paintings, furniture, women, she could fix anything. And Sverdloff himself had moved into the building next door.

On Brighton Beach Avenue I parked near a shop that sold Halloween masks. Yeltsin, Gorby, Ivan the Terrible, Stalin with fangs and a mouthful of blood. You couldn't pick a better bunch for Halloween than the Russkis, the way I saw it; you didn't need make-believe.

But even Brighton Beach looked good in this weather, even the Russians were delirious as they strolled in the sun. Fifteen miles from Frankie Pascoe's rarefied backwater on the East River, it was a foreign planet. The duplicity of her world, the cold, dry propriety, its restrictions and ambitions, the skein of lies, the sense of entitlement gave me the cosmic creeps. Someone went after Thomas Pascoe and killed him and there were still no answers.

I passed a laundromat and the jingle of slots caught my attention. I put my head in the door. It smelled of clean wash and small change. The neon on the slot machines glittered. Women, heavyset babushkas, lumbered between the dryers and the slots, sharing their quarters between necessity and hope.

I'd come to see Johnny Farone, but Farone was busy so I went to the beach to kill some time.

Along the Atlantic Ocean, Brighton Beach stretches from Sheepshead Bay to Coney Island, and tonight, because of the weather, crowds of people promenaded along the boardwalk, girls in threes and fours, arms linked, couples with kids, boys with rolled-gold chains and thick leather jackets, old men yakking through their beards. Some of the elderly, the old men and women on walkers, gabbing in Yiddish, were the last survivors of another age. Mostly it was Russian, the whispers, yells, catcalls, babies crying for supper, the noise of gossip as people trafficked in news and money, sex and snacks.

The dusky light took the edge off the hard blonde hair and brassy gold jewellery the women wore. The whiff of charcoal and burnt meat was sweet. The air was clear and turning cold. On the beach, the piroshki men heated meat pies over their little stoves. I bought one, went back up on the boardwalk, hooked my foot around the railing and watched the ocean for a while. I ate the pie; it tasted great.

'What's so funny?' a good-looking woman called out in Russian, and I realized I was laughing out loud. At myself. I had spent twenty-five years, more than twenty-five, trying to dump the past; maybe I had become a Russian all over again. Three girls, arms linked, stopped and looked at me. I complimented them in Russian, then I went to see Johnny Farone, who once gave me a tip that helped me finally put a case together.

An Italian guy, Farone sold appliances for a while, then went into the security business, a smart move if you were dealing with Russians on Brighton Beach, where the motto was if you ain't paranoid you ain't paying attention.

For a while, Farone was practically the only non-Russian for a mile in either direction, and I first knew him when he worked out of Cosmos Auto Parts.

Cosmos was always a crummy shop, beige plastic crucifix on the wall that shook when the trains went by, espresso pot in the toilet, the window sills full of second-hand fanbelts and used air con parts. Johnny's place burned down. He took the insurance, got smart and learned Russian. He got into security. He figured even Russians like Italian food once in a while and he bought a run-down place with a view of the beach and spruced it up; he hired a guy to make the pasta. He orders the mozzarella in fresh.

On the wall of his office, he'd hung the famous ad placed in *Novoye Russkoye*, the local rag. A request by the FBI for 'All facts and gossip about organized crime rackets, murders, frauds, illegal incomes, narcotics, counterfeiting and all kind of criminal activities in the United States and abroad.' Farone saw me look at it and laughed. 'I got it translated,' he said. 'It's the "all facts and gossip" that slays me. Let me show you around, Artie.'

Johnny Farone, who had traded in his short-sleeve white nylon shirt for a nifty Donna Karan suit, escorted me from his office to the restaurant; it was a large room with dark-green walls, brass lamps and oil paintings of scenes from Italian operas. There were padded leather chairs, pink linen table-cloths, a long oak bar. He gestured to a barstool and we sat and ate baked clams and homemade caponata and drank vintage Barolo. Johnny folded his jacket carefully on the next stool over.

'Very nice.'

'It's a good combination out here, you know, Artie. Food and security, boy, the Russkis are they ever paranoid, you know? Make Italians look like they're in Kansas, so to say, Artie. They love detective stuff, you know? I got a half interest in a little store over on Beach 3rd, spy toys, you know? Phone bugs, cattle prods under the welcome mat. I'm gonna be a rich man, Artie. But I got a more important surprise for you.' He turned to look at the door, then blushed as a redhead in a miniskirt walked through the door.

I squinted in the low light of the bar. 'Genia?'

My mousy cousin Genia had changed. For years she lived in a bungalow on a side street off the beach, a shabby house with broken masonry and a yard with a rusted garbage can. The atmosphere in her front room was sad and brown. Genia's father, a Red Army hero once, kept Genia and her little girl under his thumb and retailed his stories and gossip to other old men who walked on the boardwalk, ice in their beards, bitter eyes cloudy with age.

But Genia's old man was dead. And Genia, in her tight green cashmere sweater and a short black leather skirt, had emerged a

Brighton Beach butterfly. Now she put her white mink jacket carefully over her arm, kissed me three times, and said politely in Russian, 'Hello, Artemy Maximovich. It's nice to see you. How are you?'

I said I was fine, asked about her little girl. Genia sat on a barstool and crossed her ankles so the diamond ankle bracelet glittered. It turned out my cousin had sleek, sensational legs.

'She is well,' she said of her child. 'Very good at music.' She spoke English now, carefully, as if she might break it.

'Still playing the flute?

'Yes. She has scholarship. She will be big star, I think.' She sat on her barstool while Johnny poured her wine, fed her titbits from the hors d'oeuvre tray and gazed at her like he couldn't believe his luck.

Customers began arriving. The sun was gone; the ocean outside the window was black; the smell of fresh garlic bread wafted out from the kitchen.

I helped myself to another glass of wine. 'Listen, Johnny, you know a guy name of Anatoly Sverdloff?'

He picked a cracker from a tray on the bar and spread it delicately with some carponata, then popped it in Genia's mouth. She blushed again and dabbed her mouth with a napkin.

Farone said to me, 'Sure. Everyone knows Sverdloff here. Didn't I meet him with you back when?'

'If a guy like Sverdloff has a safe room in his fancy apartment in Manhattan, you know what I'm talking about, who installed it?'

'You gotta gimme some details, Artie.'

I told him and he said, interested but wary now, 'Has to be Leo Mishkin. He's the biggest in the business. I met him once. He's number one in security. He's not Brighton Beach, Artie, not anymore, not for a long time. This guy Mishkin, he's second generation, I mean I knew him once, he came first, then he brought his old man over. The old man was a rough bastard, lives in a home now. I bet he still does business. But Leo's second generation, like I said. Mishkin has ambitions.'

'Is he legit?'

Farone shrugged. 'What's that mean? There's always stories.'

'What kind of stories?'

'It's just gossip. Russians get kind of jealous one of their own does real good, you know, but I heard Mishkin keeps his own copies of safe-room blueprints.'

'Meaning he would have access.'

Johnny pushed his hair back. 'Mishkin's not my business. Out here, you mind your own business. He's Manhattan.'

Genia piped up, 'We're buying a house, Artyom. Sheepshead Bay. You'll come?' Her face lit up. 'A house with a garden. A swimming pool. A piano. A room just for TV.'

I said, 'I'll come,' but even while we talked, I was aware of people in the bar, the sullen glances, the hostile faces that shut down tight when I looked their way. There were people in Brighton Beach who probably wished I was dead. Cops, even ex-cops, were not welcome.

'Get me some stuff on Mishkin, will you, Johnny?' I spoke softly to Genia in Russian. 'Ask him to help me.' I said, 'Tell him it's a family thing.'

Johnny lowered his voice. 'I'm an outsider here, I gotta be careful, OK? You want to check out Leo Mishkin, sometimes he hangs out at the Imperial Thursday nights.'

'How come Thursday?'

'Thursday, the big guys that maybe moved to Manhattan, Montclair, whatever, they like coming home. Fridays, Saturdays, it's for manicurists and tourists, you know.'

'You know anyone who can encourage that Mishkin shows up tonight, this being Thursday, anyone who can provide a come-on?'

'I'll see what I can do.'

'I'll be over at the Imperial.'

'So take it easy, right? I mean you're not that popular around here, OK? It ain't Manhattan out here.'

The Imperial was a free-standing building that had valet parking and a phalanx of muscle in heavy leathers to guard the cars. The first thing I saw when I went inside the main room was a big blonde, black mink over her shoulders, eating off a lobster tree. It was a Brighton Beach special, a three-foot plastic tree stacked with lobsters. Hands oily with butter, vulpine eyes glittering, she sat at the table with her boyfriend, pulled the plump meat out of the red shell, dipped it in melted butter, and pinky finger held high, a massive diamond aloft on it, sucked the meat into her wet, smiling, red mouth. Then she fed some to the guy opposite her. The lively fur stayed over her bare shoulders while she ate. Another diamond sparkled in her cleavage. On the table was a magnum of Cristal Rosé.

I shifted my gun; I had taken it out of the car and it was under my jacket. People still hate you here, Farone had said. I looked around.

On the street side, you entered a lobby where there were glass Art Deco panels engraved with eagles – I figured this for an imperial motif – and pink leather banquettes where the limo drivers sat, bellies on their knees, muttering in coarse Russian and watching the babes. Through the lobby was a long bar, the main room, a huge dance floor and beyond it, set apart by an archway draped in red satin, an area that faced the ocean.

The ocean-front area had a big expanse of plate glass, eight round linen-covered tables and six high-back booths shaped like giant shells and made of cream-color naugahyde. I wondered if the glass was bulletproof. Next to the booths was a VIP entrance.

After I took a look around, I sat at the bar. The blonde eating lobster winked at me. What had changed since my last visit to a Brighton Beach nightclub, a couple years back, was the money. There was more of it. More suits that cost five grand. More women in sable, even a few Ultra-Natashas, the kind I'd seen at Mr Chow's, although you had to figure they only came to the Beach because some guy got sentimental. This was not their desired destination. No almond-eyed Natasha ever crawled out of some shithole in Russia and made her way to New York City to end up in Brighton Beach.

Used to be you saw a lot of home-made outfits and plenty of glitter. Now a lot of the women were in drop-dead black, Prada, that kind of thing. I heard more English too; a second generation had grown up here. Grandpa had been maybe a two-bit hoodlum with a tattoo on his hand who did time in the Gulag; the grandkids went to Harvard. Old story, but where it once took fifty years for a crook to shape up his American dream, now if you were a Russki with a brain, you could do it in five. I read somewhere the Russians have the highest median income of any ethnic group. Fifty grand per year for starters and that's the manicurists.

In the middle of the main room was a dance floor and a stage. In the mirror over the bar I could see a reflection of the whole room. I ordered a beer. The smell of Chanel and fur, the sound of a band playing the theme from *Titanic*, the noise of Russians talking and eating enveloped me. There were two weddings and a birthday party at long tables where maybe twenty people sat around half an acre of food and flowers and forests of booze, vodka, whiskey, also Coke and wine.

The stage show began. Twelve girls, all over six feet, in bright red jackets and fishnet tights strutted down a spiral staircase singing 'New York, New York'. The band was perched on a balcony overhead.

The noise, the smell and the raw lust and aspiration were ankle deep. A hostess in a long satin skirt, a silk T-shirt so tight you could see the nipples rise and fall, stopped by to ask if I needed anything. I gave her some money to let me know if Leo Mishkin showed up.

A waiter set down dishes of snacks on the bar – herring and pickled walnuts, Russian salads and cold meats, hard-boiled eggs, delicate slices of oily sturgeon. I had ordered vodka and the bartender put a bottle of Absolut in front of me.

Then I saw Tolya Sverdloff arrive. He didn't see me.

He was surrounded by a cordon of men. He made his way towards the private area that faced the ocean and I followed cautiously, keeping out of view. He stopped at a round table where Elem Zeitsev was drinking martinis with his wife.

Zeitsev was a quiet, vain guy who took over the big money scams when his uncle Pavel finally croaked. I'd heard Zeitsev had kept the family house in Sheepshead Bay for business, but he'd bought a big place for his wife and her show dogs in East Hampton, south of the highway.

When Sverdloff approached, Zeitsev stood up and kissed him the old-fashioned way, big smackeroo on the mouth like Brezhnev always did, and gestured to a chair. Tolya sat down and I retreated to the bar. I sipped my drink slowly. Sampled the smoked fish. And watched the hoods in Loro Piano cashmere, and wondered if any of them messed with my loft or banged me up in the Middlemarch stairwell. Looking for a particular hood out here was like looking for a grain of sand on the beach.

The show finished, the band played Barry Manilow covers now and people started to dance. Johnny Farone arrived with Genia. In her silver slip dress, she showed off her brand-new boobs: the size of grapefruits, they stayed aloft all by themselves.

Johnny and Genia were happy as clams together, him grinning, her purring, at a table not far from me. He sent me over a bottle of Haut Brion 1953. Cost a bundle. I got a waiter to open it, picked up the bottle and went over to thank Johnny, sat down uninvited, poured some wine for him and Genia. Farone's head swivelled nervously.

I sipped wine and said, 'Very very nice wine, Johnny, thanks.'

Genia touched my hand and nodded to the entrance. I looked up. The hostess and a maître d', followed by the owner, were at attention. With them was a big man in a beautiful dark-blue suit. He arrived quietly, but there was an electric field around him that made people stop eating and stare.

Genia whispered, 'Leo Mishkin.'

Mishkin walked quickly through the crowds towards the private room and disappeared into one of the high-backed booths, but I saw the face when he passed. It was the same man I'd seen at Lulu Fine's building uptown. The man talking Russian to his beautiful son. The boy in the yellow St Pete's jacket who waved to me from the park below the Middlemarch. I wanted to talk to Mishkin.

I tossed my napkin on to the table. Johnny put his hand out to stop me, but Genia took him on to the dance floor. I picked up the wine bottle and threaded my way through the dancers to Tolya Sverdloff. From the table where he sat I could get a better look at Mishkin.

The dance floor was full. The band pumped the Barbie song to a heavy disco beat, and the crowd moved to it laughing. Young guys, very smooth, danced, hands on their girls' asses. A quartet of women boogied with each other. Little kids got on the floor. A sweet-smelling girl with bright gold hair caught my arm and twirled me around, then I made my way through the rest of the couples who worked the dance floor like Fred and Ginger.

In the VIP area, beyond the big window, the ocean was black as pitch now, the yellow moon making a ladder of light on the water from the beach to the horizon. Tolya looked up from the table, caught my eye, warned me away with a gesture I ignored. I put the wine on his table, and Zeitsev shook my hand and smiled. He always figured I was bent, a dirty cop he could do business with.

The six private booths, their high backs to the room, were a few yards away. The band switched to a ballad. I reached over to shake Mrs Zeitsev's hand. Very clearly, in slo mo, I saw the huge yellow diamond on her hand. Then I saw Tolya half rise from his chair, mouth open, hand up as if to warn me or fend me off. Then a streak of blood. I was inches away from him when a shard of glass brushed my cheek. The band stopped. People screamed.

The window had imploded. The plate glass was sucked into the restaurant. Glass everywhere. I never heard it, no gunfire, no bomb, nothing. All I heard was the sound of glass and then panic, the crack and shatter, the smack of slabs of plate glass crashing, then the tinkle of the smaller pieces. I lay on the floor, tangled in a fur coat. There was blood on my cheek. I fumbled in my jacket.

Hand on my gun, I got on my feet.

I turned my head and saw I was a few feet from Leo Mishkin.

Blue suit torn by glass, he was on his hands and knees. He saw me look; there was blood on his forehead and neck, the dark curly hair seemed to sparkle with glass, but he was impervious to it all, absorbed only by the woman with him. He had thrown himself over her when the glass broke. Now he backed off carefully, and helped her up slowly, and from the way he touched her I saw he cared more about her than about himself.

Before the pandemonium in the restaurant subsided, I saw the gray slacks, the white silk shirt with the cuffs folded back over those slim freckled wrists. The woman with Leo Mishkin was Frankie Pascoe.

An arm like a tree-trunk grabbed me, pushed me towards the back door, shoved me out on to the asphalt and around the side of the restaurant to the parking lot. The gravel tripped me, but Sverdloff held on to my shoulder. I pushed him away, saw his moon face in the street light: Tolya Sverdloff's face was covered in blood. 'Get me out of here, Artyom,' he said. 'Get me the hell out.'

I didn't wait. I pushed Sverdloff into my car, he kept his head down, we got the hell out of Brooklyn. I did ninety all the way through the Battery Tunnel.

The tunnel was completely empty. The emptiness echoed around me. I drove hard until I was in Manhattan. Sverdloff was silent. I said, 'You'll stay at my place if there's a problem.'

He said, 'I'm all right now, I can go home. Lend me your phone.'

I passed him the phone, he dialled, spoke briefly in Russian.

I said, 'Farone called you?'

'Yes. He didn't like you nosing around by yourself.'

'You're a friend of Leo Mishkin, Tolya?'

He shrugged. 'We do business.'

'He installed your safe room?'

'A favor.'

'You were in Brighton Beach tonight for what?' I kept driving, watching my rearview, the empty streets.

'Looking for you. Farone called me, like I said.'

'That's all?'

'I had business.'

'With Mishkin?'

'Some of it.'

I pulled up in front of Sverdloff's building. A Russian with a square head and a crew cut opened the door. I looked out. 'The muscle is your guy?'

Sverdloff said, 'Yes,' then leaned closer to me, one arm along the back of my seat. 'Be careful, please.' He rubbed his face, smearing the blood. 'Go home. I'll be in touch.'

He was messed up. Someone was on his tail and because of him, on mine. He got out of the car. I climbed out after him.

I said, 'You think someone went for you tonight?'

He nodded. 'And someone who knows we're friends. You got in the way, Artyom. I don't want that.'

'What do you need?'

'Keep it quiet that I'm in trouble, that I do business with Mishkin. Did business. Can you do that, Artyom?'

For the first time since I met him, Sverdloff seemed to shrink. He patted my shoulder, then turned to go into the building. He looked beat.

I watched until Tolya, shadowed by his guy, disappeared. Then I walked across to the Middlemarch. It wasn't far from Tolya's building on the other side of Sutton Place and I thought how much Pascoe must have hated it, the new money, the Russians who encroached on his fiefdom. The street was dreamy and private in the mild night, shut away from the rest of the city. But if the Middlemarch was Pascoe's castle, who in God's name were the courtiers?

Chapter 13

The light slid slowly up the cast-iron building opposite mine; it seemed to paint the façade. I'd cleaned my place up, and I was standing looking out the window like I do, early mornings, smoking, thinking about the explosion the night before: it turned out to be a low-level explosive but, being Brighton Beach, no one was talking. Outside, Mike Rizzi pulled up in his station wagon, like he does every morning of his life, coming in from Brooklyn, hard-working bastard that he is, killing himself to pay for his three kids. And his wife's ambitions.

Callie Rizzi, Mike's youngest, practically fell out of the car, backpack in one hand, school blazer under her arm, pink sweatshirt tied around her neck, like the ruff on some long-legged Caribbean bird. She waited until Mike unlocked the shop, followed him in.

A few minutes later she came out again, a jelly donut in her hand, then looked up at my window – I've known Cal since she was a little kid, used to babysit her for Mike. She had her yellow blazer on now, and she saw me at the window, put her hand in front of her eyes to shade it from the sun, and slowly, donut still in her hand, waved to me. Then she turned and ran for the subway.

I shuffled the mental snapshots. Two boys in the park near the Middlemarch, their yellow jackets, one boy raising his hand in a salute. The boy who turned out to be Mishkin's son. Callie's jacket was yellow like his. It was the day Frankie Pascoe gave me the list, the day she watched me watching the boys in the park. Frankie Pascoe and Leo Mishkin in Brighton Beach together. I figured Mishkin killed Thomas Pascoe. He had the connections, motive, the muscle.

I jammed my feet into sneakers, I raced downstairs and on to the pavement. She'd turned the corner. I banged full frontal into a pair of kids trying out their Halloween gear; a six-year-old Teletubby hit me up for a buck. I caught Callie at the subway.

'Hey, Artie.' She gave me a sloppy kiss.

'You have a minute?'

'For you, always.' She grinned big – she has that infectious smile – and walked alongside me. She spotted a coffee shop and said, 'Come on, I need a hit. You can treat me.'

We sat at a table. She licked the foam off her coffee. 'Double cappuccino with skim.' She drank steadily. 'I really need my hit, you know.' She laughed. 'Caffeine's drug of choice at all the best schools. So what's up?'

Callie leaned back and yawned. Her high round breasts pushed against the school shirt. She's just fourteen, but my friend Steve says with girls like Callie, you want to look right over their heads. I see her, I think: jailbait, but I always say, 'You look very cool,' and keep the rest shut up in a real dark place. I don't look inside that place except when I'm drunk, and I'm not drinking much these days.

'How's the others? Justine? Sophie?' Callie blows hot and cold about her two older sisters. She grinned. 'The good girls, you mean? The brainiacs? They're cool. So what kind of case are you on, Artie?' She smoothed out her skirt.

'I'm working that thing at the Middlemarch, building by the river?'

'Cool,' she said. 'Guy gets his head chopped in a swimming pool – omigod, I should be like more reverent, but it's so totally weird.'

'I noticed some kids from your school hanging around the scene.'

'Warthog Park, you mean. You're interested because it's near the scene, right? Is that right?'

'Yeah, exactly.'

'Sure. We all go there a lot.'

'So, Cal, you know a kid named Mishkin?'

She polished off her coffee and blushed. 'Everybody knows Jared Mishkin. He's a junior at my school. He's pretty cool. Class President, that kind of stuff,' she said. 'I could get to know him better, if you want,' she added, then flushed again, red, like a little tomato.

I said, 'You like him?'

'Everyone likes him,' she said. 'How come you're asking?'

'Anything special about him? You ever met his family?'

'No. He doesn't ask people over. I think he's embarrassed, you know, I mean, he has like foreign parents, you know. Russians. So what?' She was defensive, then she kissed me on the cheek. 'I could get to know Jared Mishkin a lot better if you want,' she giggled. 'I'll do some undercover work today, so meet me tonight if you want. Look. Meet me tonight at the park. I'll show you.'

I left Callie at the subway. I was at my door when I heard Angie Rizzi call my name. She was across the street, leaning against the coffee shop. I went over. Angie's beautiful face was papery, ravaged, the huge dark eyes full of panic.

'Where's Mike?' I said.

'At the bank. Sneaking a smoke. You saw her.'

'Sure.'

'She won't talk to me.'

'You want me to try?'

'She says she hates being set up for conversation.'

'It's normal, Ange.'

Angie's voice rose. 'Normal? Jesus, Artie, I'm at my wits' end. Such a wasted life.'

'Callie's only fourteen.'

'They invent things. They lie all the time. You've met some of the kids she goes with, they're polite and all, but they're fourteen going on forty. I used to think anything was worth it, but with kids, from the minute they pop out you're on the rack until you die. I'm sorry, Artie, it's an unhappy atmosphere at the minute, but it's her lying. I lie in bed rigid as a board waiting for her to come home. She says she's just going out by the river. To talk. What kid goes to the river at night to talk? I smell her breath. I find a forty-ounce empty in her room.

'Everyone does it, Mom, she says, you wanted me to go to St Pete's. Then she slams her door. She'll be thrown out of school, she'll have a rap sheet that will follow her. It's not like with rich kids that got fathers who are big-time lawyers or movie producers, who can fix it for their kid. It will follow her.'

'Christ, what's she done?'

Angie whispers, 'Dope. They're smoking dope. Someone caught them in the girls' locker room. Pot.'

I smiled. I was relieved as hell. 'That's it? That's all it is?'

She was irritated. 'You and Mike, you're hopeless,' she said. 'I have to go.'

I spent all day chasing my tail. I was worried about Sverdloff. Frankie Pascoe didn't take my calls. Leo Mishkin's company, when I read the files, was big and it appeared clean. He had branches in London and Moscow. He seemed clean as a fucking whistle. Everyone at the Middlemarch had been interviewed now, residents, janitors, supers, doormen. Nothing. Nobody talked. I went to Queens to see Pindar Aguirre, the Middlemarch janitor.

Aguirre lived on a narrow street in Astoria, in a four-story house with aluminum siding. Old men sat on the stoop and smoked in the sun. When I buzzed, Pindar came out and we walked a while. He led me to the sculpture garden on the river near the old Steinway piano plant. We stared at the Noguchi sculptures for a while. On the other side of the East River you could see the Middlemarch, a tiny limestone castle. All the time we were there I had the sense someone was watching. There was no one at all in the garden. I figured the paranoia was getting me.

'You all right?' I said. 'I heard you quit.'

He snorted. 'I was fired.'

'How's that?'

I was on my way out already, you know, they didn't like it I wouldn't play ball.'

'How play ball?' I offered him cigarettes. He shook his head, took a small black cheroot out of his pocket and lit it.

'Something not right in that building. You ever see down there? You saw how lousy it looks in the basement, except the pool?'

I thought of the empty storage rooms, cafeterias, the fallout shelter.

He said, 'There was never no money for fixing stuff up. I complained.'

'The monthly maintenance must be huge.'

'Yeah, but so was the needs of certain people.'

'Board members?'

He looked nervous. 'Maybe. Maybe so.'

Aguirre tossed his cheroot down and rubbed it out with his foot. A car seemed to backfire. Nothing else. I thought it was a car until I saw a red stain on his shoulder, spreading through the material of his white T-shirt. He saw me looking and glanced down and seemed surprised. Then he grabbed his arm and held it, his fingers spread over the surface of the wound.

I spun around. Nobody. Nobody in the sculpture garden or near the river. Somebody had been there, though. Someone took a pot shot at Aguirre, I thought, as I hustled him into my car and over to a local hospital. He wasn't hurt bad. The shot grazed the fleshy part of his shoulder, but it was shocking, coming out of nowhere.

I sat with him while they dressed the wound and he said softly, 'Somebody didn't want I talk to you.'

I nodded. 'I'm sorry.' After they released him, I drove Aguirre home, gave him some cash. Apologized some more. But it stayed with me, the bullet out of nowhere on a sunny afternoon, the sudden red spot on his shirt, the fact it was probably some thug trying to threaten him because he talked to me. I couldn't stop thinking about the poor son-of-a-bitch all that day and for the day after either. I couldn't shake it.

Half a dozen dog walkers lounged on benches in the park with the bronze warthog. Their pups sniffed the earth and each other. A stream of people cruised the river front. Their chatter floated out on the night air, along with the cars that honked on the drive and the noise from a boombox and the yappy dogs. Leaves crackled underfoot and I could hear the water, and in Queens, across the river, lights twinkled. I leaned against the railing and waited.

Two flights of stairs up, along the terraced façade with its little park, was the Middlemarch. I could look up and see it through the stand of trees in the park, branches almost bare.

I leaned against the railing and waited and watched. I looked at the passing faces. Everyone smiling. Low crime, fat economy, this was fun, and even the Pascoe story added a buzz: rich people, fabulous apartments, tyrannical co-op boards, the Russians moving in, the Natashas flaunting it.

A group of teenagers drifted into the park and stood around a knotted dwarf tree. Some smoked, others stared at the water or made out in the shadows of the trees. An old Portishead number played on the boombox. The smell of pot was in the air, and the sound of beepers. Private-school kids wore beepers on their belts.

I watched them, the white kids sprawled across the park who ate French fries and Big Macs and sipped out of forty-ounce beers. They were pale, tall, long-boned kids, the best stuff the gene pool can produce.

'Hi.' Callie came up alongside me and leaned on the railing. She was in skinny black jeans and a white T-shirt.

'What happened to the bell bottoms?'

'Very last year.' She looked at the kids near the tree. 'They call it the Feeling Tree. It's OK, Artie, you can laugh.'

Nights, if they didn't go to Central Park, kids from St Pete's came here to the river, Cal told me, then she looked over at the street.

'Oh God. The Guidos, omigod.'

Music blaring, a two-tone Buick Regal, bronze and tan, pulled up alongside the park. Two boys, Guidos from Astoria, she called them, tumbled out. They were followed by a couple of their girls. The boys wore tight silky shirts and pressed jeans, the girls had bell bottoms, platform shoes, earrings through their eyebrows. Cal said they came over the Triboro or the 59th Street Bridge, Guidos like them, and cruised the rich kids. The boys from St Pete's tried to get off with the Guidettes. Sometimes it happened.

They eyeballed each other, and snickered at each other's outfits. From where I stood, the mating rituals looked harmless. One of the Guidos smoothed his hair and postured for Callie's sake.

She giggled. 'Don't tell Mom, OK? She thinks it's bad news, the Guidos, but they're OK. So, Artie?'

'What?'

'There's Jared Mishkin. By the bench.'

I said, 'Introduce me. Say I'm your uncle, whatever.'

Callie said, 'Don't be such a jerk, I'll say you're my friend.'

She introduced me to a couple of her girlfriends first. They wore tight Ts and showed cleavage and puffed on joints. The smell of pot was so thick now it clogged my nostrils. Then Callie said, 'This is Jared Mishkin.'

Up close, the Mishkin kid was dazzling. He was sixteen, tall, well built, graceful; he had a handsome face, black hair fell over his forehead and he stroked it away from his eyes, which were very light, very blue.

Jared tossed a cigarette on the grass and rubbed it out carefully with his foot, then reached down, picked up the butt and pocketed it. He smiled. He had a heartbreaking thousand-watt smile. 'The environment,' he said. 'I'm hoping to go into politics on a green ticket some day.' At first I figured him for a smartass New York kid, but he was serious. Callie watched me watch him; she was crazy about the kid.

'Where's Harry?' Callie asked him.

He said, 'Some poor bastard homeless guy got beat up, crawled out of a cash machine. Harry found a cop, took him to the shelter. Harry's still there.'

I said, 'What shelter?'

'For the homeless. Mr Pascoe's place.'

'Thomas Pascoe?'

'Yeah. Under the bridge.'

'Cal, I'll drop you home. Nice meeting you, Jared.'

'What's the hurry, Artie?' She was irritated.

A picture was forming up in my head. I was making connections and it made me tense. I wanted Callie out of here. 'Let's just go,' I said.

Jared said, 'If Callie wants to stay, I could see she gets home on time.'

Callie's eyes narrowed; don't blow this, the look said; give me some space here. I didn't want to leave her but I left, looking over my shoulder. Jared was whispering to her, his mouth near her hair. She looked young and vulnerable.

As I left the park, I looked back again and saw the kids. Callie's pals were a lot tougher than the Guidos – a couple of the boys from Queens lingered on the fringes – who only had crappy cars for turf. The St Pete's kids, Jared, his pals, who commandeered the park with a chilling sense of entitlement, owned the access routes to the bigtime. In a few years, they'd own the neighborhood.

On my way to the shelter, I called Sonny Lippert.

He snorted into the phone. 'Yeah, Pascoe and the homeless. City shelters. International rescues for the homeless, too, it eats my liver, Art, you know.'

I held my tongue.

'The goyim, a certain type WASP, they get off on that kind of thing.'

'You know anything about St Peter's?'

'The school?'

'Yeah.'

'Sure, it's where they train the kids up to inherit the parish of the privileged. The ironies of the New York rich are endless, man.'

Chapter 14

Under the bridge, near the river, a couple of homeless guys played cards on an empty crate where a flashlight was stuck upright in a coffee can. Hidden by the old tiled arches of the bridge, the makeshift camp had gone up. Cardboard boxes, tents made out of black plastic garbage bags on poles, supermarket carts. A few blocks north of the Middlemarch, but hidden in the shadows of the bridge.

Traffic roared overhead on the bridge, the boats buzzed the river, a few blocks away Callie and her pals flirted in the park, but the guys playing cards, the others who sat and smoked or snored on cardboard, were shut off from the rest of the city.

I picked my way through the cardboard and the garbage, and from out of nowhere, someone touched my arm. I jumped. He said, 'Got a smoke?'

I gave him the pack. He took three and returned it, then started for the street. Under the streetlight I saw he was a middle-aged guy, round face, dull eyes.

I said, 'You know anything about a shelter around here?'

'Come on.'

I followed him past the bridge where the arches had been restored, the turn-of-the-century tiles buffed up to a creamy glow, ready for the new market, the restaurants, food stores, shops, that would change the neighborhood. It would all change: the homeless would go; the old ladies who drank their pensions dry in bad Chinese dives on First Avenue would die off. At buildings like the Middlemarch, the co-op boards would give way; more new money would arrive. I thought about the new buildings towering over the rest of them. 'Steals our air,' Frankie had said. Somewhere a dog barked.

Near the bridge, a derelict tennis bubble loomed up and the homeless guy headed for it. The light was dull and I squinted.

Slowly, out of the dark, I saw a mass of bodies take shape in the night. It was a long line of figures that snaked its way from the camp near the river towards the converted tennis club.

I followed the moving figures up the street. In the streetlight it was a weird sight: the long line, passive, sullen, weary, shuffling, jostling on the way in, then coming out the other side of the temporary building. Now the line of people moved quickly, food clutched in their hands, people darting out of the light to eat.

The guy I gave the smokes to got in line. He said, 'Soup kitchen.'

'What's the shelter like?'

'It ain't exactly home, but it's OK, one of the best. Good neighborhood, after all.' He laughed.

By the time we got up to the shelter door, I saw a couple of cops climb out of a blue and white, the lights on it flashing. I told one my name and he said, 'Homeless guy got beat up. Crawled part way here, one of the kids that volunteers brought him in. You seen the goons they got patrolling the cash machines?'

I thought of the black guy in the bank lobby with the mayor's mask on. 'Yeah, I did.'

'Someone tried a little outreach on him. We got a situation. The New Social Order, right? Clean 'em out of the bank lobbies and you got a city that's squeaky clean. You a detective?'

I nodded.

'He's been asking for someone, you mind speaking with him? He got hurt pretty bad. He's inside, I'll take you, OK?'

On the wall of the shelter was a picture of Thomas Pascoe in a frame. Underneath it was a vase with white carnations. Everywhere was the heavy smell of soup.

The shelter had been carved out of part of the tennis club and the dome-like roof made it cavernous. At the far end were long metal tables, and a steam table where a crew of servers produced soup and sandwiches.

The young cop led me to a section of the shelter that was partitioned off from the main room. It had six beds. A man sat on one of them. The cop said, 'This is the guy that got beat up.'

He sat on the edge of the bed. Someone had patched up his

face and I sat next to him. He was young, twenty-five, not more, squat, with the biceps of a body builder but pale milky eyes that were a little vacant. His name was Dante Ramirez, he said. He held a newspaper in one hand. In the other was a cup of coffee that he set down on the floor by the bed.

'You an actual detective, man? You got some clout here?'

'I don't know.'

'Don't let them send me to the hospital, please. They make you wait all night.'

'Don't worry,' I said.

'It's been bad since the murder, you see. Then the demonstration by Gracie Mansion. Everything changed. It was OK before, then they start watching us.'

I said, 'It's pretty tough.'

He said, 'Yeah. You know how we feel, man, a lot of us that ain't insane or ripped on bad drugs? I mean, I'm a drunk, I like drinking, but I ain't crazy, you know? I finished high school. I had a job. I lost it, I lost my house, I got sent from Queens to Manhattan, this motel, that motel. I lost my baby. They took him. The city say I can't have housing 'cause I got a brother in Brooklyn, but my brother beat on the baby's head. They make you feel immoral. You're not in the game, you didn't play it right. You're a loser, man. The mayor said maybe the homeless will figure out it's easier to live in a good climate, I hear a rumor he's offering a one-way ticket south, I get this vision of us loaded on trains, south, you know what I'm saying. Trains. Camps.' He shrugged. 'You seen the shanty town down under the bridge?'

'I saw it.'

'We call 'em Rudivilles, honor of our mayor,' he said. 'We got some all over town. It's getting cold, out there, man,' he added. 'I'm scared of the cold.' He held up the newspaper. There was a picture of Thomas Pascoe. 'Pascoe.' He whispered it.

'Pascoe hurt you?'

Ramirez was shaking. 'No. No.' He picked up the styrofoam coffee cup, but the brew sloshed over the rim and he set it down on the floor. His hands shook hard.

I said, 'It's OK. Pascoe's dead. He can't hurt you.'

'Mr Pascoe, Tommy, he said we should call him Tommy, was the best human being I ever met in my fucking life.' Dante Ramirez got up and made his way to the main room, where he stopped under the portrait of Pascoe and looked up at it like an icon. He crossed himself.

'He raised the money for this shelter. He got us clothes and food and medicine. He tracked down families if people had any. He came here himself most nights. If you couldn't make it through the night any other way, he got you something to drink. He was always here.'

The words had become a eulogy, and I suddenly realized that, gradually, a group of men had clustered around us.

They began talking. Echoing Ramirez' words. Relating stories of Pascoe's good work. He was a saint, it seemed; now he was a martyr.

I looked across the room. She was there. Frankie Pascoe, a cigarette in her mouth, she was behind a cafeteria counter. She was passing out sandwiches.

Frankie stubbed out her cigarette, then lit a fresh one. Between passing the sandwiches to the growing line of homeless, she placed the smoke on the edge of the steel counter. She looked up suddenly. Saw me. Smiled.

I wanted to touch her. I walked towards her and shoved my hands in my pockets. She stripped off the latex gloves, tossed them on the table. 'It was a condition of knowing my husband, the charity work,' she said. 'I thought it was the right memorial, coming here as usual. Anyway, I can't go anyplace else, the TV people are always out there waiting. Thank God for Halloween, it will give them something else to cover.'

'Your husband was a popular man around here.'

She said, 'Here, certainly. Our neighbors weren't happy at all, a shelter on their doorstep, but Tommy said it was the right thing. He was persuasive.'

'I bet. Unhappy enough to wish him dead? Enough to kill him?'

'The worst of them were, of course, the new people. They donate their Versaces to the shelter thrift shop, then they want a cut of the profit, that's their idea of helping.'

I kept quiet.

She said, 'You like the irony, I'm sure, Tommy helping the homeless. We've got lots of irony for you around here.'

I thought of Sonny. 'So they say.'

'It keeps you from feeling,' she said. 'The irony. A very fine British habit.'

'Who else worked here?'

'All kinds. It's a day shelter for the most part. Showers. Kitchens. We've got a few emergency beds.'

'Kids from St Peter's?'

Her eyes darted away from me for the first time, unable to hold on to me, looking for someone else.

She picked up a fresh pair of gloves, put them on, unscrewed a jar of peanut butter, then another one of grape jelly. She started making sandwiches. As she passed them out, she was sober, competent, helpful, smiling.

'You asked about St Pete's?'

'Yeah.'

She spotted a freckle-faced kid with sandy hair and called, 'Harry!'

He hurried over. She said, 'This is Harry Alden. He helps out here. He helped Mr Ramirez tonight.'

Harry shook my hand. I said, 'So what's the deal here, Harry?'

Harry had a British accent. 'Mr Pascoe said we needed a wake-up call, and he was right. He made us sleep rough. We put in time at the shelter here. You see, sir, I've got almost straight As, I've got ten years on violin, I play lacrosse, I'm deputy editor of the school paper, I worked on an Indian reservation one summer, last year I was in Madrid for my Spanish. The shelter was just perfect for me.'

I said, 'Perfect for what?'

He looked up surprised and said, 'To get into Harvard.' Then he went back to fixing sandwiches.

Frankie said, 'You know what they say?'

'What do they say?'

'Charity's the new rock and roll.' She gave a small wry smile. 'I need a drink.'

'I think people would understand if you left a little early.'

'What I'd really like is a swim. They've refilled the pool.'

'A swim. You swim a lot?'

'Yes,' she said. 'I was an athlete once. Anything to keep from thinking. Swimming's especially good. Better than irony even.' She glanced at the long line of men waiting for food, for beds, for shelter. 'It gets rid of the stink too.'

So Tommy Pascoe was a saint, I thought, as we walked a couple of blocks over to First and a bar where she sometimes drank. According to the homeless guys, he was Saint Tom, and who would kill a saint and make him a martyr, unless it was random? Who? Unless he invited the killer in. I'd scratched the idea he set Ulanova up and got it in the neck instead. So who? Leo Mishkin?

I'm not sure what the hell I was doing hanging out socially with Frankie late at night. It wasn't just that I was worried about Tolya and figured Frankie could shed some light on the business with Leo Mishkin and the Russians. I smelled Frankie walking beside me and I knew I was there because I wanted her. I wanted to be around Frankie Pascoe.

The door to the bar was propped open. Frankie looked around. Three women crammed in a booth, dressed to kill, shared a bottle of Dom Perignon and talked Russian. The Natashas had cornered the neighborhood.

Frankie crossed to the other side of the room. Settling into a banquette, she grunted. Something she did whenever she sat down, I realized, like a release from the sheer effort of being upright. I sat down opposite and looked in the mirror over her head. I was always looking in mirrors now and over my shoulder, wondering who killed Pascoe, who beat me up and fucked with my loft, who shot Pindar Aguirre.

Around us, people drank their money, eyed each other and drawled their opinions. The owner was a Frenchie with a head of greasy hair and a smoke in the corner of his mouth, and he hovered over Frankie, who ordered steaks and dismissed him.

'The food here's lousy.'

'So why bother?'

Frankie ordered another vodka. 'The tribal rites,' she said. 'Habit, darling. Too much trouble to change. Also they let you smoke. Which is important, don't you think? I'm awfully tired, Artie.'

She looked unanimated, passive and beautiful, and I was thinking with my dick. I sat back in my chair, away from her.

'They read Tommy's will. It's a nightmare,' she said all of a sudden.

My mouth was dry. I picked up the water glass.

'I'm not allowed to know everything. We kept our affairs separate. But he wants the burial in England, for chrissake, and a headstone by his ghastly cousin, freaky Warren.'

'The bronze hands.'

'Yes. God, Artie, I don't know if I have the energy for it.'

A waiter slung a couple of plates of pâté on the table and a basket of bread. I asked for red wine. I was facing Frankie, my back to the room. She lifted her elegant shoulders slightly so the soft gray sweater slipped; a triangle of bare skin showed. The skin was lightly tanned.

She said, 'I suppose they've got Tommy in a fridge somewhere downtown?' She seemed suddenly fragile.

I leaned across the table; her hand quivered like a soft animal caught in a trap.

'Sometimes I get the feeling you weren't all that crazy about your husband. Why's that?'

She leaned across the table towards me again, knocked over the basket of bread, set it upright, helped herself to my drink. 'I didn't like him much, you're right.'

'How come? I mean, tell me straight.'

'He didn't make the effort for me, you know? He was a lazy fuck.'

I ate some bread and looked at her. 'Leo Mishkin installed the safe room in your apartment?'

'Yes.'

'Mr Mishkin was your husband's friend?'

'Yes.'

'A charitable guy.'

'Yes.'

'New money.'

'Yes.'

'He wanted to give the new money old veneer, so to speak, so he gave to your husband's causes?'

Frankie said, a little defensively, 'Leo's not a bad man. I met

Leo Mishkin in Moscow. Tommy was on some fact-finding mission for the British and I went and I said, we ought to help him. Tommy helped him. They came to America, we lost touch. A few years later, he called us. He had done well. He's a good Russian,' she said. 'Like you.'

I said, 'And he moved into the Staircase to Nowhere Building.'

'Yes.'

'To be close to you.'

'That's right.'

'And Mr Mishkin sends his son to St Peter's.'

'I believe he does.'

'He had your husband's help with that?'

'I expect so.'

'I'd like to know where Leo Mishkin was the night before your husband died and you weren't home. Were you with him that night?'

'I was with Leo. He'll tell you he was with me.'

'Where?'

'Leo owns a number of places. If necessary I can testify we were in one of them, and there will be proof.'

'I'm not asking about you this time, Frankie, I'm asking about him. Your alibi was Leo Mishkin? He wasn't just a friend.' I grabbed her wrist.

'Yes,' she said. 'But you knew that.'

'I knew when I saw you in Brighton Beach. You were in Brighton Beach, weren't you, Frankie? Last night.'

'Yes.'

'I saw the way he was with you. He'll make it good for you? The alibi.'

She smiled. 'Leo always made it good for me.'

'It's not a joke, Frankie. He'll make it stick?'

'He will. He will make it good because he takes care of me, and I will swear the same, if that's what you're thinking, because it's true.'

'Someone else saw you together?'

She chuckled. 'Yes, of course.'

'Who?'

'I don't know. Doormen. Waiters, skaters.'

'Skaters?'

'Yes. Sometimes we went ice skating. Ice dancing. We took lessons. We were quite good. The rink at Chelsea Piers. It was different. A time out of life.' She smiled. 'We were learning to tango.'

'Skating.'

Frankie gave a husky laugh. 'Leo was the nicest part of my life. The only part worth mentioning,' she said. She sat up straight, then reached in her bag and tossed some money on the table. 'I've lost you, haven't I?'

'You didn't lose me. You didn't have me.'

As soon as I said it, I had an insane thought that I was in love with her. I told myself it was the dark bar, the wine, the warm night, that I was pretty hurt by Lily's sudden departure. Or the soft, slurred ooze of fear, a sort of dread over the case that made me feel I was hanging by my thumbs. Maybe I'm just a lumpen guy driven by the fear I'm going die some day.

Suddenly Frankie said, 'Take me home,' and I went with her. When we got to her building, not saying anything, she went to the pool and like a dumb dog in heat, I followed.

Frankie pulled herself out of the pool. She grabbed the ledge and got out, tall, limber, naked, the water streaming off. The pool had been deserted when we got there and Frankie stripped off her clothes quickly, then dove in the water and surfaced, laughing with pleasure. She stood by the pool, naked, showing me her body.

Her nipples were hard. She touched them lightly. There was a terry cloth robe on the bench and I grabbed it and held it for her.

She laughed. 'You think I'm a femme fatale, Artie, that if you touch me, you'll die?' she said and slipped into the robe and tied the belt tight.

'Something like that,' I said.

We went upstairs and sat on the floor of the library. She dried her hair with a towel and gave me a bottle of wine that I opened.

Frankie said, 'They're not going to get whoever killed Tommy, are they?' she said.

'I don't know. I think there's a bigger picture that I'm not getting, I think there's Russians involved. You want to talk some about Leo Mishkin, his friends?'

She changed the subject. 'Do you know what Tommy left me, Artie? Do you want to know?'

'Tell me.'

'He left me his debts. He gave away so much, there were so many bequests, all he left me were his debts. And a letter of instruction to support his shelter, his work. He commended me to it. Here in New York. In London. Sanctimonious prick.'

'I don't get it.'

'He gave it away. He left huge amounts in trusts I can't touch. Blind trusts, some of them. He was obsessed with the charities, and I'm not even certain he wasn't taking a little off the top of the building fund.'

'What for?'

'Give to the shelters. It was always the shelters. They had his picture on the wall, after all. There are debts, as well. I'm his wife. I feel obliged to pay.'

I thought of Aguirre the janitor in Queens that morning. The empty rooms in the basement. 'But it wasn't you, though, Frankie. You didn't kill him. You told me you had money, that the money was yours.'

'To begin with. In the beginning. My dowry was his stake in the building. My father's money is what he used to buy property.' She snorted. 'I always thought, when he goes, it will be mine again.' She held on to my arm. 'It was mine. Is mine. What's left, that is.'

'I'm sorry for you.'

She was brisk. 'Don't be. I'm not. Let's not talk for a bit. Can I play something for you?'

I sat on her zillion-dollar rug and she played me a version of 'Stella by Starlight' I never heard, that Stan Getz recorded on an old eight-track special for her when they were an item. No one ever heard it before, she said. She'd never played it for anyone.

'You like it?'

'Oh yeah. Imagine if you could do that,' I said, and leaned my head against the sofa. Frankie sat down beside me and grunted. She leaned her head against me and we sat for a while like that.

Frankie said, 'I wish.'

'What do you wish?'

She put an arm around my shoulders and her smell made me drunk. 'I wish, Artie, that I could put the genie back in the bottle.' She added, 'But it's too late.'

Chapter 15

I left Frankie's around five Saturday morning. Halloween the next day, a week almost gone since Pascoe's murder, nothing from Tolya Sverdloff since Thursday night in Brighton Beach. I was standing on Sutton Place near my car. There was a cop on duty and I saw a garbage man hand him a bag then lean over the gutter and puke his guts out. The cop was from the local station house and he recognized me. I'd been around a lot that week.

He was a short black guy, near retirement. He held the bag tight and said 'Jesus Christ' over and over and shoved the shitty little plastic deli bag at me. I could smell the rancid coffee it once contained. The cop looked sick. I looked inside.

Inside the bag was someone's nose.

I yelled over to the garbage guy. 'Where'd you find this?'

'By that building with the scaffold,' he said. 'It was wrapped up in a nice box. Barneys. I figured I'd see if there was anything worthwhile.'

I didn't hear him. I was thinking about Sverdloff. Christ. Jesus Christ. Tolya. Oh, man, I thought, I'm sorry. I should have stuck to you. With you. Taken care. I was screwing around with Frankie Pascoe and you were over here two blocks away and dying.

I was talking to him in my head, yelling his address at the cop, running so my lungs hurt. Maybe they left him alive. Maybe they took a piece, then left him. I was yelling.

I got hold of the super, we broke into the keysafe, got the spares. Already I heard the sirens; the black cop was right behind me.

The apartment was empty.

A worker on the floor said he'd seen Sverdloff leave the night before.

'He was OK?'

'Looked OK, yeah. Why?'

'I hope to God they killed her before they did it.' Lippert showed up at the building with the staircase to nowhere, so did Homicide and Forensics. 'I could nose around for you,' she'd said. Nose around. I'd liked Lulu Fine a lot; I dragged her into it. Now they were putting her in a body bag.

Someone had forged her signature, got her extra keys out of the keysafe, gone upstairs. They took some cash, nothing else. She had been found naked, except for her blonde fur coat. A female cop let me see her. She was wrapped in the coat. Fisher. It was a Canadian fisher coat, a female cop said, and touched it furtively.

Gary, Lulu's ex, was there. He was a big man, balding, his face sorry as a faithful dog. 'We just got back together,' he said. 'We were out together last night. She wanted to walk home alone,' Gary added, his face wet. 'I said, "I'll walk you," but she said, "Come on, Gar, the city's so safe now, it's a gorgeous night, I want to walk by myself a little, think about us. I'll see you tomorrow."'

His story held up. Gary spent the night at his father-in-law's place, went there as soon as he left Lulu, stayed up late with the old man talking dyed baby lamb.

Someone left a piece of her where it would be found. There was nothing I could do. Sverdloff didn't answer his phone.

A Russian creep wanted me off the case. Sverdloff was in trouble. Pascoe was a saint to the homeless, a lazy fuck to his wife. He willed away most of his dough. And now poor bloody Lulu Fine was dead. My goddamn fault. Lulu was nosing around for me. Help me out. Oh yeah, and I had slept with Frankie Pascoe and knew I'd do it again. As soon as I could.

I pushed Sonny Lippert to one side. I told him about Lulu's dealings with the Russians. 'The way they did it, you figure it had to be some Russian shit. Keep your nose clean, lose your nose, they think it's so fucking poetic.'

'You think she got in trouble messing with the Nouveau Russkis, fixing up Russian hookers with rich guys?'

'Hookers?'

'Hookers, you know, Natashas, models, whatever. Tania from Tblisi who needs a pair of Prada sandals, what's the difference?'

I said, 'No, I think she got in trouble nosing around the Pascoe thing if you're asking.'

'You want me to believe it was the Brighton Beach crowd killed Thomas Pascoe?'

'I don't know.'

Sonny, who was wearing a double-breasted black suit and looked like an undertaker, said, 'How deep in this are you, man?'

I shrugged.

He said, 'I should have pulled you off of it.'

'It's too fucking late. You figured you'd stick me in, see what stirs, isn't that right, Sonny? You got me to babysit Frances Pascoe. I was a babysitter, wasn't I? She didn't do it.'

Sonny looked at me hard. 'You sleeping with her?'

I didn't answer him.

'It wasn't dope,' Callie Rizzi said. She was sitting in my car when I got to it. 'My mom told you it was dope, didn't she?'

'Yes. How'd you know where to find me?'

'I knew you were on the case up here. You weren't home. I walked around. I saw your car. What difference does it make?'

'So it wasn't dope.'

'I'm nervous, Artie, OK. They think I lie, you know? They think I make up stuff. So tell them it's dope, OK? Kids experimenting, like Mom thinks,' she said. 'I won't bother you anymore, OK?'

I caught her wrist. 'What?'

She whispered it very softly. 'Kids at school.'

She crossed her arms. 'The guy in the pool. I mean, is it true? They hurt Mr Pascoe with a sword? I mean killed him.'

'Where'd you hear that?'

'I don't know. Kids, we talk a lot of crap, you know?'

'A kid could do it,' I heard myself say to Sonny. Remember the Ninja sword? It could have been a kid.

'You have to give me names.'

'I can't. I didn't see. I don't know. I only heard.'

'You have to. This is real. Real people getting hurt.'

She bit on her lip.

I said, 'Don't do that, just tell me.' I turned the key. 'You want to show me your school?'

She shrugged. I pulled the car away from the curb and drove the few blocks north, then parked in front of St Peter's. It was Saturday. The building was quiet, the Gothic façade scrubbed.

I said, 'Come on.'

Callie said, 'Let's sit in the car a while.'

Saturday morning. The streets were already filled with kids trying out their costumes. Some of them wore eight-inch platforms; you could see over the crowds in them; the kids called them Double Fours. Tourists had started arriving. Halloween was Sunday. I opened the window.

'Artie?'

'What, babe?'

'They think, my mom especially, I'm a fourteen-year-old kid who's deep but cute, that if I have secrets, it's like stuff about boys, like that. They think I'm like in adolescence which is why I shut my door on them when they pester me. They don't get it, they have me in their sights all the time so that I feel like someone has a pillow over my face, I feel like I might not wake up in the morning, and they think what they feel is love, but it isn't. I wish I could have stayed in my own school in Brooklyn, but Mom wanted Manhattan. She wanted St Pete's. She didn't want me with the Guidos and Clydes, so now I'm with these rich kids, I have to fit in. That's why I go to the park at night.' She opened the car door.

'We're on the bus, one girl goes, "I don't know if I want to be a famous actress when I grow up or just a rich person." Or someone else, she screams out at some pathetic boy, "Hey, Davey, come over here and I'll give you a handjob."'

'Jesus, Cal.'

I locked the car and followed her to the school. A side door was open. She led me inside and down a flight of stairs to a locker room. Through a door I saw some boys were shooting hoops, the rhythmic thud of the ball constant, irritating, unnerving in the cavernous weekend quiet. From somewhere I heard kids shouting, their voices echoing back with the kind of metallic ring you get in a swimming pool. Then a splash. There was a pool near by.

Callie sat on a bench and I sat next to her. 'My parents, they love me. OK. Like I loved the dog, I can't even like remember its name now, but we never let it do dog things and, personally, I think that dog died from love. So at night, when they're like snoring, I go out. I have to. I can't breathe at home. They think it's sex or drugs. I'm just bored.'

'Who do you go with, Cal?'

'Can I have some coffee?'

'Sure. Later.'

She got up and wandered down the row of lockers, banged the doors open and shut, lolled against a door. Then, no warning, nothing, she began to cry. 'I need some help.'

'I'm here.'

Absently, she started pulling at the lockers. Most of them were locked. A few opened and she peered inside. 'Stuff is like happening and I don't understand.'

'Boy stuff? Guys bugging you?'

'Please! No, Artie. No. Not like that. I just said.'

'Not drugs.'

'Worse.'

'How worse?'

'You won't tell Mom, will you? Or any of them, you have to like promise me. I hate this fucking school, you know.'

'I'll talk to Mike. There's no reason you have to do anything you don't want.'

She tried to laugh, 'In your dreams,' she said, wiped her face, then went on looking in lockers.

'You looking for something, sweetheart?'

Callie turned around. 'They talk about killing, Artie. They talk about death. They read out stuff from weird books.' She looked at the lockers, the concrete floor, then at me. I've never seen such fear. 'They call the park the Killing Ground. They talk about ritual killing. Rites of passage, they say. They buy weapon catalogues in Chinatown. They practice decapitating chickens, like someone got their dad to buy some and they keep the chickens in a chicken coop in a penthouse on Central Park West, the San Remo, one of those buildings.' She was crying, but now she giggled, and I couldn't help it, I started to laugh.

I said, both of us laughing so hard she had to sit down, 'You think the co-op board knows?'

'I know, it's insane.' Callie held my arm. Then she wiped her face. 'I have to go now. I'll be late.'

'Who's involved?'

'I only hear it second hand. No one uses real names. They use names from books. They mean it. They're serious.'

'Do you think they killed Thomas Pascoe? Callie? Tell me for chrissake. If they did, it's trouble, you, me, everyone. They fucked with my loft. Did you know that? People are dead.'

She just folded her arms across her chest and said, 'I don't know. Don't ask me anymore.'

'Is Mishkin involved, and his pals?'

She looked offended. 'Of course not. It's Jared who told me about it, he said he knew you were a friend and a cop, he was worried. He's not like that. He works most nights in the shelter.'

She was a volatile kid and scared to death; now she turned belligerent. 'Anyhow, it's your fault. Your fucking fault.'

'Don't swear like that.'

'Don't come on like my parents. You curse like crazy all the time.'

My stomach turned. 'What's my fault, honey? What?'

'You dragged me into this, you did. I only asked Jared about Mr Pascoe 'cause you wanted me to.'

Callie was sullen and unforgiving when I dropped her home later that day. What she told me shook me up plenty. The kids all lied, Angie said. I didn't believe that.

As I pulled up to my building, I was suddenly fed up with the good weather. It had gone on too long. I wanted rain. In the parks, the leaves underfoot were so dry they crunched like potato chips, and upstate, forest fires had begun eating the land. After the endless Indian summer, the palmy days would end, pundits said. Boom before the bust, they said, but the mayor went on TV a lot, proclaimed New York the greatest, danced like Ali in the ring, tried to crack jokes and lost more hair.

The Pascoe case lost its juice. Lulu Fine's murder sucked the charm out of the story; two murders in a week made people edgy.

Halloween started that night. By Saturday night, a million

people, maybe two, no one knew, were moving into town. The tunnels were choked. There was gridlock on the roads, in the streets. People spilled out of bars and restaurants on to the pavement, already in costume a night early, and every window glittered with grinning pumpkins. A fancy food store down by me sold life-size skeletons made out of white chocolate.

Two of my old captains left messages on my machine to see if I could do a shift; I said I was already committed. I told Sonny Lippert I'd cover Sutton Place for him. It was rumored the President would attend a few of the parties. Security was a nightmare. West Coast gangs, the Crips and Bloods who had branches in Rockaway, were coming into Manhattan for initiation rites, someone said. If a witch slipped a box cutter out of his pocket and cut out the eye of a ghost, who was going to know? Who would see?

More cops were called in from the suburbs. Parties were scheduled on practically every block, in every club, in all the parks. Platforms went up; bands tested their equipment. You could hear the loudspeakers all over town.

For one night each year, every overlapping and separate group in New York City, Russian, Dominican, Indian, rich, poor, lawyers, bartenders, kids, was bent on the same thing, to celebrate the dead.

The parade route was changed three times. Lippert ground his teeth and called me on the hour. I tried to reach Frankie Pascoe; the maid said she was sleeping. I wanted to see her. I wanted her.

'I wish I was home.' Lily sounded mournful on the phone. 'I'm missing everything.'

'So come home then. You could get a plane tonight, be home in time for Halloween, you and Beth. We'll go on the roof. We'll have a party.'

'I can't do that,' Lily said. But it was getting cold in London. She needed some things for Beth. Could I go by her place, Fedex some things?

Sure, I said. Sure. Lily was staying on, but I didn't have much right to say anything when I'd spent the night before with Frankie Pascoe, when I wanted to do it again and would if she let me.

Lily asked, 'Everything OK?'

'Fine.'

We made small talk. When I got off the phone, I realized she never asked about the case.

'Sympathy for the Devil' was blasting out of Rick's stereo when I went upstairs that night and found him in his underpants looking at costumes that were heaped on the floor, on the sofas, strewn over the green marble kitchen counter.

'You're planning a party?'

'Several. Your friend Sverdloff's giving a party. Didn't he tell you? He called. Said for me to stop by if I got bored with the teabags.'

'He called? He's OK.' I felt a knot in my gut untie itself.

'I said that he called. He left a message for you. He's giving a party. You all right?' Rick peered at me.

'Yeah. How come he didn't call me?'

'How the hell should I know? Art? You with me? What are you going as?' He held a ruffled shirt against himself. 'I don't know about this Anglo crap.'

'Fuck that shit, Rick, I'm not going as anything. What Anglo crap?'

'Janey Cabot's giving a big bash. You know what she wants? We're all supposed to dress up as famous Brits, you know? Otherwise she might withhold her approval, that's how they say it.' Rick mimicked. 'With-hold her approval, oh dear, yata, yata.'

'You could always go as the Queen.'

'Fuck off, man.'

The doors to the terrace were open, a mild breeze rustled the orchids. Rick punched the CD and Sid Vicious came on singing 'My Way'.

'What is this, the Halloween hit parade?' I was edgy.

Rick said, 'Seriously, you OK, Art?'

'Yeah.'

He selected a shimmery blue robe thing from a pile, ran into the bedroom. I found a beer and sat on a barstool, picked up the phone and tried Frankie, then wondered what the hell I was doing.

Ricky reappeared in the long Chinese gown, a little cap on his head, a pigtail hanging down his back. I glanced at the sepia photographs on his wall, then back at Rick. He had transformed himself into one of his own ancestors. Then he burst out laughing. 'What? You think I look like a waiter in Chinatown. Who were you calling?'

'No one.'

'So, Artie, I got the perfect idea for your outfit.'

'What's that?'

'You could go as a cop.'

Chapter 16

Princess Diana and Dodi al-Fayed, blood on their clothes, danced on the roof of a Sutton Place townhouse that night, and there was John Lennon with a bloody shirt and a hole in his heart; Kenneth Starr carried Bill Clinton's head. Sutton Place was closed to traffic. It was the warmest night of the fall, sultry almost. Everywhere on Sutton Place, in the gardens, on the roofs, in the street, people partied.

I was looking out through the lens of the telescope mounted on the ledge of Sverdloff's terrace. I could see everything: A jaunty department flag hung over the back of the police boat, blue markings clear, that bobbed at the end of the Middlemarch jetty; a cop in uniform reached over the back of the boat and trailed his hand in the water, and then looked up and waved at a flotilla of boats that chugged up the East River and were caught in the arc lights rigged on the Drive and on the bridge. Green and yellow water taxis, tugs, ferryboats, a Circle Line loaded with people cruised past. It was like a movie set, the night all lit up.

I swivelled the scope: the streets were lit by more lights. The parade that had wound its way up from Sixth and Spring earlier had splintered when it left the Village, turned East, then kept on going. Ten thousand cops patrolled the streets, in uniform, on scooters and bikes, on horseback, on foot. Bands played everywhere, salsa, reggae, rap groups. A jazz orchestra on a flatbed truck wove its way up First Avenue. I could see the glint of light on the brass.

From the terrace I shifted the telescope so I could see the building tops, lighted up in orange and black. All over the city a million people bobbed and swayed. I looked down at Sutton Place again and for a second I thought I saw, on the little piazza at the Middlemarch, a figure among the stone urns with white flowers in them. Frankie Pascoe smoking a cigarette. But it wasn't her. She didn't answer my calls all day.

Suddenly, Sverdloff's building seemed to vibrate as the fireworks exploded. The crowd on his terrace pushed for places at the railing, then whistled, clapped, cheered, yelled, as gold fountains of light fell into the river. I put the telescope down.

Torches wrapped with yellow flame shivered in the breeze on Tolya's terrace; waiters snaked between the guests and hefted heavy trays of Champagne. I caught my reflection in the glass wall. In uniform, my reflection stared back, a version of the guy on my old ID card, only older. Dark blue jacket. My old cap. Light blue shirt. One of ten thousand guys in uniform that night.

'I like the outfit.' Tolya came outside and stood next to me. He wore white tie and tails and said he was dressed as Fred Astaire. He put a cold glass of Champagne into my hand and said, 'Take a drink.'

He was the good host, smiling, laughing, pushing drinks on people, feeding titbits into the mouths of the hundred gorgeous women he'd invited, but I knew him and he was worried. Tolya looked through the window and across the room. A man got up like an Orthodox priest danced with Catherine the Great. I saw Tolya look at him, then turn away.

'Who is he, Tol?'

'His name's Eddie Kievsky,' Tolya said.

'From Brighton Beach?'

'No.'

'From?'

'London. He owns a big piece of the action over there.'

I went inside, where a band played and people danced. I saw Callie Rizzi – I got her the invite – and she waved. The invitation had redeemed me. She had on a micro-miniskirt and a Soviet army shirt and cap I got for her. She was dancing with Jared Mishkin and he looked up and smiled too; he was got up as some kind of nineteenth-century gent, black frock coat, ruffled shirt. He was handsome as hell. She glowed; he smiled sweetly.

I started towards Callie and felt a hand on my arm. It was Rick. I pulled away from him and moved towards Callie. He stopped me. 'No,' he said. 'Leave her.'

In the dining room, people bobbed for apples. Water splashed on the floor. I figured I better go down to the street; I left Tolya's before midnight.

In the unfinished lobby, where the furniture was draped with dust sheets, someone had placed a pair of pumpkins on the floor: Jack and Jackie O' Lantern. Six naked guys on their way in said they were the Full Monty. A frantic Spice Girl – Back From the Dead Spice, she told me – waited for the elevator.

'You're a real cop, or it's a costume?' Dead Spice asked.

I said, 'Tough call.'

In the street, I leaned against the building, called Lippert on my cellphone. Things were pretty good, he said: a few people trampled but not injured bad on the Brooklyn Bridge; a heart attack at a Queens disco; a couple wiseguys shot each other in Brighton Beach; not much else.

I stayed on Sutton Place. By three in the morning, the crowd had thinned, the adrenalin was low. I was weary, and so were the other cops who walked down the street littered with bottles and streamers and candy corn.

I got a carton of coffee from a deli, then climbed down to the pocket park below the Middlemarch. I sat on a bench to drink the coffee.

Silently, a man sat down next to me. He was small, dark hair. He wore some kind of cheesy toga, mask over his eyes and nose, a paper plate with a slab of pumpkin pie on it in his hand. He set the plate on the pavement and pushed up the mask so I could see his face. It was Pindar Aguirre. The janitor from the Middlemarch. The guy I met in Astoria who took a flesh wound that should have been mine. I could hear how the shot cracked out from nowhere on a sunny day in Queens. I'd tried to check up on him after he got shot, but at his place nobody answered. Now I said, 'You OK?'

'Sure. It was nothing.'

'You been at a party?'

He shrugged. 'Some of my old friends at the building. Sure. They had a party. They invited me.'

For a few minutes we sat silent, staring at the water. Then he started to talk. He talked very soft, and I was tired and it took a minute until I could connect. Then my blood turned into ice.

'They swim every day,' he said. 'Every morning,' he added. Then he put his mask back on and hurried away. He left his pie on the pavement. I sat and stared at it, shivering.

I climbed down to the jetty and the police boat that rocked gently now in pitch-black water. The arc lights on the bridge were out now. The fireworks were finished. People roamed the riverfront, but the party was over.

The cops on the boat were grateful for some company. I sat with them and watched the Middlemarch and thought about Aguirre. I watched for a while, until the sky started to lighten, slowly first. An early mist covered the city like gauze.

It was just before daybreak. I was in uniform. There were still cops on the street, and when I got to the Middlemarch, no one stopped me. I was in.

It was cold. Somewhere, water leaked. It dripped on to the old, cold stone floor. I listened for footsteps in the basement of the building. No one came. I checked the room where the night super lived; the door was open. The room was empty. I had timed it right, between shifts; the pool opened at seven, Frankie said. Tommy swam at six-thirty. I looked at my watch. It was six. 'They swim every day . . . every morning,' Aguirre said.

Upstairs, the doorman, the cops, the residents, hungover from the parties, slept.

I waited. I looked at my watch. Six-ten. My lids sank over my eyes, then I thought about my loft, the way the bastards ripped it up, thought about Lulu Fine and Callie Rizzi and Sverdloff. And about Frankie. The adrenalin buzz that came with the anger woke me up. I was wide awake.

Then I heard it: the faint slap of bare feet on tiles. Slap slap slap, it was rhythmic, careless. Then a ripple of water. I walked towards the locker rooms. The smell of chlorine got in my nose.

In the men's locker room, a crumpled black coat lay on the floor. There was a wide column, floor to ceiling, just outside the locker room. I put my hand on it, felt the damp, cool, tiled surface, got a partial view of the pool. It was empty. Then I smelled the dope. It drifted towards me, I smelled it before I saw them. Heard them laughing. It was raucous, unselfconscious laughter.

They slipped into view. Except for the coats, they were still in costume: two boys in Victorian clothes. They passed a joint back and forth and grinned, then one of them rested it on the rim of the pool. They stripped quickly and dove into the water. I knew the kids. Jared Mishkin and his freckled pal Harry. Harry was freckled all over. It gave his body a weird reddish tinge.

They were good swimmers. They cut through the water while I watched, then pulled themselves out again, skin shining with water. They retrieved the marijuana.

The smell of chlorine mixed with the stink of the dope. The boys laughed, swam, came up for air. Jared and Harry. Powerful swimmers, big shoulders, muscular arms, these were boys who could kill an old man. Whack his head with a sword. A Ninja sword. A killing toy you could order from any martial arts catalogue.

'Kids talk about killing,' Callie had said. They practiced on chickens. Christ, where was she? She had been dancing with Jared. Not Jared, she had said. He was a good boy, she said. He worked at the homeless shelter most nights.

I let them see me.

'Come on in,' Jared called when he looked up and saw me. His voice had a hollow, metallic ring in the cavernous pool. I got up close, I could see he was ripped and so was his pal, and they clambered out of the pool and sat on the rim, legs over the edge, feet in the water. Both of them were naked. They had men's bodies, but boy's faces. No fear.

I said, 'How did it work?'

'What's that?' Jared picked up the joint. 'I'm sorry. We shouldn't be smoking this,' he said, and crushed it on the rim of the pool. 'How did what work?'

'Thomas Pascoe let you in to swim?'

'Mr Pascoe liked us swimming here. He liked it,' Harry said. 'He said so all the time.'

'He gave you a key.'

'Sure. That's it. He gave us the key.'

'And you forgot to give it back. After he died, you kept the key.'

Harry was nervous. 'Sure, that's it, definitely. Right.'

'Who else swam? Which other kids?'

'Mostly us. We're on the swim team at school. It was great having the extra practice time.'

'You swam the day Pascoe was murdered?'

'We left before it happened. We swam very early that day, then we left for school,' Harry said.

Jared Mishkin was silent.

'You forgot to mention you were here that day?'

'We were scared. Harry was scared, you know?' Suddenly Jared tried to get up. I put a hand on his neck where he could feel it; the kid flinched. For the first time I saw into Jared Mishkin's blue eyes; they were empty holes. There was nothing there at all.

I said to Jared Mishkin. 'How did it happen? It was Harry here, right?'

'He can't touch us,' Jared said. 'He can't.'

Harry said nervously, 'How do you know?'

'There weren't any witnesses, asshole.'

'Talk to me, Harry.'

'Will it help me?'

'Sure it will.'

Jared said. 'You're not a real cop. Callie told me. You're nothing. You can't do anything. Pascoe was driving us crazy.'

'Pascoe?'

'Yeah. At first it was fine, we showed up, we swam, we listened to a few of his numbnuts old stories, then it got really pretty boring. The old days. The war. The fucking OSS, the Cold War, Moscow, how the Russian and British people stood up to the Nazis, the Blitz, who the fuck cares, it was a zillion years ago.'

Harry piped up. 'It was working at the shelter that got to us. We didn't like the smell. Our friends made fun of us, but Tommy said it was the price we paid for privilege, some shit. He said we should get to know the people better, they were human beings, but they weren't, you know. They smelled. But we got to know them better.'

Jared egged his friend on now. 'Tell him, Harry.'

'Yes,' Harry giggled. 'Turned out they were just about as good as us. Or as bad.'

Jared Mishkin looked at his feet. Under water they were flat as fish. Then he glanced up at me. 'So Tommy told us a story once about surrogates during the Civil War. Young men of good family, their parents would buy some poor kid to go to war for them. We figured someone at the shelter could be our surrogate.'

'The guy who got beat up,' I said to Harry. 'You brought him to the shelter, but it was you who beat Ramirez up.'

'He was going to talk.' Harry's voice was petulant.

'Keep your mouth shut,' Jared said to his pal. He went on, 'We only wanted to scare Tommy, but, well, like, things happen.'

Harry looked nervous.

'Chill out,' Jared said. 'If they try and touch us we'll say Tommy abused us or some other shit. He's not a real cop. He didn't read us our rights. And we didn't kill Tommy, anyhow. Did we?'

I said, 'You got all the angles. You didn't kill him, so the devil made you do it? That's what you're saying?'

They laughed an insolent adolescent laugh, part terror, part disbelief. 'Yeah, that's right. We read a lot of stuff. It's a very good school. Nietzsche. Faust. Milton. The devil has all the good stuff, isn't that how it goes?' Harry was high. 'We thought picking a guy named Dante was a nice touch.'

I thought about their costumes. 'Like Jekyll and Hyde.'

Jared said, 'Yeah, that was kinda corny but Harry here liked it.'

I said, 'What about Mrs Fine? She bored you too?'

Harry said, 'Who is Mrs Fine?'

'She's some woman that lives in our building, you know, low-class English, always in your face, always bugging my mom,' said Jared. 'I heard someone did her, but what's she got to do with it?'

'So you had Thomas Pascoe killed because he bored you?'

Jared shifted his weight. 'Actually, I heard my dad say things would be easier if Tommy was out of the way. I heard him say it to my mom. Tommy was in everybody's way.' He looked up. 'I felt I owed it to my father to help him. I found a way to get rid of Tommy. I helped him. Didn't I?'

'And you figure your father will always take the rap for you?'

Jared got up and started for the locker room. 'He'll do anything for me.'

They were big, they were big enough to kill, and I looked at them, but I didn't feel anything except a cold dread. I yelled. 'Sit the fuck down.' I knew there was more.

Jared sat down abruptly and I took out my gun and put it against his forehead. I said, 'How did you get in here?'

'I have a key. Like you thought.'

'You stupid little fuck, there aren't any keys to the pool. The elevator comes straight down and the door is locked until seven. Only Thomas Pascoe swam earlier. Access to this pool is through the building for residents. How'd you get in Monday? How'd you sneak Ramirez in? How'd you get in today?' I was furious, looking at them, this pair of shitty kids sitting at the edge of the pool, thinking they owned the world. 'Who the fuck let you in?'

I waited for his answer. I was squatting next to the Mishkin kid, my gun still out. I wanted to hurt him. 'Who let you in?'

Chapter 17

'I did.' The voice echoed from the other side of the pool.

Wrapped in the white terry-cloth robe, Frankie Pascoe appeared, walked swiftly to Jared Mishkin, put her hand on his bare shoulder. She caressed the damp skin. She touched him as if she couldn't keep her hands off, and said, 'I did. I always let them in.' Then she looked at me with the cold light eyes and I realized they were swimmer's eyes, light, see-through green like water.

She said, 'It wasn't Tommy. It was me.' She smiled at the boy. He pushed her away hard and she reeled backwards. Frankie stumbled. I put out my hand to keep her from falling and she took it.

From the second I saw her, a week earlier now, a week ago, seven days, I knew the fallout from Pascoe's murder would go on and on, like a wave that caught everything in it.

'Get dressed,' I said and Jared leaned down to pick up his clothes. Frankie watched him. It wasn't just the father she cared about; it was the kid. She was in love with Jared Mishkin.

I was already on the phone. Before they were finished dressing, a pair of uniforms and a detective showed up. They read the kids their rights. Silently the three of them took hold of the two kids and got them in cuffs. I pushed Frankie to one side.

'You saw me watching the boys in the park that first day. That's why you gave me the list of names. To keep me busy somewhere else. You were protecting him.'

'Yes.'

She exhaled and sat on a bench. 'Can I have a cigarette please?' I gave her one. 'I got him into St Pete's, I got Tommy to spend some time with him, I didn't want him growing up a Russian hood, did I?'

'You were fucking the kid too.'

'I would have if I could, but he wouldn't let me, so I settled for watching. I watched him swim. I watched him shower in my bathroom after he swam. I told you I'm not a sentimental woman. I gave him keys to the apartment. I told Tommy if he had keys, he could come upstairs, he could use the residents' elevator to get to the pool when he liked. Tommy thought it was for the swimming.'

'And Harry?'

Frankie turned up her palms. 'Harry came along for the ride.' She looked at him. 'Harry was a joke.'

'But you were with Leo Mishkin that night, like you said?'

'Yes, of course.' She watched the cops take the boys, half dressed in their costumes. Frankie said to me, 'Will they charge them as adults?'

'If I have anything to do with it? You bet.'

'Why can't you leave things alone?' she said.

'You fucked me to find out what I knew.'

'Don't be an infant, Artie, for heaven's sake, what's that got to do with it? I liked you.'

'You were never in love with Mishkin.'

'Sure I was. When I met Leo, I was in love with everyone I met. It was the Seventies. Good times. Peace and love. I helped Mish get to America. I loved the whole wide fucking world. I helped Leo Mishkin get to America, which was pretty bloody decent of me, don't you think? It meant his son was born here, a proper American.' She laughed.

I grabbed Frankie Pascoe's wrist. 'You think you're going to work this so they don't get the kid, don't you? You'll put it on Leo Mishkin if you have to, but you'll fix it, won't you?'

'Anything.'

It was an unholy alliance. Pascoe got Mishkin's kid into the best school in town. Mishkin bailed out Pascoe with dough for his causes, his shelter. He gave him his son for a companion and fucked his wife. I remembered Mishkin coming out of the elevator with his son. I remembered how he looked at him. I played the scene back in my head: Leo Mishkin with the fine suit; the beautiful kid at his side; Mishkin's adoring look. He would do anything for the kid, like Jared said. So would Frankie.

'Did they know about each other? Did Jared know about you and Leo?'

'Yes.'

'Did Leo know how you felt about his son?'

'No. And he wouldn't believe it if he knew.'

Dante Ramirez was the sucker. He did the dirty work. Along with Lippert and a couple of precinct guys from the One Nine, we waded through beer cans, balloons, confetti, the crap left in the streets from the night before, and we picked him up at the shelter and took him to the local station house. They offered him a deal. I sat with Sonny Lippert and a homicide guy in the box while they grilled Ramirez.

The Mishkin kid told it like it happened. They made Ramirez a friend, gave him money, bought him booze, promised him a place to live.

'The shelter was nice,' Dante Ramirez said, 'but they were getting ready to tear it down. The kids told me Mr Pascoe's shutting it down. Developers moving in. I didn't wanna be on the streets.'

'Was it them that beat you that night in the bank?'

'One of them,' he said. 'I think one of them. Freckles. Red hair. They thought I might tell. Now I told.' He laughed bitterly.

'You did Pascoe for money?'

'Yeah,' he said. 'Money for a place to live. Like everyone else done around here in Manhattan. The city wouldn't give me nothing. I decided to take.'

Ramirez was the sucker all right. I went home. I had been up three nights running. I had to sleep.

In the middle of the night, late, after they charged Ramirez and I'd gone home and slept a while, Tolya Sverdloff woke me up. He was at the Holiday Inn on Tenth Avenue.

'Help me,' he said.

When I got there, he was in the crummy bar eating peanuts nervously, feeding them into his mouth like a machine. He spoke in Russian. 'Can you take me to Newark?' he said. 'To the airport. Please.' He could catch a ride with a friend who had a plane, he said. He said, 'Don't ask me who, Artyom. Just drive me, please.'

I said, 'Let's go,' and he scooped up more nuts, grabbed a

carry-on bag from the floor, put it over his shoulder, followed me outside.

I drove through the tunnel; he didn't talk. The industrial wasteland on the Jersey side of the river stank. The weather had changed. It was dank and chilly. The air was sulphurous, the lights on the power plants looked dull, and Manhattan, across the river, gave the sky an eerie glow. A few hundred yards from the airport, I rolled up the window and pulled into a gas station.

We sat in the car, me and Sverdloff. He watched his wing mirror and I thought of all the times he saved my ass. I couldn't feed Sverdloff to the cops, no matter what he did. Friends are all I have.

Sverdloff picked at a scab in his nose; blood leaked out and he stuffed some Kleenex in the nostril. He looked at his watch. 'I can get a lift in two hours,' he said.

'Whose plane?'

'I said it doesn't matter.'

'What's happening here, Tolya?'

'It goes back a long way.'

'You and Mishkin?'

'Some of it.'

'Mishkin will say he set Pascoe up, take the rap for his kid. They'll indict him as an accessory.'

'He'll go to Moscow. Trust me.'

'What about Lulu Fine?'

He shrugged. 'The same thugs who tried to warn you off the case went after her for the same reason.'

'Sent by who?'

'I don't know.'

I said, 'You have to help me here.'

'I don't know how to help you. I'm a messenger boy is all.' He looked ashen, shaky, a smear of blood on his upper lip. 'I can't even help myself. All I know is everything moves through London these days.'

'What kind of things?'

'Russians.'

'Spell it out.'

'Pull around the other side of the diner. I don't like to be near the road.'

I turned the key and pulled the car into the shadows. Visibly, Tolya relaxed. He went on talking Russian. 'One side America. The other side, the immense land mass, Europe, Russia, Asia. London is the axis for money. Body parts. The art market. Media. I do not mean individuals, Artyom, not just a few ladies who run this or that magazine, lovely English ladies that they are, of course,' he said, and because he was speaking Russian said something so dirty I laughed. From relief I laughed. For a minute, Sverdloff sounded like himself.

'What else?'

He took my cigarettes from the dashboard and unwrapped the cellophane. 'Most of all, real estate. Property. Land. You know, in Europe we killed each other for land in the old days, now we have polite economic communities, but it's all bullshit. The governments take down borders. Europe, Asia, one big party now.' He tried to laugh. 'Look at Manhattan. London. For the right apartment, flat, house, mansion, dacha, villa, castle, factory site, skyscraper, landfill, even a burned-out jungle that will be a suburban sub-division next year, people will refrain from asking the hard question. People will fuck their neighbors, cheat their clients, kill. These are guys who buy and sell hotels, whole towns; look at the new cities of Asia. Look at Vegas. It's Monopoly.' He exhaled, took one of the cigarettes and lit it with the car lighter. 'It's not just the money, it's the size of your cock. You believe me? What time is it?'

I looked at my watch. 'There's still time. You want some coffee?'

He leaned back as if to retire into deeper shadow. 'No. We did it in Hong Kong, we fucked with real estate over there, sold high, then we destroyed the market, the Asian economies went down on their knees. We'll do it where we have to. Buy up the market, flood it, sell it low. Start again. Remember the fires in Malaysia? You think we were unaware? You think Russians did not have a hand in it? Before the banks went bust and the rouble fell apart, we knew real estate was the only game. But no more rules. All up for grabs. For the first time in my capitalist life, Artyom, I am scared to death.'

'That guy Kievsky, he's a player? Is it he who scared you?'

He didn't answer. Then he leaned towards me. 'Look,

Artyom, I don't want you in trouble. You already got in the way. You were involved with Pascoe. You were my friend. They know your face. They came after me, and you were in the way, you started asking around.'

I thought of Frankie. 'It will end in London,' she had said. I said to Tolya, 'I'm not going to London, man, you know. I'm finished with this thing.'

'OK. Sure. But in case.' He shoved an envelope in my hand. A siren wailed behind me, got louder, then passed.

'What is it?'

'Keys. A place in London if you need it. It's OK. It's held through a respectable bank. No one connects me. I'll try to meet you, but I have to go home now. Moscow. My kid's in trouble.'

He had been evasive before about the kid, and I said, 'What kind?'

'Not now.' He opened the car door.

'I'll drive you.'

'No. From here I can walk. Better like that. No one sees us.'

I knew it was for my sake. He got out on the side of the road. I could see the outline of the airport a few hundred yards away against the polluted sky. I got out too, and said, 'Be careful.'

'Yes.'

I hugged him. 'You said you were scared. Of who?'

Tolya picked up his shoulder bag, stood silently for a few seconds, a huge lonely figure, then he said, 'My own greed.'

Leo Mishkin sat on the bathroom floor holding Frankie Pascoe's hand. A medic, a thin blond guy in green hospital pants, bent over where she lay on the floor in the white robe she'd worn that morning. It was soaking wet.

Mishkin had called emergency and Sonny heard the news and called me on my cellphone on my way back from Jersey. When I got to Frankie's, Stan Getz was still on the stereo; 'Falling in Love' was playing. Mishkin, whose face was raw and covered with stubble, wore a pair of jeans and a pajama top. He looked up; his face was wet. The medic stood up. Frankie Pascoe was dead.

Frankie had put the music on, poured herself a pitcher of martinis, put it on the rim of the tub and run the water. She pushed the green button in her closet. The security system was activated. The steel walls snapped into place. She trapped herself in her own bathroom. Then she slipped into the tub, still in the robe – who could say why she wore it? – and began drinking.

The maid found the room locked. Ryan Sweeney, the doorman, got hold of Mishkin because only Mishkin could get her out. He had the blueprints and knew the codes. He deactivated the system, got Frankie out, called 911.

Mishkin didn't move. I sat down next to him on Frankie's bathroom floor and we waited for Sonny Lippert.

I said, 'You knew they'd pick you up if you came here.'

'Yes.'

'It would destroy your business, letting people know a safe room you built got screwed up.'

Mishkin shrugged.

'It was a lie, wasn't it? It wasn't the room. It was Frankie.'

Mishkin didn't care. He had protected Frankie for a long time. He stayed on the floor while they covered her up and took her away. I passed him some smokes, but he shook his head.

He said, 'Can we speak in Russian? It's easier.'

I nodded.

'I don't care if they pick me up. They'll pick me up anyway,' he said.

'You'll take the blame for your son?'

'Yes, I will say I was at the pool. They will check the DNA and see mine matches. Father and son.'

I said, 'Only half the markers are the same, Leo. Father and son, it's only half.'

He put his head in his hands.

'Your son said he heard you say Thomas Pascoe was a problem. That you wanted him out of the way. Because of Frankie?'

'No,' Leo said. 'No, of course not. I loved Thomas Pascoe. He helped me. I was his friend. I tried to help him.'

'But you loved his wife also?'

'Also. Yes. It happens.'

'Who wanted him out of the way?'

'Thomas Pascoe made people nervous. He was a righteous man. He wanted it to stop.'

'Wanted what to stop?'

'I planned only to warn him. My God, I would not have killed Thomas. It was to be a warning.'

'Your son took it a lot farther than a warning.'

He didn't answer. 'You can't prove it. There was no witness.'

'You'd do anything for the boy?'

'Yes. Anything.'

'Who did Pascoe make nervous?'

Leo Mishkin looked up. 'In London, he said. People in London. They're dividing the territory, Europe, you understand? They're moving into London, west from Moscow, east from New York. Compared to New York, London is virgin territory for them. Thomas knew all this.'

'What's the scam?'

'Like always,' he said. 'Real estate. Property. Land.'

'Is Tolya Sverdloff involved?'

'Yes.'

When they took Mishkin away, I looked around Frankie's apartment. It was not exactly kosher, but I didn't care and I found her passport. She had been to London half a dozen times that year. She had lied about even that.

It wasn't over. Ramirez whacked Pascoe, it was him that did the job. But it wasn't what killed him, not the big picture. The big picture was London.

'Promise me,' Frankie had said. 'Promise me you'll finish this.'

In some way I owed Frankie, and anyway I had promised her, and in a way I had loved her. I went into the library. Out the window, it was daylight. Monday morning. I found the tape Stan Getz had made specially for Frankie and slipped it into my pocket.

Chapter 18

That night I went to Lily's. I found a bottle of Scotch, poured a couple inches in a glass, lit a cigarette and sprawled on her bed. I could smell her on her pillows. I'd slept some. I felt better.

Lily asked me to pick up some stuff for Beth. I have her keys. She has mine. I've been in and out of her place a million times, but I never looked in her stuff. A cop like me, you'd think I'm a nosey son of a bitch. I learned as a kid in Moscow there's stuff you're better off avoiding. They put that in your milk in Moscow: don't ask. Don't tell.

I stared at the ceiling. There was nothing I could do for Tolya Sverdloff. Later on I'd fill in Sonny Lippert, but I was still wasted from fatigue. I'd think about everything later. I thought I'd take a nap. It made me feel good, being here, in her place, on her bed. Normality seeped back in.

Later, I got up and went into Beth's room. Beth's clothes were neatly tucked in a dresser. It was a little dresser we bought in a junk sale on the island once. It was painted blue. I pulled out some winter things and packed them in a shopping bag. I couldn't find one of the jackets Lily asked for.

The pink loden coat – Beth's obsessed with pink right now – was in her closet. On the top shelf were four small cartons I hadn't noticed before. I pulled one of them down and put it on the floor, then I opened it.

Inside there were pictures. I sat on the floor and looked at them. I lit a cigarette and kept looking. There were pictures of Lily as a child on Long Island in a smocked summer dress. Pictures of her at school with friends I never knew. College pictures. A picture of Lily in a fringed suede vest with her fist in the air surrounded by a group of Black Panthers. Lily in big shorts in the Peace Corps. Miniskirted in London. In bell bottoms. At friends' weddings.

– 153 –

I got up and took down a second carton and found more pictures, of her parents this time. The mother was tall, thin, unsmiling. The father had a stringy patrician look, a pursed, righteous mouth. In the same box was a copy of the *Communist Manifesto*, the mother's name written in old-fashioned cursive on the flyleaf. Lily's inheritance. I didn't know if I should laugh or cry. We had that in common, anyhow: both of us had parents who were, once upon a time, true believers. A long time ago. Ten years since the Berlin Wall came down already. Time passed.

Carefully I put the pictures back. At the bottom of the second carton was a flat blue gift box. I lifted the lid. Inside was a framed picture wrapped carefully in tissue paper. I lifted it out and unpeeled the paper. The eight by ten glossy was framed in glass and silver and it was signed. It read, 'Tom to Lily, With Love.'

At first I wasn't sure what I was looking at, couldn't focus, felt numb.

Mechanically, I put the boxes back, then I took the picture and baby clothes, locked up the apartment, went out, got in my car and drove home. In the glove compartment I found the envelope Sverdloff had given me with cash and keys for an apartment in London. I shoved them in my pocket, then I looked at the picture on the seat beside me.

The man in the picture had dark hair, but the patrician forehead, the aquiline nose, the bright eyes, were all the same as the day he died in the pool of his building on Sutton Place. Except the hair was white when he died. But the picture I had beside me now, the photograph I'd found in Lily's drawer, was a carefully preserved portrait of Thomas Pascoe.

PART TWO

London, November

Chapter 19

A faint oystery light smudged the November sky outside the window. I swung my legs over the edge of the bed. I was in London, it was freezing cold and I couldn't figure how the heat worked. I ran for the shower fast, the tiled floors bare, me hopping around like a fly on a cake of ice. It was early, before seven, and I'd slept lousy after I got into London the night before, restless, displaced, tainted sleep.

At least the water was hot, and I stood under it and let it steam me back to life. Then I put on clean clothes. In my suitcase was the photograph of Thomas Pascoe. Why Pascoe died, the big picture, was here in London. I didn't tell anyone I was coming, not even Lily. I had to get my head screwed on straight. I wanted to know how she was connected to the Pascoe case and why she kept his portrait in her kid's closet. She left New York in a big hurry three days after the case broke. Maybe it really was because I was on the job. Maybe it was that simple and she was pissed off at me, or scared for me, but I didn't call her, not yet. I put it off.

If Lily was here in London – and she was here – Phillip Frye was back in her life. It was Frye who called her the day after Pascoe died. Frye who offered her a job. Frye who could sucker Lily with a call. It was only a job, she said. Said she'd finished with Frye years ago. Now, I wasn't sure. I wasn't sure I wanted to find out.

Jacket on, collar up, I went into the kitchen, made some instant because it's all there was; standing in front of the glass door to the balcony, I drank the putrid brew out of a blue and white mug. There was a radio and I switched it on. A woman's voice, poised but icy, talked politics.

The apartment in the renovated warehouse was sleek as a ship's cabin. Light wood floors, white walls, an open kitchen, a table and chairs, the bedroom with the bed, the white tiled bathroom. The balcony hung over a promenade along the river. I shoved open the balcony door.

The fog seemed to lie over the town like old soft rags; it draped itself on my hands and face and left them wet. London wrapped in its traditional weather. What else could a tourist want? I laughed and finished the coffee. Then I looked up at the roof.

The security was good: discreet video cameras, an alarm system. Anyone who got in – whoever left the dummy for me to find the night before – knew his way around. I slammed the door. What was it the cabbie said when I landed, with London lit up by bonfires like a war zone? Guy Fawkes Night.

The dummy, the Guy they call it, lay inside on a white canvas chair. It was limp and harmless now. I picked up the picture I'd ripped off the dummy's face. A *Daily News* photograph of me on a recent case. A snapshot snatched out of an Internet file, I guessed, and printed on cheap paper. I'd seen a copy before, in New York, the night the bastards wrecked my loft. Bastards!

I stuffed my Knicks cap on the dummy, made more coffee. I didn't tell anyone I was coming to London, but somebody knew. I should have gone to a hotel, but I didn't have the dough, and anyhow, if somebody was interested in me being here, I wanted to know. I wanted a gun. I didn't care if it was illegal here, and I grabbed the picture and the damp dummy, locked up the apartment, then took the elevator down.

'Yes?' He had on a Hawaiian shirt with green pineapples. He stood behind a desk in the lobby and sorted out mail.

'Who are you?'

'Porter,' he said, not looking up. Youngish guy, thirty-five tops. Going bald in the middle.

I held out the dummy and the picture. 'I found this on the balcony. It mean anything to you?'

He looked shifty, and rearranged his shirt. 'Kids. A prank. You know, man. You staying here?' He had a whiney British accent, American slang.

I put the picture in my pocket. I dumped the dummy on the porter's desk and gave him a ten-pound bill. 'See what you can find out about it, will you? Anyone been in that apartment the last couple days?'

'Only the cleaner.'

'Man? Woman?'

'A woman.'

'You talked to her?'

'She didn't speak English.'

'What did she speak?'

'Some sort of wog, I don't know, Polish, Russian.'

I gave him another ten. 'She comes regular?'

'The bank sends her in. Bank that holds the lease.'

'Bank holds a lot of leases here?'

He shrugged. 'You joking? Round here? After the crash, late Eighties, early Nineties, you could buy property here for peanuts.'

'Find her for me.'

'How much?'

'Fifty.'

'A hundred.' He moved out from behind the desk. I looked at his feet. He wore old Guccis but they were polished to a dull shine.

'Been here long?' I offered him some smokes.

'I'm the porter, like I said.' He picked up a can of Carlsberg from behind the desk where the mail lay. Swigged it.

'What else?'

'I was an estate agent. I was like heavy into Docklands property, then the market crashed, I went broke.' He shrugged, leaned back, crossed his feet, whistled tunelessly.

'You do other errands?'

'For cash.'

It was raining outside. The building was part of a complex of converted warehouses, and on the cold, humid morning, the narrow street felt ancient, shut-in, sad. It was still dark and danker than any place I could remember except Poland. I jammed my hands in my pockets and left Butler's Wharf. The passageway behind the building was empty, the restaurants and fancy food shop shut up, a few bottles of olive oil set in the windows.

A man with an umbrella hurried towards the river and I followed him up a set of narrow stairs. I looked at the map I had. Tower Bridge.

The river was so dense with fog, I couldn't see the water. Along with the keys to the apartment, Tolya Sverdloff had given me a piece of paper with an address when I took him to Newark before he disappeared through the polluted night to the airport. I fumbled in my pocket for the address, then looked up. A taxi light floated through the fog and I ran for it.

'High Ground' was the name of the house. It was written in gold leaf on the freshly painted black iron gates.

On my way up, the fog had lifted a little and I could see London soaked in the rain. Everything dripped: trees, cars, gutters that ran with water. I must have dozed. When I opened my eyes, I felt lost. We were climbing a hill. I could see a little pond, some kids, maybe on their way to school, young kids in gray shorts, older kids in big sneakers, then an immense park.

The driver turned his head, muttered, 'Bishop's Avenue, you said, right?' and pulled up to the fancy wrought-iron gate.

I pushed a buzzer. Heard a voice. Gave Tolya Sverdloff's name and my own. The gate swung open. We drove up a circular gravel drive that could accommodate a tank division. It was lined with dripping topiaries in the shape of animals, and we stopped at a massive fieldstone house with white columns out front. There was a big piece of land around it. The trees were bare, gray-green, dripping, the vista huge but bleak.

I paid the driver, asked him to wait. He lifted his shoulders in apology, glanced around, seemed uneasy, but all he said was he was due home. He handed me a printed card with the phone number of a cab company.

The door was already open. Through it I saw a hallway, warm yellow light, parquet floors, half an acre of marble.

The maid was Russian; she tried speaking English and I let her. She led me through the hall, where there was a carved fireplace twelve feet high, and into a living room that was lit up like Christmas and decorated with brocade sofas and chairs, antique tables, oil paintings. Some of the pictures were famous.

A skinny guy with blond hair and pale oily skin put down his newspaper – the *Financial Times* – got up from his chair and offered his hand. 'Eduard Kievsky,' he said, then smiled. 'Eddie.'

I recognized Kievsky from Tolya's Halloween party; he had been got up as a priest. Now Kievsky wore a good gray suit and handmade wing-tips. I don't know if he recognized me but he didn't say. I figured him for Ukrainian. He spoke bad English and educated Russian. 'We are all at breakfast,' he said politely. 'Please join us.'

He led me into the dining room where seven or eight people sat at a long mahogany table, chatting and eating. The women, most of them in their thirties, sat one end of the table; they were all cheekbones and collagen. They were dressed in fancy sports clothes – Gucci, Hermès – and their Chanel bags were on the table next to them. Picking at pastries with manicured fingers, they leaned in towards each other and chattered softly: Manolo, Versace, Donna Karan, I caught the words and figured London was as overheated by consumption as New York.

Kievsky took me around the table; everyone shook my hand and greeted me in English as if they'd learned how in etiquette class. Somewhere, a stereo played classical music, Mozart probably.

Finally, Kievsky introduced his wife Irina, who wore jewellery the size of fruit and a couple of inches of leather skirt. She held out her hand and said, 'Look what Eddie has bought. Look how beautiful.'

It was a gold egg the size of a plum, painted like a circus tent in bright enamels and studded with tiny jewels. Irina pushed an invisible mechanism and the top popped open to reveal a tiny jewelled clown on a unicycle in a circus ring. She fiddled with the mechanism and the clown went around and around on the bike, jewels glittering, enamels catching the light.

Reverent, Kievsky and his wife gazed at the little egg and the rest of the crowd gathered around him to admire it. He whispered, 'The real thing. Fabergé. Exquisite.' He looked up. 'Hello, darling.' Kievsky reached out his arm for a girl of maybe fourteen who appeared from another room. It was his daughter.

I asked the girl her name. She said her English name was Aspree. She wore riding clothes, spoke perfect English, British accent. She babbled about horses and school and her sorrow about the Spice Girls, that she was sad they were over, but, well, there was other cool stuff.

She was already a regular little courtesan and she escorted me to the sideboard, held out a plate, lifted up the covers from various hot dishes and offered to serve me. Bacon, eggs, sausages, steaks, pancakes, also caviar, cheese, smoked fish. I was hungry. I took the loaded plate and sat next to her while Kievsky disappeared to take a call.

While I ate, I listened. The group at the table, two Russians, an English guy, the women, talked about golf and racehorses. They chattered about real estate, country cottages in France, villas in Italy, property in London. A few years earlier this crowd had been second-rate Communist Party hacks or their suppliers, the men – and sometimes women – who provisioned the system. The move into real money had been natural. But the money came fast and then they yearned for the style, the big houses, the clothes. In London, it looked to me, you could find your way to a make-believe past; in London, your aristocratic fantasies could all come true.

You could treat London as your alternative home if you were a Moscow hood. You could be home in Moscow or Kiev in three and a half hours if you got homesick. You could hop over to New York. For the rising Moscow gangster, moving up meant London's high ground literally. Aspree told me about their vacation in Petersburg where they rented a whole palace and had servants who dressed up in old-time outfits to wait on them, she said.

Kievsky returned and apologized. He gestured for me to follow and we went into a huge book-lined study. The furniture was fancy inlaid stuff and the chairs were green leather with brass studs, like in Johnny Farone's restaurant in Brooklyn. A maid brought a tray with coffee and we made small talk now, about people I didn't know in New York and Moscow, and about Sverdloff. On the wall were plaques from various charities testifying to the good works of Eduard and Irina Kievsky.

Rain beat on the windows. Kievsky invited me to dinner. A standing invitation. A party the following week. A weekend to his country place to shoot birds.

I was itching to get a move on, but playing his game was like courting a high-class hooker you wanted on the cheap; you had to talk the talk. We exchanged views on the Russian Partners Fund at Paine Webber, the art market, the rouble meltdown and other investment possibilities. He switched to Russian. It was his way of asking if I was one of them; I answered in the lingo.

'Is there anything you need then, Artemy Maximovich?'

I felt a chill. The weather, the house, the company, my own need for Kievsky and his supplies. Yes, I said to him. We understood each other.

'Please.' He stood up and unlocked an old walnut breakfront. Kievsky put the little key back in his pocket and smiled. 'We worry about the children.'

In the breakfront was a dazzling array of weapons: handguns, pistols, semis. Kievsky let me know he could get me anything I needed, an AK or a complete missile, build your own, ready to go, armed. 'Big, small, what you like,' he smiled. Even nukes could be had for a price.

I selected a Gluck, he glanced at it, then picked up a phone and put the gun back into the display case. I couldn't take my eyes off Kievsky's ring. He had small, slim, pale hands and the ring was heavy on his pinkie finger.

It was square, the gold work real fancy, and in the middle was a dark brown cat's eye that shivered with light. It gave me the creeps. He saw me looking and said, 'You admire my ring?' and I said, 'Yeah, Yeah, it's great.' He said, 'I got it in Thailand. It was specially made for me. It's one of a kind.' He was pleased. I didn't tell him I knew a guy who worked a case over there on those cat's eyes.

They irradiate them a million times normal at the gem plants to make the eyes darker and more lustrous and a lot more expensive, and then the ring eats you up. One guy who died of cancer was nuked by his own ring.

Kievsky asked again if I needed anything else. A few minutes later the maid reappeared carrying a leather briefcase and handed it to Kievsky.

'Everything is here,' he said and gave me the soft leather case. Inside was a brand-new Gluck, plenty of ammo. He held it out.

'Please.' I examined the gun; there was no serial number. I thanked him. I offered to pay and he looked injured. A favor is a favor, he said. Any friend of Sverdloff's.

He walked me to the door. 'Please come again,' he said formally. His hand was soft and cold and the big ring on his little finger grazed mine.

We stood on the steps. Carrying a package wrapped in crisp brown paper and tied with string, Irina joined him. In the daylight, she was even more stunning, taller than Eddie, dark-haired, eyes slightly slanted and very blue. She smiled at me and handed Eddie the package. 'Books,' she said in English. 'The postman just comes.'

Irina Kievskaya told me they were reading a lot of books and that she was just back from a week at Philanthropist College.

'Very philosophical,' she said. 'We read Aristotle and Dr Martin Luther King, and study best charities. We learn how to give.' Irina added, 'We study poor persons.'

I kept a straight face. 'Very nice,' I said.

She said, 'Please do come again. Our daughter enjoyed your visit.'

A dark-blue Jaguar was in the driveway. The driver in a peaked hat jumped out and held the door for me. My taxi was long gone, I was in the middle of nowhere on a hill, I didn't have much choice. I wasn't crazy about the car, though; it meant Kievsky had a handle on my movements.

I got in and looked back at the house, where Kievsky and his wife still stood on the steps. She smiled and I realized Irina looked like someone I knew. It was eerie: I couldn't call the right face up. I wasn't even sure where I'd seen the face, but I had seen her face, or someone who was a dead ringer for her.

Chapter 20

Perfidious Albion, anybody's for a buck.

It was what my father always said. I was in the car leaving Kievsky's. I was looking at the crumpled picture of myself I'd ripped off the dummy. They say you pass forty, you get your father's face, and I thought how much, in the photograph, I resembled my own father. His face came into my mind very clear suddenly, young, blue-eyed, confident. He was always a young father.

Perfidious Albion. When he said it, he meant Geoffrey Gilchrist. 'The English make good spies, Artyom, but they always sell out, they have no ideology, they belong to no one. If you ever go to England, you'll understand,' and I'd laugh because the idea I'd ever go to England was so funny. I was going to America.

Years go by, I don't think about Gilchrist, then it jumps in my head and sticks, like the tune from a bad jingle. Geoff was the first Englishman I ever knew. I knew him in Moscow when my father, a young KGB officer then, had been one of his babysitters. Thirty years ago. I wondered if Gilchrist was still alive.

It was the books that made me remember. The package in Irina Kievskaya's hand wrapped in fresh brown paper. The books were what I remembered, books that came from London for Geoffrey Gilchrist wrapped in the crisp, rich brown paper, addressed in beautiful handwriting. A stream of books, all brand new.

I looked at my watch. I had time to kill while I worked out how to get a handle on Thomas Pascoe in London. I left New York in a hurry, some crazy impulse when I found the picture in Lily's drawer. Now I was somewhere in the middle of this immense wet city. No leads. No real contacts.

I yelled at the driver. 'Stop, OK. Just pull up there by that hotel.'

In the hotel lobby, I found a Yellow Pages, looked under BOOKS, recognized the name of the shop. I picked up a phone.

An English voice answered, 'Can I help you with something?'

I was as offhand as I could manage. 'You once had a customer named Gilchrist. Old friend of mine. A Moscow address. Thought I might send him a book. Geoffrey Cole Gilchrist.'

The phone line went silent for a few seconds.

'I'm frightfully sorry,' the brisk voice said. 'But I can't think of anyone with that name.'

I knew he was lying. I knew Gilchrist was alive.

I said, 'Is he still in Moscow?'

'Would you like to let me have your name?' the voice asked, but I'd put the phone back on the hook.

Geoffrey Gilchrist was alive. Son of a bitch. The past stuck a hand out and grabbed hold of me. The old bastard had survived them all and the guy in the bookstore knew. He *knew*!

Traffic was jammed up all the way down the hill from Kievsky's and the hotel where I made the call. Half an hour later, the car pulled up in front of the bookstore, I put the gun in my pocket, placed the leather case on the back seat and got out.

In the bow window of the shop were old-fashioned kids' books. The door was unlocked.

A thin, elegant man in half glasses and a good suit – I figured him for the owner – was expecting me. He smiled. 'You telephoned earlier?'

We made conversation. There were books stuffed in the shelves, floor to ceiling. Books on the floor itself, books in freestanding bookcases that spun around so you could read the titles. Round mahogany tables held more books.

In Moscow, if you wanted good books you got them under the table. My Aunt Birdie knew people. An old woman in a cardigan sweater who smoked cheap Indian cigarettes was her best contact; she saved the good stuff for Birdie, secreted under the counter, behind the dreck that passed for popular fiction, and the approved classics, and the dusty tomes on Dialectical Materialism or whatever horseshit you need to pass exams.

Hidden in these spaces were western paperback books. Here was where Birdie bought for me tattered copies of Fitzgerald and Mickey Spillane and Dashiell Hammett and *Catcher in the Rye.*

Gilchrist's books were always new. They smelled of good paper and nice bindings. I remembered helping him unwrap them, how they crackled with possibility. This was the store they came from. Its name had been magical for me as a kid.

On the table where the new books glistened in their bright pristine jackets, I spotted a biography of George Eliot. I held it up. 'Could you send this to New York?'

'Of course we can.'

I gave him Sonny Lippert's address. 'Do you still wrap your books in brown paper?'

The bookstore owner nodded slightly towards a door, and I saw it was ajar. Slowly it opened, someone pushing from the other side, there was a faint, hesitant shuffle and a man emerged, glanced in my direction, then turned away and slipped out of the front door. I grabbed some money out of my pocket, put it on the table for the book and followed him into the street.

The rain came down now in thick gray sheets, and I followed him under a low archway into a narrow passage, past a store selling fruit and vegetables. He disappeared through the door of a Lebanese restaurant. It was still shut. Through the window, I saw a waiter with a mustache polishing glasses methodically.

He shook hands with the waiter, who brought him a small cup and saucer, then he took off his coat and put it neatly over the back of a chair. He removed the soft tweed hat. He rubbed his hands together and sat down.

I walked through the door. He looked at me.

It wasn't a mistake. The gray rain that sluiced down the little restaurant window, the huge foggy city that dwarfed you, it could have been Moscow; thirty years disappeared.

'Hello, Artemy Maximovich,' he said in bad Russian. 'You have your father's face. Is he still alive?'

'No.'

He smiled. 'I heard that you were looking for me, I think. Do sit down.'

'Comrade Geoff.' I pronounced it 'Joff' like we always did; it was how we figured Americans said it and we liked showing off our knowledge of the American way of speaking.

The waiter brought me a towel and I sat down and rubbed my hair dry, found some cigarettes in my pocket and lit one. The cosy restaurant surrounded me. The waiter brought me coffee and the thick sweet brew warmed me up.

The old man looked at me. Sitting opposite him, I was plugged into a grid of memories so vivid I could smell them.

I got to know Gilchrist because my father took me places I had no business. I was the only son, only kid. He wanted me with him.

'Max,' my mother would say, 'Maxim Stefanovich, he has to practice,' and she'd stand in the doorway, the violin held out, and we'd both smile at her and run for it. Rock stars and jazzmen, in my arrogant adolescent opinion, did not take classical violin lessons from fat Russian ladies like my teacher.

In the late Sixties, when the oil still flowed, the afterglow from the Khrushchev years was still warm. Young stars like my father, KGB guys with a future, had some good times. They got the plum jobs; some of the juiciest were babysitting the British spies. My father, his best friend Gennadi Ustinov – I called him Uncle Gennadi because they were like brothers – loved it.

My father knew them all: Philby, Burgess, Vivian McFarland, and the lesser lights: Nigel Crowe, Iain Lamb, Alec Singleton. But Geoffrey Gilchrist was his favorite. The first Englishman I ever met.

'You kept the cufflinks?'

I still have them. One of the two or three things I still have from Moscow, cufflinks, a scarf from some English university so old and ratty it leaves balls of blue wool on my hands when I touch it. I don't know why I keep it.

It was in the back of my mind ever since I touched down in London and now I stared at the old man, who rolled a coffee cup between his hands as if the glass would warm them. The hands were yellow as wax paper and covered with brown spots the size and color of corroded pennies. The same gold ring he always wore was on his left pinkie. He put the cup down and held out one of his hands. It was warm from the cup.

The waiter brought pastries.

'Please, won't you eat something?' he said.

I shook my head.

'Did you recognize me?' Gilchrist spoke Russian but with a lousy English accent. He was eager. I looked at the shape of the shoulders, still square, and the light gray eyes.

'Sure, Geoff. You haven't changed that much,' I said, and he lit up like a bulb. His vanity made him lively.

'You would prefer something else for breakfast?' he said awkwardly, and I said, 'No thanks. And we can speak English, if you want.'

'You've got an American accent, Artie, may I call you Artie? It was your western name, wasn't it?'

'It still is.'

We sat in the little restaurant, rain beating down outside. Maybe it was jetlag and I was wired, but I could see them all: my father; Gennadi; my mother, when she was pretty, young, contentious, not an old woman in a nursing home in Haifa, her mind claimed by Alzheimer's. She no longer remembers my name.

I finished the heavy brew and asked for another one. 'Jesus. It's really you, isn't it? The guy in the bookstore called you? You knew it was me that called.'

'I'm not that good anymore.' He laughed. 'I do get the odd call, someone asking, usually a journalist.'

'And you answer?'

'There might be money in it.'

'So, Geoff, how the hell come you're in England?'

He pulled a handkerchief out of his cuff and wiped his mouth. 'Things change. After the Communists went we were in a very tenuous position actually, as you can well imagine. Anti-Communism was widespread, of course, in the Soviet Union, forgive me, in Russia. There was a serious disinclination to pay the upkeep on an elderly Englishman who had worked for the old oppressors. No one knew what to do with us. My sell-by date was up.' He laughed. 'They could have swept me out with the rest of the Cold War rubbish.'

'Go on.'

'I knew a few British journalists in Moscow who liked retelling my little story, the old days, the derring-do, the gossip about Philby and Burgess; it had its glamour, actually.'

'You could always make up great stuff, I remember that.'

'Thank you. I thought I'd better repackage myself for them, and one of them at least had rather good connections with the Foreign Office. The benign act of a new prime minister, I don't know, actually. A kindness, a reprieve. It took some years to arrange.'

'But you fixed it?'

'Yes.'

'How long have you been here?'

He looked at his watch, distracted now. 'Sorry?'

'How long?'

'Six months.' He grinned. The boyish grin. 'I believe they think I've come home to die.'

Gilchrist leaned over the table again.

He was past seventy, the once-handsome face drawn tight from disease. He was thin as a stick, but the eyes were bright. He gave his debonair smile; my mother thought he looked like David Niven. We'd seen Niven once in Moscow, in some lousy print of a smuggled film.

Gilchrist said, 'I do not plan to die yet, however, Artie. Your home is here now?'

'New York.'

'You really are an American?'

'Yes.'

'Of course. It was always America, wasn't it? I was quite jealous. I tried to make a little Englishman of you, but it didn't take. The only thing English you were at all interested in was the Beatles. And the whiskey.'

'Not Scotch, Artemy,' he'd say, 'Single malt. Malt whiskey. Very deep, very smoky – here, try a little, just taste with your tongue, you don't have to swallow it all, just smell it, put your tongue in the glass. Good. Good, Artyom.'

I adored the way he treated me, like a grown-up. 'Live dangerously,' he said. 'It's the best antidote.' I had no idea what the hell he meant. The only time my mother ever punished me was when she discovered he gave me booze. Deep down she despised Geoff. She couldn't understand it, these free guys from a decent place who spied for the son-of-a-bitch Soviets. My father, who enjoyed the company, the chess games and books, had lived through the war and believed in the patriotic cause. He could never grasp how a man could turn on his own country.

But mostly they made fun of the Brits: their terrible teeth, their funny accents, the incomprehensible sports they followed, like cricket.

'Joff was terribly out of sorts today,' my father would say, coming home with Uncle Gennadi, and they'd have a glass of Georgian wine at the kitchen table and laugh about him, the accent, the clothes.

'Personally I preferred Leslie Howard in *The Scarlet Pimpernel*,' my mother would say. 'He was a better kind of Englishman. I thought of naming you Leslie for a while, but it might have been difficult for a good Soviet boy.' My mother would say stuff like that, then hold on to the kitchen sink and crack up at her own private jokes. I can see her: slender, blonde, joking, but always furious. Her anger at the system got my father kicked out of the KGB later on.

I was obsessed with America, but all foreigners were exciting and England had the Beatles. When we got the news, the Beatles were everything. Somehow, someone, some kid with a father who travelled or was a Party bigwig, got an illegal print – there weren't any videos then – of *A Hard Day's Night*. I was maybe twelve years old. We sat in a dark room, someone threaded it on the projector. We were blown away. No one talked afterwards. The realization that we lived in a nowhere place hit me hard when I saw it.

I was a smarty pants Moscow kid and Geoffrey Gilchrist was an opportunity. Joff. Hallo, Joff, we'd imitate his fancy accent to each other. Talk British to us, we'd kid him. Had a hard day's night, Joff? Been working like a dog? I laughed out loud remembering. He must have thought we were crazy kids. What did Gilchrist know about the Beatles? He wasn't that kind of Englishman. Been sleeping like a log, Geoff? Geoff was a sideshow.

Gilchrist was talking now. 'What is your work?'

'I'm a cop. Was a cop. I do private work.'

'Ah,' he said. 'The family business. You are married?'

'No.'

He shifted his chair.

'Back to the wall, Geoff? You expecting someone?'

He looked at the wet window. 'Always. Shall we go?'

The waiter brought a check. I put some money on the table, Gilchrist picked up some of the coins and said, 'Too much', then put them absently into his own pocket.

Chapter 21

The rain battered the black umbrella Gilchrist held over both of us, and seeped over the edges, dripped on his tweed hat and down my neck. But I stayed with him, walking slow, in the little cocoon of the umbrella.

He shuffled up and down the curb, looking for a cab, and stuck his umbrella impatiently into the air. A black taxi pulled up. We got in and he gave an address, then closed his eyes.

Ten minutes later, we were on Ponsonby Terrace, a narrow street with pretty houses. I made a mental note of the address. The rain had turned the streets slick.

Gilchrist's house had blue window-boxes with spiky fall flowers. I followed him up the steps, he switched on the light. In it, he looked old and frail, the face cross-hatched by a million lines, the skull almost visible through the skin. The mustache was white but still thick; the eyes always saved him. They gave the face warmth, and it wasn't until you'd been seduced, that you saw the malevolent curiosity, the subversive self-obsession. The thing about Geoff I couldn't put a name on when I was a kid was the charm.

'Come in. Please.'

On a long table was a lap-top, the screen lit up, and next to it a glass bowl with two pale-skinned fish in the water. Gilchrist shut the door behind us, then reached in his pocket and tossed a coin in the bowl. 'They feed off copper,' he said. 'It bleeds the color out of them, but they can't resist. I read of this phenomenon in a marvelous book about Venice once, and felt I needed them for the irony. They've been with me for a long time, since Moscow. Do you know Venice, Artie?'

I ignored the conversational come-on, but I was pretty curious. The house consisted of the living room and kitchen. There was a small garden out back. Upstairs were two bedrooms and a bathroom.

He took off his coat and took mine and put them in the bathroom, then came back and pulled a bottle from a silver tray that was crowded with whiskey bottles and heavy crystal glasses. Laphroaig. Always the same brand.

There was a fireplace, and he switched the gas on and lit it. It kicked up a blue flame. He poured whiskey into glasses. It was an obsessive's room: the bookshelves were impeccably organized, the antique tables neatly stacked with files and paper, all of it squared off and dusted, tied with cotton string. He gestured to a deep leather chair and said, 'Sit down. Please.'

'Thank you.' He saw me look at the computer. 'Marvelous, the computer, the Internet. I'm quite good with it. All kinds of tremendously interesting things you find. Don't you think so. Tea?'

I shook my head. 'The whiskey's fine.'

He spoke like a man back from a long trip in a spaceship: his English was old-fashioned and detached.

I said, because I didn't know what else to say, 'Gennadi Ustinov is dead.'

'Yes,' he said. 'I'd heard about the general. The Americans murdered him in the end in spite of everything.'

I shrugged.

He said, 'Both of them dead. Ustinov. Your father.'

I nodded.

'How did it happen? Your father?'

'An accident. A bomb on a bus in Israel. Tourist bus. Wrong bus, wrong bomb. Nothing special. Nothing spooky. Not your kind of thing, really.'

For a while we sat and drank silently in the small comfortable room. Outside the rain came down the windows and I saw it suddenly run red, like blood; I thought I was drunk. I pulled myself out of the soft leather chair and went to the window. Thought about Thomas Pascoe. And Lily.

There was a rusty metal overhang – some kind of pipe or rain gutter – and the rust itself, brownish-red like dried blood, was flaking and had mixed with the water. It made the water coming down the pane seem bloody. Gilchrist's eyes followed me and, for a moment, as the room got hotter from the fire, his large eyelids came down over the gray eyes. I thought, for a second, he's dead. Dead.

In the hot room, while Gilchrist dozed and the blood-colored water ran down the panes, I watched him and wondered if us meeting was an accident. The mantelpiece was crowded with photographs. One showed my family in Moscow at a picnic. My father is laughing at the camera.

Gilchrist opened his eyes. 'I'm sorry,' he said. 'Forgive me for dropping off. Can I do anything for you?'

'What kind of thing did you have in mind? Can I smoke?'

He nodded. 'Your father was a considerate man. General Ustinov too. He was your godfather, your father's great friend?'

I nodded.

'It was the general who proposed I should come home. I owed him, I owed your father, I'd like to repay you. What can I give you? How can I help you?'

'What makes you think I need help? I'm a private investigator, I do light industrial cases, I report on restaurants, I'm in London because my girlfriend's here, and that's about it. I'm not a spy. I'm not CIA or KGB or MI 5, 6, 7 or 8 – whatever they call it now – or anything else. It's the end of the century. The end of the millennium.' I looked at the computer. 'You're a cyberpunk, Geoff, you know how fast things move. There's a whole generation of American kids who never heard of the Cold War. It's over.'

Gilchrist took a cigar box from a drawer, offered it to me, selected one, removed the paper ring, sniffed it, snapped the end off, lit it and said, 'It's never over. The Cold War will never end. There's always human debris. It won't be over until my sort are all dead. Maybe yours too, Artie.'

I looked at my watch.

'We've all left too much behind. Too much rubbish. Too many ghosts,' he said. 'Look at me. Look at you,' he said and he leaned forward, the cigar in his hand.

'You Americans – if that's really what you are, Artie Cohen – you left your Coca Cola, your land mines, your dollars. The Soviets left busts of Lenin, tin wind-up toys, promises of pie in the sky. We left women. Babies without fathers. Weapons without spare parts. In Havana and Hanoi, Addis, Angola, Chile, and, of course, Cuba. Cuba was our paradise and playground, good music, women, drugs, as it had been yours. There are still true believers.'

'Including you?'

'I gave up ideology for cash.'

'No wife? No kid?'

He shrugged.

'You never married, did you, not like the others? No Russian girls appealed?'

He didn't answer.

'How come they really let you back in? I don't really buy this benign prime minister stuff, Geoff. I mean, why should they care? You fucked over the Brits in a major way, they're suddenly going to care if you live or die in Moscow?'

Gilchrist shifted his shoulders as if they hurt him. His fingers were already knotted with arthritis. 'The West is frightfully sentimental.' Gilchrist spoke English most of the time. When he was angry, he switched to crude Russian. 'It's conditional, of course. I haven't got a passport.'

'You never really learned to speak, did you?' It was what my father told me: 'Englishmen don't speak other languages.' I added, 'How did you buy this place?'

'I saved up. I was quite a rich man, my father had left me a bundle, as you say. I had someone who invested for me. I had a pleasant apartment in Moscow that I was able to sell before I left. There was a KGB pension plan. After all, I was a full colonel, was I not? There were certain perks. The KGB paid my tailors. They went on paying my club membership. I'd like to take you to dinner at my club, if you'll let me. It's very nice. Nice wines.'

'Your club. Jesus.'

'And there was hard currency, of course. For a while, I was able to sell my story. Now no one cares.'

I got up. 'I don't buy it. Unless you had something to offer, I don't believe they would have let you in.'

I pulled on my jacket. Finished the whiskey in the glass. Glanced around the room one more time, then looked at the old man in the armchair. My hand was on the doorknob when I heard his voice.

'You'd be surprised if I told you the names of everyone we did business with, one way and another,' he said.

'Yeah, like who? Who is we?'

'Good question.' He got up slowly. Pulled himself out of his chair, turned to go towards the kitchen.

Suddenly I remembered: Frankie in Moscow. Her husband on missions for the West, and I said, 'Like Thomas Pascoe?'

The old clock on the carved marble mantelpiece ticked. Gilchrist disappeared into the kitchen. I waited.

'Just like dear dead Tommy,' he said, coming back into the room with a pitcher of water in one hand. 'Is that why you're really here in London, Artie?' He sat on the edge of a small stiff sofa and set the water down on the floor.

'You're not telling me Thomas Pascoe was one of yours? Come on.'

'Pascoe showed up in Moscow from time to time. Put on a show. Representing his bank, he said, but we knew he had other business.'

'You knew Tommy Pascoe was dead.'

He looked triumphant. 'Yes!'

I floated it casually. 'Do you know why he died?'

He was excited now. 'Is it yours, the case, is it?' He looked at his hands.

I didn't answer.

He said, 'You're right, don't tell me, dear. I'm not the sort of man who stands up to pressure awfully well.'

'Don't flirt with me, Geoff.'

'But why not?' He smiled. 'You met the lovely Frankie?'

'Yes.'

'She was quite something, my dear, and after your family left Moscow, she was a lifeline. She came on Peace missions. Soviet-American friendship committees. And always a bag of nice little tricks. She was a great favorite.'

'What kind of fucking tricks?'

'Things to wear. Things to eat. Books. Once my star declined a bit, I was on half-rations, so to speak.'

'Then do it for her if you want. Tommy's dead. Frankie's

dead.' I looked at him. I was angry now. 'You didn't know she was dead. She drowned herself. In her own bathtub. It took a while. It was slow for her.'

'I'm sorry.'

'So what's it going to take for us to stop talking old-time spook shit and get some information? Am I right? Was Pascoe killed to shut him up?'

'Yes.'

'Something he found out here in London?'

'I think so.'

'Know or think? You say you owe me, you owe Frankie, so what's the deal, Geoff? This involves the Russians? The creeps? Eddie Kievsky? You said you owe me.'

He didn't answer me.

'I have to go, Geoff, so can we cut the crap. Please.'

Gilchrist got out of his chair heavily and put his hand out. 'I'll have to grease some palms, as they say.'

'What?'

'You will come to see me again, won't you?'

'What will it take, Geoff, the information? What?'

He walked me to the door. He smiled and said, 'Money.'

Outside Gilchrist's front door I tried to get a cigarette lit, but the wind snatched it away. The air felt good after the hot little house, but it was raining hard and I needed a smoke. I turned the corner, ducked into a building and found myself in the lobby of a military hospital. Nobody noticed me. There was a row of plastic chairs and I sat on one and watched the old men coming and going. My feet were wet.

Seeing Gilchrist raised a tension in me like trip wires going up in my gut. You could cross the Atlantic and people still knew your business. New York and London were locked on each other in a way I didn't expect. You added Russians, the circle got smaller. Small enough everyone knew your business.

Ten, twelve days had gone by since Dante Ramirez, poor bastard, whacked Tommy Pascoe. There had been no collars that mattered before I left New York, only Ramirez, who left prints, his DNA and his soul by the side of the pool. He showed Homicide where he tossed the weapon. They offered him a deal; he didn't want it. The only deal he wanted was a place to stay when it got cold. He was crazy with fear of the cold. Even if he fried, he said, he'd still be warm.

The Mishkin kid and his sicko pal set Ramirez up. 'Our surrogate,' the kid had drawled. Later he told Homicide he had lied to me under pressure. He said him and the pal were long gone from the pool when Pascoe was murdered, and it was true. Jared Mishkin had taken his cue from his father when his father said Thomas Pascoe was a problem. Ramirez hit Pascoe, but he was only a tool. Leo Mishkin was the messenger. But who sent the message and why?

'It will end in London,' Frankie Pascoe said.

'Everything moves through London,' Tolya told me the night I left him at Newark Airport.

An old soldier shuffled up to me and asked if I needed anything, and I shook my head and headed for the door. I turned my collar up and looked out. I was an alien on an alien planet and it was raining. Still daytime, already dark.

I left the hospital and started back to Gilchrist's house. Then I noticed the dark-blue Jaguar across the street. It was the same car that took me from Kievsky's. I had been right about Geoff.

Geoffrey Gilchrist was an errand boy for the Russian mob. When he could, I was betting, he traded information about them to the Brits. What choices did he have? Gilchrist was a guy who was never in his life straight about anything. He was, like he said, Cold War scrap. Him. Tommy Pascoe. My own father.

Was it only accidental the bookstore guy calling Gilchrist? Did Gilchrist somehow know I was in town? Did Kievsky tell him? Tolya Sverdloff gave me Kievsky's name, and the dummy with my face was in the apartment Sverdloff lent me. I wondered if Tolya was in so deep he'd do anything, even shop me to his cronies. I shoved it out of my head, but I went to a phone, called Sonny Lippert and got an answering machine.

I walked back to Gilchrist's. The blue Jag was still waiting. I turned and headed in the other direction.

At a newsstand I got a cheap umbrella and a map and started walking. Along the embankment, the swollen river on my right, rain belting down now.

I'd come to London without a plan. Some kind of idiotic

impulse that I owed Frankie. It was why I went looking for Gilchrist that morning, killing time. Now I knew for sure whoever sent the message was here in London. If Gilchrist wasn't lying.

But Geoffrey Gilchrist was a guy who had lied for two countries, and would sure as shit do it again to save his own sick ass. He flirted with me and left me hanging.

Before I had left his house, Gilchrist had said, 'Have you a phone number, dear?' and I gave him the number of the apartment on the river. Maybe he'd stir things up. Flush them out. So long as I didn't drown.

Chapter 22

'Hi.'

'Hi.'

Lily Hanes stood in the doorway of the houseboat in a white turtleneck and black slacks, a gray-green silk scarf like seawater around her neck. With one hand she leaned heavily on an aluminum cane, with the other she pushed her hair off her neck like she does when she's nervous. She said, 'God, I'm glad to see you,' leaned forward and kissed me hard. 'You look like shit. What's the matter?'

'It doesn't matter now.'

'When did you get here?'

'Last night.'

'You came to London and you didn't call me? How come?'

'Where's Beth?'

'I sent her to the country with the Cleary kids for a few days, my friend Isobel, you remember? I'm having trouble with my foot. The ligament is fucking ripped. It's going to take another week, maybe more. I'm permanently high from painkillers, which ain't bad,' she joked, but it fell flat.

'Been out dancing?'

She laughed. 'Sure, with my two right feet. I tripped. I swear to God.' She laughed again.

'You didn't tell me.'

'You think I look distinguished with the cane?' She was talking too fast. 'I was worried about you, you fuck. I called you in New York yesterday, I called your cellphone. Are you OK? Why didn't you tell me you were coming?'

Lily leaned one hip against the door, then sat down heavily on a canvas chair, gesturing at the living room. 'It's wonderful. Isn't it?'

There was something territorial in her tone. She showed me

the place as if it were hers. She said it belonged to a friend of a friend, that she had rented it for a couple of weeks.

I said, 'Is it for sale?'

She nodded. 'Maybe. Do you like it?'

'Sure, but that's not what I meant.' I lit a cigarette and let the subject go.

We went on the deck where there were armchairs and a table, the cushions stowed because of the weather. Lily leaned against me, pointed out the bridges over the Thames, an old power plant on the other bank, the Embankment and Cheyne Walk. Chelsea, she said. 'I always loved it around here, it's a dumb cliché, Americans, Chelsea, but I don't care. I love it.'

Lily's was the third houseboat down in a row of boats and barges, crammed, about twenty of them, against the Embankment, each one hoisted up over the mud of the riverbank on what looked like steel sledges.

Inside, the living room had floor-to-ceiling doors to the deck outside, there was a dining area, a kitchen, two bedrooms. From the window I could see big pots on the deck next door, bushes burdened with dead hydrangeas.

The room itself was brightly lit, filled with good retro stuff, a yellow canvas butterfly chair, a bean bag, some moulded plastic stuff, not my taste, but OK. Piles of Lily's books were on the floors and chairs; her lap-top was open on the dining-room table.

She sat down again, then looked up at me. 'So you thought, OK, fuck her, I won't call, is that it?' She reached for some cigarettes, then tossed the pack on the table. When she got Beth, she quit smoking. 'Fuck. Fuck this fucking foot. I'm sorry, it's driving me nuts. I'm sorry. I'm sorry I wasn't nicer to you. I'm sorry I left home in a hurry. Please. Sit down, OK. I'll try to talk to you. I missed you, Artie, and I'm, Christ, I'm sorry.'

I'm hungry,' she said when we were still in bed. An hour after I got there, maybe two, we got up slowly, showered, dressed. I followed her up the street to the King's Road where she nabbed a taxi away from a couple of German tourists and we both collapsed in back laughing. Lily sat tight against me. She was warm. She smelled great.

I watched the streets go by, got a glimpse of squares and parks, houses, buildings, cars going on the wrong side, black taxis, red buses, Hyde Park. Most of the leaves were gone, most of it was a blur. It was night and London seemed wet, cold and handsome. We stopped in front of a brightly lit restaurant. Lily handed the driver some money and said something that made him laugh. She was all laughs; this was a brittle Lily I didn't know. The couple hours we spent in bed began to fade. She was nervous with me.

The front of the restaurant was all glass. Inside there was a bar, and near it a few tables, one in a window alcove. The rest of the big room was down a few steps.

Lily claimed the window table, sat down hard on a chair, put her bad leg on another, gestured for me to sit next to her and said, 'I'm starving. And I could use a drink. Artie? Red? White?'

I didn't answer her. She knows what I drink. I looked out of the window. Opposite the restaurant, the narrow street forked. There were fancy antique shops. One was full of chandeliers; the pellets of crystal glittered. Welcome to London.

I said, 'Can I get a real drink here?'

Lily picked the green olives out of a dish of black and green.

The martini came. I drank it and looked out the window. The rain was driving down now in sheets against the huge expanse of glass window.

'What are you going to eat?'

I glanced at the menu. 'I don't care.'

She turned on a smile and said, 'Don't sulk, OK? I'm sorry sorry sorry sorry. I am glad to see you, you know.'

Around us the room was jammed. A woman, leaving, waved at Lily, another stopped by to kiss her and exchange gossip.

I watched the scene swirl behind Lily, like figures on a screen. 'You feel like you belong in London, don't you?'

Lily said, 'I guess. I keep coming back. They like me,' she added. 'They don't know what to do with me, but they like me.'

'I like you,' I said. Then, to make it easy for her, I said, 'You're not coming home, are you? That's why you've been stalling, isn't it? Isn't it?'

She didn't answer.

'The houseboat where you're staying, you're happy there.'

She hesitated. 'I came to London because I was offered a job. I'm freelance, it was a job, no big deal. I was going to help make a documentary for HOME. It's a good organization. It shelters the homeless everywhere.' Lily smiled ruefully. 'You know I'm a guilty liberal. But it's not because of Phillip Frye, God knows, if that's what you're thinking. He's a self-obsessed jerk. Worse.'

'What's that mean, worse?'

'Nothing. Look, it's in spite of him. It's his wife who designed the Life Bubble.'

'Life Bubble?'

'It's a sort of instant shelter for the homeless, it's amazing, I swear it, Artie.'

'Oh, please, Lily!'

She ate a green olive. 'I hate your fucking cynicism. Some things matter.' Lily held her hands tight together so the knuckles looked sharp and I could count them under the white skin. 'I need to do something,' she said.

'You do do something.'

'Yeah, like what?'

'You take care of Beth. She's a happy baby. You have a million friends who depend on you. You help them out. You make them laugh. You help me. I love you. We do stuff together. Jesus, Lily, what do you want? You write stuff that's interesting. Good stuff. Useful. Funny stuff.'

'It's magazines. It's TV talk shows. It passes the time is all, nothing else. I mean, I look at what I do and I think, so fucking what?'

'You still want to save the world. You're still trying to please your parents, is that it?'

She didn't answer me.

'Where is it, this job?'

'Mostly here. Maybe a few days in Africa.'

'How long for?'

'A month or so.'

'What about Beth? She's going to be alone for a month? At least let me take her home with me.'

'She's not your child.'

'Boy, that's real tough.' I started to get up. 'But I get the message.'

'Sit down. If I need to go away for a few days, my friend Isobel's here.'

'I see. So it's still Frye, isn't it, one way or the other.'

'I just finished telling you it's much more complicated.'

'Why is it complicated, Lily? Why?'

She pressed her face against the window as if to cool it. The waiter put two plates of scallops in front of us and Lily said, 'That looks good. Thanks.' Her accent never changed, but the rhythms, the inflections, had become British. She was a ventriloquist, miming the language. I was on the other side of a glass wall watching her.

Lily ate. I put my napkin on the table. Fumbled for my cigarettes and looked around.

She said, 'You can smoke if you want.'

The waiter took away the plates and brought more food, a steak for Lily, some liver for me. It smelled great. It tasted good. I wasn't hungry.

'Why is it complicated?'

There was sweat on her forehead and she pushed her red hair off her face. She cleared her throat, played with her fork, ordered some more wine.

'Lily?'

Outside, on the rain-soaked street, the idiotic red buses lumbered up and down. Inside, the crowd sounded like animals braying.

'Artie?' Lily put her hand tentatively on my arm, like I might push her away.

'What?'

'I started coming to London when I was still a kid and I bought into it, the whole package, the writers, the accents, the bullshit, Henry James and Jimmy Hendrix and I loved it, and I kept coming back. Also, they never asked how you felt, which was perfect for me, an entire nation in denial, pre-Diana, of course. People just screwed around and had fun.' She smiled. 'I had a friend who said to me if you're an American and you're gonna be in London, there's two ways you can do it. There's Henry James or Lily Hanes. And Lily Hanes is right. So I became me. Finally.'

'And Phil Frye?'

'Phillip was my ticket. Best people, best parties, that's how I came to London in the first place. Phil was my ticket to the revolution.'

'What fucking revolution?'

'The Sixties,' she said, tone wry, but barely smiling. 'Well, it was the Seventies by then, but he introduced me to John Lennon once.'

'You didn't love Phillip when you took up with him?'

She looked at me sadly with the wide, pale, gray-blue eyes and hunched her shoulders. Lily drained her wine glass and cut a piece of meat but didn't eat it. 'I loved him. Yeah, whatever that means. Maybe I didn't tell you this – I mean, you really don't know, do you?'

'Know what? What?'

She pushed the plate away, wiped her mouth, shoved her hair off her neck for the tenth time and said, 'I didn't just take up with Phillip Frye.' Lily took a sip of her wine. 'I married him.'

I felt like someone was standing on my windpipe. I couldn't breathe right. I finished the wine in my glass. I pushed away my plate, crumbled a piece of bread, pushed it around, picked up an olive, ate it, didn't look up. It was her lying that got me. The lie. The not knowing. The casual way Lily told me about it in a public place. First the picture of Thomas Pascoe in her drawer at home, now the lie about Phillip Frye.

The rain was making me crazy. The picture of the surfer came into my head again and stuck: I was caught in a wave I couldn't handle, the board already gone in the curl, surf full of dismembered limbs: Lily, Callie Rizzi, Sverdloff, Gilchrist. I had jumped in and dragged them with me, and I figured if I didn't get out from under, we'd all drown.

A Beach Boys tune started up, incongruous as hell, in my head. I'd heard someone sing it that morning they found Pascoe's body at the Middlemarch pool. 'Little Surfer Girl' played over and over. The noise was deafening in the restaurant. But all I said to Lily was, 'Is there anything else? Anything you feel you want to tell me? Any other surprises? Anything else you forgot to mention?'

She took something out of her bag and handed it to me.

I looked at the envelope. 'What is this?'

'Keys.'

'Keys.'

'Keys to the place we're staying, Beth and me, and the address, and all the phone numbers.'

I felt the gun in my pocket. I didn't belong here. The place was so noisy my head hurt; I pushed my chair back. 'I don't want your fucking keys, Lily.'

'What do you want?'

'Like I said, I want to know if you got any more surprises for me. I want to know how come you change the rules all the time but I'm not allowed to. It's like getting beat up, you know. One day things are fine, we're OK, you, me, Beth, the next thing I know you're leaving for London. Now I can't see Beth because you've sent her to the country. What was it, she was the accessory of the year you had to have, the handbag of choice, like all the other over-forty girls? Or was it me, the accessory?'

'You don't have to yell at me.'

'I'm not yelling at you.'

'It's over. Phillip Frye and me. It's been over for years. We got married, we got divorced. Phil remarried. OK, I know I saw him some after that, but it's over. I swear to God. Whatever else you think about me, that's the truth.' Her eyes filled up. She reached for my hand. 'Don't pull away from me. Please. Artie? I hate this. I miss you. Let me talk to you.'

Lily's eyes were wet. She rarely cries. I didn't care. She had a right to her life, but I didn't have to like it.

I pushed the keys back across the table. 'Like I said, I really don't think I'll be using these.'

Head bent slightly at an awkward angle, eyes avoiding mine, Lily said, 'What surprises?'

I wanted to say, 'How come you have a framed picture of Thomas Pascoe in your drawer, like a relic, like some icon. You fucked him too? Or what?' I wanted to push the picture in her face and say, 'Tell me', but I didn't. I didn't want to hear the lies. I didn't ask.

She said, 'I'm glad you're in London. I want you here, I do, honest. OK? Tell me about the case. Please. Artie? I don't want to hurt you.'

I zipped my jacket. 'You're doing a lousy job. What is it? I'm embarrassing you? I get the lingo wrong? I don't fit in here?' I looked around the restaurant. 'You know what, Lily? I'm just a regular American, an ex-cop, OK? I can't read all this shit and I don't care. That's all I am.'

'You get a lot of stuff wrong,' she said quietly, 'but it's not about the lingo. It's not about London.'

'Then what is it I get wrong?'

'Me.'

Outside, rain dripping down my neck, searching for a cab, I turned to look through the window where Lily sat, and I saw her, alone at the table, her bad foot propped on a chair. She saw me look and raised her wine glass and tried to smile.

I went back to the apartment and switched on the radio. Risk of flooding, the radio voice whispered. Spring tides. Gale force winds. Tyne, Dogger, Fair Isle, Cromarty, Rockall, Faroes, Humpty Dumpty, what's going on, I thought. I was so groggy I couldn't focus. It was late. I was restless. I put on the TV and there was an old movie and I went and got some Scotch and climbed under the covers.

I flipped the TV channels, got the weather on BBC. A nerdy weatherman appeared on the box wearing a jacket like I'd never seen on TV, or in real life: a short bad jacket like a clown would wear, buttoned tight across his stomach.

There were gale warnings, he said. Stuff coming across the Atlantic, some kind of hump under a low, that was causing heavy rains followed by 'spits and spots'. Just fucking tell me, I thought: is it gonna rain? I figured maybe he was a joke weatherman; maybe like we got fat weather guys, they have geeks. If I'd been with Lily, we would have laughed about it. Or maybe it wasn't funny for her anymore. Maybe it was only part of the scenery for her in a town where she belonged.

The time difference had caught up with me. The windows rattled like animals caught in a cage. I got up, but the windows were locked. I poured an inch of Scotch in the coffee mug, took it back in the bedroom, sprawled on the bed, turned on the TV.

My legs burned from walking. On cable, I found an ancient Hitchcock picture with Tallulah Bankhead I'd never seen.

Lifeboat. Tallulah, William Bendix, they swam in front of me, but I fell asleep with the sound on before anyone in the picture went overboard.

Chapter 23

God, it's cold, I thought the next morning as I climbed the factory stairs to Warren Pascoe's studio. It was the coldest place I was ever in, an empty factory building on a stretch of waste ground. Paradise Street. Not far from the river. Signs announcing redevelopment of the area into 'Luxury apartments' dangled from metal fencing. Rolls of barbed wire were stacked and left to rust.

I don't know what I expected, but Warren was a link to Thomas Pascoe, and when I'd crawled out of bed that morning, I made my way east from my place on the river. I had the bronze begging hands Frankie gave me in my jacket.

Past the fancy shops and restaurants and design firms, along Shad Thames through canyons of warehouses. On the left, as I walked, was the river. Most of the buildings looked nineteenth century. The warehouses reminded me of Soho in New York before it was a tourist trap. Names, half rubbed out, were the only vestiges of a working port: Gun Wharf. Tea. Sugar. Wheat. Spice. Once this place had belched with life. I read plenty of Dickens when I was a kid; he was always big with the resident propaganda chiefs in Moscow. This was Dickens country, most of it bulldozed now, but I remembered: *Bleak House* for the river, *Oliver Twist* for the slums – 'every imaginable desolation and neglect'.

I crossed a footbridge spun out of glistening steel, then headed a few blocks inland. On the right, I passed bleak cement storage centers stained with damp and angry graffiti. NO HELIPORT HERE, someone had scrawled on a building that said COLD STORES. Broken-down housing projects. Tooley Street, a broad desolate avenue that was deserted. A woman, clutching an umbrella, wheeled a baby in a cheap stroller. She wobbled quickly by on high-heeled pumps through the leaky day; the heels were broken; her legs, even on a cold morning, were bare. She saw me look at her. She walked faster and one of her heels caught in the broken pavement.

Everywhere there were building sites, but the cranes were still. It was Sunday and the place felt empty of life, and I walked faster towards Warren's and felt the gun, comforting, weighty, in my waistband.

By the time I reached Warren's building it was raining again, and as I hurried up the rough, cold stone steps, I could hear the wind and the river. The building had four floors; Warren's studio was on the second floor. Somewhere remote a radio played.

I pushed on the door, but it was open. The studio was badly lit, the walls half soaked. Wind rattled the old factory windows set high in the streaky walls. But there was a halogen lamp on a work table and in its light I saw that plaster cast of a head with vacant eyes and a sweet smile. A man bundled in an overcoat was bent over it. He didn't hear me. He wasn't expecting me.

The studio stank of dope and cigars and sour wine. I looked around. The cavernous studio was full of half-made sculpture in plaster and bronze, body parts, shoulders, arms, hands, torsos, heads. They littered the work table that ran the length of the long wall. Taped to the dank cement-block walls were large sheets of white paper with sketches of more bodies, some in pencil, a few in colored chalk.

The sculptures were beautiful, the limbs graceful, the faces sweet and placid, the arms and hands reaching and elegant.

I looked closely at some of the heads. The expressions were sweet but closed, impassive, as if the subjects were finished with life. From a high shelf, a series of heads in bronze stared down. In the middle of the long table where Warren Pascoe was working was the head and torso of an elderly man half formed in white plaster.

The huge tweedy overcoat draped around him, Warren worked carefully at the piece with a small steel knife. He wore wool gloves with the fingers cut off. He heard me, looked up and said, 'Who the fuck are you?'

He was a small thickset man, sixtyish, partly bald, but the deft way he worked his subject made you watch. He hummed to himself like jazz musicians do, listening to a track inside his own head.

I pulled the little bronze hands out of my pocket and put them on his work table.

He looked at them. 'Where'd you get these?'

'Frankie Pascoe gave them to me.'

Warren Pascoe sat down suddenly. 'You're some sort of cop, are you?'

'Some kind.'

'I wish you people would leave me the fuck alone, you know. I don't do anything Leonardo didn't do, or Caravaggio or Holbein.'

I realized Warren was probably a headcase, and I said, 'I don't know what the hell you're talking about. I'm here because of Thomas Pascoe.'

Warren pulled off a glove and fumbled in a stack of newspapers on the floor. He tossed me one.

Warren Pascoe had been snitching bodies, or doing deals to get them. Dead prisoners mostly. Got them sent from the morgue so he could make casts. Christ, I thought. Warren, cousin of Tommy, was a bodysnatcher. The guy was using cadavers for his models because he thinks he's Caravaggio or Leonardo. In the newspaper piece, a local cop was quoted saying he had seen 'bits of human remains around the place.'

'I hate the bloody thing. I think it's repellent,' Frankie Pascoe had said about the bronze hands. This was why; the hands weren't art; they were practically flesh.

'Pretty creepy stuff,' I said.

Warren said, 'I think death has a sweetness all its own. I look at the decomposing bodies and I consider how we all finish up.'

'Look, I don't care what you're doing, or who, or if you've got bodies in your backyard.' I said. 'I want to talk about Cousin Tommy.'

Warren Pascoe got up. 'Is this going to help me, do you think, talking to you?' he said, then offered me coffee out of an espresso pot he had on a hotplate. He rolled a joint and held it out to me.

He said again, 'Is it? Talking to you? I've talked to all of them, you know. I'm a fucking artist, man, and I wish they'd bloody leave me alone. Artists have always used death as a model. Always. Do you want the coffee?'

I shuffled the truth. 'It can't hurt, talking to me,' I said. 'You help me out, I'll do what I can.'

'Yeah, what the fuck,' Warren said. 'Why should I let the establishment fuck me over any worse than they already have, right. Isn't that right? They're already looking to put me out of this place, the money boys, that is, they want to tear it down.'

I said, 'Development guys?'

Warren laughed. 'No, no one wants to live in this shithole. It's the charities. The aid people. Homeless shelters. Warehouses for the bastards, the poor fucking homeless sods, out here on the riverfront where no one notices. You like the little irony? They want to make me homeless so they can stuff this place with other homeless bastards.' He gestured at the bronze hands. 'I've even done some work for them, you know. And gratis.' He scratched his head. 'Look, man, the wanker you really want, the chap with the answers, if you ask me, is Cousin Tommy's fucking nephew.'

'Cousin Tommy was a close relative of yours?'

'No.'

I said, 'So how come he left it in his will that you do the memorial? I assume you knew he was dead.'

'I'd heard, yes. I don't know about his fucking will, but I'm not involved. I gave Frankie the bronze hands. I liked Frankie. I wanted her to pose for me.'

'Did she?'

He grinned. 'In the old days she did. I liked my models alive then.'

'She was here?'

'She was here.' He squatted on his haunches and rummaged through a filing cabinet. The cabinet was missing part of a leg and it wobbled when he touched it. Finally, he found what he wanted and stood up. 'Here.'

It was a piece of thick paper about ten by fourteen. On it was a beautiful line drawing of a nude. A woman. I squinted at it in the dull light. 'Frankie?'

He said, 'Yes. She was something.'

'Can I keep it?'

He reached over. 'No, it's all I've got.'

'Tommy's being dead surprised you? And Frankie?'

He shrugged. 'Cousin Tommy made a lot of noise. Always leaning on people, do the Christian thing. He never shut up.'

'This nephew, is he someone who could have profited from Tommy's death?'

He looked uneasy. 'I don't like to say. I'm in enough trouble.'

'You mean you're looking for a deal, is that it? Warren?' I was at the end of my rope, so I let him see the gun. 'I can make more trouble or I can try to make it go away.'

Warren reached for his coffee. 'If you ask me, I think it's where all Tommy's money went.'

'What's his name?'

Warren picked up the little bronze hands and gave them to me. 'Keep these if you like. If Frankie made you a present of it, then it's yours,' he said.

I took the bronze. 'So, Warren, just whisper me the relevant name, will you? OK?'

'I'm not going to drop some fucker in the shit if it's not doing me any good, you understand me?'

The noise of the rain distracted me. Warren finally lit the joint in his hand, pulled on it hard, made some kind of calculation and said finally, 'All right.'

'So?'

'His mother was Thomas Pascoe's sister. Tommy was his uncle. Is that any use to you? Is that what you were after? Is there anything else?'

'Is there?'

'Yeah, the guy in question would run down his mother for a bigger slice of the action.'

'What action?'

'Charity, man, actually.' He opened a drawer under the table and took out a tube, extracted a poster, then unrolled it. There was a picture of the begging hands, and the logo HOME.

'Gimme the name, Warren.'

'It's going to get me into frightful shit if I tell you.'

I said, 'Worse if you don't. Much worse. You been stealing dead bodies, Warren.' I looked at the newspaper. 'You need help here. So what's his fucking name?'

Warren tossed the remains of the joint into a glass jar half full of paint-stained water, pulled his thick coat around him and smiled his half-sweet smile. 'His name,' he said as the wind bleated outside, 'His name is Phillip Frye.'

Phillip Frye. Phillip Frye. I started walking, the name repeating over and over in my head. I looked for a phone, then walked back in the direction I had come, the river on my right. Everything was shut up tight as a drum. It was Sunday. If Frye was Pascoe's nephew, if Frye got the money and Lily had Pascoe's picture in her closet, where did she fit? What was she doing here? I looked for a phone.

I looked around me. Before I got here, I didn't figure London for a river city. I didn't really figure it for anything much. The rain let up some. Up on the high pebbly beach that skirted the water here, a houseboat seemed stranded by the low tides. On the deck a young couple, her in a big sweater and a long skirt, him in a red parka, made repairs on their boat. I heard the hammering. A boombox played an old, sad Willie Nelson tune. The two of them saw me and yelled did I want a beer, and held up bottles. I waved back. Kept walking. Then I saw a pub.

From a phone in the pub, I called information and got Frye's office, but it was Sunday and a machine answered. I conned an operator into giving me his unlisted home number and a woman with a soft, shy voice said he was out of the country. I tried Tolya Sverdloff on every number I had for him. I wanted money so Gilchrist would talk to me. Sverdloff had money, but no one answered. I needed a drink.

The pub was smack on the river, seventeenth-century maybe, a two-story wooden building with a galleried deck on the water. Inside it was warm. I found a seat at a table near a window. I could hear the water lap the seawall.

I drank the beer, which was OK, and they let you smoke. The bartender had an amiable face; he looked like the fat guy in *The Full Monty*. It was almost lunchtime and I ordered some sausages and cheese and bread. The cheese was sharp and the bread was good. I switched to red wine.

The noise of people doing regular stuff made me feel better. I watched them, shaking out their coats, glad to be inside, getting cozy, drinking, talking, flirting, stuff you saw any town, any day. Sinatra soared on the sound system singing 'Come Fly With Me'.

A yuppie guy with round steel glasses and a good sweater was hitting on a girl in a long skirt and a brown jacket, talking at her about trees and the environment. Two men sat at the bar and drank pints of beer and talked about work. A couple of cute women, twenty-something, bare legs, short skirts, black sweaters, nasal voices, shared my table briefly, told me they loved New York, and were going over to do their Christmas shopping next month, although London was pretty cool these days, they said.

They flirted, giggled, offered me potato chips that tasted of vinegar out of little cellophane bags, and bought me a glass of wine. We toasted Bloomingdales. Toasted London. I bought them some drinks in return. The bartender yakked with his friends. He had an accent like Michael Caine, and he cranked it up special, I figured, for the tourists. I could hear its ebb and flow as he made the rounds of the tables.

I sat in the window of the pub and watched the action inside and out. London crept up on me. The river especially. The idea of it. The idea of Europe.

When we left Moscow for good, we went by train to Rome for processing on our way to Israel. There were immigration forms that felt like toilet paper, there was a lousy third-class compartment and my mother crying, her lap piled with Agatha Christies. Dog-eared and stained, those books, and she read them over and over.

My father wore a vacant expression and his crappy old officer's coat without the decorations. Me, I was embarrassed: we were refugees. When he pulled his head back into the compartment that day, his face was wet. Now he was dead. I was an American. You didn't get tired of America.

I never get tired of New York, but I was liking London. I liked the river. I liked the people and the old buildings and the beer. Except for the Beatles, until now the idea of England never moved me. Until now. I looked out of the pub window at the river. London had scale and history and people who played their parts and made you laugh. In spite of the tangle I was in with the Pascoe case – I didn't know how the hell to get the money to make Gilchrist talk to me – in spite of Lily, in spite of the weather, I liked it. I could feel myself seduced by it.

The bartender brought me a refill; I offered him a drink. 'Nice place,' I said.

He put out his hand. 'Charlie Diamond,' he said.

'Artie Cohen.'

'You here for long?'

'Maybe.' I drank some of the wine.

He said, 'Come and see us again.'

I finished the wine and set off for home. The sky had cleared. Outside, I looked for the name of the pub and saw a plaque on the other side of the door. *The Mayflower*. From this spot the men of the *Mayflower* set sail and ended up in the Americas. I went back in and asked Charlie about it, and he tossed a dish cloth over his chubby shoulder, grinned and said, 'This version? Nineteen fifty-eight.'

I said goodbye to Charlie again, and the girls in the pub, then I went back to the apartment and called Jack Cotton.

Chapter 24

I didn't want to plug into officialdom, but I needed help, I needed access to information, and Jack Cotton was a cop I had a connection with. We'd done business together long-distance over the years, so I called Jack on the off-chance he was in on a Sunday. The line to his station house was busy.

I was going in circles. Gilchrist wanted money. Sverdloff had disappeared off the map. Warren Pascoe was stealing bodies. Frye didn't answer.

Phillip Frye was Tommy Pascoe's nephew. Was that the link between Lily and Pascoe? Lily had been married to Frye; she never told me. I didn't call her because I was hurt and I nursed it. I missed Lily, but these days I missed her even when she was there.

I picked up the picture of Pascoe I'd found in her apartment for the hundredth time and propped it against the coffee pot. By now I knew every line in the handsome, sanguine face, every wrinkle, every pore, every hair in his nose. Dead, Thomas Pascoe's face haunted me like the icons of the saints that stare back at you from the walls of the religious. I put it away and went outside.

Standing on the balcony, the wind blowing, I felt I was looking at the edge of the world. The volatile weather was making me nuts. Rain, fog, then the wind and a sudden glimpse of blue sky. Below me on the promenade, a couple guys were putting sandbags against the railing.

I went in the bedroom and pulled a sweater out of my suitcase, then hung up my good jacket; I had never really unpacked.

We were already packed.

Frankie had said it the first morning I met her, in the Middlemarch lobby.

Pascoe was killed just before he left. Before he could get to

London. Ramirez the homeless guy killed Pascoe, sure. But someone else didn't want him getting on the plane. Someone stopped him leaving. I knew the case would end here in London, but now I saw it sharp that Pascoe died so he wouldn't get on the plane.

We were already packed.

I went out, found a subway stop, and trotted down the stairs. Moneywise, the cabs were killing me.

For ten minutes I stood in the hole in the ground waiting for a train. The floor of the station swilled with dirty water. In a couple of places along the platform, the puddles were two inches deep. There was a steady drip and I peered at the ceiling where I saw water leaking through the cracks. It could make you nuts, the drip. The platform was nearly empty. Then the train shunted into the station.

In the lobby of the police station, Paddington Green they called it, a couple sat on plastic chairs, a broken umbrella on the floor between them, leaking water. The grim building stank. A procession of cops hauled their suspects in and out of the front door and down a flight at the back of the lobby. Somewhere there was a holding cell, I figured. The station house stank of Saturday night vomit and Sunday's blues.

The woman on the chair was white. The guy was black. She held a baby that squalled; he edged away as if the distance freed him up from her, the kid, the broken umbrella on the floor. Behind the cage a fat white cop dozed, a radio droned on about the weather. Storm warnings. The fat cop snored loud as a death rattle.

Two kids with Rasta braids and big red and green knitted berets walked in nervously and asked about a friend. Behind the cage, the cop opened his eyes. He was an angry man. I craned my neck and saw he had a plate of food in front of him, and he glanced at the kids a long time, and looked over their brand-new sneaks; you could see from his expression he decided the kids swiped the sneakers. He picked up a phone.

The kids waited. A cheap electric clock ticked. The umbrella dripped. Eventually the cop in the cage told them their friend was at another station house, and they left. They had been sent from one station house to another all night long. The cop in the cage resumed eating French fries. I could smell the grease.

'Artie, hey! Welcome to London, man. Like the weather?' Jack Cotton bounded down the stairs, his hand out. 'Nice to meet you finally,' he said, escorting me up to his office, settling me in an armchair the other side of his metal desk. He buzzed a console, asked for coffee. 'This is a phenomenal pleasure – I mean, after all these years we've been talking – to actually meet you.'

I hooked up with Jack Cotton when I was still in the department. I kept in touch after I went freelance, but I'd never met him in the flesh. He was the best contact I ever found overseas. John Ivan Looksmart Cotton; calls himself Jack. He was an easy-going guy, medium size, medium height, medium brown, compact, muscular but comfortable, and humorous. I liked him. He wore black jeans, denim shirt, knitted silk tie, battered leather jacket.

I must have talked to Jack a hundred times on the phone. There's a lot of heavy traffic between New York and London, it's the big money axis in pretty much every area: drugs, industrials, communications, illegals, people and body parts, intellectual property – meaning books and movies, stuff like that – even plain old money. And real estate.

You can't investigate in New York these days without overseas connections, and London's a clearing house for Europe, Asia, Africa. I can get information plenty of places, computer stuff, police files, but you need a guy like Jack to help you read it. I used him when I could. The Brits, they don't let their coppers, like they call them, do outside work: no running bars, no paid commerce. Ask me, it's a lousy idea. Anyhow, it was limited to official stuff, more or less, and I was hoping we could find something official, more or less.

I looked around the office, plain walls, bulletin board, the metal desk, couple of chairs. Jack Cotton buzzed the intercom again – it looked like something out of the 1930s – and a few minutes later a young woman appeared with a pot of good-smelling coffee.

On the phone, he has a great voice, rich and British, but with the lilt of Jamaica where he was born. In person, it got buried in an urban nasal drawl. He had been partly raised in London, partly in Detroit by a grandmother, so his accent was a fuck-up: part south London, part West Indies, part Motown, whatever came in handy.

'Yo, mon,' he said, 'if you know what I mean,' and he laughed when he said it and pushed a red and gold box of Dunhills across the desk. I took one. Nice smoke, I thought and figured I'd quit next week.

'Where you staying, man?' he asked and I told him. He raised an eyebrow slowly. 'Very nice. Very nice indeed. Cops like me couldn't afford a toilet around there, not anymore, not unless you got into the Docklands thing early on, back in the Eighties, though my Nina would say it's the dark side of the moon. Londoners are very attached to their own part of town. Nice views. So what can I do for you?'

I tossed the picture I'd pulled off the dummy onto Jack's desk.

He picked it up. 'Where did you get this?'

'Off a dummy someone left for me.'

He said, 'Yeah, I've seen this stuff before. Guy Fawkes pranks. Who knew you were coming?'

I didn't know Jack well enough yet to throw him Tolya Sverdloff, so I shrugged. 'I don't know.'

'You want to tell me why you're here?'

'Jack, can we do this unofficial? You heard about the Pascoe murder?'

'Thomas Pascoe? I read something in the papers.' Jack was suddenly cautious; there was the buzz of ambition. He lit a cigarette.

'He was coming over here the day they killed him. He wanted his burial here. Had a cousin, a sculptor name of Warren Pascoe. Ring any bells?'

'Yeah, colleague of mine picked him up. They let him out. Bail. Some rich wankers helped him. Did it for art, they said. Hard to pin anything on Warren unless you put your hands on the bodies, so to speak.' He laughed. 'Gives new meaning to the phrase *habeas corpus*, Warren does. You think he sat there and drew them, had them pose for him, so to speak, like models? The particular dead guys?'

I laughed. 'I don't know.'

'Pretty freaky stuff, using corpses for models. But he sells the shit and he likes the attention. You think he's part of the landscape in the Thomas Pascoe thing?'

'A small hill maybe.'

'Anything else I can help you with?'

'He had a nephew. I'm guessing the nephew was named in the will. Name of Phillip Frye. Runs a charity named HOME. Thomas Pascoe was into homeless causes.'

Jack was interested. 'I've heard of Frye somewhere. He's got a number of shelters on the river, I think.' He picked up the phone. 'I've got an idea.'

Jack listened for a while, then spoke softly into the phone. He got up from his desk and put the phone down. 'Come on,' he said, 'there's someone who might help with Frye.' He hesitated. 'I actually figured you being here in London was for your lady.'

I was pretty surprised. 'How come you know about that?'

'I think I actually met her at a party. A tall redhead, right? Very smart. Funny. Great legs, if you'll excuse me saying so.'

I didn't answer for a minute, just sucked up the smoke. Then I said, 'So how come you and Lily hobnobbing at the same parties, Jack?'

He looked uncomfortable; he must have figured Lily told me. I kept my mouth shut and followed him to the parking lot.

'You got any Russian activity in London lately, Jack?' I said.

'Sure. Always.'

'What area?'

'Dope. Petrol scams. Property more than anything. You need something specific, man?'

In the parking lot, we climbed into a silver BMW. The rain was belting on the hood. He backed out of the lot fast, cop style, never looking back. I said, 'So how come you and Lily were at the same party?'

'Small town. I'm the luvvies' favorite cop. Book parties for crime novels coming out, that kind of thing. I get the right invites. Soho Club. Groucho Club. The Ivy. I could take you.' Jack's tone was wry.

The windshield wipers started their beat. What the hell did he mean, 'luvvies', for chrissake? 'It came out you knew me, Jack?'

'Sure. Of course, man. She said you had mentioned my name once upon a time and she had remembered, which is how it came out.'

I reached on to the dashboard for his smokes.

Jack stepped on the gas. The town passed in a blur, but what I saw I liked. It was clean, handsome, spacious, assured, street after street of red brick houses, or tall white stuccos, squares and crescents, cul-de-sacs and ovals. And parks. Big boulevards, the Parliament building.

We drove through the financial district they call The City. It was washed down and beautiful in a monumental way. St Paul's Cathedral. The banks and trading houses, imperial, chilly, awesome. Money here was sunk deep. I was still trying to put London together geographically. It was big and I was out of my depth. I was edgy; there was a steady drip of anxiety in my veins.

'You want to say where we're going, Jack?'

'Sorry. I thought I'd take you over to Wapping. River police. They look like a lot of guys playing around in boats, but they're actually brilliant. They work all kinds of cases both sides of the river. I thought they might give you a line on Frye and his shelters.'

'You do boats, Jack?'

He laughed. 'I hate fucking boats. But I spent some years in Contingency Planning at Scotland Yard, and one of my colleagues, she works out at Wapping.' He peered through the windshield. 'Weather,' he laughed. 'Just so you'll know you're in England.'

'What's she like?'

'I always show willing with Tessa Stiles. Minorities stick together, that kind of thing.'

'You don't like her?'

'She's all right.' Jack shrugged. 'I'm the black chap, she's the woman, we sit on a lot of panels together. She's smart but tetchy. Doesn't like Americans. Thinks you treat us like a third world country. Thinks you throw money at every problem, send in the Marines.'

'She probably prefers a good old-fashioned war, honorable killing, noble death, that kind of thing.'

'Something like that. Her brother was killed in the Falklands. Don't take it personal, man, She doesn't like me either.'

Stiles's station house was on the river. You could hear the water, the wind at your back. We went in from the street, she met us on the ground floor and took us into the canteen. I was hungry, so was Jack. We ordered baked beans and burgers; a pretty black woman who cooked added on fries and served us; we ate alongside six other cops in the small room.

Tessa Stiles was a handsome, stocky woman with a square face and curly brown hair, but her face was dragged down by peasant genes and worry. She wore a dark-blue sweater, a shirt and tie, a plain skirt that ended below her knees, sheer panty hose and expensive pumps. Her legs were terrific and she was vain about them, you could see that; she crossed her ankles.

We ate, Jack said I was a friend from New York. Visiting. An old pal. She said, 'Why don't I give you the tour, Mr Cohen? Jack?'

'Don't lay too much propaganda on him, Tess, OK?'

Stiles led us out a side door and down a wooden walkway to the jetty where a pair of police boats were moored. She looked at the river.

'London is old and a lot of it is broken. Like New York,' she said. 'I had a fellowship that took me across to the States for a bit, the Winston Churchill Fellowship, in fact.' She lifted her chin a little. 'Tell me what you see.'

I followed her gaze. Located Tower Bridge. The apartment at Butler's Wharf on the other side of the river. I said, 'What I can make out, I'm by the Thames River, the Tower of London on my right here, the bridge, boats, lot of development. But you didn't bring me out here for this, Inspector. You tell me, you're the expert.'

Jack stood slightly apart, watching the water.

Stiles said, 'The Thames is tidal. I look out, and five thousand acres of disaster is what I see. Cheap buildings, land reclaimed that should have been let alone, tidal walls that crumble.' She walked to the end of the jetty and I followed.

'Until the Sixties, Seventies, even the early Eighties, this was a working riverside. Docks. Wharves. Factories. Both sides of the river. It was heavily unionized,' she smiled. 'Do you know what Spanish practices are?'

'No, ma'am.'

'Semi-legalized pilfering was how they ran it. They were all men, Englishmen, big muscles, small brains a lot of them, no blacks, no women.'

'Racist bastards is what they were,' Jack said.

Stiles said, 'My dad was one of the good guys. He tried to open up the unions, they cut him up. Poor people like him lived here all their lives.' She pulled her sweater tight. 'You ought to meet my dad. He was a good bloke, but he made trouble.'

'How's that?'

Stiles smiled. 'For one thing, he was an Irish fella who married a Jewish girl.'

'Something like mine.'

'What?'

'It doesn't matter.'

Stiles tugged at her own uniform sleeve. 'There's never been a woman with the river police, not at my level. There's no women worked on the river, except the daughters of men who'd got no sons. No need for women in the police. None of it matters anymore.'

'How come?'

'Shipping was containerized, moved downriver to Tilbury, the whole place felt apart. My dad had put himself on the line for nothing. The biggest wasteland in Europe. Developers moved in, corrupt Labour guys, like your Tammany Hall, but nothing happened until Mrs Thatcher. Tax breaks for all. Old people were kicked out, everything was upgraded for the bastard yuppies who bought in here, crap apartments most of them. Two hundred grand. More. Newspapers moved in, Murdoch first here at Wapping, then Canary Wharf.'

It was her subject. I let her rant. She stepped over the side of one of the boats and sat on the back of it. I went and sat next to her. The boat rocked; I lit up a cigarette.

Stiles said, 'End of the Eighties, the crash came, the whole thing could have fallen into the river, it would have been better. A few developers, foreign most of them, bought it cheap. Real scum.'

'What kind of scum?'

She smiled sourly, 'All kinds. Money scum. Stock market scum. Canadian, Australian, British scum.'

'Russian?'

'Oh yes. The Russians bought. They built two hotels on the waterfront. Isle of Dogs. A new heliport. The old days, they said the Jews landed up in Stepney because it's as far as they could walk from the boat with a suitcase. The Russians like to be close to their point of arrival too, only they don't walk.'

Jack called out from the jetty, 'Hey, Tess, I have to get back some time tonight.'

She ignored him. 'I'll tell you what I see. I look at this river, I see the biggest concentration of risk in the urban world. Big as the San Andreas Fault.'

'You're losing me here,' I said.

Almost dreamily, she said, 'If the Thames ever floods, and it will flood, London's fucked for a decade. Britain is sinking, the world is getting warmer and wetter and Britain is sinking. Think about it. Even now, it's been raining some of every day since September. The tributaries of the Thames are already full. Say we get some freak weather during the spring tides this month, a surge tide, a failure in weather reporting, London floods. The telecommunications go first, and the financial systems, gas, electricity, newspapers, the Underground, all property on the river right down to Westminster, Chelsea, floods. You can't evacuate nine million people. People start to hoard. There's a run on the banks. Raw sewage everywhere. We pump our sewage uphill out of London, if there's a flood the pumps go, the town fills up with shit.' She waved her arms towards the night. 'And all this. All Docklands.'

The wind blew her hair and she clutched at it, but her face lit up with excitement; Tessa Stiles was a zealot. 'Even the Thames Barrier can't help.'

'The what?'

'Barrier's a steel wall they put up in bad weather, not far downriver from here. What if the Barrier doesn't work? What if someone takes the wife of the Barrier's controller hostage? What if a plane from City Airport – look just over there, you can see the plane going in – what if it crashes? The airport was supposed to be for short-haul props, now it flies big jets. The landing strip is a hundred meters from the Barrier.'

Stiles talked rapidly. 'I don't even need a major flood. A small device breaches an underwater tunnel, we've got four trains with two thousand people each at Waterloo Station, water starts to pour in. Our tubes – subways to you – haven't got proper ventilation. It's the motion of the train that moves the air, but suppose a train's flooded. There are no fans. Carbon monoxide poisoning sets in.'

'Tess!' Jack was impatient.

It was freezing now, the wind bitter, but Tessa Stiles was wrapped up in her rhetoric. I looked in her eyes. They were dark and large and inward looking. It was as if she had an internal screen where she played her doomsday scenarios over and over, like video games. Stiles crackled with excitement. I thought she was desperate and doomed. I wanted to say: stop. For chrissake, stop. Please. But she was lost.

She put her hand on my shoulder and climbed off the boat, then looked up at me. 'I see a wall of water coming down on London.'

Chapter 25

Inside Stiles's office, Jack said to her, 'You ever come across anyone named Phillip Frye?'

She looked up. 'I see. That's why you've come, is it? He runs that organization HOME out of a converted factory over by Rotherhithe. It's not strictly speaking my territory, being the other side of the river, but I keep an eye on both sides and I know something about Frye and I hate the way he gets his hands on derelict docks property, what's left of it, before anyone else does.'

Jack, who had been smoking and looking bored, perked up. He said to Stiles, 'What's he want all the property for?'

'His homeless.'

'His?'

Stiles picked up a thermos and poured coffee in a mug. 'I think it, but I can't prove it yet, that Frye's involved, and I don't know how, in pressurizing people to give him money for his shelters. In exchange he helps them – and some of them are real thugs – get permits for development on land no one else can touch. He's connected. It's sick stuff.'

'I don't get it.'

She said, 'The hotter the property market got, the more homeless there were. The more homeless, the bigger Frye's operation.'

'That's crazy.'

'Perhaps, then, Mr Frye is crazy. Do you want some coffee?'

'Enjoy the lecture?' Jack, laughing, pulled out of the parking lot behind Stiles's station. 'You hungry at all?'

'I'm still eating that burger, man,' I said. 'Let me buy you a drink if you have time, Jack. There's a decent bar near where I'm staying.'

I got the impression Jack was happy to hang out. We were near the bridge when his cellphone rang.

'Bloody phone,' he said, but he was listening now, face intent, eyes small and black and impenetrable.

'What is it?'

'I don't know. I'm going to have to drop you off, Art, OK? I got to take this. It looks like we have a problem.'

'I'll come with you,' I said, and he was already revving the car, crossing the bridge, heading into a bleak broken area of ramshackle buildings and wasteland. He said, 'You'll have to keep out of it if I take you, OK? I can't have any cowboys on this.'

A bonfire lit up the broken ground. It was surrounded by squat, busted buildings. It looked like hell. The crummy apartments, the long stretch of rolled barbed wire, the garbage that spilled out of metal cans and left its sour stink. The graffiti on greasy tile walls shimmered in the firelight. On the fire was half-burned furniture – a chair flared and crumbled, the flames fed on the stuffing. Five or six homeless guys, most of them drunk or ripped, I couldn't tell, crawled out of their cardboard huts and circled the perimeter, edgy, nervous, scared. A group of boys, teenagers, thirteen, fourteen, faced off with them.

A boombox pumped out rap music. On the balconies of the building, people screamed at the kids. One boy started throwing bottles into the fire.

The glass shattered, the flames spurted higher. Sirens screamed. The pumping waa waa of the sirens was foreign, unnerving, like sirens in a war movie. Police cars were parked everywhere around the housing project. The sirens tore up the night and cracked any veneer of civility. The flames lit the faces of the boys; all of them were black. I saw now some of them were only nine or ten. Backlit, they looked like ash.

Jack kept to the sidelines. His body tensed up. Arms stiff at his side, he walked slowly to one of the uniforms and spoke to him quietly.

I got out of the car, leaned on the hood, watching. He turned back to me, and I said, 'You all right?'

'Yeah. Sure. I've just got to show my face for a few minutes and we can get the fuck out. They need a black face to show up when this kind of stuff happens. Calm the natives, so to speak.'

'They got no one else?'

Jack, heading towards the kids, turned around, his compact body, outlined by the flames. 'At my level? In the Met – that's NYPD to you, man – at my level, there's no one else black.'

I leaned against Jack's car and watched him walk towards the fire. The white cops watched too. He talked to one of the boys, but I couldn't hear, and then I saw another kid raise a knife. It happened fast. I saw the blade glint. I put my hand on my gun.

A couple of white cops, faces raddled with anger, headed towards the kid with the knife. A wind had come up and it whipped the flames now. Jack was in front of the rest of the cops. He moved towards the kids; Jack looked like cannon fodder.

Then it started raining.

We sat in Jack's car after that and the windshield wipers swiped at the car. He lit a cigarette, then pulled away from the waste ground. The fires were out. The kids had disappeared. So had the cops. All that was left was the garbage and the rain.

I said again, 'You OK?'

'Yeah.'

'What's going on here?'

'They're tearing down the council flats – projects to you – to make way for new development, shutting out the poor. People are angry about it, but it's the name of the game. Docklands is used up. They're moving south, the development people, the property blokes. I don't know why in the fuck anyone wants to live out here anyhow, on a piece of reclaimed marshlands that never drains. You get a bad storm, the place fucking floods over.'

I didn't care about the weather. I cared about the spectacle, the angry kids, Jack's showing himself to them, the angry white cops. Jack had no weapon but he went in anyhow.

'But how come you felt obliged, you personally?'

'Another time, Artie, OK? I need that drink.' He glanced back at the desolate scene.

Suddenly, a small white man pushed his face against the car window. Jack rolled it down. The man had a sweet moon-shaped face and no teeth and he held his hand out. 'Can you help me out?' he said. Jack rolled the window back up and pulled away.

'Bloody homeless. They'd be better off if they got themselves some work to do.' Jack grinned his beguiling grin. 'You thought all black people were on the Left, did you? Me, I fucking loved Mrs Thatcher. On your bike. Get a job. My parents did it. My dad worked forty years for Ford. Us kids did it. No one gave us a handout. Never mind. Anyhow, this lot are OK. Pretty much the same as before. Same film studio, different head, you know? Business as usual. Which is a good thing.'

'What lot?'

'Government, man. You're not into politics?'

'Politics bore the shit out of me. I'm not interested.'

'You will be. Politics, that is. You spend a little time here, you will be.'

I didn't know what he was talking about, I don't give a fuck about British politics or any other kind.

Jack changed his tone. 'So, Artie, man, you going to buy me that drink or what?' He drove silently for a while, the streets opened up again. I could see the river.

We closed the bar at one of the restaurants along the promenade. London was feeling like a night city to me, always dark and wet, but full of warm, light, boozy places, bars and pubs and restaurants and clubs where people congregated to cheer themselves up. Or maybe it was the company I'd been keeping since I got off the plane.

Even while the waiters stacked the chairs, we stayed on, sitting in front of the window. Fog was coming in now and it ate up the river. The promenade was deserted. A thin stream of traffic was barely visible on the bridge.

Jack was not completely comfortable with me, maybe it was the incident on the waste ground. He was a black cop in a white town. Maybe it was his meeting up with Lily. His eyes moved to the river then back to me. The sound of laughter from a couple of waiters working the other side of the room seemed to startle him.

I said, 'Something else on your mind?'

He finished off his drink quickly and said, 'Nothing I can think of. Look, about Lily Hanes. She didn't tell you we'd met or about that party, did she?'

I finished my drink and kept my mouth shut.

Cotton was nervous and he stuttered some. 'We met at the party. She's a nice lady, Artie, but she's messed up with a bunch of charity wankers who like to imagine they're doing good things for poor people and I'm sorry for you.'

'You got something to be sorry about?'

'OK.' He reached for his drink and swallowed it down. 'We almost had a scene. Now that's the fucking truth, and I'm telling you because if you want my help on Pascoe, there has to be some trust between us. She was a little frightened. She was on painkillers and a little high, her leg all messed up and I've got some stuff I'm working out at home, but fucking nothing happened. Nothing. I swear to God. I'm a pretty big bastard but I'm not a big enough shit to sit here drinking with you if there was anything.'

'I didn't ask.'

'Well,' he said. 'So tomorrow I'll track down whatever I can on Pascoe for you, OK?'

'Yeah, fine.'

'I'll help you where I can, man. But even if I got you attached formally, which there's no point, you know you would not be allowed to do much, not to interrogate, for one thing, but most of all, no guns. We can welcome you, we can offer you all kinds of courtesy as a brother of the badge, so to speak – you like my phrasing?' He grinned. 'Being as how you were a New York City detective, and my friend, but what's the point of a formal attachment?'

'I operate pretty much on my own. I'm here as a tourist. I'd just as soon keep it that way. What I'm looking for is who stopped Pascoe coming to London. Him, his wife, they were packed. Ready to go. There's Russians in it hip deep. New York, we've got Russians manipulating real estate prices same as they eat borscht, and some of them wanted Tommy Pascoe dead. People are getting killed for living space and nobody who matters gets indicted.' I lit up one of my own cigarettes.

'Here too. Plenty of them. Russians with money, the babes

who drop a hundred thousand grand, that's pounds, man, at Harrods in an afternoon, Russians that got a string of race-horses. Casinos. Some of them buying up the big houses that belonged to Arabs, up around Highgate, Hampstead, some in Mayfair and Knightsbridge.'

'Anything else?'

'I bet you'll like this one. Since the Prime Minister went to visit Yeltsin in Moscow, we've got our KGB brothers walking the beat in London looking for Russian gangsters.'

We laughed, and I thought of Geoffrey Gilchrist.

'One thing you should know, Artie, you'll forgive my sounding patronizing, is that London is a very small town. Very. Areas of relationship cross over that might be different from New York City. Politicians. Money. Lawyers. The aid business, you know, charity. Good works.' Jack's tone was sardonic.

'I want something on Phillip Frye real bad.'

'I understand.' He looked at his watch. 'Why don't we pay Phillip Frye a visit together tomorrow?'

Jack's phone rang. He wandered to the other side of the room while he talked. I got the check and paid for the drinks.

Jack said, 'I have to go.'

I walked with him around the corner and watched while he got in his car, then leaned out the window. 'Maybe we'll play some golf.'

I didn't want to insult his game by saying I thought, Tiger Woods notwithstanding, golf's a game for guys with prostate trouble, so I nodded.

'And Nina's hoping you'll come round for supper too, next week? And Lily, of course, if you like. You're all welcome.'

Jack was trying hard, so I said, 'I'll let you know. About the golf. And dinner. Thanks.'

'Roast lamb, the works.'

'Nina doesn't cook Caribbean?'

'Nina?' Jack laughed. 'She's as English as it gets. You think I wanted to marry my mum? Christ, when I met Nina and she told her old man she was marrying a black chappie, the next time I went to call, her dad met me at the front gate with a shotgun. You think I'm joking? Like I said, this is England. They can change the labels all they want, old Britain, new Britain, it's always the smell of England getting up your nostrils.'

'Yeah. So thanks. Hey, it's good to meet you, you know?'

He backed out of the alley, then before he turned towards the street, he stopped and leaned on his horn to get my attention. I went after him.

'Jack?'

He said, 'Tell me for sure you're not thinking about carrying some kind of weapon, Art.'

'For sure, Jack.'

'You do that, I can't help you. You carry a gun, you put yourself in real jeopardy here in London, OK?'

'Yes,' I said and he put his foot on the pedal and disappeared.

Chapter 26

I didn't wait for Jack Cotton the next day when I barged into the renovated warehouse where Frye had his office. Jack had other business and I didn't want him knowing I had a gun in my pocket.

A brass plate on the wall of Frye's warehouse was engraved with the words 'Charity begins at HOME'. There was an outline of Warren Pascoe's begging hands. The building in an area nemed Rotherhithe consisted of two warehouses joined by a courtyard with a view of the river. It wasn't far from Warren Pascoe's studio and the pub where I had eaten lunch the day before. Over the front door were security cameras.

The lobby was designed to play off the Victorian warehouse it had been: high ceilings, wooden pigeon-holes on one wall, a long front desk, a corrugated tin roof overhead where you could hear the rain. The receptionist behind the desk was probably seventy and volunteered her name. Ida Pink, she said and told me to wait, then returned to her main occupation which was egging on a black handyman. He was on his knees, cutting with a pocket knife the frayed cord on a battered electric heater.

Somewhere through a sound system Sting was singing 'An Englishman in New York'.

Princess Diana in Capri pants and a land-mine shield inspecting a blasted hut with Phillip Frye. Crippled kids shaking hands with Phillip Frye. Frye with Nelson Mandela. Jimmy Carter in a hardhat with a hammer on a building site, putting up a house, and next to him Phillip Frye. The waiting room at home, Frye's organization, was a shrine to Phil Frye, the stuff of a self-made saint, an icon of do-good, a right-on guy who believed he could save the world. No wonder he had a grip on Lily she couldn't shake.

I looked at the wall again: Frye was pictured at Paul Newman's cancer camp where he apparently donated housing materials. There wasn't anyone or any place on the planet where Philly Frye didn't help out, not when it came to housing, not when it came to shelters.

Phillip Frye and Thomas Pascoe. A perfect pair. Maybe I was just feeling sour, seeing as how Frye knew Lily a lot longer and better than I ever did; maybe I was just pissed off about that.

'Keith and Mick over there,' said Ida Pink. 'Gimme shelter, you know,' she said. 'You can sit down if you want.'

I ignored Ida and headed up a flight of stairs. At the top of it, in a large square room with windows that looked out on to the central courtyard were four women. They sat, all of them, in front of computers, with phones in their hands, all chattering in the phones and at each other like birds that landed on the same branch and enjoyed the company. Punching keyboards, drinking coffee, two of them smoking. They were in their twenties. Dressed in black. All of them pretty, a black woman in cornrows with colored beads that jiggled, an Asian with long hair, two white girls with studs in their tongues and commas of hair over their eyes. Who was it who said age and treachery sure beats youth and exuberance?

In that room, where the walls were covered with bright posters advertising HOME, there was so much youth and exuberance that all I wanted was a Scotch.

A couple of doors led off the room, and one swung open now. A tall woman with a big ambitious mouth and a short leather skirt strode through it and looked me over. She introduced herself. Prudence Vane, she said. In charge of PR, she added. I asked her where Frye was. She nodded toward the other door and when I opened it and stuck my head in, I saw Phillip Frye. He was on the phone.

Frye lifted off from his chair, but kept on talking, the phone under his chin. He shook my hand with the regular guy shake of a rugby player. I remembered that about him, the one time we had met. He gestured to a chair.

I'd met Frye once, at a party on Long Island. He worked in New York for a while; he ran a publishing company. He had a long ruddy face with a high forehead and curly brown hair that was turning gray. The hair was too long, the face was cheerful and closed.

He had Thomas Pascoe's forehead and nose, but Pascoe's was an international British face – the silver hair, the polished look. Frye's face was old fashioned and secretive. Now he put the receiver back on the phone and shook my hand for the second time.

'Artie Cohen, isn't it? Good to see you again. We met in East Hampton, didn't we? Yes, I was still in New York then, I do remember, of course. Coffee?'

The Asian girl appeared with a tray and two mugs. The coffee was lukewarm. The instant brew had been made under a tap and undissolved crystals floated on the milky surface. I put the mug on Phil's desk. He didn't mention Lily. Neither did I.

The three windows in Frye's office looked on to the river. Inside, the room was jammed with books, floor to ceiling, and there was promotional material on every surface.

Modern leather chairs were heaped with posters, brochures, boxes. The tables held tangled computer gear and empty coffee cups. Under the windows was some kind of plastic tent about ten feet long, six feet high, and Frye, following my gaze, ambled over to show it off. His socks didn't match. His shoes were brown and suede. I felt better.

'Come and look at this. This is going to change the world, actually. It's the Life Bubble. It's a portable living space for the homeless, or refugees. It's insulated like a thermos, warm in winter, cool in hot climates. You can hook it up and filter clean air in environmental emergencies. It folds up flat, it weighs only a few pounds, it fits in a backpack, it's cheap to make, it's weather resistant. It's quite brilliant, don't you think so?' Behind the little round glasses with steel rims, his eyes shone like a convert.

Frye, who wore a pin-striped suit with bell-bottom pants and a nylon velvet shirt, foraged in a box on the floor, pulled out a green bottle of white wine, opened it and poured some in two sticky glasses he found on his desk.

He offered one to me, the phone rang again, he picked it up, talking, pacing, flexing his hands back and forth. He was charged up like someone stuck him into a socket. He talked beautiful English, though, rippling, elegant, lustrous; he talked it in whole paragraphs, like a talking book. He finished the call, and said, 'I'm sorry,' picked up the glass and drank the wine.

'Look,' he said, as if he had finally clocked my presence. 'Maybe you can help me. Someone's stealing from this office, blueprints for projects, my personal notes, address books. Stealing donors' names. You've no idea how difficult it all is these days, people moving on to your turf.'

'Turf?'

'There are some of my contributors, if they think their names have been sold on, will leave me, and God knows there are plenty of other charities with their hands out.' He looked at me. 'But you're not interested in a minor theft, are you? I've got the wrong policeman.' He laughed. 'You haven't come over from New York to help me track down an address book, have you, Artie? What can I really do for you?'

I said, 'Tell me about your relationship with Thomas Pascoe. Uncle Tommy, wasn't it?' I shoved a pile of books on the floor and sat on a leather chair. There was a full pack of cigarettes in my jacket.

'He gave us money.'

'For this bubble thing?'

'Yes. Can we walk if you're going to smoke? I want some air,' he said.

'It's raining.'

'I don't care.'

'I care.'

He shoved open the window.

I stubbed the smoke out in the wine glass.

Frye said, 'I put Tommy Pascoe on my board.'

'He came to the meetings. Here? In London?'

'Yes. Always. It made him feel important. And he was quite useful, but I had to keep it quiet.'

'Why's that?'

'Some of my more left-wing members didn't approve of Uncle Tommy.'

'But he had the dough.'

'Yes. Exactly.'

'You were named in the will, I heard.' I wasn't sure, not until I said it, I was trying it out. But Frye nodded, and I thought: Bingo!

'Yes, I was. Thank God. We need the money. I just hope to Christ it doesn't take too long to expedite.' Frye pulled a jacket off a hook and said, 'Come on. I'll show you something interesting and you can smoke all you like.'

I followed him through the room full of young women, who all looked up hopefully when he passed, then out the door. We walked two blocks to a derelict stretch of riverfront. Planks were set across the puddles. The rain had slowed to a drizzle, but the wind howled. Frye didn't seem to notice.

I said again, 'So you profited by Uncle Tommy's death.'

'Then he died for a cause. He'd have liked that.'

'How much?'

'That's none of your business.'

'Come on, Philly, what's the harm? I mean, you'd like to know who killed Uncle Tommy, wouldn't you?'

'I understood they'd arrested someone in New York.'

'You wouldn't want to see some homeless bastard take the whole rap would you? I thought you were king of help the homeless.'

'What's that got to do with it? I let Tommy work with me because it suited us both. He was enlarged by it. He showed me how to work the money – we are a global organization – and it's in New York where people know how to give properly. He showed me how to – what's the ghastly American term? – how to grow it.'

'Names? He gave you names?'

'Yes.'

'Rich assholes you could rip off?'

'We don't rip them off. They contribute.'

'Russians?'

He looked up. 'Some. I suppose there are some. What difference does it make?'

'Is Eddie Kievsky one of them?'

For less than a second Frye hesitated, then he said, 'Why the fuck in all the world should I give you my names, my people? I'm not going to do that.'

'Why is because I'm wondering if you leaned on Tommy Pascoe to introduce you to people who gave you money and that it went wrong with the Russians. If you don't help me, I'll get the word out, which will make you real unpopular, OK? So do this thing for me, Philly,' I said.

He was impervious. His face remained smooth. Getting at Frye was like punching jello. You put your fist in and broke the surface, it jiggled back, bland and gelatinous.

He stopped suddenly in front of a run-down building. There was scaffolding on it. The door was painted blue. Half a dozen bikes were hitched to a metal rack out front. From inside came the noise of hammering.

The hallway was an inch deep in water. There was a hole in one of the walls. Frye walked into a puddle and started yelling for someone.

A guy, his pants falling down past the crack in his ass, a yellow hardhat perched high on his head, appeared. He dragged a cigarette out of his mouth, flipped it into the puddle where Frye stood and said, 'This ain't gonna work, guv. This place is under the water line. This part of the old docks is marshy, it's shit, I can't do nothing with it.'

Frye looked at him and said briefly, 'Yes, you can.'

I said, 'What is this place?'

'One of my shelters,' he said. 'The Americans worked it out first. You've got to privatize the shelters to make them work. That's precisely what I'm doing here. That's why I needed Tommy's money.'

Frye led me through a series of rooms, some with rows of beds, the mattresses folded back over themselves. In a kitchen area, about a dozen men sat gloomily around a table. A black and white TV played in the corner.

'Someone has to do it.' Frye nodded at the men. 'We've already got people here and we're not open. There's a tremendous overload on the system. I've got six more shelters in the works.'

I looked at the guys at the table. They were a forlorn group, ragged, lonely men huddled together in the cavernous space drinking out of thick mugs. Water dripped through the old warehouse ceiling.

'Yeah well, Phil, I wouldn't call this home exactly,' but he said, 'You're wrong. You're just wrong.'

Without any warning, one of the men at the table got up. You could smell the stink. He ran at Frye and stuck his fist in Frye's face. His hand was like a skeleton, he was so thin.

Frye made for the door. The man followed him, and the three of us stood in the doorway, half in, half out, fetid water swirling around our feet. The rain was heavy now. The man punched Frye's arm. He was almost incoherent but I caught the drift: how much he hated the shelter, why he was transferred from a place he liked closer to town. He had a cleft palate and when he screamed, the noise came out of a hole in the middle of his face. But he was too weak and the effort made him crumple. He fell down. Two guys dragged him away.

'Poor bugger,' Frye said.

'He didn't like this shelter. You have a hierarchy? Who gets the best beds.'

'Something like that. He's a dead man. He could be dead tonight. Liver disease. Brain tumor.'

We went back to Frye's office, where he pulled a bottle of Scotch out of a drawer and poured it into the wine glasses.

I said, 'Frankie Pascoe was happy with it, that Tommy left you so much dough, that he put you in the will?'

'I don't know.' Frye shrugged. 'I don't actually care much. Frankie was a silly, spoiled woman. Besides, she had plenty of her own. The money was for this.' His gesture included his whole empire. 'It was for all this, and more, it wasn't for me.'

'What's more?'

'The shelter I showed you. Other shelters all over town.'

'On the river here?'

'Yes. Abroad too. Wherever we're needed.'

'Thomas Pascoe's dead, so is Frankie, but you're not really interested. I wonder who gets her money? I wonder who gets the apartment?'

Frye looked at his watch. 'I'm late,' he said.

The phone started ringing again. He took it off the hook and listened.

'Lily?' he said. 'Goddamn it, I've been trying to reach you. Don't you pick up your phone?' He covered the mouthpiece and said to me, 'What else is it exactly that you want from me?'

I said, 'Whatever Thomas Pascoe knew that got him killed.'

Prudence Vane stuck her head in his door, and Frye said to

her, 'Show Mr Cohen out, Pru, will you? And be nice to him. He's what they call a private eye. Maybe he'll help us find our missing address books.'

I headed for the door. I'd heard enough. I turned up my collar, but Pru Vane kept step with me.

She was tall, thin, angular, handsome. She had a small head and slick, short hair dyed platinum. She was probably thirty. When she hitched up her thousand-dollar leather skirt, I could see she had on stockings. The flesh between her garters and her stocking tops was bare. Smooth. She gave me a real good look at the thighs.

'Can I buy you a drink later, Mr Cohen? Dinner?'

'Why not? It's Artie.'

She puckered up. 'Superb,' she said. 'And look, we're having a party, a launch for the Life Bubble at the Waterclub. Great new restaurant on the river, everyone's coming. I'll have an invitation biked round to you,' she said.

I wrote my address down for her, and let her believe I was up for a drink. 'Tell Phil thanks. And do me a favor.'

'What's that?'

'Get me the date of your last board meeting.'

But Pru's eyes had drifted. She was looking over my shoulder. 'Hello, Jack,' she said.

I turned around. Jack Cotton stood in the doorway.

'You know each other?'

Under his breath, Jack said to me, 'I thought we were doing this together, Artie. I called by your place, you'd gone.'

'So, Jack, you'll be at the party, then?' Pru said. 'Jack's at every party.'

I went out the door and Jack followed me. We stood in the courtyard under a metal overhang.

'What's going on here, Jack? You know these people? You know more about all this than you let on. What am I, your stalking horse?'

Jack lit a cigarette. 'I made a few calls last night. As far as New York's concerned, the Pascoe case is wrapped and you know it. They've got a confession from Ramirez. You brought the case to London, Artie. You put it in your suitcase and imported it, and I'm not at all sure you declared it at customs, know what I mean.

Now I didn't mention it, man, I didn't even mention you, but you came to me for help, remember?' He took a couple of drags on his smoke, then tossed it in the gutter.

I said, 'Someone stole Frye's address book. People been leaning on his contributors. Some of them are Russians. I don't get it. And I don't like him.'

'I don't like him either. Let me work this with you.'

'I have to go, Jack.'

'I'll drop you.'

'I'll walk.'

I thought about Jack Cotton on my way back to the apartment. I didn't figure him for a wrong guy, but he didn't make me easy either. I stopped at the pub on the river for some lunch, and by the time I got home, the invitation from Pru Vane was already under the door. A couple of other letters too, addressed to a bank I never heard of.

The apartment spooked me now, like jujus lived in the walls, and I dumped some groceries, coffee, Coke, beer on the table along with the invitation and the letters. Slammed the windows shut. Replaced the batteries in the shortwave, and opened the mail.

The first letter was a foreclosure notice, as far as I could make out. The second was a bill for some work on the apartment and I tossed it in the garbage can and looked at the first one again. One bank defaulting on another. It didn't take me long to track down the bank that held the mortgage, or to find out its main shareholder was Anatoly Sverdloff. I tried the phone numbers on the letter. It didn't surprise me a hell of a lot when a machine answered in Russian and English.

Sverdloff was in more kinds of trouble than I knew. I sat at the table and methodically I tried every number I had for him again. Moscow. New York. Hong Kong. Nothing. Come on! Come on!

Tessa Stiles said Russians bought up property cheap in Docklands in the early Nineties. Sverdloff was one of them. Eddie Kievsky, who I first saw at Sverdloff's Halloween party in New York, sold me a gun because I was Sverdloff's friend. And Kievsky had a testimonial on his wall from HOME. I'd seen the plaque when the kid showed me her father's room. Kievsky and Frye. I wondered who made the introduction.

When I'd left Kievsky's Saturday morning, the wife Irina stood in the doorway. Irina with the dark hair and fabulous blue eyes. Suddenly I knew what bugged me: Irina Kievskaya resembled Jared Mishkin.

I put in a call to Sonny Lippert. Asked him to track down any connections between Kievsky and Mishkin.

'Where the hell are you, Art? I've been calling you all weekend.'

'Please, just do this, Sonny, will you?' I was tensing up. I wanted this thing over.

On the radio, people were yakking, yakkety yak, talk talk talk, it gave me a headache, all the talk: a new adaptation of Chekhov; questions of moral ambiguity; more freak weather; rumor of a sell-off of some speculative building on the river. Someone read a short story while I wondered who had ripped off Frye's addresses.

It was still early. I got out the map and found my way to Lily's houseboat. I had to ask her about Pascoe's picture. About her and Frye. I was mad and scared. I suddenly thought: Lily was in trouble and I wasn't there for her. I got it wrong, like she said.

I couldn't wait. When I got there, the lights were on.

Nobody answered the door. I banged harder, then I climbed over the railing of the deck and peered in the window. The lights were on. The living room was a mess, papers on the yellow canvas butterfly chair, a half-eaten meal on the table, a bottle of wine and a couple of glasses on the dining room table. The radio played faintly, and I tapped on the window. 'Lily?'

No one answered.

'Lily?' I was shouting.

At the houseboat next to Lily's, the door opened and a man in a red sweater and jeans came out on deck and looked at me. He said, 'Everything all right?'

'I'm looking for Lily Hanes.'

'I saw Lily go out earlier,' he said. 'I had the sense she was in a hurry. Can I help?'

'No thanks.' I climbed back off the deck. 'It's OK,' I said. 'You didn't see if she was by herself?'

He said, 'I did. She wasn't. There was somebody with her. A man, I think.'

'Black or white? A white guy?'

'White,' he said.

On the embankment I found a payphone, called up Pru Vane and said I'd take her up on the drink. She was eager.

Chapter 27

The Groucho Club, she had said. It was wet, cold and windy
that night, but the streets were jammed with people. Clubs, coffee places, restaurants, people streamed in and out, some of
them stylish as New Yorkers, the same brotherhood of black
clothing, same pumped-up gay guys, some great women. London stayed up late. In spite of the mess I was in, I liked the
nights here, the bright lights in club windows, the smoky pubs
where people spilled on to the sidewalk, the noisy restaurants.

Most of the men, poking their faces out from umbrellas,
looking for cabs or addresses, were in soft shoulder suits and
little round glasses. Everyone moved fast. They talked into
snappy little phones – the place had New York beat for cellphones ten to one.

At the entrance to the club stood a knot of people laughing.
On the ground, on a nest of cardboard boxes, was a pair of
homeless guys. Young guys. I pushed a pound coin into one
hand; they were doing excellent business. Must have been a
prize claim they'd staked, this venue outside the club. I wished
them luck and pushed through a revolving door.

A good-looking man with a crew cut and a high style four-
button jacket told me Pru was in the bar if I was looking for her.
He had a faint German accent. People dumped wet coats in the
coat room, humped packages and briefcases.

'What's so funny?' Pru Vane said when she saw me in the bar.

I wanted to say, 'You think I should have checked my gun?' I
kept my mouth shut.

The place, long bar, armchairs, a fellow playing some pretty
good piano, was awash with noise. Pru wore a weird little cardigan sweater in dull green and a sheer long dress.

She fingered the dress fondly. 'Voyage, darling,' she said. She
draped her arm around my shoulder, ordered a bottle of Cham-

pagne, grabbed it by its neck, exchanged wisecracks with a waiter, and led me upstairs to a room where a couple of women played some desultory pool and sat in the corner. 'Not pool, darling. Snooker.'

'Whatever.' I sat next to her. She hitched up her dress and showed me the great legs. Pru's white-blonde hair, slicked back earlier, fell over one eye.

I said, 'What is this place?'

'A club. We all come here.'

'Who?'

'People. You know.' She laughed. 'So, like Artie, once you've been here with me, you'll like know everyone in London. And Everyone will know you. Like lucky you.'

I knocked back some wine and lit a cigarette. 'Lucky me. How the hell old are you, Pru?'

'Twenty-six. So.' She chugged some Champagne out of the bottle. 'So you're Lily Hanes's cop.'

'What?'

'Oh, come on, darling, everyone knows about you. Lily, when she came over to help us with a HOME project last year, she told Isobel Cleary she was in love with you, and of course it wasn't Iz, she didn't let on because she's graveyard, whatever you tell her, but someone heard them talking, and you know. Anyway, it's ace, isn't it, I mean, being a cop.'

'Sure. Laugh a minute.' I picked up a Champagne glass, shifted my thighs on the couch. I could hear Rick's voice in my ear: 'You're a slut, you know.' He always says it when I work a case like this. Now I looked at Pru and thought, yeah well, fulfill my destiny.

'It's very very exciting, Pru. Guns. Gangsters. Tell me about HOME, what you do.'

'I'm freelance, of course. I have other accounts. I help out because Phillip's like connected, but he's in the shit, I have to tell you, and the big party coming up, and this fucking weather.'

'Connected?'

'Very. To everyone. Which is why he's so upset. Should we get another bottle? Let's do. Someone's taking stuff out of the office.'

'He told me.'

'He makes this like huge fucking great fuss about it, calls the police. Someone stealing Phillip's addresses. I don't believe it. I'll tell you what I think, shall I?'

'What do you think?'

She ordered a second bottle. 'There's a quid pro quo.'

'Which is?'

She grabbed the bottle by the neck and poured it so it fizzed over the tops of the glasses, the froth running down the sides. She drank some, foraged in her tiny, shiny handbag the color of a cantaloupe, and offered me a pill.

'What is it?'

'Like a Quaalude, only better, second generation. Oh go on, take it,' she said. 'Quid pro quo. Right. We go back to your place and fuck our brains out.'

'And I was expecting Miss Marple.'

'Who?'

From downstairs I heard the piano player do some early Ellington. I kissed Pru's cheek. 'Tell me now and I'll show you my gun.'

She said, 'Look, I have to do a little business, OK? So the board meeting, right? There was a board meeting the week Phillip's Uncle Tommy Pascoe died, two days afterwards in fact. Is that what you wanted? Give me ten minutes, I'll be back. Like love the gun. Very *noir*.'

I squeezed her arm harder than I should; that turned her on too. The evening had turned into a cartoon. With an arch little wave, Pru Vane disappeared. Left me watching the crowd. I strolled out on to the stair landing and glanced into a dining room with candles on the tables; their reflection played in a sky-light overhead.

'Artie Cohen?' I turned and saw a tall man get up from a crowded table. He said my name again. I went in.

He was a good-looking, saturnine guy about fifty, neat beard, brown eyes, and he was holding out his hand. 'You probably don't remember me, but I'm Keir Cleary. Isobel's husband? Isobel, Lily Hanes's friend? We met in New York once.'

I shook his hand. He introduced me to some guys at his table – two French, a Brit, an American, a Russian – and they invited me to sit with them. Keir was an orthopedic surgeon with a sideline in real estate, he said, and he was eating with the guys in his consortium. I realized I was hungry. Keir must have noticed. He said why didn't I order.

I was conscious I had about ten minutes before Pru reappeared. A waiter brought a menu, I ordered some cheese and a glass of Merlot. Keir and his friends, jackets on the backs of their chairs, sleeves rolled up, discussed leases and profits, a six-part sell-and-buy deal they were celebrating, the shortage of decent space in London, the necessity of surveys and conveyancing deals. One of them mentioned rumors of a small downturn, a sell-off, another said it was temporary, insignificant, and they toasted themselves again. It was a foreign language, so I just sat and ate and listened in. I thought about the letter under the door and I leaned over to Keir. 'Ever come across the Joint Eurobank?'

'Yes,' said Keir. 'They're crooks.'

But Isobel suddenly arrived, breathless, face red, hair wet, said she had been kept in court late and ordered a glass of Champagne.

She kissed everyone at the table, then sat next to me. Keir was on her other side. Without turning away from me, she reached back and touched her husband's hand and I was jealous, of both of them.

Iz Cleary was prettier than I remembered, an impish woman, short hair, freckles, Irish accent. She told some very funny jokes, and I bought everyone some more wine and hoped Pru Vane had disappeared for good. While the men huddled and finished their business, Iz turned her chair so we were facing each other.

The candles on the tables flickered. The rain drummed on glass overhead. Isobel sipped her drink, looked around and smiled at me.

I said, 'So how about leaving your husband and marrying me?'

She laughed. 'You American guys don't beat around the bush, do you?'

'Not like here,' I said.

She wolfed down some bread and cheese now, then drank more Champagne. 'Tell me about it. I was in law school at New

Haven for a bit. Americans normally mean what they say. They say ABC, they mean it. The English, they say ABC, you say, oh I get it, it's ABC, and they burst out laughing. Sarcasm, diffidence, self-deprecation, lying, spying, betrayal. Of course, post-Diana, they, and I mean they – the non-verbal classes – have been released from all of this. Now they say everything. They're like Americans now. They spill their guts on the telly. They hold vigils for the hopeless. They talk about how they feel. We're a caring sharing nation now, we use words like proud, like Americans or John Bull Brits of a century ago. Outstanding, we cry. Proud to be you and me.' She laughed.

I said, 'What about you?'

'I'm Irish, not English.'

'It's so different?'

'You bet it is.'

'What's Lily?'

'Lily's a complicated woman, you know? She feels at home here and not at home. She loves that child – Beth, I mean, of course – to distraction but she's restless. She's crazy about you, Artie. In her way.'

'Yeah?' I was unconvinced.

'Yes.'

I felt like a kid. 'How do you know?'

'She talks to me. She sends me pictures.'

'What of?'

'Of you, you idiot. Look, we've known each other twenty-five years, I met her in the States, she came to London for the network, we shared a flat for a while, we worked for the cause.'

'What cause?'

She grinned. 'Peace and Love. Women's Rights. Anti-nukes. Anti-war. Amnesty. South Africa. Homeless. Black Panthers. Whatever there was. She's lovely, but she's troubled, Artie. Ease up on her, if you can. Meanwhile, come and have lunch with me tomorrow. Maybe I can help. I'll be in court.'

'You work much with the cops here?'

'A bit.'

'Guy name of Jack Cotton?'

'I've met Jack once or twice. In London, it's hard to avoid. Jack gets around.' She was only half sarcastic.

'Is he an OK guy?'

'He's a policeman. He's maybe a little right-wing for my taste, but by the nature of what he is, you'd expect it.'

'I'm a policeman. Was.'

'I know. But my friend's in love with you.'

'So you forgive me.'

'Look, Jack is a black man who's made his way, we're talking a pretty fucking racist country, OK? Cotton stands out. There are only three per cent of the police who are ethnic minority all told. Worse still, he's Jamaican.'

'So?'

'So around here, Jamaican means criminal. Yardies. Jack's got a tough row to hoe. If there's a black problem, Jack Cotton has to show his face. You've met his wife?' She pursed her lips.

'No. Should I?'

'Nina Cotton wouldn't be my first choice of port in a storm, but then you never know, do you?'

'You trust Jack?'

'As much as I trust any cop.' She gestured at the low-lit room full of wine-flushed people making happy talk. 'We can't really talk with these guys around, so why don't you meet me tomorrow? Give me your number. I'll call you as soon as I can break out. Meet me, Artie, OK? I want to talk to you about Lily.'

'You're busy later?'

'Yes.' Without turning around, she leaned back against Keir and blushed. 'The kids are all in the country and I expect to be busy.'

'Too bad.'

'Fuck off.' She laughed. 'Meet me tomorrow.'

I took Isobel's hand, which was small and warm. 'You've known Lily practically forever, Iz. Did you know Thomas Pascoe? His wife Frances? Did you know Phillip Frye was Pascoe's nephew?'

She picked up her glass and held it in front of a candle. 'Lily doesn't give a rat's ass about Phillip Frye.'

'Then tell me why Lily had Pascoe's picture in her kid's closet and how come I know if I ask her she about it she'll lie.'

Before Isobel answered, her husband reclaimed her attention. But not before I got a good look at her lucid brown eyes.

– 231 –

She was worried. Isobel was a woman with rosy skin, but when I mentioned Pascoe's picture, the color drained away, literally. A sheer film of sweat appeared on her forehead.

'What is it?' I said.

Iz shook her head. 'Just leave it until tomorrow. Just go back to where you're staying and we'll talk then.' She looked up and saw Pru Vane coming towards us. Iz leaned over and whispered, 'Stay away from Prudence Vane, Artie, OK? You tell her stuff, she'll use it. She'll mess you up, darling. She's poison.'

'Well, what's like eating Isobel?' Pru Vane said when we were in a taxi.

'Forget it.' I put my arm around her and said, 'Forget about it and tell me who's stealing Frye's stuff, the names, the contributors. Tell me.'

'You ask a fucking lot of stupid fucking questions, don't you, sweetheart? You drive a hard bargain,' she said.

I swear like a sewer, so does Lily. Everyone at home in New York swears plenty, but in London, it was an epidemic. 'Fuck' lived its own life here, adjective, verb, noun. There was enough of the Moscow puritan left in me that I was still startled by the mouth on Pru Vane.

We got to my place. I paid the taxi. She was all over me. By the time we got upstairs, she had half her clothes off. I was a sucker. She had a great body. She was on the floor now, naked, cross-legged, looking through her bag. She found a baggie smudged with white powder. Pru turned the bag inside out and rubbed the plastic along her gums.

I faked disinterest for a while. 'I'm getting bored, Pru, so why don't you tell me who stole Frye's address, OK?'

She licked the crumbs of cocaine off the plastic.

I crouched down next to her. 'Who is it?'

'It's bloody Phillip Frye.'

'Frye?'

'He's stealing his own stuff. Do we have to talk about Phillip?'

'Yes.'

'OK. He makes it look like someone's doing it, but he's faking the theft himself.'

'What for?'

'It's superb. A ruse. Gets him attention. He makes a fuss, calls the police. Free PR for the cause. Meantime, he plays fast and loose with the names. He leans on people who think the request is coming from somewhere else. From someone who stole the names.'

'The calls, the pressure, he does it himself?'

'Of course not. He has people.'

'For money.'

'What else?'

'That's extortion.'

'So? Do you think Phillip's incapable? You think that?'

'You're in love with Phil Frye and he fucked you over. Didn't he? He rejected you.'

'You're not listening. I don't care who Phillip fucks, he fucks everyone. He's obsessed. He'll take anything from anyone. It's a big deal here, this aid business, ever since she died. Diana, you know. Very competitive. I mean, Christ, Phil sent me on a course for philanthropists.' She lolled against the sofa now. It was the second time I'd heard about the course. Irina Kievskaya, now Pru Vane.

Pru sucked up the dope and put her hand in my pants. Then she giggled. 'I swear to God. Learn how to give. Learn how to sucker the rich, you ask me.' She climbed on me and said, 'It's like cool, you know what I mean? Like Phillip says, charity's the new rock and roll.'

It was three in the morning and Pru Vane lay on her side, naked, asleep, and I had been real careless. Sometime during the night we'd moved to the bed. I didn't remember much.

I got out of bed and looked back at her. Her hair was a mess. Face smeared with make-up. She said she was twenty-six. I was betting less. She looked like a kid. Like jailbait. Jesus, I thought, and yanked on some jeans, prodded her, got her up and made coffee.

She was hung-over and pissed off at me. I looked in the phone book and called a taxi, got her downstairs, sent her home. Not exactly romantic, but she was too drunk to care. For now. I went back to sleep for a few hours, woke up, saw the gun on the table and thought how much I hated it all.

I hated dealing with a Russian creep to get an illegal gun, I hated feeling vulnerable without a weapon and suspect having one. I hated knowing the language and not knowing it. I knew Phillip Frye was up to his tight ass in Tommy Pascoe's murder and would get a pile of dough out of Tommy's will. Frye ripped off his own contributors if I believed Pru Vane. He had offered Lily a job and Lily had jumped for him.

I believed Pru.

I pulled a blanket over my shoulders and stood in front of the window. It was raining. It was always raining. The phone rang. It was Sonny Lippert.

I said, 'What time is it?'

'What difference does it make?'

'Where are you, Sonny?'

'It's daytime, OK, New York City daytime, man, I'm at work like you should be, OK, now shut up and listen to me. You called me, you wanted to know about Leo Mishkin and some-body name of Kievsky?'

'Yeah.'

'Eduard Kievsky, right?'

'Yeah.'

'Yeah, well, you suspected right. Irina Kievskaya is Leo Mishkin's sister. Which makes Eddie Kievsky his brother-in-law. That what you wanted?'

'Which is why she resembles the kid.'

'What?'

'Nothing.'

'When are you coming home?'

Mishkin and Kievsky were connected. Tolya Sverdloff did business with Leo Mishkin. I felt swamped, stuck in the mud, and I said to Sonny, 'Find me Sverdloff if you can. Tell him I need him. And fast.'

Sonny was distracted. 'He's not mine to find.'

'He's in bad trouble, Sonny. Real deep,' I said, and thought: so am I.

A few hours later, I went out. Steel shutters were down on a couple of restaurants that faced the promenade. A pair of cops, bleary-eyed from lack of sleep – they'd been up half the night, one said, picking crud from the corner of his eye – inspected a damaged railing along the embankment. A couple of others unlocked a storage box, dragged out an inflatable boat and looked it over. More sandbags had appeared overnight, stacked neatly against the wall of the museum further down the promenade.

London looked rough. A police boat heaved up and down on the heavy river. Some workers appeared and started on the damaged railing. One of them grabbed his blue hardhat, but it blew off his head and into the water, where it bobbed up and down like a toy. I knew I'd been stupid with Pru Vane; she was loose now, like the hat in the river.

Jack Cotton showed up at the apartment around ten – my watch had stopped – and I followed him out and saw Tessa Stiles was in the car. She was looking at the cops working on the sandbags and the boat, and snickered. 'They've got boats like that stored all over London, and they reckon that's meaningful risk prevention in case of flood. Fools.'

Jack said, 'Get in.' We drove over the bridge. The traffic was a mess. We sat in the car, Jack and Tessa swearing and tense, me silent.

Up by the Parliament buildings, near the river, the cop cars were parked everywhere. A gang of TV people hovered close by. Sound men hugged their furry mikes against the wind.

Stiles leaned over the ledge of the Embankment. 'It's what I was telling you. It wasn't a hoax, not this time. Take a look.'

A small, brutal hole had been blown into the embankment wall just above the water line. Cops in uniform and plain clothes, and divers in rubber suits, were hanging over the edge. Hurriedly, some electricians rigged special lights. It was morning, but the sky was the color of graphite.

'Jack?'

'No one knows who set the device.'

'Is it bad?'

'Not in itself. It was a very small explosion, nobody was hurt, not yet. The old brickwork is really soft, some of it's already eroded. It's contained now, but when it blew, water flooded a tube tunnel. Underground. Subway to you,' he said.

'It's OK, you don't have to translate for me all the time,' I said.

Jack's mild stutter got worse when he was wired, and he said, carefully now, 'District Line. The weather gives this place a pounding.' He glanced at the Parliament building. 'Government doesn't like it when the water level rises around here,' he said, and a couple of cops near by laughed and gave Jack a thumbs-up.

Tessa Stiles had disappeared into the clutch of cops and reporters. I said to Jack, 'What's Tessa's business with this?'

'The river. Contingency planning. She always has her hand in.'

'You know who did it?'

Jack shook his head.

I said, 'So what's your business with it, Jack?'

He looked at me. 'You. I thought you might have some idea about this. Do you, Artie? Do you have any idea?'

'I don't know what you're talking about.'

Jack said, 'The creep who phoned it in was Russian.'

Chapter 28

'Someone murdered Pru Vane.' Isobel Cleary took off her wig. I met her later that day in a locker room at the Old Bailey courthouse and she looked plenty rattled. I had a bad taste in my mouth like someone stuck a pistol in it. I slept with Pru, I sent her home, she was dead. Jack Cotton didn't mention it that morning, but maybe he didn't know.

'How? When did it happen?'

Isobel was whispering. 'Late last night. This morning, really, early. She got home, someone was waiting, they beat her up. They took her to hospital. It didn't help. They say she had a lot of stuff in her system, coke, heroin, I'm not sure. No one's sure if she died from the beating or an overdose.'

'Any marks on her?' I thought of the Russian thugs who liked to cut their victims.

'I don't know. Do you know anything at all about this, Artie?

I was silent.

Around us in the hallway, people came up to Iz, tried to talk or joke, she forced a smile, pointed out famous judges and lawyers in black robes and crusty wigs to me, but her attention was somewhere else.

She hurried me into the street, then into a pub. A woman there looked up and waved eagerly.

I said, 'Who was that?'

'Nobody. Let's get out of here,' Isobel said, and went back outside where she snapped up a black umbrella, held it over us and said, 'Come on, Artie. Please.' We walked to a hotel near by.

The hotel lobby was full of tourists. Isobel skirted them, found a bar, sat at a table in a dim corner, ordered a bottle of white wine and sandwiches. 'Is this OK?' She draped her coat over the back of the chair, and asked for a cigarette. I ordered a beer.

Isobel wore a plain black suit and a white shirt; her face was creased with worry.

I lit her cigarette and said, 'Who killed Pru? What's going on?'

'She was with you last night, Artie. Pru's the kind of woman who puts herself in harm's way, but this was different. Someone hurt her. It made me think that everyone who comes into contact with Phillip Frye's organization gets into trouble.'

Everyone who came into contact with me, she meant.

Isobel put her hands on the table, palms up. 'I am scared for Lily, which is why I wanted us to meet.'

The food and wine came and Iz gobbled half a sandwich and gulped a glass of white wine. 'You heard about the bodies that washed up this morning?'

'What bodies?'

'This storm is much worse than they've said. There's flooding near the river. Some of the homeless are living down there.'

'Frye's shelters?'

She nodded. 'Keir's on a couple of boards of big property outfits, so he hears. From what I can tell, London has got itself into trouble over bad property deals. Everyone's lost money, the government as well. They were supposed to change the laws to keep some kind of handle on the market, but there were political contributions and hacks asked the wrong questions and foreigners came into London in droves and bought everything. Flats, houses, buildings, old warehouses, even the less desirable stuff and the prices went up. Like New York. Is that right, Artie, like New York?'

'Yeah. There's people say they're related.'

'Global markets, right?'

I thought of Sverdloff.

She said, 'The real panic buying in property started a few years ago. It's out of control now.' Iz stopped for breath, stubbed out her cigarette, pulled another one from my pack, tried to smile. 'I quit.'

'I can tell.'

She drank another glass of wine. 'The hotter the market got, the more people were squeezed on to the streets. It's become the dirty little secret of Britain's boom years. Anyway, my business makes me paranoid, and when I heard there were two dead men at Frye's new shelter because of flooding, I thought something's terribly wrong. I asked around. The shelters aren't safe.'

'Last night I said Lily had a picture of Thomas Pascoe in her closet, and you turned white. Iz?'

'Yes.'

'Why?'

'I met him a few times with Lily. I thought him an ass, a self-obsessed old man who had once lived the high life and had vague left-wing ideas, and he was arrogant. Felt he could do anything so long as it had a moral imperative. But he didn't deserve to die. I think you have a lead on some of this. Am I right?'

I thought of Geoffrey Gilchrist. 'Not a reliable one.'

'Use it.'

'I need money I haven't got to make it work.'

'I'll talk to Keir. Maybe he can help.'

'You wanted to talk about Lily.'

'If you can't forgive Lily, I don't know what she's done to you, not really, but if you can't love her anymore, at least help her. I want you to get Lily out of London. And Beth, of course. Take them home, Artie. Lily seems to believe Phillip Frye's operation is some sort of mission. She's in way over her head here.' She held my hand for a few seconds, and said, face tensing up. 'Please.'

'I'll try.' I pulled a notebook out of my pocket. 'Write down for me where the dead guys washed up. Write it down.'

'If you're going out there, get hold of Jack Cotton. Don't do this by yourself.'

'Frye's a creep, isn't he, Iz?'

'Yes. He's a man who likes mayhem. He's a man who thinks you can create something useful out of chaos.'

'You still haven't really told me why Lily having Pascoe's picture scared you. She knew him too well? She was involved?'

'Not him.'

'Who?'

'The wife.' She paused. 'Frances Pascoe.'

I picked up a rental car and a cellphone and drove uneasily on the wrong side of the road. I had no goddamn idea where I was headed, but I was full of Pru Vane's death; somewhere along the line someone would figure I'd been with her the night before. Someone was going to ask questions. I wanted Frye in a hurry now. After I left Isobel, I went to his office. He was out. I conned one of the girls and she told me he was at the new shelter on the river where two men drowned and gave me the address. The same address Isobel gave me.

On the radio, people talked about politicians I didn't know and told jokes I didn't get. Outside, as I rubbed the cold side-window clear, an ugly waste land stretched for miles. I peered at a sign. Woolwich Road.

The windshield wipers beat a counterpoint to the rain, as I drove past broken streets and shitty houses. Once in a while I saw a grocery store, a pub, a hardware store; they were grim and shabby, some of them boarded up against the storm.

At one of the stores I pulled up and went looking for some smokes. An Indian guy in a yellow sweatshirt sold me the cigarettes, but he was occupied with a small TV and a cricket game in another continent where the sun shone.

Through the rain, I saw the river. The conical top of a skyscraper pierced the gloom. A sign pointed to the Thames Flood Barrier and I pulled into the visitors' lot and got out.

I walked up to the river. Faint shapes rose out of the water, a row of curved steel caps, like hoods over giants' stoves. They stretched across the river until they disappeared into the fog. I walked a while, then glanced at the map. Hiroshima Promenade, Nagasaki Walk, they were labelled. Then I walked in the other direction and I could see where the water had come up over the banks and stained a cement bench. There was steel under the grass here and I figured it was some kind of flood wall.

It was raining lightly and I thought about Tessa Stiles, then the rain came down heavier and I ran for the car.

Further east along Woolwich Road, I found Frye's shelter. Westminster Industrial Estates, the sign said. I almost missed it.

Fog rolled in so thick now I couldn't see the road in front of me. I thought I saw an airplane, but the airplane disappeared into the fog. Out of nowhere, as I turned into Frye's place, a truck loomed up. I could just make out it was a TV van. Frye's warehouse was where the dead bodies washed up, Isobel Cleary said. The brakes shrieked. I jammed on my own brakes and got out of the car.

A TO LET sign dangled from a pole in front of the six-story warehouse at the dead end of a narrow road. It had a corrugated iron roof and exterior stairs like a fire escape. I left the car where it was and walked.

The warehouse itself was near the edge of the river; there was an old jetty, crumbling now, as far as I could see. The building had been freshly painted, but there were already damp stains on it. A hand-painted sign announced it was a shelter provided by HOME. A truck was backed up to a loading dock. Figures in green slickers were unloading a pile of flat plastic bundles, dragging them out of the truck, dumping them on the raw ground. Frye's Life Bubbles. They lay, limp and oily in the rain, like used condoms.

Water sloshed on the ground in the courtyard where more trucks and vans were parked. More women – I recognized some of them from Frye's office – unloaded crates. Mattresses and cooking pots were covered by plastic sheets.

Nobody noticed me. Around the side of the building, I dragged an empty crate under a window and climbed up. There was dull light from inside the window, the scuffle of feet, the sound of hammering, the drip of water. I scrambled on to my feet. With my sleeve, I scrubbed at the mist on the window and looked in.

Under the window, a woman sat at a makeshift desk and talked frantically into a phone. She sat cross-legged on her chair. She arched her back as if to get relief from the stiff chair that was too small for her and put her hand in the hollow of it. The phone was tucked under her chin. With the other hand, she lifted the red hair off her neck. I shifted to one side. If she turned around, she'd see me. I didn't want her to see me, not here.

Frye appeared. He wore black jeans and a shirt with purple stripes and white collar and cuffs. He sat on the edge of the desk and leaned over her, then whispered to her. His demeanor changed, became intimate. He reached down and rubbed her back. Christ, I thought, Lily was in it, whatever it was, up to her armpits.

– 241 –

I don't know if Frye saw me. I stepped back off the crate, turned, pulled my jacket over my head – the rain was coming down in buckets – and ran for the rental car. It wasn't just the rain that made me run; I didn't want a fight with Phillip Frye, not then, not when he was rubbing Lily's back.

I could wait. I wanted Frye on his own, stealing, extorting, setting up some patsy, like I knew he set up Pru Vane but couldn't prove. First I had to get Lily out of the way, out of Frye's path. I couldn't make a move, not until then.

I drove away from the shelter, returned the rental car, went to Gilchrist's house and picked open the lock on his front foor. I went looking for a lead.

The files were tied with string and I worked my way through them, but there were only tidy stacks of bills and letters and notes for a memoir. The house was clean as if experts had worked it over. There wasn't a scrap of paper that gave up anything about its owner. The albino goldfish stared at me.

While I turned over the files, I listened for a car or cab. I poked around his closet, where you could smell tobacco on the tweed, but there was nothing else. But Gilchrist was a smart old bastard. He would know I'd been in his house, and that's what I wanted.

I wanted him alert. I wanted him in touch with Kievsky and the rest of them. He was a messenger boy; he could send my message for me. I wanted them – whoever wanted me – out in the open where I could see them. London had too many secrets.

Five minutes later, after I'd locked the house and walked to the end of the street, Gilchrist showed up in a taxi. I cornered him.

For a minute he fought his umbrella. I grabbed it from him and opened it and held it over us with one hand. With the other, I held his arm. 'Give me something, Geoff.'

'Is it a threat, dear? What shall I give you, Artie?'

'Something I can work with. Some kind of information. I'll get you money when I can, but I need a handle on this case, so unless it was all bullshit about my father and you and me, give me something to work with here. I'm drowning here. You get it? You want to repay the family, here's your chance.'

The umbrella turned inside out in the wind. I fixed it, and while I pulled the metal struts into place, Gilchrist put his hand in his pocket. I gave him the umbrella. He held up a keyring, removed the keys and gave it to me.

'Frankie Pascoe gave me this, actually,' he said. 'Sent it to me as a little gift. Perhaps it looks familiar to you,' he said. 'Does it look familiar, Artie? It's something, isn't it, dear? Take it, and let me give you some lunch Thursday, all right?' he said. 'The Reform Club,' he added, and hurried up the steps into his house.

I looked at the keyring in my hand. From it dangled a miniature version of the bronze begging hands.

Chapter 29

The white-hot desert sun beating down. A big aquamarine pool, shape of a kidney. Golf on emerald-green links. The awesome purple crack in the planet that was the Grand Canyon, and Sigfried and Roy with the white tigers, and Shirley Bassey, Tom Jones, Wayne Newton. Memories of Sinatra's rat pack and the *thrill* of the slots when you scored.

The rain beat down, gray rain, gray streets, and the cabbie regaled me with his annual trips to Vegas past and present. 'Rio Suites,' he purred. His ambition was to stay at Rio Suites. Or the Bellagio. I played with the keyring Gilchrist gave me like worry beads.

'Give me something, Geoff,' I'd said and he'd given me the keyring with the begging hands. There was a connection between Warren and Tommy and Frye. Blood connected them. Pru Vane worked for Frye and Pru was dead. As the cab ploughed through the rain, I felt myself dragged down in it all. The tangled relationships seemed to spread like dry rot. Lily was in this with Phillip Frye and I didn't know how to talk to her. Did Warren know how it played, was that why Gilchrist sent me? I was on my way back to Warren Pascoe's studio in a hurry.

The driver scanned the street, then pulled up at the building where Warren worked. 'You sure this is it?'

'Yeah. Can you wait for me?'

He lit a cigarette, pulled a fat brochure from under the seat, waved it at me – it was a brightly colored Vegas brochure – and said, 'Sure, mate.'

'Warren? Warren Pascoe?' I shouted into the studio and my voice hit the concrete walls and died. A piece of paper landed on my face, it was soft and wet, it felt alive as it blinded me. I tore it off. The old wood floor creaked under my feet.

The building was silent except for the echo of my own feet. I took the gun out of my belt and put it in my jacket pocket. I fumbled on the wall and found a light switch, but nothing happened.

'Warren? You here?' A faint streak of artificial light came through the windows high up – a streetlight, the beam of a passing car – otherwise it was black as pitch. There was the incessant sound of dripping water. One of the windows was open and I could smell the wetness of the place.

I flicked my lighter on, found the work table and a piece of a candle on it. I got the candle lit.

In the shadowy light, the half-made sculptures made eerie shapes, entwined arms reaching up, a torso draped in damp pale cloth, the heads smiling down at me from the high shelf.

'Warren?'

No one answered. I took out my gun. Somewhere in the building, very faint, like a signal from another planet, a talk radio station started up; in the silent studio I could hear it, indistinct, polite. No human sounds; only a radio. Thunder rumbled outside. Outside were miles of empty streets, waste ground, demolition crews, cranes, the swollen river and the rain.

I picked up the candle and worked my way around the place, my back to the wall; the candle gave me enough light so that before I stumbled on the body, I saw the blood.

Where the floor sloped down, water seeped in and formed a puddle that was black with dirt, red with blood. Warren Pascoe was lying in it, a crumpled figure, wrapped in a sheet of plastic. When I touched it, water poured off the slick surface.

Soaked, he was hard to move. When I got the plastic off his head, in the creepy half-light, Warren Pascoe's face turned into Thomas Pascoe's, the head bobbing in water, the swimming pool slick with blood in the basement of the Middlemarch.

Grand Guignol, Lily said I called Thomas Pascoe's murder. She was wrong. I never thought death was a joke. Not then, not here, three thousand miles from home in this stone-cold place. First Pru Vane, now Warren. There was nothing to make me laugh here.

I tried to untangle more of the plastic sheet, then the old tweed coat. Warren was dead. Small, bald, the skin waxy. I stared at the face some more. I saw the family resemblance even better now: the distinctive Pascoe nose – Thomas had it, so did Phillip Frye – the long forehead. I replaced the plastic and backed off.

I wanted out. Gilchrist as good as sent me to Warren's and Warren was dead. I left him on the floor. The scene was intact. I headed for the door. Then I tripped. A plaster head crashed on to the floor. It split at the mouth so the sweet smile came apart. The plaster was damp, I could smell it.

Water came up over my ankles and seeped into my shoes. I tried to pick the head up, but it had cracked into two pieces, and I put them carefully on a work bench. I held the two halves together. I held the candle closer to the head.

It was a cast of the homeless man who had attacked Phillip Frye. The man with the cleft palate who fell in the mud. A dead man, Frye had said. Won't last the night. The man I'd seen in the shelter the day before had been Warren's last model. Or maybe I hallucinated.

Did Warren use him after he died? Did Warren Pascoe get bodies from Frye's shelters? Was that what Gilchrist meant when he tossed me the keyring with the begging hands? Why did he send me here? Get me out of the way? Who gave Geoffrey Gilchrist his orders?

Suddenly, a leak opened up in the ceiling. Rain poured in.

I was drowning. Somewhere, I lost my balance. Someone pushed me or I fell. I lost my footing and my head was on the floor. The floor. Sidewalk. Steps. Cold stone.

There was the taste of blood. Sewage. In my mouth and nose. I could smell the river, the fetid smell of oil and garbage, feel the wind, taste the menace. It was dark. Someone banged my head on the ground again, and now I was only half conscious.

My head was under water. I saw everything drift by and I was freezing cold. I thought: If I pass out, it's over. I thought how cold it was. Hypothermia, isn't that what they called it on TV when little kids fell through the ice somewhere? Minnesota. Canada. Somewhere. Where was I?

I was cold. My lungs ached. I thought about the swimming pool out back of Kievsky's house up on the hill. The river. A lake. I thought someone dragged me down some slimy steps to the river. I had seen steps when I was out walking, steps, metal moorings, floating pontoons, tugs, boats, a houseboat. The Beach Boys' 'Little Surfer Girl' ran in my head.

Staten Island Ferry, fishing off Long Island, my sailboat in pieces on the roof of my building in New York, the pool at the Middlemarch where they got Tommy Pascoe. Frankie in the bathtub, full of gin, dying. Frankie naked in the swimming pool.

I heard the smack of water against a seawall, felt the stone surface under me; it was slick with shit and dead vegetables. I could feel metal. I couldn't move. My head was under water. Someone yanked it up by the hair, then shoved it back. Lungs hurt.

I couldn't move. I realized they'd dragged me out of Warren's studio, down to the river, banged me around good, then dumped me back in the studio. They wanted someone to find me. Things went gray. My body relaxed and I tried to breath in, except there was water inside me. I was drowning.

Chapter 30

Water streamed out of me, mouth, nose. It choked me. Arms holding me let go. When I forced my eyes open, I saw a concrete ceiling. A skylight where rain drummed on the murky glass. Plaster casts of dead men, covered in cheesecloth. I was in Warren's studio. A bucket on the floor was half full of water. Blood in it. My blood. It floats, I thought, looking at it.

Somehow I crawled out, down the stairs, into the street and found the taxi still waiting. The driver was fast asleep, the Vegas brochure over his face. I tapped on the window.

He dragged me into the cab. Unloaded me at some hospital. There was some change in my pocket and I gave him everything I had. The creeps didn't take my money, but the gun was gone. My passport was gone.

The next time I looked around, I was in the corridor of an emergency ward that resembled something out of Dickens. The stink of the linoleum. Carbolic. I tried to crawl off the steel gurney, then half-fell, half-sprawled on a plastic chair. My legs shook.

Half-conscious, I stayed on the chair alongside the poor, drunk and hopeless; you could smell the misery. It smelled like Moscow.

Snatches of conversation drifted towards me, then away. People cracked their bones slipping, a doctor said. His lungs fucked, someone else muttered. Bad weather. Damp. TB on the rise again. People coughing. Carbon monoxide. Train stuck in a station. Station flooded. No air.

The gabble of anxious voices surrounded me, the quibbling, contentious sounds of a public hospital. I was too tired to care. Maybe I dozed. When I finally came to the surface, standing over me, in a Burberry raincoat the size of a tent, was Tolya Sverdloff.

'You set me up.'

Tolya looked at me. 'Don't be an idiot.'

I grabbed his arm. 'Swear on your kids.'

'Yes. On my kids.'

I believed him because I had to.

We were in a big car, a Rolls-Royce, me wrapped in a blanket, Tolya next to me. I was shaking. I could hear my own teeth. The soft leather in the back smelled nice. He said again, in Russian this time, 'Bastards.'

I looked at him. He looked lousy, the skin gray, a gash over his one eye that someone stitched in a hurry, a purple bruise on the other; the bruised eye was half shut.

'You look like shit,' I said. 'What happened?'

'Makes two of us. They banged you around some, put your head in a bucket. Not fun guys.'

'Who were they?'

'The usual creeps.'

'Russian? Ukrainian?'

'Maybe.'

'How do you know?'

'Someone at the hospital found a list of numbers on you. My cellphone was one of them. I got into London a few hours ago. They had the driver's name, and I got to him. We talked Las Vegas. He showed me where it happened. The style was familiar. They were stupid, these creeps; they went drinking in a bar near by to get out of the rain. I found them.'

'How many?'

'Two.'

'Jesus, Tol, what time is it? How long have I been like this?'

He looked at his Rolex. 'One a.m. Five, six hours you're like this, I guess. Maybe more.'

'The same assholes that killed Warren Pascoe and Prudence Vane came for me?'

'Who is Prudence Vane?'

'Never mind. How come they didn't kill me?'

'Luck. You're an American. They don't want extra problems maybe.'

'They're alive?'

Tolya didn't answer.

'Answer me.'

'Don't ask me, OK? What's the difference? They were nobody. Small little people.'

'Where are we?'

'My car.'

'We're going someplace?'

'Hotel.'

'How come? You got apartments here, buildings, the one I'm using. We can go there.'

'No.'

I hurt worse now I was really conscious. I mumbled, 'Tell me some jokes.'

He told me some very old jokes in Russian about sex and politicians and cheap sausages. The blinding rain made it impossible to see, and by the time he finished the jokes, we were in a hotel garage.

There was a glossy brochure on a table. River Palace, five stars. Canary Wharf. Tolya stood in the doorway to an adjoining room. 'You want a doctor?'

'I had enough doctors.'

Tolya shoved me towards the bathroom. Out of the window I could see the river. It was high and bruised, the rain drove down on it and made it pitch right up against the embankment. Somewhere in the distance, I could hear the waa waa of the sirens.

In the bathroom that filled softly up with steam, I lay in the tub, hot water up to my neck. It took all my energy to soak a washcloth and spread it over my face. After a while, my frozen joints began to thaw. Tolya squatted on the toilet holding a bottle of brandy, pouring it into big glasses. He said, 'Drink,' and I drank and said, 'Gimme a smoke, OK?'

He went into the other room and came back with a carton, an ashtray, his gold lighter.

I looked at him. 'You're in trouble, man. Aren't you?'

He said, 'I'm in trouble? You should talk,' but he didn't laugh.

'You do business with Leo Mishkin and Leo is Eddie Kievsky's brother-in-law.'

He reached up to a radio on a shelf and turned it to a music station. 'We will speak English now, but softly,' he said. 'And I will order some food.'

There were no querulous medics, no stinking creeps, no radio voices. Just the lovely liquid piano, Oscar Peterson and his trio and Rogers and Hart. Oscar played 'I'll Take Manhattan.'

The steam was thick on the mirrors and ceiling. My lungs were still sore.

After I got out of the bathtub, I found a thick terry-cloth robe and put it on. I went into Tolya's room, which connected with mine. A waiter rolled a table in; it was loaded with food – soup, roast chicken, hot rolls, heavy Barolo. I couldn't lift the spoon. I stumbled back into my room and on to the bed, and switched on the TV.

On the tube, a guy with a big nose, curly hair and a pinky ring came on and began interrogating a couple of politicians. Was there flooding near the Dome? Had the excavation for the Dome damaged the old tidal walls? I never heard an interviewer so rough in my life. He commented on the guests' ages and ailments and frailties, and I thought, Jesus, you'd never get a New York cop to go one on one with him for a million bucks after taxes. But it made me laugh, and laughing hurt. I switched off the set and turned the radio back on. I fell asleep just before dawn with only Oscar playing faintly from the radio.

When I woke up, it was dark again. I reached for a light. The door opened.

'What time is it?'

'Six o'clock,' Tolya said. I had slept through the tag end of the night and most of the day after. He said, 'You are feeling better?'

'I'm good.' I sat up. Reached for my jeans, felt in the pockets, then got out of bed in a panic. My passport was gone.

'I fix,' said Tolya. 'Tomorrow.'

I looked at him. 'Yeah, OK.'

'Now we party.'

'Party?'

'Eat. Party. Meet people. Makes us feel good, see what we hear, who we see, have fun. I'll call Lily.'

'No.'

'Don't be one giant asshole, Artyom. This girl loves you. You need her.'

'Mind your own fucking business. You have no idea what you're taking about.'

'We go out together then, you, me.'

'Why are we talking English?'

He shrugged. 'Between possibility of Russian bastards listening in or British asshole, I pick British asshole.'

'I need some clothes.'

'Clothes are here. I sent driver already.' He pulled on his cashmere blazer. 'Let's go to party.'

The windshield wipers beat the panes, Tolya's beefy driver drove carefully and the car rolled smooth as cream down the road. My ribs were sore. Tolya handed me his phone and I tried Lily because I was scared for her. Missed her. There was no one home. I left a message with Isobel Cleary.

On the back seat was a pile of papers. All the papers carried Pru Vane's murder. I scanned them fast. No one mentioned me. I had disappeared.

We cruised London a while, stopping in a couple of fancy hotel bars. More than before I had the sense of a place that changed at night – you pulled up out of the dark, wet, vast city, and light spilled out of bars and pubs and restaurants, and everywhere, people knew Tolya. Hands reached out for him. Booze appeared. At a restaurant with stained-glass windows, we ate Chateaubriand so rare it was practically alive. At a fancy nightclub in a townhouse, we ran into Eddie Kievsky, who shook my hand and showed Sverdloff the Fabergé egg. He kept it in his pocket. Kievsky was smooth; Sverdloff looked uneasy, and we moved on.

The car pulled away and a few minutes later, I said to him, 'You have any ready cash, Tolya?'

He laughed, but bitterly, and said in Russian, 'Big picture is, I'm broke.'

Tolya Sverdloff liked the night. He liked to work it, and he was never so broke or so drunk he couldn't enjoy himself. He put his ear to the ground, he said; listening for news, gossip, information, entertainment. 'At night, people looking for contacts,' he said. He switched constantly from Russian to English and back, and as he got drunker, his Russian got better and his English fell apart.

In the second club, a casino with mauve silk walls, he listened to a woman in a green dress. Even while he put the make on her, he listened sympathetically. Then we got back in the car and sped down the embankment towards Docklands, Canary Wharf, Isle of Dogs. I knew my way better here. I could follow the routes.

Tolya talked. He had a piece of apartment buildings along the Thames down to Teddington and up to the Barrier, he crowed. He talked about property like it was sex. Manhattan on the Thames, he said. London's Hong Kong. But I knew him. He was nervous. We stayed north of the river most of the time, the other side from the apartment on Butler's Wharf. Over here, this side, the north side of the river, Sverdloff said, was a boom town in a boom town, Tolya said.

East from Tower Bridge all the way to the estuary, he added. Plenty of room left. Isle of Dogs. Surrey Docks. Silvertown. Millennium Mills.

We drove, he talked. There were thousands of acres of eerie landscape, a few decayed remnants of the massive Royal Docks, the waterways, canals where the big ships once unloaded. Once, there were chemical plants and rubber processing and no one cared how toxic any of it was, not then, when the chemical manufacturers came in the 1870s. There were railheads next door and a ton of money to be made. For a hundred years, even more, there had been a seething, belching, filthy, noisy life to this place; now it was creepily quiet. You wondered how much toxic crap remained in the soil, the riverbed, the air.

A few skyscrapers loomed. There was some open space, but the landscape was half finished, the parks rough, the buildings covered with scaffolding. The apartment houses looked like Lego. Sverdloff showed me the Tate and Lyle plant at the edge of the river. 'Sugar,' he said. 'My great grandfather traded sugar in Petersburg.'

Through the wet car window, he watched closely. He pointed out the Millennium Dome, a huge erector set of a monument, a flying saucer set upside down, legs in the air.

Foreigners liked it here, he said. They felt happiest here. They could fly in and out fast. Short-haul airports. Private strips. Heliports. Marinas. Here was a whole new city dedicated to skyscrapers, money and tax breaks. Here, in the slick apartments and anonymous office buildings and the brass and glass hotels and restaurants, among the babble of foreign voices, England seemed to disappear.

The façade of the massive hotel was copper colored. The doorman, rigged out in a Tsarist uniform, looked like an extra from a Mosfilm epic. He spun the door for us, and tipped his fur hat to Sverdloff.

In the lobby, nightclub, casino, all of them jammed, there were Russian voices. Rich Russians. Russians circling the tables, tossing down chips for bets like they were candy. Sverdloff reached casually in his pocket, found a couple of hundred pounds, picked up a few chips, then tossed them on the roulette table.

'I thought you were broke.'

'Don't be so bourgeois, Artyom.'

Then he hit. He picked up the money and stuffed it in his pocket and moved on.

Tolya glanced around and said, 'At night, people take off their faces. No illusion. Everything is on table.'

He took a corner table and ordered wine. A band played elevator muzak.

I said, 'So we learned something from the night? We learned the birch trees are weeping, or what? Can you fucking return from Planet Russian Fantasy and talk to me? Why don't you tell me about your so-called bank and the foreclosures, Tolya? It's Eddie Kievsky's bank. Isn't it? You can drop the bullshit act.'

I bought too much, Artyom,' he said in English. 'All over Docklands I buy in Eighties, early Nineties, when was dying here. Good stuff. Bad stuff. Doesn't matter, I buy cheap. Ninety-eight, Russia on its knees, rouble falls apart, I am laughing. My money is in property. Now the market is swollen, fat, bloated.' His voice fell.

I kept quiet.

'Say someone pulls plug. Say real-estate market tumbles.

Rumors here. Rumors there. Market goes belly up, everything goes down like dominoes. It was plan. Listen to me.'

'Is that what the foreclosure notices were about?'

'Maybe. I'm trying to fix something, OK?'

'Something here?'

'Here, yes. Mob chiefs – all of them, Russian, Jap, Chinese, Mafia – two, three years ago, they met in Beaune to divide Europe, no one even noticed, the locals were at a goddamn wine auction.' He laughed mirthlessly. 'The Russians asked for Britain. Russians always like London, I was already in. I already buy Docklands, land, building, apartment, office.'

'You were in on it?'

'Sure. I'm real-estate guy, I'm in. We borrow from banks we also own.'

'Russian banks? Eddie Kievsky's banks?'

'Yes. Now market is volatile, up, down, up.'

'You're telling me the banks foreclose on purpose?'

'We sell a little. Markets get nervous. We sell some more. We take financial reporter to nice lunch at Pont de la Tour. Discuss overbuilding on river. Discuss overheated market. Article appears, maybe *FT*, *Herald Tribune*.'

'Christ, so you fuck with the market and start all over again?'

He looked nervous, twisting his head constantly.

I said, 'Eddie Kievsky makes you nervous.'

'Yes.'

'You knew all along he was Leo Mishkin's brother in law?'

'Sure.'

'When I got to London, to your apartment, there was a dummy with my face on it. It was a message to stay away from you? A message for me. Who from?'

He turned away. 'Kievsky's creeps. I'm sorry.'

'You're in bed with these guy, Tolya? You do business with them?'

'I did.' Tolya switched back to Russian. 'I am trying to fix it now, but it's hard to put the genie back in her bottle. Listen to me. Tomorrow I've got to go back to Moscow. See the kid, OK. I got a problem. They came for me, they beat him up again. Knocked his teeth out. How's he going to work as an actor without his teeth? I'm bad luck right now. Stay away. Go home to New York.' He leaned in my face. 'Go home.'

'What about Phillip Frye? Is he also in bed with Kievsky?'

'Kievsky gave him money for his charity.'

'What's he been giving Kievsky?'

'I'm working on it.'

We finished the night in the hotel strip joint. It was called the Sugar Reef. One wall was made of glass. On the other side was a huge pool. There was a wave machine and colored lights, neon fish and make-believe coral reef and strands of seagrass that waved seductively to the lights and music.

Tolya took a front-row seat, put his face up against the glass, was transfixed. The girls in the pool were got up like mermaid or fish. They stripped in the pool, then bobbed up above the water line for tips.

Customers threw the girls bills and they caught them in their hands or fins or sometimes their teeth. More guys, eyes moist, put money at the end of toy fishing reels like bait. I laughed. Tolya shoved an elbow in my ribs. He takes his strippers serious, as he informed me a long time back when we were in a Brighton Beach club in Brooklyn and I made the mistake of laughing at the girls. I asked for Scotch; he ordered the bottle.

A girl with enormous melons hung on her chest smooched him through the glass. He raised his eyebrow, grinned at a naked woman with a tail who swam up alongside the other babe and kissed the glass. Tolya leaned forward, his face dimpling, and kissed her back.

I put my hand on the glass. A lobster swam up to me and winked. Tolya leaned over and kissed her, then turned to me and stuffed the thick wad of cash he won earlier in my hand. He said softly, 'Will this buy you the information you want?'

I thought about Gilchrist. 'Yes,' I said. 'So tell me, these guys, Mishkin, Kievsky, tell me yes or no because I'm getting nervous here, man, did they kill people we both know about? Are you in business with them, in or out?'

He got up to go. 'This is problem for me, Artyom. I must go now. I will call you.'

'In or out?'

'Half in, half out.'

Chapter 31

My passport lay on Jack Cotton's bare metal desk at his station house next to a crude poster. I had slept badly after I left Sverdloff at the strip club and went back to the apartment. I dreamed too much and couldn't remember what I dreamed. A polite young guy in uniform showed up the next morning and said Jack couldn't come himself, but he had something for me.

I picked my passport up. 'Thank you.'

He said, 'You'll need a new one. This one's fucked.' It was stained with water. I leaned against the desk.

'Sit down, Artie, OK. We have to talk.'

'I don't want to talk, Jack. I'm on vacation. Remember? I'm a tourist.'

'You're an American. All Americans want to talk.' He pushed the red and gold Dunhills towards me.

'Fuck you.'

He grabbed my wrist. 'Sit down. Please. And listen to me.'

I sat down. 'I'm listening.'

Jack Cotton said, 'Prudence Vane is dead. It turns out you were out with her the night before. People saw you, man. Warren Pascoe is murdered. Your passport turns up at his studio. We find a pair of Russians near by, one also dead, the other as good as. I get a message from a casualty unit, they've got an American. Now, I never mentioned your name when we heard about the Vane woman. Or Warren Pascoe's death. Or the Russians. None of this is my territory, but I covered for you. You're in London, what, five, six days, Artie, and people die.'

I looked at the cup Cotton's assistant brought me and said, 'What is this shit?'

'Tea.'

'Please.'

'You want coffee instead?'

'I don't want anything.'

Quietly, Cotton said, 'I'm not saying anything about anything, but help me out here, Artie, man, OK?' He reached over and shut his door with his foot. Jack Cotton wore black suede shoes with rubber soles. He took the thick mug and drank the tea himself. 'We're on the same side, Art.'

'Are we? Can I go?'

'No. You asked me to help you out on Phillip Frye. We know he stinks. I want us to work on this. We will get him if you work with me.'

'Especially if he's faking the theft of his own address book so he can extort his own contributors.'

Jack looked up. 'Christ, Artie, is that what it is?'

'That's what Pru thought.'

He said, 'She told you?'

'Yes.'

'You'd testify?'

I didn't answer. I said, 'You got a pal at the morgue?'

'I need one.'

'A guy with a cleft palate that lived in one of Frye's shelters, brain tumor, liver disease, they must have paper on him, ask when he died, and if any of Warren's models came via Frye's shelters.'

'My God. Frye's supplying bodies?'

'Yeah.'

'You think Warren was in the middle of this?'

'A sideshow.'

'But Frye's contributors ain't gonna be happy if he was supplying homeless dead guys for Warren's art. Least we can hope for is getting Frye some lousy publicity.'

'I'll call you tomorrow, Jack. I'll have some stuff for you. Probably we can do business.'

'You want a lift?'

'I'm all right.'

'Do you think, Artie, I should put someone on Phillip Frye straight away?'

'It's your call. Me, I wouldn't. I'd give him another couple days, see if he jumps overboard all by himself.'

'Anything else?'

'I hear Philly's having a big party tonight, and I got myself an invite, I figured they might cancel because of Pru's death, but I checked. So you want to be my date?'

Jack smiled. 'A lot of excellent women will attend.'

I grinned. 'How old before we outgrow this shit?'

Jack said, 'When our dicks drop off.'

'So what's the poster?'

Jack leaned back in his chair. 'I'm thinking of quitting this.' He gestured at the room. 'I've been putting the word out quietly.'

'You want to tell me about the poster?'

He reached over to the desk and unrolled it. It was a rough drawing in crayon that showed a black cop with Asian features. It was addressed to the 'Eleven Black and Asian Cops' and said they should have their heads cut off.

Jack tore it in half. 'Forget it,' he said. 'I'm way past this kind of shit, you know? Hey, I had a boss who told me straight out – I mean, we're having breakfast – he says most black men are uneducated and uneducable and because there's no overt violence in Britain like there is in America, there's only a simmering rage. He said, you give me any seven-year-old black male, I can write his future for you right now because he doesn't have one.'

'Jesus.'

'Yeah, well, fuck them all, Art, you know. I'm busy with other stuff. So one more thing.' He picked up a thick brown envelope and opened it, then pulled out a gun.

'What's that?'

'You don't have to say anything, OK, just take it as from a friend, which I am, but they picked up this weapon near Warren Pascoe's studio. A Gluck. Brand new. Never been used. No serial number. Sadly for us, the prints got wiped off.'

'Thanks, Jack. Thank you.'

'I didn't hear that, so if you know anything about it, don't tell me, just think about it. OK?'

'OK.'

Gilchrist's club was in a building on a grand scale, high ceilings, pillars, beautiful woodwork, a library, men in leather armchairs. Soft voices. Old books. Gilchrist sat in front of a fire.

The flames were bright, warm. He held out his hands.

I said, 'So the KGB kept it all going for you. All this.'

He laughed merrily. 'Absolutely. Fees paid, post collected, friends memorialized even. If I asked for flowers to be sent to a funeral, it was done. They understood. It was all much more banal and much more surreal than people imagined, but I suspect you know that. It's in your blood.'

I sat down next to him. For a moment he seemed lost in his history. 'Do you know, Artie, that there was an occasion when I was summoned by the conductor of the KGB house band. Someone had discovered I had a liking for swing music, and could play a little clarinet. They were keen on Glenn Miller, you see.' He hummed 'In the Mood' and looked for a waiter.

I looked around the room, then at Gilchrist; it didn't get a lot more surreal than this, and I leaned closer to him and watched the fire. I pulled the cash Sverdloff gave me out of my pocket and put it on the low table in front of us. Geoff picked it up slowly, then put it in his pocket.

'Listen, Geoff, I took your previous advice. I went to see Warren Pascoe.' I tossed his keyring with the bronze hands on the table. 'And Warren was dead as his models. I don't know if you sent me to Warren Pascoe's to fucking set me up or not, or whose errand boy you really are, and I don't really give a crap right now. I got you some money. So either you have something to tell me or not.'

Gilchrist said, 'I sent you to Warren because I think Warren knew where the bodies were buried, so to speak. I didn't set you up. If someone followed you from my house, I am sorry. I want you to believe me.' He leaned forward and added, 'I don't want to lose you. Can't I get you a drink?' He rose from the chair and padded across the carpet.

Suddenly, it was the other Gilchrist, the Geoff of my childhood, the sprightly man in his forties who got up out of the old man's body. He was light, easy, agile. I thought he might do a little dance step on his way across the floor.

I saw Frank Sinatra do that once at a concert a few years before he quit singing. He was already an old man, but he got up on stage and pulled his own fabulous youth out of a hat and, for one number, sang like he was forty. I miss Frank.

Gilchrist disappeared into another room, then came back with a waiter in his wake. There was Scotch for me and brandy for him, and a bowl of potato chips that he placed on the table between us.

'You always liked snacks as a boy, I think. Have I got that right? You ate all my Twiglets,' he said.

Animated, Gilchrist sipped his drink. He looked at me as if he could divine some secret in my face, could find something he'd lost. 'I said I owed you. I meant it. I'm not sure I would have managed those first couple of years in Moscow without your father's kindnesses.'

'No more nostalgia, please.'

'I never thanked him.' He craned his neck towards the door.

'Waiting for someone?'

'Always. I'm not privy to everything that goes on. I'm an errand boy, as I'm sure you've worked out. But I do errands for all of them, you see. I take whatever I can get from them, the creeps, as you call them. The other side too. Everyone's terribly worried about the Russian mafia, so-called, and after all, who knows the Russians as well as I? I'm quite good on the new mafia, you'd be surprised, an expert witness, actually.'

I looked into the fire.

'None of them trusts me particularly, but they can't give me up entirely and with what time I've got, I thought I'd help myself to a few of the goodies. I was always rather good at getting information.'

My pulse started racing. Someone in the corner of the room, someone with too much muscle for such a civilized venue, was watching us. I shifted my chair out of his sight lines. 'And what's the information you've got now?'

He smiled a little triumphant smile, and said, 'Someone has been waiting for this opportunity.'

'What opportunity?' I hated the games. 'What?'

He laughed, the tinkly, charming laugh again, and gestured for the waiter, then saluted a youngish man in a pinstripe three piece on the other side of the room. Playing the conspirator, voice low, eyes alight, Gilchrist giggled and said, 'The weather.'

'What?'

'It's marvelous, isn't it? I loved the Russian winters. It was proper weather, sharp, clean. London soaked your bones and made you a crank.'

He was on a roll. The waiter brought refills. The man in pin-stripes stopped by to chat. More people, on their way to eat or drink, came by. Gilchrist soaked it up. And I watched the man in the corner whose eyes never left us; Gilchrist had his back to him.

I said, 'What did you mean by opportunity?'

'You know, in my business, there are always a dozen plans on the back burner. Opportunity. Natural disaster. Nuclear spills. Someone trips up or a diplomat goes to bed with the wrong woman or the wrong man or there's a murder, but if something happens, you ought to have a plan so that you can exploit it. Opportunity.'

'You're losing me,' I said. 'I thought we were talking about the fucking weather.'

'We are. That's the point. Someone is planning, has been planning for years maybe, various tiny little terrorist acts if the opportunity arises, which is perhaps to mess about with the soft brick embankments along the Thames. You heard about the device set near Parliament the other day?'

'Yes.'

'Greenwich was to be next, where the Dome is. One of the options. Do you understand now?'

'No.'

'Certain conditions, spring tides, usually in November. It doesn't take much, either; in the right conditions you get floods. London is built on reclaimed marshlands. Britain's got a pretty stable climate, but it's sinking quite fast. Global warming. Overbuilding. We're not vulnerable to volcanoes or earthquakes, but there are the floods.' He laughed and laughed and drank the brandy. 'Britain is sinking.'

Tessa Stiles said it was how she saw it: a wall of water coming down on London.

Gilchrist added, 'Anyway, it's yours, the information.'

'Why? Who are the hostages? What's the point?'

'Oh, Artie, you don't understand. It's never so clear cut, never so obvious. This isn't about ideology, it's about money. Greed. This is about land. Think about it. The property market was overcooked. It went sky-high. Volatile. You've heard there have been some sell-offs, a few foreclosures.'

I thought of Sverdloff. Him and his cronies buying up Docklands. Buying everything. Push the market up. Sell. Watch it fall. Buy again.

'A bad flood, even the threat, suddenly depresses property prices. Someone starts a rumor. It's like dominoes. And Artie?'

'What else?'

'I don't care, actually. I'll be happy to watch the whole bloody place sink, a nice way to end it for me, but not for you. If you want to stop it – unless the weather breaks – you'll have to find someone in power who will believe you.'

I changed the subject. 'You've heard of Phillip Frye?'

'Possibly. Tell me.'

I told him. Gilchrist stayed in his deep chair, eyes half-closed, until I mentioned Thomas Pascoe. Until I said that Frye was Pascoe's nephew.

Geoffrey Gilchrist leaned forward, put his hand on my arm and said, 'If this man Frye is involved and if he profited from Pascoe's death, I'll get you anything you need.'

'Why the sudden enthusiasm, Geoff?'

Gilchrist looked up. The watcher in the corner seemed to have moved closer. I said to Gilchrist, 'Your muscle? Over there in the corner?'

He looked up. Saw the man. Tried to hide his fear. He lowered his voice, 'Eddie Kievsky's.'

'And you're Eddie's boy?'

'Yes. I am, as you say, Eddie's boy. Finish your drink, dear, and we'll go.' He patted the pocket where he'd put the money and moved slowly towards the door. When we got there, he picked up his hat and coat from a little room. Kievsky's guy stayed a few yards back.

Gilchrist said, 'I'll get you your proof, if I can, but check the weather forecasts.' He held out his hand.

'Do we have any time left?'

'Not a lot.'

Gilchrist suddenly hugged me and I had the feeling I'd never see him again. We went out of the front door, he opened his umbrella, trotted down the steps, then looked over his shoulder. 'Goodbye, Artie.'

The dark-blue Jaguar was waiting for him in the street. He climbed in with a wave, leaned out again and laughing to himself, called out, 'The weather.'

I looked at the sky. I was sick of it. Sick of the rain and wind, sick of the heavy sky, sick of the bloody weather.

Chapter 32

The band on the barge played 'Blue Skies' that night. Everyone laughed. People danced, drank pink Champagne, strolled in and out of the restaurant, through the sand-blasted glass doors, on to the broad planks of the deck.

Gilchrist was wrong. The weather had changed. It was windy, but clear and very mild. The sure-footed waiters carried trays of Champagne aloft, and the decks of the barge were lined with fruit trees in tubs. Oranges and lemons, like Christmas tree balls, bounced merrily in the breeze.

WATERCLUB, the name of the restaurant, was picked out in a silver neon banner that seemed to change shape like water. The river barge had glass walls and ceiling, and a mirrored bar. The glass rippled with reflected water and sky. There were stars and the moon out, and after days of vicious storms, lead-colored sky, a sodden city and swollen river, it was a soft seductive night.

'It won't last,' I heard someone say. Someone else laughed and said, 'Who cares?'

It was opening night. A party for HOME. A brand-new restaurant that was moored near Butler's Wharf. In good weather it could sail too. On the deck, people stood, glasses in hand, yakking. A dinner boat sailed by and partygoers waved to us and called out. It was surreal, the sudden mild night, the stars.

Jack Cotton looked up from his glass. 'French probably, that boat. They sail right out the Thames Estuary and back. Corporate shit. Names like *Symphony, Silver Sturgeon, Golden Salmon*. A hundred quid for a bad meal and a boat ride,' he added, not quite bitter.

'Where's Nina?'

He shrugged. 'We've got some problems, like I said.'

There was plenty to drink; Jack was drinking his share. In my time, I put plenty away, but London – Christ, they really knocked it back. Jack stopped a waiter now and pulled a bottle of Lanson off the tray, resting it on the railing of the deck.

I leaned against the side of the barge and stretched. The volatile weather that had made me nuts really was over. Geoffrey Gilchrist was just a paranoid old man looking for a handout. The weather! Come on, Geoff, I thought. But it left me hanging on the Pascoe case all over again. Frye was a prick, but what kind?

Inside, a band did a jazzy version of 'Sunny Side of the Street', and I looked for Lily and said to Jack, 'Nice party.'

Jack puffed on a little stogie and said, 'Yeah, well, you're either at the party, eating good, drinking plenty, or you're out at some shithole hoping no one dies in the crossfire.'

'Nothing else, huh?'

'Yeah, sure, dying yourself, usually of boredom in the middle-class rectitude of a London semi or a suburban cottage and mortgaged for life,' he said.

On the wharf below, people arrived in cabs, cars, limos. Jack pointed out the cast of characters as they disembarked in front of a stand of lights that had been rigged by a camera crew. A medium-size pack of paparazzi jiggled around the edge of the scene, calling the stars by name, popping their bulbs. 'Over here, darling. Over here.' There was a buzz.

I looked for Lily in the crowd again. The sight of her at Frye's warehouse made me nuts, but I'd come to the party for her, dressed up, too. I'd seen the jacket in a store and bought it with some of the cash Tolya lent me after I lost my wallet.

'Nice jacket, Art,' Jack said and looked at the crowd. He pointed out a large man in a dark-blue suit with a cigar in one hand. The owner, said Jack. Famous restaurant guy.

Jack had an eye for style – you could see from his clothes – and he pointed out the features of the boat. I said, 'You shoulda been in PR,' and he told me, half serious, that the ashtrays alone were a work of art.

'Or a decorator.' I ribbed him some about it. He smiled coolly and we watched a woman in an orange velvet Gucci that probably cost three grand, watched her drop an ashtray casually into her Prada shoulder bag.

By nine there were three hundred people on the barge. There was a toot from a whistle and a gang of sailors appeared suddenly – in outfits no real sailor ever wore – and cast off.

The barge moved at a stately pace. The band played 'Let the River Run'. The noise of the crowd grew.

I said to Jack, 'How come you're so popular, Jack?'

Jack laughed. 'I told you. Celebrity cop. Celebrity black guy. Two for the price of one when it comes to these gigs. Anyhow, I'm a lot of fun, Art.' He raised an eyebrow. 'Still, the drink's free.'

'And good.'

'Very good. What's more, Phillip Frye's our boy, isn't he? Let's go eat some of Phil's food.'

But we stayed on the deck, drinking, watching the crowd. Phillip Frye was the emcee. He stood in the middle of the room glad-handing all comers. He wore a purple velvet suit with bell bottoms and a red silk shirt embroidered with lurex houses.

Jack saw me look. 'Nothing like an Englishman trying for hip,' he laughed.

I said, 'Who's that with him?'

Jack said enviously, 'The wife. Shashi. She's Ethiopian.'

Shashi Frye was very tall and ravishingly beautiful. A coffee-colored woman, her hair in corn rows, she wore a traditional gauzy white dress that blew around her like sails on a slender boat.

We went inside and the noise hit me. The talk was loud, people greeting each other, laughing, kissing. Jack introduced me around: Benedict, Nick, Tristan, Georgia, Jeremy, names like something off of *Masterpiece Theater*. There were Russian voices in the crowd: Irina Kievskaya appeared and kissed me three times.

I tuned in to the chatter. There was talk about property. I heard a man mention a rumor of sell-offs in Docklands, and a woman said in a piercing voice, 'Don't be a party pooper, darling, it's nothing to do with us.'

While everyone circled around Phillip Frye and praised his project for the homeless, they talked about leases and renovations and profit margins, and architects who charged a grand just to pick up the phone and corrupt estate agents and how you couldn't get anything in W11 for under a mill.

The irony wasn't lost on them either; they were cool. They laughed at their own ambitions, but I knew Tolya Sverdloff was right: people would kill for real estate.

Then I saw Isobel Cleary. Iz wore a green silk dress and high heels and Lily was with her, the two of them arm in arm, heads together. They were laughing uproariously at something, shaking with laughter. It was why I had come, but Lily had her back to me and then she walked off in the other direction before I could call her name or wave or get to her.

'Micro celebs,' I heard someone say, and I looked around and recognized a few actors. Isobel came over to me and kissed me and pointed out some politicians, a couple of rock stars, a famous chef, some writers. I never heard of any of them except for David Bowie and Michael Caine. No one seemed to notice the way the wind suddenly came up strong or the river lapped the deck outside.

There was food: little crunchy birds and spicy polenta, hot breads, salsas. Jack got me by the elbow and shoved a plate into my hand, and we loaded up and sat down at one of the tables in the center of the restaurant. The band, which was really good, played 'Moonlight in Vermont' and 'Summertime', and people ate, drank and danced.

Afterwards, waiters appeared with silver trays heaped up with little chocolate houses. People scooped them up and munched the houses and I watched and listened the way you'd watch a circus, all three rings going at the same time: the light and shadow on the dance floor and couples dancing; a red-headed man in a loud checked suit and big black glasses surrounded by serious men in suits, a security man with a finger in his ear near by; a pack of druggy models with smudged eyes; the oldest was maybe sixteen. The semi-famous huddled together.

And Lily. On the other side of the room, in a tight black velvet pants suit. She looked great. I looked again. She shrugged and pointed to her leg, which was free of the velcro and bandages, and she smiled mournfully and waved, and I looked down at my glass, then looked up and raised it in her direction. But a guy in a tux pulled her on to the dance floor.

I danced with Isobel, and she said, 'You OK?'

'I'm OK.'

'You want to talk about Pru?'

'Not tonight.'

Iz nodded. 'So how do we look through your eyes? What's it like for you?'

'Like being an alien.'

'Dance with Lily,' she said.

I went back to Jack's table. People came and went, sat for a while, got up to dance, moved around, smoked. 'We closed Indonesia,' someone said. 'We did. It was the last great party before the end, then they closed the country.' The conversations were the same you heard in New York, only the inflexion and the details were different, the barbs more vicious, the sarcasm fiercer, the talk more political.

Snatches of talk reached me: Russian fascists at Austrian spas, the price of a villa in Tuscany for the summer – or was it a village?

Models and party girls, men in khakis and tux jackets, three hundred people stuffed themselves with chocolate houses now. A handsome man in a silk suit and black silk shirt sat down at our table, ate mashed potatoes and talked French to the woman next to him. They covered Japanese Fusion chefs, varieties of Champagne and if there really was what one of them called 'anti-Semiticism'.

Jack reached out as a waiter passed, pulled a fresh glass off his tray and muttered to me, 'I've just had a mine shaft into the rest of the world, man, you know, we're in here and everyone else is out there in the howling void, and I wonder if I should be doing something about it, but it doesn't matter so I won't bother.' Jack was drunk. When he was drunk the mild speech impediment disappeared and the chip fell off his shoulder; charm was Jack Cotton's middle name.

Then there was a drum roll.

On the outside deck, bright blue and gold cloth covered a hulking shape. Phillip Frye stood on a chair, and people gathered. The wind blew harder now off the river, and people clutched at their clothes. The women's tiny skirts blew up; you could see a lot of great ass.

Frye toasted Pru Vane's memory and everyone murmured politely and shifted their feet. Then Frye spoke about the Life Bubble and how it would withstand even this wind, and someone said the word '*Titanic*' and we all laughed.

Two of the girls from Frye's office pulled the gold and blue cloth off, the Bubble was revealed and everyone clapped and whistled. Then Frye introduced his wife.

'Shashi Frye,' Isobel Cleary said in my ear. 'She's a bloody sight too good for him.'

Mrs Frye, who had designed the Life Bubble, smiled. Cameras flashed. The conversation turned to the homeless and Ethiopia, and how much good Phillip and Shashi did, how the Bubble would change things; it was the beginning of a new age, a proper start-up for the millennium, someone said. It was terrific, it looked good, it was a testament to modern Britain, a new age of great design, and they circled the thing and ran their hands over the surface, congratulated Phil, drank his Champagne.

Shashi Frye moved gracefully around the windy deck, the white dress blowing.

I leaned over the front of the boat alongside Jack. In front of us was the row of massive silver hoods I'd seen from the road. It was foggy then. Now, the Thames Barrier gleamed under the stars and looked beautiful, mysterious, glamorous, London's first great monument if you came in by sea.

A few hundred yards from the Barrier, the barge turned slowly. Clouds moved across the sky. A spatter of rain tinkled on the glass walls.

The rain came down harder. On the deck, people picked up their glasses and ran inside. The Bubble shivered. Two waiters grabbed at it, but a huge gust of wind came down the river, and the Bubble pulled loose from the ropes that held it to the deck. More waiters hurriedly set down their trays and reached for it. Frye himself grabbed it. Jack ran to help.

It was too late.

The Life Bubble sailed off the deck and into the river. We stood in the rain and watched it float away.

By midnight we were almost back at the wharf; you could feel the barge vibrate. The disaster with the Bubble put an edge on things, people were excited and nervous; they got drunker.

I was at the bar. Without looking, I suddenly knew Lily was beside me. I saw her reflection next to mine in the mirror, but I knew she was there before I looked. I could smell her. She put her arm around my shoulders.

I said, 'How's the foot?'

'I'm fine. We're all such event freaks.' She leaned closer and giggled. 'I'm sorry but I loved it when the Bubble blew into the water, I can't help it.' She put her face against mine. She pulled my head around and kissed me hard. Said, 'Do you want me to introduce you? I'll introduce you. Come on. Who do you want to meet?' Lily had her arms around my neck.

I said, 'Let's just dance.'

The band played 'Stormy Weather' and I held on to Lily on the crowded dance floor and we laughed at the music. We danced for a long time, not talking at all. The band finished 'Autumn Leaves' and started another tune.

I didn't plan on feeling happy as soon as I saw her, but I felt happy. I had planned on making it tougher for her; Lily makes me nuts, but without her I feel like my oxygen's running on low. On empty.

Whatever she'd done, however she knew Pascoe or Frye, who she'd been before I met her, right now I didn't care. Didn't care at all; it's not at all rational, this stuff; it's just how things are.

She said in my ear, 'What's this song called?'

Over Lily's shoulder I saw Phillip Frye watching us. His expression was vacant. He was a pissed-off guy and I didn't think it was just the Bubble. 'Why is Frye watching us?'

'Is he watching?'

'He looks mad as hell. His Bubble went overboard so he's pissed.'

'Who's with him?'

'Russian babe in Versace.' I moved us around so she could see for herself.

Lily looked over my shoulder. She grew less mellow. She said, 'Please, can we go home? Artie?'

'Yes.'

She put her chin on my shoulder and said again, 'And tell me what it's called.'

'What?'

'The song.'

We moved towards the door, and I said, 'The song is called "Love and the Weather."'

Chapter 33

'Tommy's dead. He's dead, Lily.'

'I heard you, Frankie. I'm sorry.'

'What's his name? I need a name.'

'Whose name?'

'The boyfriend. Your cop. Tell me.'

'What on earth for?'

'Help me here, Lily, please, I've never asked you for anything. Not for a very long time. I need someone. I'm alone. Tell me what his name is.'

'His name's Artie Cohen.'

'Thank you.'

'Why do you need to know?'

'Tommy was murdered.'

'Christ, Frankie. Jesus Christ.'

'They found him in the swimming pool downstairs in our building. He's dead. They tried to cut his head off.'

'I'm sorry. But leave Artie be, OK? Just leave Artie out of this, you understand? Please. You've done enough damage for one lifetime. Frankie?'

The stilted conversation ended. The line went dead.

In the living room of the houseboat where we sat on the floor, Lily switched off her tape recorder. 'So now you know.'

'You knew her as Frankie?'

'I knew her as Frankie.'

'You taped her?'

'I guess it's habit. I was working, the tape recorder was there, I heard trouble coming down the phone, I pressed Record. I hadn't heard from Frankie Pascoe in several years. She was trouble.'

'What kind?'

'Booze. Sex. She was a sexual compulsive, some doctor told

– 273 –

Tommy. Femme fatale. Killed with a touch.'

'Killed?'

'Metaphorically.'

'It wasn't just accidental me being on the case?'

'No. I tried to stop her. I couldn't. By the time you told me you were on it, it was too late. Frankie had that kind of clout. She knew who to call. She knew how to press the buttons that made Sonny Lippert put you on the case. She would have figured she could control you because there was a relationship with me.' Lily looked at me. 'Did she control you?'

I didn't answer. I said, 'Sonny didn't fucking tell me.'

'He wouldn't necessarily know,' she said. 'God, I am sorry. I should have told you. I got scared and ran.'

I put my arms around her. 'Scared of what?'

She said, 'My own fucked-up past. Do you want a drink? I want a drink.' She found a bottle of Scotch and poured some in a glass. 'I know I've made you crazy, and I'm sorry, but I need you.'

Outside, the rain that had started earlier pelted the roof. But it was warm inside. Safe. I held her tighter. 'It's OK.'

'I'm scared. Someone killed Pru Vane. Phillip's PR woman.'

'I met Pru.'

'Met?'

'No one's going to touch you.'

'Pru knew about Phillip's business. So do I.'

'You want to tell me?'

'I wanted to tell you all along, but I was afraid.'

Lily took her drink and leaned against me. 'It's not always that easy, you know, when you get caught up in work.' She was weeping now; I made her drink the Scotch.

'Where's Beth?'

'She's all right. She's still in the country with the Cleary kids and their aunt. I'm going to get her tomorrow, but she's OK. She's OK.' She repeated it, like a mantra.

I said, 'Are you sure?'

Lily sat up and pushed me away. 'I take care of her, I really do.'

'I know you do.'

'I'm glad you're here. I was glad the minute I saw you.'

'I figured you didn't want me here. I thought you had a different life in London.'

'I did, though. Want you. I almost always do.' She looked up from her glass. 'I wanted you here because I was frightened, but I was afraid to say anything, to mention Phillip's name. I knew something was wrong with his project. I knew but I couldn't believe it. I figured I'd play along.' She was shaking. 'I got over him a long time ago, just like I told you, long long ago. I'm drunk, Artie, I was drunk last night, I've had too much to drink and too many pills because my foot hurt, and I want more. I'm telling you the truth, you know? I'll quit the Scotch. Just give me some of that wine? The red. Thanks.'

She drank nervously and scratched her leg. Lily got up, looked out the window, made sure the door to the deck was locked. 'Give me a cigarette.'

I found a pack, and she pushed her hair off her face, sat down, this time in an armchair opposite me, lit up and started talking again.

'I was in the Peace Corps. I was in Ethiopia, in the middle of the country, in a region named Asela, they call it the Bread Basket of Africa. That was OK. It was a shithole, but it was some kind of town, there was a market, there was a kind of motel, even if the bathrooms had actual holes in the wall. And the countryside was gorgeous, like New Mexico, you know, you remember the high desert, how it goes gold and green in the fall?

'That was OK. But after some indoctrination crap, they moved three of us south to a village near a lake. It's very empty there, real bush. No maps, no roads, lakes full of hippos, scrubby bush, and whole tribes who live on islands in the lake. It was the kids I saw first, each one had a kayak for coming to school on our side of the lake. We were suppose to help these people, you know, but we were kids ourselves. American kids. We didn't know shit.

'I was out there on the edge of the world, literally, and I thought I'd never make it, I'd never get through two years. I lay awake all night listening to wild dogs and seeing my mother's face all pursed up and sour with disappointment in me, my father so smug and knowing. He said I'd never cut the mustard when it mattered.

'And Phillip shows up. Literally. A big mud-spattered Land Rover comes bouncing over the hill, like a tank, down the embankment, we're in these *tukuls*, these mud huts, me and two other hopeless kids, and we're reading instructions in a book on how to build a well, getting ready to screw up these poor villagers, doing more harm than good, and there he is. I swear to God, the whole works right down to the khaki bush jacket. Tall, handsome, ruddy face, like something out of a history book, an old-fashioned face, with a great accent, he's a documentary film-maker, or was back then, but with private money, so he does what he wants. Also, he wore a hat.'

'A hat.'

'Yeah, a hat. Like Bogart. Like Indiana Jones, only there wasn't any Indiana Jones yet, so he was an original.'

'You fell for his hat?'

'Yeah, I did.' Lily was rueful and ironic, but also wistful, caught up in the romance of her own story. She went on. 'And he says, come back to my camp, and we go and he's got a generator hooked up and a canvas shower and camp chairs and a fridge, very *Out of Africa*. I'd been reading Isaak Dinesen, I'm full of, you know, me woman, this Africa. Except I didn't have the guy. Then he opens the refrigerator and it's completely jammed with Veuve Clicquot. I swear to God. In the middle of the bush.'

'So you took up with him.'

'And the Champagne and the camp, and the fact that he rescued me and showed me how to dig a well and how to survive in Africa. By the time I left I could do it, I could manage. I did my whole stint in the Peace Corps and came off looking great. You know what, Artie? Even my father was impressed. Stringy, self-righteous son-of-a-bitch that he was.'

'You never talk about your father.'

'He was a lapsed Catholic who replaced the church with left-wing causes. The worst kind of zealous bastard, and even he was impressed by Phillip. He used to think I was a spoiled brat without any politics, he figured every guy I dated was an imperialist running dog. Phil Frye won him over. I didn't mention the Champagne to Daddy, of course. So I fell for Phil, and eventually I came to London with him.' She pushed her hair off her face. 'We got married.'

'You stayed with him a long time?'

'Even after we split up, yes. He had a way.'

'What kind of way?'

Lily's face was slick with pale sweat now, and she said, 'Whenever I shook free of him, he got to me. He was good at it.'

'How did he get to you?'

'He said he needed me. I told you once. You don't remember.' She flushed, turned away again and pressed her face to the window as if to cool it down.

I reached over and took Lily's hand. My pulse was racing. 'It doesn't matter. It's over. I love you. It's OK.'

'It isn't over. We started this, we might as well finish,' she said and tried to laugh. 'I think Phillip's whole set-up here is shitty.'

'How?'

'I'm not sure, I just know.'

'You knew this when you came to London?'

'I suspected as soon as I got here. He called and offered me a job doing a documentary on his new project. Tommy had just died. Frankie got your name out of me, you were on the case, I hated the way everything was getting dragged down in this. I figured I'd get out of town for a few days. As soon as I got here, I knew it was fishy. I started poking around. Artie?'

'What, sweetheart?'

'I wasn't suckered by Phillip, you know. I had to find out for myself, but I knew. He's been using cheesy building materials, putting shelters on bad land by the river. That's why the men died out there. He takes money from crooks. I couldn't even tell Isobel.' She saw me pick up the phone.

'Who are you calling?'

'Jack Cotton. I want to leave a message where we are.'

She smiled. 'Jack's a nice man. He tried to cheer me up. I met Jack, you know, but nothing happened. Between us, I mean.'

I hung up the phone. 'I don't care. I love you.'

'Can you stay with me?'

I kissed her. 'Let's go to bed.'

'Can you lock the windows, please? Are they locked? And check the back door, will you? The decks too, OK? This place makes me nuts. Warren Pascoe's dead, they killed Pru. Am I next, Artie? Am I on the list?'

I held on to her. 'You knew Warren?'

'I met him once.'

'It looked like a simple hit.'

'You think it was simple, first Tommy, then Warren and Pru? They wanted Warren's warehouse. He wouldn't budge. I'm guessing Phillip threatened to expose him. There were more dead bodies than anyone knew. Warren was a collector! He was a contentious old bastard, and talented. I thought the sculptures were beautiful. Warren was a freakshow but he didn't deserve to die. I think Phillip knows I'm on to him. I think Pru opened her big mouth and someone shut it up for her. Sometimes I think someone's watching me and this bloody houseboat makes me crazy.'

'Let's go back to my place, or a hotel if you want.'

'I can't. I gave the Clearys this number, this address. I have to be here in case someone wants me for Beth. She's due back tomorrow.' Lily glanced at her watch. 'Today. It's today. In a few hours, Keir will have the kids back from the country. Please. It's OK. You're here. It's always OK when you're here.' Lily shivered and fooled with her hair.

'I found a picture of Thomas Pascoe in your drawer.'

'You went in my stuff?'

I touched her hair. 'You asked me to.'

'Yes, I did.'

'The best thing about marrying Phillip was the two of them, the Pascoes. I was still only a kid. They spoiled me. My own parents never had any time for comfort or good food or nice clothes. After Stalin died, my mother got really messed up. I was a baby, but I remember she ran around wild. She never believed the bad stuff. Later on, she actually used to say, "If only Stalin had known, if only someone had told him." Eventually she killed herself. I didn't tell you that part, did I?'

'You didn't tell me.'

'Yeah, well, she couldn't take it. She could take it OK that I was miserable. She could take it that I got left with my grandma most of the time, and that I – Christ, you know why I hate this time of year?' Lily's voice was dry. 'After Thanksgiving, this real dread would come over me, you know? Because it was December. And in December, all the other kids were getting ready for

Christmas. Or Hanukkah. But not me. We didn't celebrate. We were atheists. The holidays came and went and there was nothing, and you know what?' She looked at me.

'Tell me.'

'I wasn't all that sad when my mother topped herself, OK?'

'Cold War scrap?'

Lily looked up, startled. 'Who said that?'

'I'll tell you later.'

'They loved me, Tommy and Frances, they really did. But we drifted apart after a while. Somewhere along the line, she started drinking. He got old. Then Frankie decided I was having an affair with Tommy, and I didn't see them anymore.'

'Were you?'

'Was I what?'

'I take it back,' I said.

She said, 'Thank you. I told Frankie to leave you be. You heard on the tape.'

'It's OK now.'

'I'm frightened.'

'What of?'

'Fucking storm. Listen to it.' Lily's hands were ice-cold.

'Get into bed.'

She looked at me. 'I know it was some homeless guy who whacked Tommy. But it was Phillip who killed him.'

We lay in bed. Lily said, 'Hold me, will you? If I could get a little bit of sleep I could make it more coherent for you. I don't think I've slept for a week.'

'Then sleep. We'll talk some more later.' I put my arms around her and she turned away, her face to the wall, and I knew she was crying. I wondered if I should have told her about Frankie and me, but Frankie was dead and I'm a coward. I couldn't lose Lily again.

In the middle of the night, I sat up. The wind was ferocious. Lily was restless. She got up and pulled on a ratty pink bathrobe, sat on the bed, fumbled for my cigarettes and lit one. I reached for the radio. A voice droned shipping information. I thought of the poor bastards out in boats tonight.

I looked at my watch. It was five past four. Lily had left the lights on in the bathroom and in the hall. At ten past, they flickered and went out. Lily fumbled for my hand. 'What is it?'

'Must be the power's out. It's nothing, sweetheart, it's the storm. You have a flashlight? Some candles?'

'In the kitchen.'

It was pitch black in the living room. I scrambled for the flashlight in a drawer and switched it on. In the beam, I saw the room was a mess. Papers flying, pillows on the floor. The door to the deck was open. I yanked it shut and pushed a chair against it. The wind rocked the boat harder. There was the cracking of glass and after it, a shower of shattered splinters. I peered through the window; the window on the houseboat next door was bust.

I skidded on the kitchen floor and felt the water come over the tops of my shoes. The floor was flooded. The windows had blown open here too, and rain poured in. I stumbled around, scrambling in drawers, found some candles. I got the door shut. I locked the window and retreated to the bedroom.

'Lily?'

There was no answer.

'Lily?'

But she was in the bathroom. I yelled, 'You all right?'

Somehow we got the candles lit, turned the radio up and sat in the bed, wide awake now, smoking, listening to news of the worst storm since the fall of 1987. Worse. Britain was more vulnerable now, said the radio voice. It was shaping up as the worst storm since '53, by some accounts. Global warming. Britain sinking. Overbuilding along the Thames. Carbons. Polar ice cap melting. A pumping system that failed in Thamesmead. Hangover from El Nino.

I said, 'Let's get out of here.'

'I have to wait for Beth.'

'I'll call Isobel.' I picked up the phone. It was dead.

The rest of the night, the voices from the shortwave played in the dark. I reached over and touched Lily's face. She was soaked in cold sweat. She gripped my hand. 'Artie?'

'I'm here.'

'I love you, you know.'

'I know you do.'

'I love you as much as I can love anyone,' she said quietly. 'Sometimes I'm so disengaged from everybody it scares me. I go into a room, a party, I think, oh these are perfectly nice people, really nice, good, interesting people, and then I start thinking, how soon can I get out of here? You're the only person who makes me feel. I mean it. That's the best I can do, Artie. I don't think I have anymore to give you.'

Chapter 34

Before it was light, we were up and dressed, trying to put the place back together, me working phones which were dead. Lily's, mine, the landline to the houseboat, dead. The weather, I kept thinking. Gilchrist said it was the weather, but he was a man who ate paranoia for breakfast.

The houseboat was a mess. I went out on the deck. The rain and wind slammed into the sides of the boat, which sat high on the steel sledge. But the river was rising and water slapped the deck and sloshed over it. The river, in front of me, what I could see through curtains of rain and fog, was an angry purple-gray swell, sloshing the Embankment, still rising. Somewhere near by were sirens, and the honking, cars, trucks, insistent, relentless. It wasn't a noise you heard a lot in London – I had noticed the quiet hum of the place my first night – but now the horns screamed.

I switched on the flashlight. The thin beam of light showed the wreckage on the boat next door. The widows were smashed. Part of the roof had caved in. The man I'd seen the night I came looking for Lily – he had on the same red sweater – came out on his deck, lifted his shoulders in despair and tried to smile.

On the Embankment, the ghosts of emergency crews appeared. Trucks. Soldiers climbing down, unpacking inflatable boats. From the roof of a building across the street, someone waved a flashlight.

Wearing a yellow slicker, Lily came outside. She held the radio. 'Listen,' she said. It had rained for months on and off, the weather geek said. The Thames tributaries were full. The rain the week before pushed them over the top and there had been minor flooding – I thought of the dead men near Frye's shelter on the river. During the night there were freak gales, and if the winds shifted and a surge tide occurred, it meant trouble.

Four hours, a reporter noted. Four hours was the minimum warning needed to close the Barrier, to shut off London from the river.

Even the weather geek was anxious. You could hear it in his voice. There was news of hoarding. The stock market computer system had shorted out before trading opened; for half an hour there was pandemonium while a back-up system booted up. Incoming flights were diverted to Paris. Everything else was canceled.

In the middle of the night, when the winds were blowing a hundred miles an hour, a train carrying nuclear material derailed outside a place named Stratford East. Canisters of hot stuff tumbled along the railway tracks and down to the river. A guard tried to get hold of one of the barrels and it killed him. They found him soaked, his skin peeling, his face half flayed by the contact with the radioactive spill. Then one of the containers burst; some of the contents were soaked up by the soil, some of it spilled into puddles and was carried into the river.

There was no let-up in sight: more rain was predicted. The worst weather in fifty years. The weather. I thought of Gilchrist. Christ, I thought. Maybe he knew. I said to Lily, 'I have to go. I have to. Call Isobel and tell her and come with me.'

She went inside and tried Isobel. I stood on the deck in the rain and watched the traffic grow. Lights spinning through the fog. The shapes of cops, firemen, soldiers.

Lily reappeared with coffee. 'The phone's still dead.'

We drank from the thermos. Then Lily said, 'I'm going to find a phone.' She shoved her hair under a plastic hat, climbed up on to the Embankment.

Ten minutes later, she was back. She got a phone off one of the emergency crews, but Isobel's phone was dead.

'Keir will bring the kids to their house. I know he will. I have to go.' She looked at me. 'It will be OK. It's higher ground at Notting Hill. It will be fine.' She was convincing herself. 'I have to. I can read between the lines. What they're not saying on the radio. They're withholding news. It's bad. I have to get Beth.'

My arms tight around her, I said, 'How will you get there?'

'I'll walk if I have to.'

I hesitated. 'I'll come with you.'

'If there's someone you have to see, then do it.'

I followed her off the boat and on to the pavement. The street was jammed now. A young cop struggled to inflate a dinghy by blowing on its tube like it was a balloon. His face swelled up with effort.

I held Lily. 'You get Beth and I'll meet you. We'll go home to New York. I'll find you both at Isobel's. Give me the address and I'll get there. You listening, sweetheart?'

She found a piece of paper and scribbled an address, and we walked fast, together, up the block, past a line of people waiting at a payphone. Lily pulled the yellow hat down hard. 'I'm going to leave you here, Artie, OK. I'm going.'

I wrote down Tessa Stiles's number. 'Leave me a message there, if you can get through.'

'I promise.'

The rain and wind blew sideways now and Lily stumbled against me. 'I have to go,' she said over and over, and started up the street. Then she ran back. 'Tell Jack Cotton. Tell your cop friends. Tell them to get Phillip Frye.'

'Tell me.'

'I told you last night. He knows everything. The dead men near his shelter. Something stinks. And Tommy knew. He knew, Artie. Tommy Pascoe knew about Phillip, and it killed him, and Frankie, too, and the rest of them.'

'I was out there. At the warehouse.'

'You saw me?'

'Yes.'

'I tried to talk to him. It's why I stayed in London.'

'Lily?'

'What?'

'You're telling me Frye's a killer?'

'Have you ever really looked into Phillip's eyes?'

'You're not gonna take him on, swear to me, Lil.' I grabbed her wrist. 'Tell me you're really going to Isobel's.'

Head bent against the rain, Lily set off. I called out, 'I love you,' but Lily disappeared, her yellow slicker sucked up by the fog.

Carrying the shortwave radio I grabbed from the houseboat, I got to the King's Road and hitched a ride up towards the sub-way. On the street, I found a payphone that was still working and left a message for Jack: Get to Frye. Get Phillip Frye. I didn't figure he'd get it, a day like this, but I left it, and left another message with his wife, who I never met after all, never ate her roast lamb, and a third for Tessa Stiles.

There was a supermarket and I went in and grabbed some smokes. People packed the aisles, dripping dirty water behind them. They pushed carts methodically up and down the aisles, eyes intent, searching the shelves. Some of the shelves were already empty. People piled water, milk, sardines. There was a pile of dusty bags of charcoal, left over from the summer maybe, and people grabbed at them and piled their carts until the carts wobbled.

Kids ran alongside their parents, laughing, pulling candy off the shelves; the schools were shut. The kids inspected fancy cereal and ice cream. One of them snitched a bag of M&Ms, tore it open, tipped his head back and poured the candy down his throat. People called out to each other and cracked anxious jokes.

'Cooking up a storm, are you?' A woman shouted out to a guy who passed, his own cart towering with food.

There was a ripple of unease. Not fear; not yet. But it infected you, and I bought batteries for the radio and more cigarettes, chocolate bars and a pint of Scotch that I stuck in my raincoat pocket. I was a kid during some bad winters in Moscow when there was a food shortage. In Moscow, no one had laughed and there was nothing you could hoard.

In front of the supermarket, people shifted bags into their cars. One woman dropped a shopping bag on the pavement. Rolls of toilet paper fell out. The rain soaked them before she could pick them up.

Through the window of a bakery I saw people eating crois-sants at the counter and drinking coffee. A man strolled into a video store, as if nothing much had happened, as if he might be required to spend another night at home and wanted a couple of movies. Another guy came out of a hardware store, a mop over his shoulder, laughing. Everyone draped with raincoats, slickers, plastic sheets.

The daylight showed the damage. Garbage cans were over-turned. Trees were ripped up – one lay across the sidewalk – and buses were stranded in water up to their hubcaps. The window of a big department store had blown out; the bed in the window was drenched.

Up and down the main drag here, people wandered around looking for supplies. It had a surreal quality. Some people smiled and joked. This was London, they seemed to say. Civilization. But they were nervous. The street resembled a tiny war zone.

I kept the radio on, holding it to my ear as I walked. In an appliance store, TV sets showed multiple images of London. In other parts of town, the electricity was out and a slow drip of real panic had started. There were more reports that the river would rise higher than 1953. Reports that the pumps had failed in Thamesmead and the whole place was under water, drown-ing in its own reclaimed marshes. Some residents on the Isle of Dogs were evacuated. Someone else reported they were loading kids on the last trains out of Waterloo before the station shut down. The financial markets opened, there was panic selling, then they shut. The sewage pumps were breaking down. People who lived along the river itself were instructed to go to the upper floors or to the roof. Somewhere safe.

Everywhere on the street, like me, people carried their radios. They held them to their ear as if it were a big sports event. The noise of the radios jammed its sound into the morning along with the sound of hammers as people boarded up stores and the jackhammers that ripped the streets open. Men dug for power lines, rain dripping off their hardhats, and the sirens wailed and cars honked.

Sloane Square, where the subway stopped, was littered with wet flowers. A sign posted at the subway entrance announced one line was already out. I ran down the stairs, but the platform was jammed. The crowd looked restless, wet, angry. I pushed my way back up and got a lift on a truck that took me to the river again. Cop cars, fire engines, ambulances were everywhere.

There were soldiers out now, piling sandbags along the embankment. The river looked vicious. High. Choppy. I wished I had gone with Lily. Where was she? Did she really go to Isobel's, or did she head to the river and Frye's shelter? I tried Jack again. No answer. The networks were jammed or broken. I had to get to Gilchrist.

Geoffrey Gilchrist sat on the roof of his little house on a canvas stool. He held an umbrella over himself and he was bent down, peering at the roof. My ribs hurt from where the creeps worked me over and I was breathless from running. I yelled up to him.

He looked at me, pointed to the roof and said, 'It's leaking. Come up. The front door is open.'

I climbed over a broken window box on the pavement and went in the house. In the living room, buckets stood on the floor and the rain pinged through the roof on to the metal.

There was a ladder on the top floor that led to a trapdoor and the roof.

Gilchrist, wrapped in his raincoat, dropped the umbrella. He was trying to put a sheet of plastic over a hole in the roof. I helped him nail it down. Then he looked up and said, 'It's the Barrier. The Thames Flood Barrier.'

'What about it?'

'They're going to ram it. Set an explosive device on it. The forecast is bad. There's an assumption of a four-hour weather warning, but it's a false assumption. And if there's a problem with the Barrier, if it can't be raised, the Thames will flood.'

I pulled at his sleeve. 'Who? Who is they?'

Gilchrist said, 'What's the difference?'

'What's your price, Geoff?'

'This is free.'

'Rammed with what?'

'A Russian paper ship, maybe. Crewed by cowboys who will risk the weather. Illegals on it. A stash of AKs for the British market. I've seen the Barrier, Artie, I've seen the plans. The concrete walls have ladders for maintenance and rings for mooring repair dinghies. There is terribly easy access from the water.'

I looked out at the river that was choked with fog.

'What kind of cowboy's gonna offer up his life on some crazed kamikaze mission? I don't buy this shit.' I turned to go.

'A ship crashed the Barrier a few years ago. No one saw it or heard it in the fog until it was too late. The crew didn't die, did they? They were conveniently fished out of the river, dried off, fed, tucked up and sent home.'

'What's the fucking point?'

'The flood.'

'The point of the fucking flood, Geoff, what's the gain?'

He looked at me and said, 'Chaos. Mayhem.' He was laughing. 'Fear.'

'The Russians don't care about terror unless there's profit. Fear of what?'

'You think there isn't profit in fear? It's got very deep pockets.' He leaned over me and said softly, urgently, 'I don't care, you know. For all I care the whole bloody city can wash away, but I promised you, and I am telling you. Find someone who will believe you, Artyom. Make them put the gates up. Do it now.' He dug in a pocket and pulled out a cellphone, then handed it to me.

There was a faint signal, and I got Stiles's station house and left her another message, and I should have run like hell after that, to the police, the Barrier, Frye, but I didn't. I had to know.

'Is this what Thomas Pascoe knew? About the Barrier?'

Gilchrist said, 'He knew what the Russians were. He knew about the options, the opportunities. In a sense, it was his fault, of course – which has a rather nice moral symmetry, actually – because it was Tommy Pascoe who introduced Phillip Frye to the Russians. They had the money, he said. They wanted a stake in the legitimate social system. Tommy set it in motion. He thought he would make them better citizens. He thought they'd give him and Mr Frye money for their good works, and they did, but it also gave them entrée to all sorts of deals. And Tommy didn't know what Frye was, and he couldn't stop what he had started.'

'You knew and you didn't tell me?'

'I didn't know it all until this morning. Not all of it. Not the Barrier.'

'That's not enough,' I said. 'You said you owed me. I want a payback. Is this why Leo Mishkin said Thomas Pascoe was a problem, that it was better if he was out of the way?'

Gilchrist shrugged. 'I don't know any Mishkin.'

'He's Eddie Kievsky's brother-in-law.'

'Then I'm sure you're right.'

'You could have stopped it, Pascoe's murder.'

He shrugged. 'That was my opportunity, you might say. I overheard things. Perhaps I even knew enough to warn Tommy, but I let it pass. Anyway, dear, who on earth would believe me? I should imagine I'm the least trustworthy man on the planet.' Gilchrist was bareheaded. Water poured down his collar.

I said, 'Come inside, Geoff.'

'No, I'm enjoying this.' He gestured at the rough, gray city, the heaving river, the scurrying figures, bent under ripped umbrellas.

'Yesterday, at your club, I said Phillip Frye was going to inherit Pascoe's money. It made you talk. Who the hell cares if Frye profits from Pascoe's death, I mean, you didn't expect the dough, did you?'

Gilchrist looked at me. 'Oh no. Quite the opposite. I wanted Tommy's death to be pure. I wanted it to be meaningless. A hole in the universe.'

I tried to light a cigarette, but the pack was soaked. I crouched next to Gilchrist on the roof; I was close enough to smell his sour breath.

'Why?'

'Years ago, in Moscow, Tommy Pascoe decided I had betrayed this country, him, the whole shooting match, he took it personally. We were all so young and full of ideas.'

'What ideas?'

'You're too young to remember. Silly ideas. Exploding cigars. The weather. Sex. The Americans once tried to destroy Fidel Castro by putting poison in his boot polish so his beard would fall out, that sort of thing. We responded in kind.'

'Just tell me straight.'

'Once upon a time, Tommy Pascoe tried to have me killed.'

'What, with an exploding cigar?'

He said, 'I wish. It would have made a better story. You ought to go now, Artie.'

'What?'

Gilchrist looked out over London again. 'Find someone who

will believe you,' he said again. 'It will happen soon, it's happening now,' he said dreamily. 'Now.'

I was running. I ran along the river, still holding the radio, Gilchrist's words banging in my head. I stumbled. I barged into an army truck that was stranded in water. Subways were out everywhere, you heard it on the radio, the stations knee-deep in water and sludge. A sewer had burst. I could smell the shit.

Screaming sirens cut through the fog. Suddenly, a yard from me, as I ran, a metal sign flew off a pole and sliced through a woman's arm. She stood. Watched her arm hanging from her shoulder. Then she started to scream. I couldn't hear the noise anymore.

Lily being alone on foot somewhere in London scared me. I was worried for Sverdloff. He was involved with Kievsky's crowd, with bad real-estate deals. He bought into the syndicate that bought up Docklands intending to fix the markets. He was 'Half in, half out', but when he found out the Russians would use terror to depress the market, he tried to stop them. I believed that, and anyway, I love the big prick and I owed him.

They would kill him. They would rip him into pieces and they'd do it slow.

The Savoy Hotel loomed up in front of me and I hurried in, dripping. Pushed my way through the tourists milling nervously in the lobby, found a hotel operator, scribbled a list of Sverdloff's numbers and shoved it at her with a wad of money. 'Try these. Now. Please.' Something in my face convinced her and she worked the phones for me.

Eventually I got a signal. I left Tolya frenzied messages everywhere: Stay away. Keep away from London, I yelled, then realized someone could clone his cellphone, someone was listening.

I called Tessa Stiles again. She picked up the phone herself and I told her: the Barrier; Frye; the Russians. I told her because what choice did I have, and who else except a paranoid cop would believe me?

'Christ, look at this.' Tessa Stiles was in her office, crouched in front of the TV, eating her cuticles, drinking tea out of a mug. Jack was with her. He finished his cigarette, dropped the butt into an empty cup, lit another one. They stared at the TV. On it, a man with patent-leather hair, Brylcreem slick, black button eyes, pencil mustache, was talking earnestly in an accent that could crack old Coke bottles.

Stiles was waving at the TV. 'It's the only instructional film we could find about flooding. It was made in 1954.'

She looked up as if she suddenly realized I was there. Her face was red, excited, triumphant, scared. 'Are you certain about the Barrier, Artie? I hope you're bloody certain, what you said on the phone. Because we called the chief on your say-so and we put it to him, so it's our ass, mine, Jack's. Yours, too.'

I collapsed on to a chair and glanced out of the window. The front of the police station was sandbagged up to the second floor. I couldn't see the jetty or the police boats. I got a lift part of the way but most of the time I ran and it took me hours from Gilchrist's.

'I need a car,' I said to Stiles. 'I have to get to Phillip Frye.'

She ignored me, intent on the video, while the door to her office opened and shut, cops barged in and out looking frantic. Someone brought me a mug of coffee. Snatches of talk – low pressure, north-east gales, three days of storms. The phones rang constantly.

I grabbed Jack by his collar. 'I have to get to Frye.'

Stiles said, 'You'll wait for the chief with us. You laid it out for us, you called me, do you understand? I took your phone call, I took what you said at face value, you'll fucking stick around to back me up, me and Jack both.'

I picked up a phone and tried Sverdloff again. I tried Lily. The phones were dead everywhere. Rain battered the window.

Jack said, 'Christ, Tess, I hope to fuck you know what you're doing,' he said. 'You, me, a couple of middle-ranking nobodies, one black, one female, we tell him, "Sir, I've got it on awfully good advice that there's going to be an event at the Barrier." Based on what? On information from an ex-New York cop who got it from someone he won't name. He's going to come over all sarcastic, I know that look. "Been to the pictures too often, inspector?" That's what he said to me once.'

Stiles looked at me. 'It's our jobs on the line. Tell us who your source is.'

If I gave them Gilchrist, he'd be dogmeat. A messenger for the Russian mob doesn't get to retire to a fancy club and drink good booze. I wasn't selling them Geoff. Not unless I had to. I said, 'What's the difference who? I'm telling you.'

Stiles looked outside. 'I can't even see the fucking river anymore, the fog's so thick.'

I looked at the clock. Jack got up.

Tessa said, 'Sit down. I'm not doing this alone. Cohen's your bloody friend.'

'He's going to blow his top.'

'What can I do?' she said. 'He's Welsh.'

For a while – it seemed like a month – we waited in the office, drinking horrible coffee, watching the rain. Stiles took emergency phone calls, and Jack and me, we sat and smoked. I worked the one remaining phone. Came up empty. I was chain smoking now, listening to the rain and my own pulse. It was dark out.

Suddenly a uniformed cop put his head through the door. 'He's here.'

Cotton and Stiles jumped up. A handsome man in a raincoat, about fifty, slammed into the office. 'Christ, I hope this is good,' he said. 'Convince me.'

'There isn't time, sir,' Jack said. 'We want to get on the boat while there's time. I'm on the line here, I know. But can we please talk on the way?'

'This is Commander Evans,' Cotton said to me. 'Forward Planning. Scotland Yard.' Jack was smooth. He cut the tension in that room in half.

Evans shook my hand. Stiles and Cotton spelled it out for him again. He said, 'Can we get a helicopter out there?'

Stiles said, 'No.'

'A car?'

'The traffic's murder. We can use the new boat. The radar's good, I've got my best team ready to roll with it, sir.'

She opened the door and Evans went out and started down the stairs and we clattered behind him, pulling on coats, running now out of the door, into the fog that enveloped the jetty. A couple of river cops were waiting for us as we climbed on board. Both of them were young, good-looking guys. Their expressions were grim.

Jack looked nervous. 'I can't see the water.'

One of the cops smiled briefly. 'We have radar,' he said, and revved the engine.

'You're sure of this?' Evans said to Tessa Stiles. 'Because I've already sent word, I've already put out alerts, you'd better be bloody sure you're bloody sure.'

'Yessir,' Stiles said. 'Tell them to raise the Barrier, sir, please. Before it's too late. Before it's damaged by the explosive device.'

'It's your word against the rest of them. It's your necks.'

Jack Cotton looked at me, then back at Evans. 'Yessir.'

'Persuade me,' he said, and they started to lay it out for him again when his cellphone rang. He pulled it out of his pocket, listened briefly, put out his hand to steady himself as the boat started to move. 'Let's go, then,' he said. We were already on the river.

Stiles said, 'The Barrier?'

He looked at us all and said, 'There's been a crash.'

'The Barrier?' Jack repeated it.

'Yes.'

'What is it?'

'A ship.'

'What time?'

'It's happening now.' Evans talked softly and I thought of Gilchrist. Did he really know? Could he have stopped it? Face tense, voice low and angry, Evans went on. 'They're not sure. No one heard it. An hour, two, it's unclear when the ship hit.'

Spray from the river, the rain and fog sluiced down the windows of the police boat and it bucked wildly on the rough water.

I said to Evans, 'What happened?'

'All I know is a ship rammed the barrier, it smashed up, there are forty men in the water, though what the fuck kind of hubris people have getting on board a boat in this weather.'

'Can't they fish them out?'

'There's zero visibility. This is a freak. The Barrier has to go up.'

'Otherwise?'

'Otherwise, London will flood. We'll lose most of the power for London, City Airport, Parliament, half the underground lines, most of the telecommunications.' He said, 'When there's a tidal surge, and the winds shift, the Barrier has to go up. The winds have shifted.'

Tessa Stiles said, 'And when the Barrier goes up, sir, the people in the water?'

Evans looked grim. 'They're fucked, poor bastards. They'll be caught in the tide and smashed against the steel Barrier gate, they haven't got a bloody snowball's chance in hell.' His voice rose.

'Christ,' Jack said.

Evans said, 'Maybe they thought we wouldn't raise the Barrier if there were human beings at risk, maybe they figured we don't have the balls, that we'll leave it too late, let the place flood. Maybe what started as a little mayhem got out of hand, and they couldn't turn off the taps.'

'How long?'

Evans looked at his watch. 'Two hours tops. If we can get them out before the gates go up, there's a chance.'

Tessa looked at him. 'You don't believe that, sir.'

Face drained, Evans sat down suddenly on a bench at the back of the cabin and put his head in his hands. The boat rocked. Water splashed high up on the windows. He looked up. 'How long until we get there?'

Stiles said, 'Twenty minutes. Half an hour.'

Evans's phone rang again and he held it to one ear, grunting assent into it while he listened. Then he said to us, 'Well, then, you can all be there when I give the order to kill forty people.'

Chapter 35

Blinded by the thick fog that choked the river, the Polish captain of a Lithuanian cargo ship, the ship allegedly carrying paper, had crashed into the concrete piles of the Thames Barrier. From what Evans heard from the Barrier, what he passed on to us, it was unclear if the crash was intentional. The captain of the ship had ignored the red warning lights, had navigated badly, was marginally out of the lane when it crashed. Radio contact with the control tower was out when the ship approached. It was chaotic, then it hit. The men on board scrambled for life rafts. The ship was already listing badly. On deck the men prized open the white canisters to get the life rafts. People shouting, panic setting in. They open the canisters. There are no life rafts inside.

Only vodka. Smuggled booze where the life rafts should have been.

'Vodka,' Evans said, laughing bitterly until his face was wet from laughing so hard. 'Vodka. I hope the poor sods had time to drink it before they went in the river.' He held on to the side of the boat and Jack and Tessa watched him, Jack looking green – if a black guy could look green – his lips the color of ash.

We were in the middle of the river, wrapped in the fog and rain. The boat bounced crazily on the waves. When we came down, the riptides seem to drag at us. The only sign there was anything alive outside was the sudden bleating of a siren from another cop boat.

'Vodka.' Evans wiped his face with his sleeve.

No one on the river heard the crash. Silently, the Lithuanian ship had smacked the concrete that was sunk deep in the riverbed. It had happened before, like Gilchrist said. There had been a model. Back in '97, '98. Someone on a shipping channel picked up a radio message, but it was too late.

Evans was still talking. There was no explosion. No one knew if there even was a device on board the Lithuanian ship; there was no way to tell. There was only minor damage to the Barrier so far, paint stripped, concrete chipped. I thought about the huge, hulking, silent ship loaded with paper or timber, illegals in the hold, cowering, frightened, then the hit. Men scrambling against the tide in the freezing water. Terrified. London waiting for the flood. A wall of water coming down, like Stiles said.

'Fear,' Gilchrist had said. The point was fear.

'Look.' Tessa pointed to the front window. Through the dense fog, there was a faint light and in it, the outline of a silver hood. We had reached the Barrier.

One of the young cops – I never even got their names – said to Evans, 'I'll try to get you as close to Barrier control as I can,' he said.

A wave sloshed over the side of the boat and it bucked up high and then down and I half fell on Jack. We pulled ourselves up and I said to him, 'Listen, when we get off this thing, there's a homeless shelter. Down the road from the barrier. Not far. Next to Westminster Industrial Estates. Frye's place. I'm going.'

Jack glanced at the Barrier, then at Evans. He said to me, 'You can't arrest Frye, man. You're unofficial. I'll go. You stay with this lot, this was your call. I'll go after Frye. If we make it off this fucking boat, that is.'

I grabbed his sleeve. 'Do it.'

We crept, like moles, under the riverbed, underneath the Barrier. It was the only way up onto the Barrier itself. The steel gates were sunk into concrete piles that stretched from one side of the Thames to the other. Electrically driven, they were powered by hydraulic packs concealed overhead by those silver shells I'd seen from the water the night of the party. Raised, the gates made a solid steel wall across the river.

We hurried now, panic drifting between us. Stiles carried the walkie-talkie, but it crackled and went dead. Evans had gone to the Control Centre. I looked at my watch. How long until the Barrier was raised and the men in the water were smashed against it and drowned? An hour? Half?

The tunnels were light and sleek, the interior tubes glossy with paint, spick and span like the guts of an Edwardian steamship. It was man-made, huge, mechanical. If the tunnels were damaged, water would pour through and crush us; it made me feel tiny and wild.

Except for the regular hum of the generators, under the river, inside the tunnels that service the Thames Barrier, it was deep and quiet as a tomb.

We moved in a line, Stiles and two Barrier officials ahead, a BBC pool reporter whose name I never got, her cameraman, and a PR guy whose name was Gordon. The reporter repeated her questions about the men in the water. She started to run, anxious to get her story, anxious to see what was going on in the water, and Gordon, jogging to keep up, tried to slow her down. He had a job, he had to get out the word that the Barrier was invincible, that things were all right, keep the population calm, even when we knew there were forty sorry bastards outside in the freezing river and the only way to rescue them was to leave the gates open and let London flood.

I was at the back of the line. Gordon's rap got on my nerves; he had the pinched, pimply face, the obsequious style of a low-level apparatchik. He wore a yellow slicker and his brown corduroy pants were too big for him. One of his hands kept creeping down to hitch them up.

He led us through a second series of passageways and tunnels, deeper and deeper under the riverbed, under the Barrier itself. The image of the surfer tumbling in a tidal wave came back to me: the broken limbs, the on-coming surf. Along the tunnels, emergency crews popped up suddenly at various junctions, then moved on, efficient, intent; I felt as if I was suffocating down there.

It was surreal under the river. Outside, men drowning. Inside, Gordon, grasping his pants, scrambling to keep up with the rest of us, delivered the party line in a loud voice for the benefit of the TV reporter: the Thames Barrier, Gordon said proudly, was a perfect machine. He had the stats, he knew the dimensions, not just the Barrier itself, the billion bucks it cost to build, the eight years it took, how much that was in today's money, and why it was an important part of London's infrastructure. The soft, unironic voice, the rote recitation of the information, had the opposite effect he intended: it made the place seem less secure. The Barrier was Gordon's home team; for ten minutes, while we hurried through the tunnels, we were his hostages.

He kept up the patter as we went down more stairs and then started up, and I followed him because I didn't have any choice. I thought about the men in the water and listened to Gordon's history of twentieth-century floods. The flood in 1928 when fourteen people drowned. The big flood in 1953 when a depression in the north Atlantic flowed around the tip of Scotland, into the gap between England and the Continent, when the water funneled, was forced higher and higher at the Thames Estuary.

He knew about the daily tides that lap at London, and the tension between London as a trading port and the need to protect the town, and how the city came within an inch of disaster in '53, the year he was born, Gordon said. The only alternative to the Barrier would be a ten-foot wall the length of London. Lying low on the river, London was vulnerable. Most of its 125 miles of bank were made of old, soft brickwork. It didn't matter. The Barrier would prevail, he added. He talked, and all I saw were people drowning in a wall of water.

Finally, Tessa Stiles grabbed him by the sleeves of his yellow jacket and said, 'Just shut up, will you?', and Gordon, the fixer's smile fading, pushed a button. An elevator door opened and he said, 'We'll go up now.'

The silver hood was above us; we stood on the Barrier itself now. The river was wide down here. Standing on the concrete pile, we were an assortment of tiny figures, dwarfed by the silver hood and the concrete piles.

I could barely make out the ship below, or the men in the water, but on the next platform, where more lights were rigged, divers in rubber suits waited. Gordon pointed out there was no damage except to the ship. This was his real purpose. This was why, in lousy weather like this, he was here, delivering the news to the reporter and the rest of us. The Ford plant was just downriver at Dagenham, Gordon added. 'It has massive flood gates of its own.'

What about the current storm, I yelled. He smiled and put his hands behind his back. It's all right, he yelled back at me. There was still time. There was time. Get the men out, raise the Barrier. I looked into his soft bland face; I knew even he was worried.

There were nine concrete piles, nine curved wooden hoods capped with silvery metal. When all the gates were raised, it made a solid steel wall across the river sixty feet high. Five stories. On one side, the river would be violent, turbulent, a killing machine. When the gate shut, the water would rise suddenly, like a bathtub filling fast. It would rise thirty feet and spill over the banks, over the concrete bench where I'd sat a few days earlier, where the grass hid a steel bank. Then it would subside. But the men in the water would drown.

Behind me, Gordon went on talking, whispering in the reporter's ear. The silver hoods were decoration, Gordon said. 'A landmark. The first thing the ships see when they sail towards London.' He was proud of the Barrier, of the environmental advances that had gone with it. He talked softly about the return of river fish and bird life, the sanctuaries along the banks, the mud banks that were a source of food for fish and birds, the fish nursery. The river had been dead; now there were 115 species lived off it. He murmured in the reporter's ear.

I had seen enough. A cold sweat dripped down my neck and I grabbed Gordon by the arm, and said, 'Get me out of here.'

'I can't do that.' He looked down at the water. 'My God.' Excitedly now, he whispered, 'Look, they're raising one of the gates. On the left.'

Huge arc lights were directed at the water now, one after another they snapped on until the fog seemed lighted up from inside. I could make out the ship, listing, disappearing under the water. The light picked out faces staring up, bobbing on the water, glowing through the weird fog. The sailors in the water seemed to cling to each other.

Then I saw the steel gate. It rose up out of the water like a monster in a movie. It rumbled, shuddered, the gears grinding, linking one concrete station with the next.

I turned my head away, then I looked back in time to see the sailors in the water smashed against the steel gate, like surfers breaking up in a tide.

Chapter 36

The water around Frye's shelter was knee deep. It was dark out now, and the riverfront was a mess: water, mud, cops, firemen, officials, camera crews. Emergency rafts floated in the stinking puddles.

This was where the dead men had washed up that week, the TV crews already knew their way around. Here you could see the scale of the flooding. If the fog lifted, you could see the Barrier. Reporters stood waiting. Photographers climbed on makeshift stands and watched the river and waited.

I thought of the forty bastards who slipped under the water, who smashed into the steel gates. A bunch of guys out to make some kind of life, most of them. They opened the canisters on deck and instead of life rafts, they found vodka.

Jack appeared and grabbed me and said, 'I heard on the radio they raised the gate.'

'Yeah.'

'Jesus, Artie. Jesus Christ.'

'Where's Frye?'

'There's nothing you can do about him, man. I'm telling you.'

Jack's phone rang, and he listened in. 'Wait here for me, will you?' He shoved some binoculars in my hand and ran in the direction of the road. I headed for the shelter.

Outside the shelter, a dozen homeless men and two women sat on a flatbed truck in the courtyard. Inside, where a foot of water splashed over the bare floorboards, crews of people worked frantically, humping beds and equipment. A woman told me she'd seen Frye. He was here.

I looked for Lily. She hadn't come. She had gone to Isobel's after all, like she said. She went to Isobel's. Thank God.

On the side of the building was a fire escape and I hauled

myself up on to it and began to climb. I was looking for Frye.

The rain battered the building, but the fog was lifting. I stood on the edge of the roof and held up Jack's binoculars and I could see the white lights on the Barrier and the silver hoods. I reached in my pocket for cigarettes. A sharp wind came up.

A trapdoor opened and Frye appeared in his shirtsleeves. He was soaking wet. 'Artie Cohen. You were looking for me?'

The cigarettes were in my hand; I lit one to keep from killing him.

I said, 'There's forty guys dead in the river who never had a chance.'

Frye – I could see his eyes glitter – looked out at the water. 'They did the job for the money. It was a job. They knew the risk.'

'They planned to plant explosives.'

He shrugged. 'So I imagine.'

'You fucking bastard.'

'Maybe so, but I've done something, haven't I? I've made things better. I've made shelters for thousands of people. Haven't I?'

'It's bullshit, Philly, is what it is. It's crap.' I wanted him riled. The bile got into my mouth and I could taste it. 'It was you who had Thomas Pascoe killed. And the rest of them. You let it all happen. Why, he threatened to change his will? Cut you out?'

'For one thing, yes. But people had the wrong idea about Uncle Tommy, you know? He was a stupid old man. He didn't understand the priorities. As soon as he discovered what the Russians were up to with the property market, he wanted to report them. I thought it rather brilliant. Buy cheap, push up the prices, sell high, start the rumor mill turning, the whole bloody market falls on its knees, you begin all over again. Brilliant. And who suffers? Only a few rich people, bastards like Uncle Tommy.' He turned his head.

'But you wanted their money, the Russian mob, the rich bastards?'

'Yes. And why not? They were gangsters, weren't they, on both sides of the aisle? Of course I wanted their money.'

'So you let Eddie Kievsky know what Uncle Tommy knew.'

He shrugged. 'It was Tommy who put me on to the Russians in the first place.'

'Leo Mishkin,' I said. 'And Kievsky let Mishkin know Pascoe was trouble, and Mishkin's kid overheard him and bought himself a homeless guy to kill Pascoe. Very nice, Philly. Real sweet.'

'Is that how it worked? Well, it's your chum Sverdloff. It's his kind who fix the markets. And pretty much everyone else who's in it, for that matter. Who wants controls on property when there's so much money to make? Not me. Not you. Not any of our pals.'

Frye's sense of entitlement made him fearless; he was a fool. He walked towards me, rain pouring down his neck.

I tossed my cigarette on the roof. 'What about Warren?'

Frye laughed. 'Warren was nothing. A freak. I bought the bronze hands for our logo, he knew my business, he talked too much, I found a way to shut him up.'

'You supplied the cadavers. Homeless men.'

'It wasn't enough for him. It kept him quiet for a bit, then you showed up. You asked too many questions, Warren had a big mouth.'

'So Eddie Kievsky sent his goons.'

Frye shrugged and didn't answer.

'And Pru Vane?'

'Silly bitch,' he said. I'd heard it before that week. The British insult: 'Silly bitch. Silly bitch.'

'Gilchrist?'

'Who?'

Like Warren Pascoe, Geoffrey Gilchrist was a freak, a sideshow. But Gilchrist survived.

Frye suddenly held his hand out, palm upturned, and looked at the sky. It had stopped raining.

The roof was slippery; I edged towards Frye. 'You ripped off everyone, you as good as killed Thomas Pascoe, and you inherited. It was win win, wasn't it?'

Frye's face shone. 'He absolutely had to go before he changed his mind. Or his will for that matter. What's the difference? His kind was finished. He was a silly sentimental old man, he never saw the real pain out there. I house people, I shelter them – what difference does it make how I get the money? The rich prefer to give when there's some glamor to it, film stars are nice, foreign places, missionary zeal. Imagine what it takes to shelter the ordinary homeless. I don't care where I get the money. Or how.'

Tessa Stiles had said it: 'The hotter the property market gets, the more homeless there are. The more homeless, the bigger Frye's operations.' I said to Frye, 'You're crazy.'

He laughed. 'You don't know anything. You haven't been out there and seen the desolation.' He looked at me. 'We're going away. Shashi and I, we'll go to Ethiopia for a bit, work there, let the kids see the real world. There's nothing you can do to me.'

'What about Lily?'

Frye grimaced. 'She always wanted you in a way she never wanted me.'

'Yeah, Phil, she does.' I taunted him. 'We talk about you all the time, Philly, and what an asshole she thinks you are, so fuck you.'

Frye's face changed. The flesh tightened up, as if he felt some pain.

'That's really it, isn't it? This is about me and Lily.'

The wind howled down the river suddenly, moving the clouds. I lifted the binoculars and looked at the sky like I did the night Pascoe died in New York and I sat on my own roof with Lily and Beth and watched the stars.

I thought of Thomas Pascoe in the swimming pool on Sutton Place. And Frankie. 'Stella by Starlight' ran in my head. The buzz of a helicopter distracted me.

In the split second, when I shifted the binoculars to look at the chopper overhead, Frye lunged. It was what I wanted. The binoculars were a ploy. He figured I wasn't watching him, but I knew he was coming. Could feel him.

I dropped the binoculars and slugged Frye as hard as I could, and the feel of my fist on his face felt good. He looked surprised as he sat down heavy on his foot. He held his hands in front of his face. He tried to get up and couldn't.

I moved in his direction. I wanted to feel the flesh on my knuckles again. Without any warning, one of the men I'd seen earlier walked through the open door to the roof. I didn't know if he was Frye's muscle or a homeless man looking for a smoke. Plastic raincoat. Old hat. Face hidden under it. He stood near the door and watched us and lit a cigarette.

Frye sprawled on the roof. He looked at his leg twisted under him. He held out a hand to the homeless man, who only took the cigarette out of his mouth and spat at Frye. He spat again and disappeared.

I looked down at Phillip Frye. He'd set up Thomas Pascoe. And the others and he did business with thugs. Now, on the roof, ankle smashed, face smeared with pain, he looked up at me and said, 'At least I built my shelters. At least I did something.' I saw he believed it.

Frye held up his hand to me. 'Help me up, will you?'

I looked down at him. For a second I thought I might kill him, but the only thing I could feel was contempt. Let someone else have him, I thought. Let it go. I pushed his outstretched hand away and left him, and then I went to get Lily and Beth and take them home.

New York: November

We were home in time for Thanksgiving. Rick made the turkey upstairs at his place. His parents brought the trimmings. Tolya Sverdloff showed up with oysters in a barrel, ten dozen shrimp, each one the size of the baby's hand, magnums of Champagne and Bordeaux and a new wardrobe for Beth, everything pink, who showed it off for everyone.

Lily, being as she always says the world's most unmotivated cook, bought the pies from Eileens on Lafayette, apple, pecan, pumpkin, and a cheesecake, and she made some kind of peace with Sonny Lippert, but only, she said, because she liked his wife. I watched her and Jennifer Lippert, and heard them cook up schemes for a soup kitchen; I hoped to God they planned on doing it at home, here in New York, not some cockamamie country halfway around the world. But I wasn't betting on it.

Keir and Iz Cleary came over from London with their kids to have Thanksgiving with us, and Isobel told me Jack Cotton, like me, quit being a cop and went private. Geoffrey Gilchrist seemed to have disappeared off the face of the earth, though his club reported his bills were still paid on time.

In London, in spite of the weather and the beating the town took from the flood, in spite of global rumors of terrorism, the bad land deals, the volatile stock market, the homeless riots in New York notwithstanding, real estate went up everywhere; it went sky-high. The creeps made a mistake about that. They sold too soon. People bought apartments and houses and agonized about the mortgage and what color to paint the walls, Decorator White or Gardenia, like they always did. In my loft, my floors cleaned up good as new. Phillip Frye was honored for his work with the homeless and the Life Bubble was patented. One day I'd make Phillip Frye weep.

There was a memorial service for Frankie Pascoe. Lily never

forgave her and didn't come, but I went. Leo Mishkin sat alone in the last row. His face was wet. I let him be. The kid, the son, wasn't even there.

Lily said it freed her up though, Phillip Frye out of her life, the Pascoes dead. It cut her loose from the past, she said. The next day, I sent Lily a box of Cracker Jacks with a message inside; I wished it was a huge diamond ring in there; I once read that Frank Sinatra put a diamond in the Cracker Jacks when he proposed.

Anyhow, Lily said she ate it all, and we figured maybe we'd get married around Christmas. I said to her over a beer that night, 'Honeymoon in London?' and she laughed.